Enjoy

AWARD-WINNING AUTHOR

KIMBERLY
KILLION

Kimberly Killion

CARIBBEAN
SCOT

Cover and book design by
Hot DAMN DESIGNS
www.hotdamndesigns.com

Visit Kimberly Killion online at:
www.kimberlykillion.com

Prologue

~ Taken ~

Southwest of Glenstrae, Scotland, Summer—1603

At ten and six, Reid MacGregor only had one person occupying his mind, and she stood at his boot tips preparing him for the dive into Loch Long.

"Think ye a bit of treasure might be worth one kiss?" Reid snapped a wink at the lass tying the leather straps at his neck and ignored the gagging noises Eoin and Fergus made behind them.

Torchlight filled the cavern with a yellow glow and showed the blush tinting her fair skin. She pulled the laces tight. A wee bit too tight. "'Tis just like a Mac-Gregor to bargain without means of payment."

Mary-Robena Wallace had always been quick of wit, especially when it came to tossing barbs at Reid. She didn't give him the answer he wanted, but neither did she tell him no.

Anticipation and excitement tickled his stomach. He'd never actually kissed a lass, save for Nanna, and that wasn't the kind of kiss he wanted to share with

Robbie. Nay, he wanted the kind of kiss the kinswom-
en gave the warriors when they returned from battle.
The kind of kiss that involved a wee bit of tongue.

Reid squirmed inside his leather suit, swallowed,
and slipped a gloved finger between the ties and his
neck to make room for the knot in his throat. But
Robbie slapped his hand away, flipped her red-blonde
braid over her shoulder, and then picked up a pail of
tar off the cavern floor. She smeared the thick black
pitch around his wrists and then his ankles, sealing
the leather suit to his iron boots so water wouldn't
seep in. The pungent smell of turpentine burned his
nostrils as she circled the warm tar around his throat.

Not once did Robbie attempt to hide her dimples as
she glued his hair to his neck. He would have to soak
in animal fat for a sennight to remove the sticky substance. But it would be worth it if he found evidence of
the treasure Robbie's grandda assured them was in
the depths of Loch Long. Robbie had mapped out a
grid based on her grandda's theories, and they'd covered more than half the area where he believed a
Spanish lieutenant might have hidden treasure he'd
stolen from Cristóbal Colón's new land. In the past
three months, they'd found little, save for a boot and a
piece of armor.

Robbie's brother, Fergus, checked the iron weights
hanging from the base of the wooden bell-shaped diving barrel then released the crank and eased the
wooden vessel into the water until it disappeared from
view. "Why would ye be wantin' kisses from my sister
anyway? Robbie has yet to get her titties."

Emerald eyes flashed just as Robbie slopped a dol-
lop of tar at her brother. "Ye should learn to hold your
wheesht. Grandda will take a switch to your duff for
saying such things." The tips of her ears shone bright
red when she looked into the gapping bodice of her

wool kirtle and sighed.

Reid wanted to console her, to tell her she would get her titties soon, but he wasn't that dim of wit.

Fergus wiped the tar from his round face and turned the crank that lowered the barrel into the water. "All I'm sayin' is the Gregarach can have any maiden this side o' the loch. Why would he choose the likes o' ye?"

Robbie stared at the cavern floor, no doubt hurt by Fergus's words, but Reid saw something her brother didn't. She was smart. She knew more about the diving barrel at ten and three than the boys combined. And Reid, Eoin, and Fergus were all three years her senior.

The quartet had been friends for forever, but lately when Robbie had occupied his mind, he no longer saw her as just Fergus's sister. He saw a blossoming beauty—a caterpillar before her change. He chuckled inside at the comparison, thinking himself besotted and not really caring that Fergus and Eoin thought it, too.

Eoin skipped a rock across the water's surface. "I can think of at least a dozen things I intend to purchase with the Spaniard's gold. The first of which will be a pistol to protect the keep from those murderin' Colquhouns." His cousin drew up a wad of snot and spit it in the water Reid was about to enter.

"Think ye can blow your hawkers onto the rock?" Of all the habits Eoin had, the way he constantly chucked his snot irritated Reid the most.

Eoin responded by drawing up another lunger and launched it into Robbie's pail of tar. The wretch had good aim, if nothing else.

"Keep it up, and I'll drag your arse down with me."

Eoin shrank back, and mayhap even turned a shade green. The sop still wasn't overly fond of water.

Robbie stepped closer and tied a rope around Reid's

waist. The bones in his legs liquefied. She smelled the same as the rest of them, like fish and tar, but when she exhaled, he caught a whiff of the rowan berries she'd eaten on the way to the cavern.

He raised her chin with the tip of his gloved finger and dropped his gaze to her heart-shaped lips. "What say ye, Mary-Robena Wallace? If I surface with proof of the Spaniard's gold, will ye grant me a taste of your sweet lips?" Da said similar words to a bar wench in a tippling house just before he set out to sea, still Reid felt ridiculous repeating such drivel.

Robbie's entire face flamed red. Her smile split, exposing teeth too big for her mouth. "Bring me the gold, MacGregor, and I'll give ye your kiss."

Heat whipped through his insides just before she pushed him into the pool of frigid water. The slap of cold to his face was quickly forgotten when the weight of his iron boots pulled his legs taut. The rest of his body followed, dragging him downward into a black abyss. The darkness didn't bother him overmuch, but he'd never been terribly fond of the drop.

Eyes closed, cheeks puffed, he waited for his feet to touch the bottom. Robbie had measured the distance and cut the rope accordingly. The loch bed would come.

Eventually.

Several dives back when Eoin nigh drowned, Reid had learned not to panic, regardless of the pressure popping in his ears, regardless of the tightening in his chest, regardless of the rapid beat of—

His feet connected to the silt floor. A rush of bubbles tickled his face.

Moving his arms side to side, he searched for the diving barrel. Robbie's calculations were never wrong. In six steps, he found the sides of the wooden drum.

Lungs already burning, he swam between the

weights hanging from the bottom of the diving barrel and slipped into the hollow. His movements echoed inside the drum. He sucked in cool air but knew better than to dally. Robbie had explained to him last summer how a person's exhales would quickly turn the air to poison, so he stole a second breath and dove back into the water.

Surrounded by total blackness, he searched the mud and rock for jewels, trinkets, cups, coffers. Any evidence would satisfy Robbie and earn him his kiss.

His pulse remained steady, beating a staccato in his ears. He moved further away from the safety of the barrel, determined to find proof to take back to the surface. Of course, anything valuable would be used to buy their way back into the king's good graces. Three months had passed since King James issued the proscription against Reid's clan.

He returned to the diving barrel often, sneaking bits of air a breath at a time. Mayhap he was being selfish, but he cared little about what his uncle would do with the treasure. All he could think about was that damn kiss.

He searched the loch bed a square patch at a time, then something caught his thumb.

Something smooth. Something man-made.

Mayhap the hilt of a sword or a tool. He inspected the area for more and felt the square edge of a large coffer. He wrapped his arms around it, but the strongbox was massive. The Spaniard's gold was inside. He knew it. Twisting his body, he pulled his knee to his chest and then rammed his iron boot into the rotted wood.

It gave way.

In a mad rush, he stuffed his fingers between the splintered wood and felt something circular.

A coin.

Satan's stones! Robbie's grandda wasn't adder-bitten.

The excitement of his find invigorated him. He could practically hear the blood racing through his veins. Unfortunately, he could also feel the squeeze of his lungs.

He needed air. Now!

Reid wrapped his hand around what he hoped was gold, then pushed water behind him to return to the vessel. He stood inside the drum and filled his lungs with air. One breath, two, then three. He was greedy with the remaining air. Part of him already celebrated his victorious quest.

The MacGregors would no longer be forced to take false names, and the border raids could cease altogether. Da could return to his rightful place as chieftain at Kilchurn Castle, and Reid wouldn't have to stomach another day watching Eoin flaunt his status with the warriors on the training field. Being the appointed chieftain's son had swollen Eoin's head to annoying proportions.

Reid's mind raced full circle, leading him back to the one thing he'd been dreaming about since the day Mary-Robena Wallace batted her cinnamon lashes at him—that kiss.

With the hand not fisted around his small treasure, Reid located the horn Robbie had fastened to the top of the drum. He inhaled and blew three times, anxious to rise to the surface.

Would she kiss him, or would he have to kiss her? And how did one go about starting a kiss? Was he supposed to smash both his lips to hers? Was he supposed to suck her top lip and she his bottom? Or was it the other way around? And when exactly was he supposed to use his tongue? He struggled with all the options while he held tight to a crossbar over his head and waited.

Nothing happened.

"Raise the barrel," he yelled and emptied his lungs into the horn again.

But no one turned the crank. No one gave the rope around his waist a swift tug as was their signal. Nothing happened.

Unable to prevent his panic, Reid inhaled through his nose in short, quick draws. How long did he have before the air turned to poison?

He blew on the horn again and counted to sixty.

Still, nothing.

He put the coin in his mouth, slipped out from beneath the rim, and reached for the rope attached to the top of the barrel. Hand over hand, Reid pulled himself toward the surface. His iron boots felt like boulders beneath him. Even if he thought he could get them off, the water would leak into his leather suit, and Nanna would make him drink that wretched tonic to prevent him from passing a fever onto his half brother and sister.

His head grew light, his body weak, but anger kept his arms pulling him upward. He would put the itching weed in their *plaides* and toads in Robbie's bed. Nay. Spiders. Robbie hated the wee creatures.

Light rippled above him, still meters away. He felt the tearing in his chest. His body demanded he breathe, but he bit on the coin and pulled himself toward the surface.

Seconds later, he burst out of the water and gasped for fresh air, nearly choking on the coin lodged between his back teeth. He spit the gold piece into his hand. "God's legions! I'll tar and feather each one o' ye cockgnats."

Before he could push the hair from his eyes, two massive hands clutched the shoulders of his leather suit and yanked him out of the water. "'Tis good to see ye've not lost your spirit, son."

"Da?" Reid was only slightly surprised by Da's appearance. While the clan thought Calum MacGregor a coward for not fighting the Colquhouns, Reid always knew Da would return from sea and to his rightful place as chieftain.

Eoin would be furious.

"Did ye come back to lead the clan?" Reid asked hopeful.

"I came back for ye and none too soon."

Reid followed Da's gaze to a man slumped over against the rock wall. Reid recognized the Colquhouns' blue and green *plaide*. At his feet lie Fergus, sprawled out on the cavern floor with a wound opening him from gullet to navel.

Fergus! His thick fingers clutched the butt of a club and blood soaked the green and red crossbarred garment he wore so proudly. His round face was gray, save for the bright red blood pooled in his mouth. He was dead.

Tears blurred Reid's vision as salty bile crawled up his throat. *Why? Why Fergus?* He pinched his eyes tight, bent over his knees, and vomited onto the cavern floor.

A high-pitched scream knifed through his ears. *Robbie.*

Reid's heart pounded against his ribs. Wiping his mouth, he scanned the cavern, but the hollows were empty. "Where are the others? Eoin and Robbie?"

"They ran. Come, we must make haste." With one hand fisted around his bloody basket sword and the other clamped around Reid's wrist, Da pulled him out of the cavern and into the dying light of dusk. A massive black mare stood at the mouth of the cavern, saddled and waiting.

Another scream ripped down the knoll.

Reid's heavy feet froze in place. "Robbie," he whispered and looked up the hillock where the mist spread over the ancient standing stones. Wind slowly pushed the haze aside and exposed two Colquhoun warriors garbed in blue and green *plaides*. One of them held a torch while the other scabbit pinned Robbie to the ground with a foot on her back.

"No!" Reid yelled and broke free of Da. He ran toward the enemy, forcing the muscles in his legs to bear the heavy weight of his boots.

The Colquhoun pulled an iron rod from the torch; its tip glowed like a tiny sun.

"Let her alone!" Reid clawed up the base of the hillock not caring that they saw him. Terror gripped his insides. He shook. He cried.

Robbie stared at him, her mouth stretched wide, but her scream was silent when they laid the rod across her cheek.

"No!" he roared, just as the Colquhoun stepping on her back started toward him, sword drawn. Reid would kill him; he didn't care that the man was twice his size. He would rip the flesh from his bones and burn it. "Ye bastaird! I'll—"

The remainder of his curse was forced from his lungs when two hands yanked him off the ground and laid him belly down over the neck of a monstrous steed.

"I'm taking ye to a better place, son. A land that knows less hatred."

"But what of the clan? Of Nanna?" *What of Robbie?*

"I cannot save those who dinnae want to be saved."

"Ye can save Robbie!" Reid kicked his heavy legs and flailed his arms, but he remained trapped in Da's grip. "I cannae leave her behind." Reid sobbed as Robbie's cries lessened behind them, drowned out by the thunderous hoof beats pursuing them.

1

●

~ REUNION ~

Early Fall—Eleven years later

Robbie gasped for air. Not because the devilishly braw man squatting over her stole her breath, but because her lungs were on fire from the dive.

She held tight to the rock ledge and wiped her eyes enough to study him. Clean black hair, long lashes, thick brows—one of which was currently raised—strong jaw and lips far too sensual for a man.

"Holy Loki!" Recognition nigh stopped her heart in her chest. She would know those silver eyes on a troll. The last person she expected to await her when she rose from the dive was…"Reid MacGregor." Alive and in the flesh—sun-baked flesh.

She'd prayed for his soul when she hadn't been cursing him to Hell and back. She'd thought him dead all these years. It was easier to accept than the fact that he and his da had abandoned the clan.

Wherever he'd been, it hadn't been on a battlefield. Not one scar marked his clean-shaven face, and his nose was arrow straight. She didn't know any man who hadn't had his nose broken at least twice.

Starting at his pinkie, he rolled a coin from knuckle to knuckle, then caught the piece of gold between his thumb and index finger. "I've come to collect my kiss."

She gawked at him, recollecting their bargain, but she needed no time to form her opinion. "Ye pompous, craven-born scut. I would sooner kiss a bluidy sow than the likes o' ye." She might have tossed another barb or two—or three—at him, but he hauled her out of the water and onto the cavern floor with a thunk of her iron boots.

The man might be as strong as an ox, but she took great satisfaction in knowing she nearly met his height.

"God's legions, Robbie. You're all legs," he jested with a twinkle in his eyes and pushed the hair from her face. A darkness stole his merriment in an instant when his gaze settled on the scar—the brand that marked her as a MacGregor.

The same brand she'd lived with since the day he left. She cupped her cold cheek and turned away. She hadn't hidden her scar in years and damned him for making her do so now. "Leave."

"Robbie, I'm—"

She waited, thinking he might beg her forgiveness, but no words followed. "Leave. Go back where ye came from." With trembling fingers, she bent and released the latches on the boots then poked her frigid feet into the same pair of brogues she'd worn since she was ten and six. She refused to think about what could have been and peeled the laces out of the tar at her neck. She stripped out of the leather suit which left her standing in her thread-bare kirtle. Blood stained the skirt where she'd cleaned a rabbit a sennight ago and tar clung to the bodice, making her look like a filthy beggar.

She peeked over her shoulder to assess Reid's finery.

He wore no *plaide*. Instead, he was garbed in violent colors; a purple surcoat clung to his broad shoulders over a white *lèine* shirt. Tight black breeks tucked into shiny black boots rolled to a perfect crease at the knee. Two red sashes painted more color into the ensemble—one at his waist, the other at his knee. What purpose they served she knew not, lest it was to hide his weapons.

S'truth, he looked like a giant jester. He belonged at the border faire, not here. She would never admit it aloud, but she envied his obvious good fortune. Why would he return to this bleak land, if he'd found prosperity?

Little thought was needed for her to answer her own question. He'd come back to claim the chieftainship. "Eoin leads the clan now. Ye've no place here." She tucked herself inside her *arisaid*, wrapping the wool tight around her and fighting the need to shiver. Her jaw ached from the effort it took to keep her teeth from chattering. When she tried to step passed him, he grabbed her arm and drew her close.

He was warm. So warm.

Silver eyes rimmed with sapphire blue held her gaze. "I did not return to lead the clan. I came for you."

For me? Blast him! Robbie reared back and slapped him hard. Her next two heartbeats seemed to pass painfully slow. The stinging crawled into her hand as Reid rolled his head atop his shoulders and wiped a drop of blood from his lip. He said nothing, but his gaze fell, and the rise and fall of his chest increased the longer they stood in silence.

"Ye have no honor, and ye dinnae deserve me. Ye

are a coward the same as your da."

"Da was not a coward," he defended, but not in a harsh voice.

Trembling, Robbie jerked out of his grasp. "Nay? What other name would ye give a man who flees his people, knowing his enemy intended to seize his lands?"

"'Tis not true. Da did not flee. He went in search of a better place." Denial darkened Reid's pale eyes.

She assessed him from the top of his head to the tips of his polished black boots. "Well, I suspect he found it."

"He did, and I want to take ye there, Robbie."

Galled by his assumptions, she retrieved the torch and stomped toward the mouth of the cavern. Blast him to Hell and back! The man had dung for brains if he thought she would just leave with him. Too many people depended on her. The same people he'd left behind.

She rubbed her stinging hand against her skirt and demanded her quivering legs to carry her far away from Reid bluidy MacGregor. Turning her back to him, she exited the cavern into a night black as pitch, but a dark-skinned demon stepped into her path.

She dug her heels into the dirt. Her breath turned into a lump in her throat. She held the torch in front of her, more as a weapon than a means of light.

The man blocking her way wore a heavy fur and was like no one she'd ever seen. He was bald, save for a single black tassel of hair atop his head. His skull was marked with black symbols, and his face was pierced with bits of ivory. Or were they bones?

Grandda had told her stories of the savages from the New World, but the man before her didn't resemble the image she'd conjured up from those tales.

He reached out to touch her hair.

Robbie reared back, her pulse quickened in her throat and nigh burst through her neck.

"*Sak kan* woman?" His black eyes shifted from her face over her shoulder.

"Aye." Reid positioned himself beside her. "This is Mary-Robena Wallace. Robbie, meet Yaxkin. He is known by his people as Running Spirit, but I call him Jax."

Running Spirit? What breed of man bore the name Running Spirit?

This man, Running Spirit...Yax...Jax, cocked his head and studied her. He raised her skirt off the ground and bent to examine her feet, then without warning he squeezed her small breast.

"Ack!" She jerked backward and was about to shove her torch up his nose when Reid latched onto the savage's wrist.

"Nay." Reid calmly eased him back. "'Tis not their way."

Jax shrugged. "*Sak kan* woman, too *bek´ech*."

She blamed curiosity for why she remained in their circle and turned toward Reid. "What is a *sak kan* woman?"

"*Sak kan* means white serpent." Reid's mouth lifted at the corner into a crooked grin. "The Mopán people call me White Serpent."

Jax pointed at Reid. "White Serpent." Then he pointed at Robbie. "White Serpent's woman."

"Nay." Robbie held out her hand and shook her head. "I. Am. Not. White Serpent's woman."

Jax's smile deepened the lines at his eyes. "Then I call you *C'ak'is Ak'*."

The heathen insulted her. She could tell by the way Reid laughed. "What did he call me?"

"Fire Tongue."

Robbie growled between her clenched teeth, then

stomped away. "S'help me Odin. If I had a blade..."

• • •

"I suspect my Robbie is not fond of her new name."
Reid walked alongside Jax, following a grumbling
Robbie at a distance up the hillock and into a blinding
mist. Nay longer was Mary-Robena Wallace a wean to
be certain. In truth, she'd aged quite nicely. Reid fiddled with the gold doubloon he'd found years ago and
wondered how much groveling it would take to convince Robbie and her grandda to come with him.

Picturing her long legs on the Yucatán's white
sandy beach made him ache in places a man didn't
need to be aching given her obvious disdain for him. If
he could get her on the ship, he would take her back to
Rukux and away from this cold barren place. He
would show her a new land. A warm land filled with
exotic fruits and food aplenty. But he was far from deluded. It would take more than a ripe guava to get her
stubborn arse on the *Obsidian*.

He would have to tell her about the gold.

"Fire Tongue scrawny." Jax's blatant opinion interrupted Reid's musing. "Too thin. Not at all like Black
Dove."

Jax's woman was full of figure, so Reid couldn't argue the comparison. He'd seen skeletons with more
flesh than Robbie. He'd caught a glimpse of her sharp-
ly defined collarbone before she covered herself with
her *arisaid*, not to mention the hollows beneath her
high cheek bones. Robbie's grandda needed to spend
less time with his experiments and more time putting
meat in the kettle.

Reid hesitated on that thought. When he and Jax
first arrived, they'd gone to Kilchurn Castle only to
find the keep had been taken over by scores of
Colquhouns. Cautiously, they'd climbed the bailey

wall protecting the stronghold and paid visit to Argyle Wallace's small cot-house, but Robbie's childhood home had new occupants.

What other name would ye give a man who flees his people, knowing his enemy intended to seize his lands? Robbie's words echoed through his head. He knew she was wrong. Da had tried to save them, but they'd called him a coward and accused him of madness. S'truth, it was madness to think Da could have saved the entire clan.

Argyle Wallace had been one of Da's accusers. Only now did it occur to Reid that Robbie's grandda might have passed. He'd been feeble eleven years ago, always complaining about his aching bones. Her mam had died when Robbie was a wean, and her da died fighting the Colquhouns not long after. She had no one else. If Argyle was dead, how long had Robbie been on her own? And where was the rest of the clan?

Jax shivered beside him, causing the bones in his ears to rattle. "We steal White Serpent's woman and go back to the Yucatán. Too cold here."

"Aye, Scotland is not—"

"Nok ol." Jax's hand flattened against Reid's chest.

He narrowed his eyes, searching for the enemy. His instincts sharpened instantly. The first of which was to protect Robbie. He strained against Jax's hold, but stilled as he watched the flame of her torch bob up the hillock then dissipate into the fog.

The mist prevented him from seeing more than ten feet in any direction, so he tuned his ears to his surroundings.

The hoof beats of multiple riders circled them. The rattle of harness jingled, then the smell of horseflesh thickened beneath his nose. A horse's whinny didn't hide the whisper of a blade hissing from its sheath.

Positioning himself back to back with Jax, Reid retrieved his basket sword and waited for the enemy ghosts to show themselves. He'd never been one for warfare, but few surpassed his skill as a hunter. However, the land in Scotland was different than the jungle he'd grown accustomed to. Still and all, he'd cut his fighting teeth on this land.

The tip of a sword broke through the mist before the Scot holding the weapon came into focus. Three other men materialized on horseback behind them, each wearing the *plaide*.

"Lay down your weapons and state your name."

"Duncan Montgomery," Reid lied, giving the name of a Scottish laddie employed on the *Obsidian*. After overhearing a few vagrants blathering in Rosneath where he'd anchored the ship, he knew the edict against the clan was strictly enforced. Any man bearing the name MacGregor either renounced it or suffered pain of death.

"Duncan Montgomery, aye." The bastaird raised Reid's chin with the tip of his sword. "Ye dinnae look like a Montgomery."

"This one is no son o' Scotland to be certain," another man added behind him the same time Jax disappeared from Reid's rear guard. His Mopán friend had earned the name Running Spirit for a reason. Jax would hold his enemy's heart in his hand before the wretch realized it no longer beat inside him.

Just then a man vanished from atop his steed with a grunt followed by a boyish scream.

"Cease! Cease!" Robbie burst into their circle. Torchlight exploded on the scene and shone down on a frightened lad sprawled on the ground. Jax held the boy by his throat with one arm, while his other raised hand was poised with lethal intentions.

"'Tis the devil," the boy choked and squirmed like a beetle trapped on its back.

"Please." Robbie turned to Reid. "'Tis Shane." Her voice trembled, and her torch cast shadows beneath eyes filled with fear.

Shane was still in the nursery when Reid last walked these lands. 'Twas no doubt the lad was wishing for Nanna's skirts right now. "Release him, Jax. He's my half-brother."

Grinning, Jax pulled Shane to his feet, wrapped thick arms around the lad and squeezed. "White Serpent's brother is my brother, too."

"Brother?" Their presumed leader cocked his head and studied Reid further. "Who the devil are ye?"

"'Tis Reid MacGregor," Robbie supplied, her wide green eyes fixed on the man still holding a blade on Reid. Her delicate brows drew tight in the middle, and she held the corner of her bottom lip between her teeth.

When he realized she was fretting over his well-being, he warmed inside and out. His smile couldn't have been more ill-timed.

"Reid MacGregor." The Scot sheathed his sword and spit a wad of mucus at Reid's boot tips. "'Tis been a long time. To what honor are we privy to your return, *cousin?*"

"Eoin?" Recognition took hold. Reid's cousin was no longer a gangly grunt. S'truth, the man had grown into a bull.

The warble of a fake bird sounded in the woodland. 'Twas a signal, one he'd used in his youth to call upon his kinsmen just before a raid. It seemed the MacGregors were still reaping mayhem across their borders. Years ago, they'd run the raids to repel their enemies from Kilchurn Castle, but Reid suspected the reasons were altogether different now.

Much had changed.

However one thing stayed the same. Eoin still held

the same confident demeanor he had in their youth.
His cousin didn't seem the least bit concerned with
Reid's return.

"Join us. 'Twill be like old times." Eoin cocked a
crooked grin and ran his narrowed gaze over Jax.
"Bring your friend. He has proven to be resourceful."

Reid looked at Robbie and wished she would walk
away with him. He wished he didn't have to prove
himself according to their code. "I did not come here to
pillage. I came for..."

Robbie glared at him and shook her head. A warning.

One he did not take. "...Robbie."

Silence followed. Every man atop his steed stared at
Eoin.

The man drew up another hawker and blew this
one over his shoulder. "And what makes ye think my
Robbie would be goin' anywhere with ye?"

My Robbie?

Reid's gut fell to his toes. He immediately searched
Robbie's hand for a ring, but she wore gloves. He
thought he'd prepared himself for every possibility,
even her death. He'd vowed to not interfere should he
find her married with bairns. If she'd given herself
over to the Church, he swore he wouldn't take her
from the cloister. However, finding Robbie wed to his
cousin had not been a scenario he'd prepared for.

He should leave. He needed to think. "I have gold."

If his offer tempted Eoin, the man hid his reaction.
He scrubbed his beard, lingering a moment in
thought, then pulled the slack from his steed's reins.
"We've gold as weel. We just have to steal it."

He turned to Shane. "Lend your brother your
horse."

"Aye, m'laird." Shane immediately complied and
awaited further instruction.

"Gather the clan at Leckie's old estate and put the fattest calf on the spit. Let them know their lost son has returned, and we've reason to celebrate." Eoin pulled Robbie onto the back of his steed. "Let's ride."

2

•   •

~ PILLAGE ~

"Did he take you to wife?" Reid asked in a demanding tone. He was certainly every bit as forthright as he'd been in his youth.

Eoin had positioned Reid alongside the road north of the brook and Jax in a tall birch tree overhanging the pass, but the moment Eoin went into the valley, Reid deserted his post. He now stood at Robbie's back where she leaned heavily against a solid tree trunk and prayed for strength.

He'd abandoned the clan. She hadn't thought about him in years, but now that he'd returned, she couldn't help but wonder what might have been. Would he have fought to save Kilchurn Castle from the Colquhouns' invasion? Would she be his woman instead of Eoin's?

"'Tis a simple question." He stepped so close she could feel the heat of his body through her *arisaid*. "Did Eoin take you to wife or no?"

She focused on the approaching carriage, wanting to lie to him. "Not yet."

Reid's exhale felt like a gust of hot wind beside her cheek. Why did he think he could return and claim her so easily? "Your relief is unwarranted."

"I feared I was too late." His fingertips lightly touched her lower back and filled her empty stomach with fluttering emotions.

She didn't want him to touch her, or breathe on her, or make her recall unwanted memories—foolish memories of poetic words and butterfly wings. 'Twas drivel. Childhood whimsies reminiscent of a carefree lass who nigh swooned every time Reid MacGregor set a dead moth in her palm and filled her head with honeyed words about beauty and transformation.

Her fingernails dug into the bark. She would not betray Eoin. "Ye *are* too late."

"Vows have not been spoken. You do not wear his ring." Reid's strong hot hand covered hers and sparked a thousand feelings of regret inside her. She'd lain with Eoin. She cared for him, and he'd been good to her. They had plans to build a home in Rannoch once the proscription was repealed. They intended to raise a hundred head of cattle on the small farm outside Glenstrae, and he'd promised to give her a half dozen bairns. She would not risk her relationship with Eoin simply because Reid bluidy MacGregor came back from the dead.

She pulled her hand out from beneath Reid's and spun around to face him. His perfection was distracting. The man was positively beautiful. Her heart gave a little jump. 'Twas not her heart aflutter but that of an innocent girl unscathed by reality. The hold between their gazes felt bold, daring…wrong. She licked her dry lips and fisted her hands to cease their trembling. "I am Eoin's wife in every sense of the word, save for the marital contract, which we cannae get lest we use false names. He promised to set the banns for a wedding as soon as we've enough coin to petition the king."

"Do you love him?"

His question caught her unguarded. Love was a foolish sentiment. A word used by poets at court. A word used for wooing the weak of mind into bed. If Reid gave credence to such an emotion, then he was a greater fool than she.

"Aye," she finally answered after long seconds, but her hesitation sparked a glimmer of hope in his steel-gray eyes.

The scrutiny of his narrowed gaze was suffocating.

She pulled air into her lungs and with it came the smell of salt and sea. But hidden beneath his scent was something exotic, something not of this land, something forbidden.

Holding her breath, she slipped away from him. "Eoin protects the clan. He is honorable and treats me as an equal. He keeps me safe."

"He involves you in raids. Uses ye as a pawn to stop unsuspecting victims." Reid gestured toward the approaching carriage. The valley was free of mist, and the moon shone down on a driver guiding four horses along the path. "What if the conveyance is filled with vigilantes? Do ye know they are selling pardons in the tippling houses in Rosneath? Any vagrant can purchase the right to hunt a MacGregor."

Did he think her ignorant? She wouldn't take such risks if she didn't believe in the cause. "Things will be different once King James—"

"King James hated the MacGregors when he sat on the throne in Scotland. Now he sits on England's throne as well. Do ye truly believe you could ever plunder enough gold to buy the clan back its name?" Reid growled and ripped his fingers through his black hair. "Damn the Devil, Robbie! Are ye adder-bitten?"

Blast him! Her fingers itched to smack him again. "Every man has a price. Even a king." She turned away from him, raised her skirts, and raced through the wood. Determined to uphold her role in the raid, she jumped the ditch and flattened herself on the road. The cold seeped into her bones as she lay on the ground awaiting the carriage. He was wrong, and he betrayed the clan—his clan—with his cowardly words. The man had no honor, no pride. Like his da, he was concerned only about himself and his wants. She would pay no heed to his words.

The creak of wheels and the clopping of horse hooves drew close then came to a slow stop. A horse nickered. A tail swooshed.

"What is it?" a man asked. Through the slits of her eyes, Robbie saw soft yellow light glowing inside the carriage.

The driver stood and studied her. "There's something in the road."

The man leaning out the side of the carriage craned his neck for a better view. His head jerked to the left to survey the wood.

An owl hooted—their signal to attack. A rustle of leaves followed. Her fingers wrapped tightly around the hilt of her dirk as she waited for her kinsmen to emerge from the woodland and pounce.

"'Tis a trap," the man shrieked and pounded on the side of the carriage. "Move forward, I say. Run over it."

The crack of reins exploded against horseflesh. One of the beasts reared and then jerked against its harness.

Holy Loki! Robbie pushed to her knees, but before she could gain her feet, a force from behind knocked her to the side of the road and landed atop her. Air rushed from her lungs in a whoosh. The passing wind of the carriage pulled her skirts over her calves and the wheel nipped at the tip of one boot. Fortunately her toes had been tightly curled.

A mass of muscle rolled off her. "Ye call this safe?" Reid didn't wait for her reply and raced after the conveyance just as Jax fell from the branches and landed in a squatting position atop the moving carriage.

Trembling from a fright only seconds old, Robbie sat up wide-eyed and watched Jax pluck the driver out of his seat then effortlessly fling him to the ground. Undoubtedly spooked by the attack, the horses whinnied in protest. The carriage came to a sudden halt where her kinsmen had piled boulders at the entrance to the bridge.

She ran toward the scene and only then did she see the cross mounted to the back of the carriage. Candle lamps hanging from four corners of the carriage glowed behind the cross like a religious halo. They were men of God. While disturbed by this knowledge, she selfishly felt relieved they were not vigilantes come to hunt the MacGregors.

Atop their steeds the MacGregors surrounded the conveyance, blades in hand flashing beneath the moonlight. Eoin dismounted and approached the carriage then jerked the door open with a force that startled even her.

Screams erupted inside, both male and female.

Without compassion, Eoin reached inside, pulled a man out by his garments and tossed him to the ground. He scurried to regain his feet but tripped over his crimson robes—bishop's robes.

Robbie felt instant misgivings. She waited for an omen. Mayhap lightning would strike her down for this deed. While Grandda held a certain fascination for the Norse gods, he'd raised her in the Church after her parents died. They'd attended mass in the kirk every morn until the Colquhouns burned it down and killed Father MacCrouther.

"Repent! Repent sinners!" the bishop wailed just before Eoin's favored kinsman, Lyall, drove the butt of his dirk into the bishop's temple.

He sprawled out onto his back unconscious.

Robbie fought the remorse drawing out her sympathies. Clergyman or no, the man had given his driver the order to run her over. His actions were by no means righteous or compassionate. While Robbie justified their actions, Eoin yanked a woman dressed in eels of silk out of the carriage. A young girl with matching white-blonde hair followed and clung to the woman Robbie could only assume was her mam.

"Release the horses from the carriage. Lyall, gather any valuables inside." Eoin gave the orders, which were followed without pause, then walked an intimidating circle around the sobbing twosome. He didn't have to speak to instill fear in them.

"We are people of God," the woman deemed with a haughty lift of her chin that demanded they be treated with respect.

"And what man of God travels in the secrecy of night with a woman and child?" Eoin asked in a tone filled with accusation.

"We have nothing of value." Their full skirts, trimmed in silver and gold threads, mocked her words. The soft plume bobbing out of her wide hat could buy twenty loaves of bread for the clan.

Eoin looked down his nose at her, then ripped a gold button from her high-necked collar. "Remove your garments and your boots. Both of ye."

Robbie shook her head, lips parted to oppose Eoin's order, but in truth, their garments combined would bring forty or fifty pounds from the right merchant.

Lyall ransacked the interior of the carriage while

Robbie's kinsmen untethered the horses. Without further protest, the woman and young girl stripped down to clean white sarks and then watched Eoin stuff their heavy skirts and footwear into a wool sack. The girl's sobs eased, but in their place came the incessant chatter of her teeth.

When Eoin stood and stared at them, as if to imply they were not yet finished, Robbie found her tongue. "'Tis enough."

"Leave them their dignity." Reid rounded the front of the carriage. The candle lamp fixed to the corner filled his sharply-boned face with shadows. His scowl was dark and full of contempt.

Eoin narrowed his eyes on Reid, but instead of flaunting his status as the man was want to do, he yanked a gold crucifix from the bishop's neck and mounted one of the mares bareback. "Stay behind to soothe them if ye choose, but when you're done playing the martyr," he gestured toward the remaining unsaddled horse, "confiscate the mare." Eoin then directed his attention toward Robbie. "Ride Thor and try to keep up. Let's move out." Eoin kicked the mare's belly with his heels, not waiting to see if his orders were carried out. He didn't need to.

The MacGregors followed him through the brook like pups to a bitch, and with their departure came a tense silence.

Wanting nothing more than to distance herself from the raid, Robbie hooked her toe in the stirrup and mounted the enormous black stallion Eoin had stolen from the Laird of Luss last fall. She watched in wonder as Jax removed his fur which exposed his dark muscled body. Black images covered his back and the side of one leg, and most likely represented his achievements or his status within his clan. He stood naked save for the scrap of rawhide covering his pillicock and offered his heavy fur to the woman and her child.

"Begone from us, you wicked son of Satan!" She slapped his hand away as well as his offering and hugged the girl tighter.

Jax pivoted on his heel, leaving the fur at their feet. "White women are not smart."

Reid looked up at Robbie, his icy eyes filled with a disappointment that made her want to run to the nearest kirk and confess her sins.

"This was far from honorable." He walked away from her without so much as a backward glance.

3

● ● ●

~ CONSEQUENCE ~

Mayhap he was too late.

With his hands clasped behind his back, Reid walked up the hillock beside Jax. The moon had guided them over the moor, but his memory of the land now led them through the mist-covered hills of Glenstrae—the land that once belonged to the powerful MacGregor clan. A force of nigh four hundred kinsfolk used to protect this land. His land.

There had been a time when Da believed the Mac-Gregors would always reap the splendors of victory, but something had changed. Something made Da give up his status and turn his back on the clan. Mayhap Da had simply grown tired of the fighting. He'd never wielded the sword with much expertise. Had Da made different choices, Reid might be leading Clan Mac-Gregor instead of Eoin.

God's legions! He hadn't come here to pine over his lost status, nor had he returned to lead the clan. But what if that was the only way to prove his worth to Robbie? Would he hold her respect as well as her affections if he helped regain the MacGregor name? Or would she remain loyal to Eoin?

He didn't want to accept that she was in love with the man or content with her life, but mayhap she was. Mayhap she was happy with Eoin, though Reid was surprised she'd forgiven his cousin for what had happened that night in the cavern.

The years had changed her. She didn't look at Reid the way she once had in her youth. The spark in her emerald eyes was gone, no doubt dimmed by defeat and pessimism. She wasn't the woman he'd created in his fantasies. She wasn't soft or whimsical. Instead, she was bitter, angry, and obstinate.

Mayhap he should leave as she suggested and go back to Rukux, back to the Yucatán. He was respected there. The Mopán people didn't see him as a coward. He was an esteemed warrior, a brother, a son. They were his family and had been for eleven years.

Reid crested the knoll where the ancient stones still stood proud and tall. The smell of smoke clung to the wet haze surrounding them and guided him toward a fire burning in the middle of Leckie's cattle yard. Three sides of the barn remained, but they were charred from fire like so many of the MacGregors' homes he'd passed along the way. Eighty, mayhap a hundred men, women and bairns bustled round the fire. Reid estimated the clan had decreased by three-fourths. Had they died fighting the Colquhouns? Or had they left in search of a better life like Da?

Oddly enough, they appeared jovial, no doubt telling lies of their victory, and he wasn't certain he wanted to be a part of their merriment.

"Did White Serpent make good decisions?" Jax rubbed the gooseflesh from his arms and waited patiently for Reid's answer. For hours the man held his tongue while they walked the Scottish landscape. His friend knew the way Reid's mind worked. He wasn't impulsive, nor did he ever make decisions with haste.

"We eat and drink." Reid slapped Jax on the back and grinned.

"We eat and drink?" Jax's flat nose flared wider as he pointed in the general direction from where they'd crossed acres of land. "White Serpent thinks too much. We steal Fire Tongue and go back to the Yucatán."

Reid laughed outright at Jax's persistence. "Mayhap, but not this night. Tonight we eat and drink." Reid jumped a broken fence, but the instant he stepped into the firelight, silence wrapped around him like a cold blanket.

The women stared at him, the bairns stared at Jax, and the men narrowed their eyes and reached for their weapons. Huddled by the fire, Robbie sat atop a thick log beside Eoin. Her honey-red hair glowed in the firelight, and her fair skin pinked with warmth. She was beautiful. She always had been.

Her eyes met his and after a long painful moment she surprised him with a small smile.

His heart skipped a beat, then picked back up again in double time. The world vanished, as if the sun and moon revolved around this woman. He imagined what it would be like to return from the hunt and have her waiting for him. In the vision he conjured up, she stood barefoot at the edge of his jungle with a bairn on her hip and another swollen in her belly. Of course, thousands of butterflies decorated the scene inside his head; yellow, blue, orange—

"Where's my horse?" Eoin's question slammed the gates shut on Reid's fantasy. His cousin swallowed and wiped the grease from his mouth on his already soiled sleeve.

"'Twas not your horse," Reid stated matter-of-factly, managing to pull himself back to reality.

"I stole it and gave orders for ye to return with it." Eoin sat up taller beside Robbie who twisted her hair round and round her index finger like she'd always done in her youth.

"I decided it best not to leave a man of God stranded without means of travel."

"'Twas not your decision to make."

Reid knew Eoin flaunted his status, and he had to remind himself of his goals—none of which involved leading Clan MacGregor.

Eoin cleared his throat and spit into the flames. "I suspect ye cost the clan a great deal of coin. What say ye, Lyall? Think ye we could have gotten five hundred shillings for the mare?"

"Oh, aye, m'laird. Mayhap more." Lyall stood and tossed another log on the fire. Sparks flickered upward like orange stars out of the flames.

Reid pulled in a long breath and then exhaled. He didn't have to let them goad him. He reached inside his surcoat, withdrew a small bag of coins, and tossed the satchel between Eoin's boots. "Forty doubloons should cover the loss of your stolen goods." *And mayhap buy the women new kirtles and brogues,* he wanted to add when he saw a dozen young girls drying wooden troughs with their thin skirts. He didn't recognize any of them. But what he did recognize was the brand on their cheeks. He quickly glanced over scores of kinsfolk. Every woman in the yard, young and old, was marked the same as Robbie.

Guilt made him turn back to Eoin, who scoffed at Reid's offer but tucked the small satchel into his *plaide.* What the man did with the coin was out of Reid's control, so he kept his suggestions to himself. He was more interested in the way Robbie hid her bemused smirk.

"Reid MacGregor," a woman bellowed with a voice

coarse enough to peel paint. "Merciful Moses." Not until the bone-thin woman rushed toward him did he
recognize Nanna. The waistband of her soiled kirtle
undoubtedly kept her sagging bosom from falling to
her navel, but he would have expected nothing less
from a woman who'd teat-fed half his kin for nigh
three decades.

Long after the plague took Reid's mam, Da took
Nanna to his bed and sired both her bairns, although
she was beyond her birthing years. As she stood before
Reid with soft, fawn-colored eyes filling with tears, he
wondered if she regretted not accepting Da's offer to
take her, Shane, and Kelsa to the Yucatán.

"Ye look well, Nanna." He wiped a tear from her
branded cheek as a rush of remorse spiraled through
him. The same life-sucking guilt he'd felt when he first
saw Robbie.

"'Tis good to have ye home, laddie." She pressed her
trembling hand against his and peeked around his
shoulder. "Did Calum return with ye?"

Reid shook his head, wishing he could spare her his
next words. "Da died three years past."

She inhaled a shaky breath, raised her chin, then
as fast as a snake spit venom she transformed.
"Shane! Bryson!" she bawled over her shoulder. "Fetch
our Reid and his friend some fare." She guided him to
a log and then waved in Jax while the laddies retrieved meat from a young calf speared on a spit.
"Come. Sit. Eat."

Nanna showed no prejudice toward his friend, but
Reid wasn't so delusional to believe the rest of the
kinsfolk would treat Jax in like.

Argyle Wallace limped around the fire, his crippled
hands gripping the handle of a crooked walking stick.
The right side of his face was smooth and lacked emotion, but the left pinched tight with wrinkles. "Mary-

Robena tells me ye assisted m'laird on the raid this eve." He fell onto the log beside Reid with a grunt.

How in God's name had these people survived?

While Reid was glad to find Robbie's grandda alive, the man had to be knocking on death's door. Nay, he corrected. Argyle Wallace was standing beneath the archway.

"You'd have been impressed with Reid's friend, Grandda." Robbie spoke over the fire between them. "Jax jumped out of the trees and landed like a cat atop the moving carriage."

Argyle leaned forward and studied Jax who was currently masticating a haunch of cooked meat. "Is he one o' those savages?"

Jax swallowed and pointed at himself. "Jax is not savage. Savage is a wild man who rapes and pillage." He directed his black eyes toward Eoin. "White man is savage."

Jax really needed to practice the art of biting his tongue.

"Holy Christ! Think ye I choose to live this way?" Eoin's tone set a babe to screaming.

Reid waited for one of the younger women to tend the bairn. Instead, Nanna rushed to a bundle wrapped in wool and cooed the wee bit back to sleep.

Robbie inched away from Eoin, but he set his hand on her leg. "'Tis my duty to feed the clan. A duty that was not handed to me so much as forced down my throat. What would ye do? Please, pray tell. I welcome your opinion."

Reid's gaze fixed on Eoin's hand curled around Robbie's knee.

Jealousy rendered him speechless. It ate at his gut and tightened his muscles into knots of envy. He knew his cousin awaited a response. He could feel Eoin's eyes on him, but couldn't pry his stare from that simple intimacy.

Eoin's hand slid lower, cupping the inside of Robbie's knee, then he angled his arrogant chin and watched Reid like the hunter stalked his prey. The scabbit taunted him on purpose.

Reid bit down hard on his back teeth and suppressed the urge to lunge over the fire. He had no right to feel such anger. Robbie wasn't his woman.

She laced her fingers in Eoin's and set their clasped hands back atop her knee. "If ye were the Gregarach what would ye do?" Robbie's question was not delivered in a defensive tone so much as a genuine inquiry.

Reid controlled his breathing and glanced at those around him who awaited his input with the utmost interest. He was not the clan's enemy, nor was he their savior, but something in between. For now, he accepted this undefined position. Patience was one of his greatest qualities.

He untied the red sash around his calf and used it to wipe the sheen of sweat from his brow. "Mayhap you should consider uniting with your neighbors?"

"Your memory obviously fails ye. We border the Colquhouns," Lyall answered and stroked his dark beard, oblivious to the tension rolling through Reid's veins. Lyall had been the youngest member of the council when Da resided as chieftain. The man had proven exceptional with numbers at a young age and was most likely acting as Eoin's seneschal now. "'Tis doubtful they would align with us, given we killed two hundred of their kin at Glen Fruin."

'Twas Reid's first battle and not one he would soon forget. "Then what of the MacThomases?"

Lyall settled beside Eoin and drank from a tin cup. "The MacThomases already pay us not to steal their livestock, but we cannae call them our allies, nor would we benefit from an alliance with them. They are small in number. The Colquhouns are our greatest concern. Not only do they control the borders and reside in the MacGregor stronghold, they also hold the king's commission."

"Then 'tis the Colquhouns you need in your pocket." Reid paused to accept a flask of drink from Argyle. "It is my opinion that your raids will never prove profitable enough to fill a king's purse. Mayhap you should seek protection from the enemy by the enemy."

Lyall's bushy brows rose. "'Tis doubtful any amount of coin would settle the bad blood between our clans."

"Every man has a price." Reid repeated Robbie's words from earlier but didn't dare look at her. "Offer the Colquhoun chieftain a sum of money for Rannoch or Auchingaich. If he accepts, you know he can be bought, and you will have land to build a home for the clan."

Lyall turned toward Eoin. "What kind o' coin do ye think the Laird of Luss would require to comply?"

"Fifty-four thousand pounds for Rannoch." Eoin popped off the sum relatively quickly. "Forty-two for the fruitless moss of Auchingaich." His words set the kinsfolk into upheaval. Some whispered their opinion, while others simply snorted and guffawed. They sounded like migrating birds squawking their protests.

Ignoring their cynicism, Reid retrieved the coin from inside his surcoat and rolled it across the ridges of his fingers. He'd always found the repetition soothing. It helped him think, but this night he need not argue with the pessimist inside him. Eoin didn't pull those figures out of his arse. He'd already bartered with the Colquhoun chieftain. While the MacGregors may not be capable of attaining such a sum, Reid was. He had the opportunity to provide for the clan, and mayhap earn Robbie's forgiveness and respect in the process.

Eoin raised his hand to settle the kinsfolk. "Your ideas are entertaining, cousin, but we dinnae have that kind of coin."

"I do." Reid twirled the gold piece through his fingers a final time then caught the coin in his fist. He looked at Robbie. "I just need a wee bit of help attaining it."

She pulled the corner of her bottom lip between her teeth and lowered pale lashes to hide her eyes.

"Go on," Argyle nudged him.

"Southeast of Cristóbal Colón's New World, there is a land called the Yucatán not yet settled by the Spaniards. Ancient Maya once ruled this land now inhabited by different tribes. They are much like Scotland's clans in their divisions, but they live by different ideals, different beliefs. There are great stone pyramids inside their woods."

"Like our ancient stones?" Argyle asked.

"In many ways I suspect."

"And the gold ye seek is inside these pyramids, untouched, unclaimed by anyone." Eoin's mocking assumptions were no more than an attempt to discredit Reid, but he wouldn't be swayed by his cousin's skepticism.

"The pyramids were once religious sanctuaries for the dead. Temples for the Maya gods and goddesses. Some of the tribes fear disrupting these temples for they do not wish to anger the gods." Reid could easily blather on for hours about ancient cultures and the ways of the Mopán people, but the MacGregors cared naught about Jax's people, nor would they hold any interest in learning about an ancient Maya priestess's lost library. They wanted gold. Something substantial they could barter with. He wouldn't waste his breath lecturing them on the value of the ideals Xitali might have left behind. "The treasure I seek is not within these temples. It is below in an underground river."

The fire popped. The intensity of their anticipation was reward in and of itself. Reid was certain Robbie's eyes could get no rounder. If he was a betting man, he'd wager she was nigh salivating at the opportunity to seek out a hidden treasure. She was still diving, which meant she still searched for the Spaniard's gold.

"And ye need the diving barrel to get to this treasure?" Robbie asked in a soft tone he didn't expect.

If all he wanted was the diving barrel, he would have built one himself. "I need your expertise as well as Argyle's."

Robbie swallowed hard, her delicate brows shot up. Murmurs escalated.

Eoin glared at her, no doubt gauging her reaction.

Argyle cleared his throat, and Reid prepared for Robbie's grandda to protest, but he merely inquired, "How long would such an expedition take?"

"Three months." Reid thought the time period reasonable, given two of those months would be spent aboard the *Obsidian*. "And I leave on the morrow."

Eoin stood, putting an end to further discussion. "Then it is on the morrow when ye shall have my answer." He pulled Robbie to her feet and led her toward the burned out barn.

The envy that consumed Reid earlier was naught but a scale on the serpent of jealousy coiling inside him now.

● ● ●

Robbie was certain she'd never seen Eoin quite so enraged. She had to run to keep up with his strides as he practically dragged her through the yard toward the barn. The moment he released his grip, stinging settled in her fingers like she'd just swiped her hand through the nettles.

He climbed the ladder to the old loft, and for a fleeting moment she contemplated not following. Not because she feared him, but because of the argument she would undoubtedly lose. She wanted to learn more about Reid's treasure. The idea of hunting for gold filled her with an excitement she hadn't felt since her youth. It had nothing to do with Reid. Nothing at all.

They would need to retrieve the barrel and the boots and the leather suit. Did they even need the suit where they were going or would it be warm? Would they need two or more? How many would be diving?

Robbie closed her eyes and forced the chaos from her head. She needed to focus on what was important, and that was convincing Eoin to swallow his pride and accept Reid's help. The gold would benefit the clan. Naught else mattered.

She drew in a breath of courage and ascended into the loft one rung at a time.

Eoin stood in his red and green crossbarred *plaide*, legs braced, arms crossed, staring into a moonlit night through a splintered window. Silver light shone down on his hardened face and outlined his massive form. He was a big man. Mayhap even bigger than Reid.

Robbie stared at him and saw a man who'd always been saddled with responsibility. He rarely laughed. He never prayed. He held himself with constant dignity as the leader of a dying kingdom. She respected him as a leader and would always be indebted to him for his devotion to the clan and his protection of those dear to her.

"You're not going with him. I'll not allow it." Eoin words didn't shock her.

Pulling the seams of her *arisaid* around her, she shuffled through the sour hay and settled in his shadow. "Should we not at least consider his offer?"

"I'll not give coin to my enemy. Da was executed in Edinburgh because of those bastairds. The Colquhouns are the reason we live like starving dogs. Think of what they did to Kelsa, and the other lassies, and ye. They marked ye, Robbie, and are responsible for the deaths of hundreds of MacGregors, including your da. Can ye forgive such crimes?"

"If it meant we could start anew."

He snorted and shook his head. "I might have known you'd take his side."

This had nothing to do with Reid. Nothing at all. "This is not about taking sides." She stepped beside him. "We are talking about a means to provide for the clan. We have the opportunity to change our livelihood as well as those who have paid ye loyalty."

He uncrossed his arms, pulled a hand through his wiry hair, and turned toward her. The moonlight outlined his features—tight lips, pinched jaw, dark angry eyes. "The kin of Clan MacGregor have paid me their loyalty because I have earned it. When all the others fled, I stayed. I should be living in Kilchurn Castle and commanding the kinsfolk of Glenstrae. Instead, I sleep in rotted hay while the Colquhouns seek their slumber in my bed and warm their faces by my fire. A chieftain should not live as I do." He turned back toward the night. "I should have coffers brimming with siller and sons on the training field, but no. God has not blessed me with the riches I deserve."

Mayhap it was the self-righteous tone he'd used in his delivery, but Robbie missed the part where she was included in his glorified plans. Not once had he mentioned Rannoch or the life they'd talked about once the proscription was repealed. Eoin didn't want to purchase Rannoch or Auchingaich for that matter. He didn't want to be the lord of the manor. He wanted to be the king of his castle. He wanted the stronghold returned, and she doubted anything less would appease him. "And am I your lady at Kilchurn Castle? Did I provide ye with your sons? Or did ye marry according to your bluidy status to strengthen ties between *your* clan?"

"Holy Christ, Robbie! How can ye even speak such drivel? I love ye."

Just as he loved the miller's wife and scores of fair maidens who were loose with their favors. Robbie wanted to scoff at his words. She wanted to accuse him of being unfaithful, but she had no proof, so she said naught.

Eoin rubbed the heavy sacs beneath his eyes. "Ye know why we are not wed, and we both agreed not to bring a bairn into this world if the doing was at all preventable."

"We could have pledged our troth years ago and for every year that passes, I grow farther and farther beyond my birthing years." She'd given him her loyalty as well as her affections, and she deserved a family.

"We have been through this, Robbie. Ye know why we cannae go to the Highlands and live with our MacGregor kin."

They'd argued often enough about why they should remain in Glenstrae. Eoin gave her many reasons— some justifiable, some not. He'd said Grandda wouldn't survive the trip, nor would auld Angus or the babe, Alana, who was so frail at just six months old. Robbie disagreed with him wholeheartedly as so many of their kin had traveled to the Highlands to seek a new home. She'd held her tongue, choosing her battles, but this night she would call him on the real reason she suspected he didn't leave. "Because ye would not be the Gregarach in the Highlands, nor would ye have your castle."

"Hold your wheesht!" Eoin's jaw clenched. A vein

whelped in his neck. "I have never laid a hand to ye, Mary-Robena Wallace, but never have I wanted to more than I do right now."

Robbie raised her chin, tempting him to do so. "Tell me I am wrong."

"Ye accuse me of a selfishness I dinnae deserve. I stay in the glen because of them." He stabbed a finger in the general direction of the yard where the MacGregor kinsfolk gathered round the fire. "I did not leave because I felt it my place to save them. 'Twas a duty entrusted to your precious Reid and he left. He is the one who acted selfishly. He is the one who betrayed the clan."

"And he has returned to offer an assistance ye are too proud to accept." Robbie suppressed the urge to shout as loud as he did. She needed to proceed with caution. Reid's presence alone bruised Eoin's pride.

"He is no savior," Eoin hissed between his teeth and bent low. "Think ye I am a fool? He dinnae return to save the godforsaken clan. He returned for you."

Her heart beat so loud in her ears, she feared Eoin would hear it pounding. She grabbed hold of the sides of her kirtle to keep her fingers out of her hair. "He needs my assistance with the diving barrel. And Grandda, too. And—"

"I am not blind. I see the way he looks at ye. He was besotted with ye in his youth, and he is besotted with ye now."

Mayhap this *was* about Reid.

No one, save for Lyall, had ever shown an interest in Robbie. The clan knew Eoin had claimed her for his own and didn't dare challenge him for her hand. Jealousy was an emotion she'd never seen on him, and he didn't wear it well. S'truth, she found it ugly. "Ye dinnae trust me."

"I do not trust him!" Eoin yelled and turned away

from her.

Long moments passed in awkward silence, then Eoin laughed. 'Twas a disturbing chuckle that made her question the man's sanity.

"The mon returns for one day and has the clan contemplating an alliance with our greatest enemy. He has ye warring with me in his stead, and all for a treasure he doesnae even possess." The arrogant lift returned to his chin. "For argument's sake, let's say ye go with him and return with this treasure. We pay the Colquhouns for lands that already belong to us. How long do ye think it would take them to gut us?"

"If ye dinnae trust the Laird of Luss, then take the coin and petition King James." 'Twas what she wanted in the first place. Lands wouldn't free the MacGregor women of the prison of their brands.

"What happens after our lands are returned and the proscription against our name is lifted? Where does that leave Reid?"

"I know not." She hadn't thought that far ahead. "Mayhap he will return to this Yucatán he speaks of." A sadness washed over her. A sadness she'd long ago buried inside her.

"I think not." Eoin spun, and she didn't much care for his snarl. "He'll expect restitution for his act of generosity."

"Think ye he will want to reclaim the chieftainship?" The instant she posed the question, she realized Eoin had already contemplated what it would cost him. He would never give up his status.

"Nay, Robbie. I can assure ye, he will never lay claim to Clan MacGregor, but what is to stop him from laying claim to ye?"

She wanted to spit fire on him. Eoin insulted her with his insinuations. She'd been faithful to him for three bluidy years. Never had she strayed from his bed or given him reason to distrust her. Yet, he stood before her and questioned her loyalty. Reid might have returned to claim her, but she possessed enough will to ward off his charm. "I am."

Eoin's shoulders fell with an exhale that sounded much like defeat. He pushed the hair from her eyes and traced her brow. "Ye've always done what ye wanted. I tried to stop ye from running the raids, but ye insisted on playing your part. I tried to stop ye from diving after what happened to Kelsa, but ye dinnae listen. Ye've always acted out against my will. I trust ye will do so again."

Eoin cradled the back of her head in his hand and kissed her. His touch was familiar and safe, yet something in his kiss felt like farewell. She pulled away. "Grandda and I will bring back the gold, and we'll petition the king. Ye will see. All will be right."

He walked passed her and started to descend the ladder. "I need to think."

Which translated into "I need a drink." The man was no stranger at the tippling houses. He was known as John Murray. It angered her that he snuck away from camp and spent what little coin the clan had on such frivolity without conscience, but what hurt more was his decision to spend their last night together getting blootered.

Out the window, she watched him guide Thor into the wood until blackness hid him from her vision. She pulled her *arisaid* tighter and contemplated going back to the fire. She was tired of being cold and tired of being alone.

A silver-eyed devil flashed through her mind's eye, and for a moment she let herself think about what it would be like to be Reid's woman. She wondered what his touch would feel like, what his kiss would taste like.

Oh, this *was* about Reid MacGregor.

She twirled a curl round and round her finger and prayed she possessed the strength she needed to resist temptation when she boarded his ship on the morrow.

4

~ DECISIONS ~

Reid rubbed his stinging eyes. Mayhap the fire he'd glared at throughout the night burned a permanent image onto his mind, but the way Robbie stood behind the barn staring into the wood made him think of the fire-goddess he'd named his ship for. Robbie's golden-red hair hung in loose waves to her waist and nigh glowed beneath the sun's morning rays. Every breath she blew curled around her in opaque ribbons and made her appear ethereal, dreamlike...untouchable.

An orange butterfly, too afraid to land, danced around her. He knew not if the insect was real or part of a memory from his dreams. Nonetheless, he smiled.

He couldn't see what held her attention. No doe returned her gaze. No enemy hid in the timber as far as he could tell. All was quiet, save for the crackling sound of a wood creature burrowing through autumn's leaves.

When she had emerged from the barn and went to the brook to tend her morning ablutions, Reid forced himself not to race after her, but now he intended to have private words with her. He wanted to hear her decision from her lips, not Eoin's.

The crunching beneath his boots announced his approach and sent Robbie into fidgets. Her hands flew to her face, scrubbed, then fisted into the sides of her kirtle.

"Robbie." He side-stepped around her, but she pivoted and inhaled a shaky breath.

When he spun her around to face him, she pinned her chin to her chest and avoided his eyes. 'Twas not like Robbie to act so demure. He angled his head and saw the dampness turning her thick lashes to cinnamon spikes just before she looked at him with red swollen eyes.

A fierce pain exploded in his chest. "You're crying."

"I amnae crying."

"You lie. Your eyes are red."

"As are yours."

"I've been staring at the fire."

"I've been staring into the wood."

Damn the Devil! The woman was ill-tempered. Reid pulled in a breath that was soft and sweet, like flowers covered in morning dew. As if her scent alone had the power to calm him, the tension fell away from his neck, then without thought, he reached out to touch her cheek.

She jerked away from him like a beaten dog.

"Has Eoin hurt ye?" Reid's breathing increased again while he awaited her answer. *Give me a reason to kill the bastaird.*

She shook her head. "Eoin has never struck me."

"A man does not have to strike a woman to hurt her. Has something happened?"

She turned back toward the woodland. "Yester morn I awoke in a different valley." She twisted her finger through a coil of hair. "It was just as cold and just as barren. I helped Grandda to his feet as his knees dinnae work the way they used to, and then I did the same with auld Angus. I cooked eggs Shane and Bryson stole from the MacThomases, and then warmed milk to feed Alana. After noontide, I went to the brook to assist Nanna and the other kinswomen with the laundry." A tear dripped from her cheek and splashed onto her sharp collarbone.

She wasn't going with him. She didn't have to say the words. "Why are ye telling me this?"

She turned toward him, her green eyes brimming with unshed tears. "Because this morn when I awoke, I wondered if mayhap I deserved more."

Aye, she deserved so much more than God had given her thus far. This time when he reached out to push her hair behind her ear, she didn't stop him. He held the back of her head with his fingers and drew a half circle around the rim of her dainty ear.

His gaze fell to her quivering lips. He desperately wanted to kiss her, but 'twas too soon. "Come with me, Robbie. The Yucatán is unlike any land you've every seen. It is warm and green all year round. There is much to be discovered, and I want for naught more than to find it with you." Of course Reid thought of Xitali's library, but he chose to tempt Robbie with talk of treasure for now.

Leaves crunched in the timber. A horse snorted.

Like a startled cat, Robbie jumped backward and pulled the seams of her *arisaid* tight.

Reid turned and with his next breath, he realized what Robbie had been searching for. Eoin emerged from the woodland on his beastly stallion whose neck shone slick with perspiration. He dismounted between them, and then scrutinized Robbie from head to toe with heavy-lidded eyes. "Did I interrupt?"

The man smelled like he'd bathed in sour whisky.

Had Reid known the fool spent his eve in a tippling house, he might have taken Robbie and her grandda away last night.

"We were talking about the expedition." Robbie's spine lengthened and her chin raised another inch. "I was on my way to rouse Grandda and gather a satchel of toiletries."

She's going! Reid's insides danced in jubilation, but he reined in his excitement and held a somber face. He would not gloat. He didn't care if Robbie was going to spite Eoin. Reid only cared that she was going.

"Weel then." Eoin grinned at her and pat her backside. "Make haste. We'll be waiting."

"We?" Both Reid and Robbie questioned in unison.

Eoin popped an arrogant brow. "Ye must think me a complete dunderheid to trust either of ye to return with the gold. In fact, I think it best if Argyle stayed in Scotland. 'Twill give ye a reason to return."

• • •

The morning had nigh defeated Robbie. Every muscle inside her wanted to push Eoin off Thor and leave his duff in an alleyway, but she didn't dare invite more attention to their entourage. She'd elbowed him in the ribs several times, hoping she might rouse the ox and free her aching back of his weight. But the drunkard continued to snore in her ear and blow his whisky-soaked breath down her neck. She sighed and pulled the hood of her *arisaid* close to her face while she guided Thor behind Reid and Lyall through the crowded port of Rosneath.

A young boy rushed by them rolling a barrel down a narrow boardwalk. Another followed with coils of ropes draped over both shoulders. Gulls cried overhead, but Robbie kept her head bowed and her eyes forward. The wagon carrying the diving barrel drew a

few curious stares, and Jax caught the eye of a couple
bystanders, but at least Reid's friend could hide inside
his hooded cloak.

Most were interested in the corpse-like body draped
over Robbie's back. 'Twould take little effort for someone to see the brand on her cheek and name them
MacGregors. This was why she hadn't been in public
since she was ten and three, and Eoin was in no condition to wield a sword to defend her.

She didn't know what angered her more; the fact
that Eoin didn't trust her or the fact that everyone
seemed to share his skepticism. Even Grandda.

*Someday is now, Mary-Robena. Reid can make ye
happy,* Grandda had said before he hugged her with
his crippled hands and kissed her forehead.

Did no one believe her capable of resisting Reid
MacGregor?

She didn't want to know the answer to that. S'truth,
she wasn't certain she trusted herself. Reid almost
kissed her that morn, and she couldn't say whether or
not she would have stopped him.

When Reid looked at her, she felt like that giddy
young girl awaiting him to come up from the dive and
collect his kiss. She nudged Thor onto a wooden land-
ing beside the water and refused to think about that
girl. She no longer existed, nor did any of her foolish
dreams. Robbie would never marry a king and live in
a castle. She would never sleep in a bed draped in eels
of colorful silks. And she mustn't forget the most un-
realistic dream of all: she would never be a mermaid
who breathed underwater and searched for buried
treasure.

She laughed a little on the inside. That last bit of
foolishness had always been Fergus's dream, but he
let her share it. Her throat tightened a little as it always did when she thought of her brother. Fergus

would have given his sword arm to go on this expedition.

Reid stopped in front of her, pulling her out of her musings. He rose up in the stirrups in his tight black breeks, kicked a leg over his steed's rump, and then dismounted.

Robbie's gaze locked on his duff. And a nice duff it was indeed—sweetly rounded into thick thighs.

Blast it! She slammed her eyes shut, then opened one. Why shouldn't she look? Eoin would never know. By the time she made the decision to ogle Reid, he was walking toward her. Actually, she would more call his walk a swagger. Neglect on his part to tighten the laces of his shirt exposed the swells of his muscular chest. His sleeves were rolled to the elbow and thin red marks covered his forearms. Not so deep they were scars, but scratches. Like he'd dragged his arms through a thorn bush. His polished boots outlined his brawny calves and clicked on the wooden planks in time with a ringing bell in the background.

"Is something in your eye?" He looked up at her.

"Nay." She popped the eye open she'd been hiding behind as a rush of heat warmed her cheeks. Embarrassment? Mayhap. Or was it guilt? Either way, the attraction she had to Reid needed to cease before she boarded his ship.

Thankfully his gaze left her to study Eoin. "Think we could slip you out without his knowing? We could be at sea before the drink wore off."

Robbie forced a disapproving look, knowing the smile she suppressed would only encourage Reid. "Eoin sleeps during the day because we raid at night."

Reid snorted at her lie. "He sleeps because he drowned himself in the cups."

"And I suspect you've never been overcome by the drink?" She didn't know why she defended Eoin. He certainly didn't deserve it.

"I'm no saint, Robbie, but I can assure you, if I had ye in my bed, I'd not be spending my eves tossing back drams o' whisky with the drunkards." Reid didn't wait for her response, which was fortunate because she hadn't paid much attention beyond the words "in my bed."

Why did the man have to say such things? And why did he have to look so perfectly braw? And why couldn't she remember all the reasons she hated Reid MacGregor?

A grunt ended the string of questions piling up in her head, then the weight that had been Eoin was wrenched off her back. When she twisted in the saddle, her spine popped in three different places.

"Holy Christ!" Eoin assumed a warrior's stance, drew his dirk, and swayed. "I swear on the cross I'll gut ye down, mon."

"Easy, cousin." Reid slapped Eoin on the back— hard. "Conserve your energy. You're going to need it."

While Eoin gathered his wits and struggled to become familiar with his surroundings, Reid stepped back to Robbie's left and offered his hand. "Come, m'lady. Your ship awaits."

She shouldn't find humor in Eoin's suffering, nor should she accept Reid's offering, but she did both. She set her small hand in his much larger one and when he wrapped his strong fingers around hers, she bit back a giggle that made her eyes water.

Control yourself, ye wantwit! She dismounted and followed Reid in front of Thor.

He made a sweeping gesture toward a single-masted vessel tied to the dock. "May I present the *Obsidian*."

Though it had a bow and a stern and even a bit of open deck, Robbie would hardly call it a ship. 'Twas more of a boat really. Her disappointment would be difficult to hide. "It...is...lovely."

"Surely ye jest." Eoin laughed outright and exchanged a look with Lyall who'd joined them at the dock's edge. "I dare say your *ship* might buckle beneath the weight of the diving barrel."

"That is the ferry boat, you dunderheid." Reid raised Robbie's chin with the tip of his index finger and pointed at a much larger vessel anchored in the Firth of Clyde. "*That* is the *Obsidian*."

"Oh," was all she said. 'Twas all she could say really as words failed her.

"She's a three-masted carrack, weighing well over six-hundred tons. She's armed with three cannons on the starboard side and three on the larboard side. It takes a crew of fifty men to row her," Reid listed the *Obsidian's* attributes with a lilt of pride. "She's named after a warrior fire-goddess who often appeared in the form of a black, clawed butterfly."

She could feel his penetrating eyes on her, but before she could comment, Eoin curled his arm around Robbie's waist and drew her close to his side—a blatant reminder of who she belonged to. "Impressive, cousin. I'm curious about one thing. Is the *Obsidian* the same ship ye and Uncle Calum fled Scotland on?"

She felt her eyes widen. Did Eoin feel so inferior that he had to browbeat Reid at every opportunity? At the very least, Eoin could attempt to be amiable. S'truth, Reid abandoned the clan, and she would always hate him for doing so, but now was not the time or the place for a fisticuff.

"Nay." Reid leaned in toward Eoin which squashed her between their chests. "I obtained the *Obsidian* shortly after Da died."

"Ye *obtained* it or ye stole it?"

"Enough." Robbie pressed a palm against each of

their stomachs and pushed. A rumble of frustration sounded low in her throat. They'd actually made her growl like some rabid beastie. They were the ones behaving like bluidy animals.

"S'help me Odin," she grumbled, disgusted with them both, then stepped out from between them and approached Lyall. She inhaled deeply, cocked her head slightly, and smiled. "See that Thor and the other horses get back safely, and if I might trouble ye with a task. Pay Grandda and auld Angus a visit in the mornings. They have difficulty getting going most days."

Lyall dipped his head once and bent to Robbie's ear. "If they kill each other, my offer to take ye to the Highlands still stands," he whispered and then kissed her scarred cheek. "God speed, lass."

5

———

~ DEPARTURE ~

After hoisting the diving barrel over the rail of the *Obsidian*, Reid strode across the main deck and gave instructions to the boatswain. "Prepare the launching crew, Henrik."

"Aye, Captain."

"*Captain* is it?" Eoin leaned against the rail and spit a hawker over the edge. He scratched a beard that was four, mayhap five, days old. "I hope ye dinnae expect *me* to refer to ye as such."

"I'll not be referring to you as 'm'laird,' so I suspect that makes us square." Had Reid been holding a chicken by its neck, the head would have shot off. Normally, he wasn't a violent man, but the day had him thoroughly vexed. Eoin wasn't even supposed to be here. Reid intended to make the guzzle-guts wish he'd never stepped foot aboard his ship.

Then he looked at Robbie and changed his mind. As much as he wanted to smash his fist into his cousin's arrogant mouth, 'twas not the way to earn her respect.

Eoin hadn't changed. He was still a pompous arse.

He might hold the respect of the clan. He might even be a decent leader, but he wasn't the leader aboard the *Obsidian.* On this ship he was naught more than another bilgemate, and that was the powder that would ignite his vanity.

"Is there aught we can do to assist?" Robbie twisted her hair with one hand and strangled the single satchel she'd brought on board with the other. When she raised her soft green eyes to him, the storm inside him subsided.

"'Twould be best if you just stay out of the way."

Robbie's brows stitched together, and her lips thickened into a pout.

God's legions! He'd insulted her. She wanted to do her part just like in the raid, but what duty could he give her? He looked overhead at the topmen swarming the rigging, some of them Mopán natives, some of them vagrants Reid retained from various port-of-calls. They untied the canvas from the yardarms, which left a mess of ropes dangling onto the deck. "Now that I think on it, mayhap I could use your assistance."

She smiled and Eoin rolled his eyes.

"Tie the lines off larboard."

"The left?

"Aye." Reid left her to her task and climbed the center mast to assist with the mainsail. Every now and again, he would glance her way to see if she was watching—which she was. If naught else, the launching was an impressive show. Organized chaos at its best.

Reid dropped from a yardarm and landed beside his first mate. "Good den, Jean-Pierre."

"Salut, Capitaine." The man twirled his thick black mustache and looked down his long pointed nose at Reid. "I trust the *fille* making a mess of our ropes is

your Robbie?"

"Aye. But dinnae tell her. She does not yet know it."
Reid grinned and clapped the man on the back. "Raise
the anchor before the Scots discover I brought a
French renegade into their waters."

Reid took his position at the helm and gave the signal to the boatswain overhead to hoist the sails while
Jean-Pierre assisted five men turning the capstan.

Canvas snapped like gunshot. The sails filled with a
nor'wester gale that hurled the *Obsidian* into an unsteady quiver.

Robbie held tight to the rail and gawked at the
spectacle overhead. The wind blew her honey-red hair
in haphazard directions, but she didn't bother to control it. Aye, she was impressed. Reid was certain of it.

Eoin on the other hand had missed the show, as he
was spewing his guts over the side of the ship. A wee
bit of seasickness should keep the man occupied.

Reid tried not to gloat, but the task was nigh impossible.

● ● ●

This wasn't the first time Robbie had seen Eoin
green in the gills. The steady to and fro rocking of the
ship must have been more than his whisky-soaked gut
could take. The sun had just dipped beneath the horizon when she'd left him resting in a rope bed on the
deck near the bow of the ship. However, Eoin would
undoubtedly rise with the moon, full of spit and piss—
which brought to mind a pressing matter she needed
to tend.

Robbie snatched up her toiletries and raised her
skirts. Cool wind pushed against her and sea spray
misted her face as she followed the polished rail toward the helm.

"Good den, miss." A man tipped a three-cornered

cocked hat spilling light-brown curls as she passed. She recognized him from the launch but didn't know his—

"The name's Henrik," he verbalized her unfinished thought.

"The name's Robbie," she offered over her shoulder, then realized how rude she must appear for not stopping. "I've a matter to discuss with your captain, but I'll be back a ten, and we'll chew the fat." Grandda had always said that to auld Angus, but Henrik's face squished up like a withered grape. She didn't have time to explain Grandda's expression, so she kept walking—in fact, she more ran to the helm.

Reid brushed his hands together, chewed whatever he'd been eating, then swallowed, all the while sporting a scowl. "Is something amiss?" He looked over her shoulder and swept the deck with a nervous stare.

She crossed her legs at the knees beneath her kirtle and searched for words to explain her predicament without turning ten shades of red. "Not exactly." Pulling the corner of her bottom lip between her teeth, she stared at his boot tips and prayed a puddle wouldn't form at her feet.

"Robbie?" He raised her chin and the pressure on her innards intensified.

The skin around her knuckles grew taut as she squeezed the neck of her satchel. "It seems the men have no qualms about relieving themselves over the rail, but I fear I'm not quite so talented."

He laughed and popped the tip of her nose with his index finger. "You had me fretting." He pointed over his shoulder with his thumb. "There's a privy pot in my cabin. Have you need for an escort?"

"Nay," she practically squealed, but had no time for niceties. She rushed passed him and climbed the companionway in four steps, then burst through the cabin door. A low-burning oil lamp provided her enough light to glance over the furnishings; a desk, a bed, a fabric-screened partition. She tossed her toiletries atop the bed and raced toward the partition where she found the blessed privy pot.

Once she'd tended her needs, she carried the pot through a small door at the rear of the cabin that lead to a narrow balcony where she discarded the contents over a rail. Reid paid her far too much attention as it was. The last thing she needed was for the man to start playing chamber maid.

She located a basin and washed the day's dust away, then dried her face with a towel. *His* towel. A tangy, yet woodsy scent filled her nose and sent tingles over her spine. She rubbed her arms. She was cold, she told herself, refusing to believe the gooseflesh covering her skin had anything to do with his scent.

She walked across a fur rug to fetch her satchel, but when she plucked it off the bed, she grabbed hold of the corner of a red silk sheet. A matching red coverlet lay twisted across a down-filled mattress tucked securely in its hold. The silk was softer than anything she'd ever slept on. Boldly, she slid her fingers through his bedding, and before she could stop the image, she saw a man tangled within those sheets. His thick muscular calf lay on the outside of the coverlet exposing his hip and the sweet curve of his duff. A muscular arm wrapped around her tiny waist, then the man turned and looked at her with silver eyes.

Brown. Brown eyes. Eoin had brown eyes.

Blast it! She snatched her hand out of the silk as if it had scalded her and fanned her hot face. 'Twas bad enough she was imagining Reid naked, now she was naked with him. And how could her nipples be so hard when she felt so hot?

Without thought, she scurried around the giant

wooden berth fluffing the bolsters and making up the bed. 'Twas not proper to have such lust-filled thoughts about a man other than Eoin. Just because Reid bluidy MacGregor looked delicious and smelled delicious and would undoubtedly taste delicious—

Ack! Enough, Mary-Robena Wallace! Enough.

Content with her mental scolding, Robbie again started for the door, but another curiosity caught the corner of her eye. In the center of Reid's desk lie a map weighted down by carved stones. The shape of the land was unfamiliar to her and the numbers and lines inked atop land and water could be no more than Reid's charts for their voyage. Or mayhap it was more? Beside the map was an open log book filled margin to margin with a record of daily distances. She flipped through the yellowed pages and found a section filled with symbols similar to those she'd seen tattooed on Jax's skin.

An entirely different excitement rushed beneath her skin, but this bout of gooseflesh was safe, for it had naught to do with Reid MacGregor's body. She rolled the wick on the brass lantern bolted to the desktop to increase the flame, then bent over the desk eager to analyze the journal. She was lost within seconds.

Just as she'd decided the triangles represented mountains, a low growl interrupted her exploration. She should probably eat, but her stomach had not yet cramped.

The growl turned into a steady vibrating rumble behind her.

What in the name of Odin? Her heart jumped into her throat. She swallowed, scared to turn around, but scared not to. She slowly swiveled. With her buttocks pressed against the edge of the desk, she came face to face with a spotted cat the size of a goat. Black stripes painted its brown and white face, and curved teeth hooked over its bottom lip.

It leapt onto the bed, stared at her with huge golden-brown eyes, then it opened its toothy mouth and screamed.

Robbie gripped the edge of the desk and screamed back.

The cat lunged from the bed and pinned Robbie to the desktop. Its heavy paws held her shoulders down and its pink nose hovered over her face.

Robbie screamed two more times.

Just as she was certain her heart would explode through her ribs, the feline beastie dragged its thick raspy tongue over her cheek.

A pounding of footsteps preceded the whoosh of the cabin door. "Damn the Devil, lass!" An audible breath followed. "I feared you were under attack."

Was the man soft in the skull? "I *am* under attack. Get this beastie off me!"

The said beastie licked her again and set a heavy paw on her throat. Its purr vibrated against her chest, but now seemed less menacing combined with Reid's chuckle.

"Oscar, come." Reid clicked his tongue and bent down on one knee. "He was simply curious. 'Tis all."

The instant the cat bounced off her, Robbie shot upright and then backed up against a row of lockers built into the bulkhead. "Curious? Curious as to what I tasted like before it bit my face off?" She held her burning chest and watched the cat crawl onto Reid's shoulders and rub its forehead against his bristled chin.

"I'll wager she tasted sweet. What say you, Oscar? Did she taste of honey or was she bitter like new wine?" Reid scrubbed the cat's ears, but received comeuppance for his remark when the beastie knocked him to the planked floor. Its long tail whipped side to side as its wide jaw wrapped around Reid's forearm, but not so hard it drew blood. They were playing.

She'd seen Reid's smile, but this one was different. The smile he wore now set dimples high up on his cheeks just beneath his eyes. He really was easy to look at. She watched them wrestle until she felt brave enough to leave the safety of the wall. "What is he?"

"He's a cat. A rather big cat I s'pose." Reid motioned her toward him. "Come, he'll not hurt you."

Oscar wrapped its paws around Reid's forearm as he scratched its furry belly. 'Twas obvious to her now how Reid had acquired all the scratches. Robbie had never known the affections of a pet. The clan ate anything with a face that wasn't human. Just last spring Shane and Bryson gave a couple barn cats to auld Angus's granddaughters, but Cait and Anice set them free into the wood knowing auld Angus would turn them into vittles.

The connection between Reid and his feline beastie warmed her in a way that was unfamiliar, yet safe. Robbie knelt down and cautiously stroked Oscar's soft fur. "'Tis like no cat I've ever seen."

"He's not quite a jaguar. I've heard him named an ocelot, but I simply call him Oscar. His mother was killed during a hunt in the jungle. Jax and I found two kits after the fact. One died, but Oscar learned to like goat's milk and has been with me ever since."

"I'm certain ye make a fine mam," Robbie jested as Oscar flipped to his feet and slinked about the cabin until he found a resting place in the center of the bed where he began to bathe himself.

"Did ye make the bed?" Reid asked.

"'Twas unmade." Robbie realized her propensity for order might not be welcome.

"'Tis because I'll be getting back in it shortly."

Must he talk about the bed? The image she'd conjured up earlier slammed back into her mind's eye just as she turned toward him. His heavy-lidded eyes held hers, but she couldn't bring herself to look away. She suddenly became very aware of her position. Oscar's absence left her kneeling between Reid's splayed legs on the floor and an uncontrollable force seemed to draw them closer. The same force that had been present behind the barn. A force she admitted was desire.

Awkward silence settled between them.

A giggle tickled her throat, a nervous attribute she'd never outgrown. She swallowed and licked her lips while her stomach did flip-flops, and her fingernails dug into her palms.

Reid's gaze fell to her mouth.

He was going to kiss her. And she didn't possess the strength to stop him.

"Are ye hungry?" His jarring question ripped her out of the moment but saved her from making a reprehensible mistake.

"Aye." She shot to her feet and looked out the open door into total darkness. What if Eoin had seen her? If she betrayed him, then she betrayed the MacGregors. She needed to control herself and put all the people she held close to her heart to the forefront of her mind. She didn't want to think about what Eoin would do, or worse, wouldn't do. Whether Robbie wanted to admit it or not, she needed Eoin. She needed his protection, not only for herself, but for the weak of the clan.

As Robbie followed Reid out of the cabin, she focused on all the reasons she was with Eoin. The greatest of his qualities was his loyalty to the clan. He loved them. He loved being their leader. She would not destroy what she had with Eoin on adolescent lust.

● ● ●

Are ye hungry? Reid shook his head. He could have

kissed her. She wasn't pulling back and he asked, "Are ye hungry?" What an oaf. He'd been close enough to count the freckles on her pixie nose, and he killed the moment.

In an effort to justify his idiocy, Reid decided it was for the best. Regardless of what his aching cock wanted, he didn't want stolen kisses, nor did he want Robbie to have regrets. When they did kiss—and they would—she would not regret her actions.

Reid led her down the companionway and walked toward the yellow glow of the binnacle lamp.

"Is everything in order, *Capitaine?*" Jean-Pierre stood at the helm with one hand holding the tiller that steered the ship.

Reid counted the strokes on the slate where the gromet lad kept track of the time. "You have another half hour before the change of guard."

"I'm early." Jean-Pierre grinned wide, side-stepped Reid, and dipped an exaggerated bow before Robbie. He then cradled her hand and brushed a kiss across her knuckles. "I am Jean-Pierre. I am the *Capitaine* when the *Capitaine* is not the *Capitaine,*" the Frenchman spouted his foolishness overtop her hand, then had the gall to kiss her knuckles a second time.

Robbie batted her thick lashes. "'Tis a pleasure. I am Mary-Robena Wallace, but I insist ye call me Robbie."

"The pleasure is mine, I can assure you, *ma chaton.*"

My kitten was Jean-Pierre's favorite endearment for women, but Robbie was no sweet kitten. Reid suspected the woman was sharpening her claws right now.

A giggle bubbled out of her throat just before she retrieved her hand and proceeded to twirl her hair round and round her finger.

Aghast, Reid gawked at the scene. Jean-Pierre

wasn't uncomely. He'd never had issue wooing the lassies at the port-of-calls, but Robbie's response surprised him. Mayhap she simply wasn't accustomed to
the attention.

The last thing Reid needed was another man fawning over his woman. He swiped a bowl of salted nuts
off a wooden crate and shoved it in Robbie's hands.
"Nuts?"

Robbie wasted no time stuffing a generous handful
of cashews into her mouth, freeing her from further
conversation with Jean-Pierre. Smart lass.

"As my first mate has generously relieved me of my
duties early, mayhap we could walk." Reid didn't wait
for her agreement. A gentle shove encouraged her footing and their escape from Jean-Pierre.

Robbie swallowed hard and peeked back over her
shoulder. "He seems likeable for a Frenchman."

"I dare say King Louie might disagree. It seems
Jean-Pierre has been tried and convicted of various
counts of treason. Should they ever catch him, I suspect—" Reid drew his finger across his throat.

Robbie laughed, which was the reaction he'd hoped
for. "Do ye strive to employ the wicked?" She set another nut between her full lips, and Reid swore he
wouldn't taint their time together with lecherous
thoughts.

"I'll tell you a secret, but dinnae be blathering it
about." He checked over his shoulder for drama. "Henrik is English."

Robbie feigned shock. "Satan will no doubt strike ye
dead."

Reid chuckled and clasped his hands behind his
back, escorting her toward the bow. This was what he
wanted. Someone to talk to. Someone to share his life
with. And he'd always dreamed that someone would
be Robbie. "S'truth?"

Robbie eyed him and licked the salt from her finger-tips before dipping her hand back into the bowl.

"They are loyal to me. Some of them have been with me for years. Mayhap because they have nowhere else to go, as is the case with Jean-Pierre and Henrik. The Mopán people assist me because I have earned their respect."

"One might call them your clan."

"I suspect."

Reid wanted to brush the hair from her cheek and take her hand, but he controlled his urges and simply walked beside her beneath the billowing sails. He introduced her to a dozen men and explained the workings of the ship in nautical terms, not because he wanted to flaunt his expertise, but because she wouldn't stop asking questions.

Their stroll ended on the prow where they shared a moment of silence as the sun dipped below a pink and yellow horizon. As if the sun's disappearance altered her mood, she turned toward him, and stared him boldly in the eyes. "Why did ye wait so long to return?"

Reid had prepared himself for that question. He wished he could tell her he'd been in captivity or that some act of God had prevented him from returning sooner, but naught was true, and he wouldn't lie to her. He would offer his reasons and pray she saw the right of it, then forgive him. He pulled in a breath of salty air and rested his forearms over the forward rail. "When Da returned to Scotland, he tried to convince the elders to move the clan, but Uncle Alasdair refused to leave Kilchurn Castle."

"Did your da know the Colquhouns were going to invade?"

"Mayhap. If he did, he never told me. When Da took me away, the clan was being safeguarded inside the walls of Kilchurn Castle. He pleaded with Nanna to return to the Yucatán with him, but she refused. He tried to save them, Robbie, but they didn't want to be saved." He paused to gauge her reaction, but her expression was guarded so he continued, "For eleven years, I have belonged to another clan. I accepted the ways of the Mopán people, studied their symbols, learned their religion. The jungle became my home, and the people, my family. Three years past, when Da died, I returned his ship to the Crown and purchased the *Obsidian*. I had intentions of going to Scotland then, but I went back to the Yucatán instead."

"Why?"

Reid focused on the bow wave below. "I was three and twenty and had naught to my name. No home, no land…" His words trailed off, and he waited for Robbie to respond, but she held silent. "With the Mopán's help, I built Rukux. 'Tis no castle of stone, no keep protected by scores of men, but a humble dwelling when compared to Kilchurn Castle. While falling trees in the jungle, I located a tomb where I found a treasure worthy of a king's dowry."

"And ye thought I would have ye because ye found gold and built a home?" Her tone was sharp, scolding.

Reid had battled on Scots' soil. He'd protected the *Obsidian* from pirates on multiple occasions. He'd fought against the Kekchí tribe. But it took far greater courage than he'd ever possessed to face this one wee woman. "Ye said yourself you deserved more. Would ye have come with me if I was a broken man with no pride and no life to offer you?"

A scowl narrowed her green eyes. The rise and fall of her chest increased. "What I might have done is of no consequence. I am with Eoin now, and I would never abandon the clan."

"Like I did?"

She didn't have to respond for him to know her

opinion of him. With her chin jutted outright and her spine stiff, she handed him the empty bowl and held herself with dignity. "My thanks for the fare. I've had a trying day and wish to seek my slumber."

"You're welcome to sleep in my bed." That hadn't come out the way he intended. An awkward pause fell between them.

Robbie's eyes rounded, her lips tightened. "I'm inclined to think that is a bad idea."

While Reid thought it a splendid idea, she didn't appear to be in the mood for jests. "I meant to offer you a comfortable place to sleep—alone."

"'Tis on rare occasion that I sleep in a bed. I'll be quite comfortable on the deck. Good eve, Captain." Robbie pivoted with a jerk, her crossbarred kirtle spun wide with the action then settled as she walked away.

"The watch is called, the glass floweth." A dozen rungs up on the mainmast, Henrik belted out the verse that announced the change of guard. "We shall make a good voyage, if God willeth." In his whisky tenor voice, Henrik proceeded to sing the *Salve Regina* in Latin. The song suited Reid's mood—sullen and dark.

He raked his fingers through his hair and set out on a mission which led him below deck. In the keel of the ship, he lit a lantern and searched their provisions; barrels of salted sardines, pickled beef, cheese, casks of wine, water, and blessed brandy. With a flask filled with enough spirits to kill a horse and a tinderbox containing the Mopán's sweet tobacco, he settled atop a keg of molasses to soak his bruised heart.

A familiar drawing up of mucus grated over Reid's last nerve just before Eoin spoke. "Robbie is by far the most loyal person I know. She has dedicated her life to aiding the clan. 'Twill take more than charm to break her."

"Your color has improved." Reid didn't possess the energy to pick a fight with his cousin. Instead, he lit the tobacco in the lantern and offered Eoin the flask. "Brandy?"

The man snatched the drink from Reid's hand like a drunkard addicted to laudanum then settled atop a barrel to Reid's left. Eoin readjusted his *plaide* and studied the ribbon of smoke with a curious eye. "What is that?"

"The Mopán call it *sikar*. But because the damn English want credit for everything, they call it a cigar. I call it an escape from reality." Reid thought it best he and Eoin come to some sort of mutual terms. If a bit of smoke and a dram of drink built the foundation of that amnesty, so be it. He lit a second cigar for Eoin and passed it to his cousin. "Truce."

"For now." Eoin watched Reid take another long draw, then mimicked the action. He coughed, but only once, took a long swill of brandy, and then sucked his cigar until the embers burned a bright orange. "'Tis good. 'Tis verra good."

"Aye." Reid leaned against the wall and propped his ankles atop another barrel. He closed his eyes and made a mental attempt to flush the frustration from his body.

'Twill take more than charm to break her. Eoin's words echoed in Reid's head. He didn't want to break her. Her loyalty and pride were qualities he admired, but feared those same qualities would prevent her from ever forgiving him.

He drew on the cigar and rolled the smooth silky smoke over his tongue before he exhaled. "How did ye do it, cousin?"

"Do what?"

"Gain Robbie's forgiveness for what happened in the cavern." Reid half expected the man to mock him.

What he was unprepared for was Eoin's intensity.

The scruff of brown curls hanging over Eoin's brow didn't hide the narrowing of his eyes. "Ye should've died in that cavern. Not Fergus."

"Is that how you justified it? You blamed me?"

"The Colquhouns came for ye."

"Nay," Reid corrected strongly. "They came for us— the sons of the MacGregor chieftains."

"I'm not to blame for their error."

Astounded, Reid sat up and gawked at Eoin. "You're solely to blame."

"What would ye know of it? Ye werenae there." Eoin turned away, but his eyes slipped to the corners.

God's legions! Understanding chilled Reid like a bucket of ice water. True, he hadn't been at the surface, but he knew what had transpired. "You never told her, did ye?"

If Eoin had a comment, he drowned it in brandy. He propped his elbows on his knees, spit between his boots, and glared at Reid. "Think ye can taint Robbie's opinion of me with lies?"

"They are not lies. Da was there, outside the cavern."

"Your da is dead. It is your word against mine."

The bastaird was delusional. Reid shook his head with minimal effort. "Have ye no conscience?"

"Men with conscience make poor leaders. If a king relied on his conscience, he wouldnae win wars. What I did protected the MacGregor bloodline. Fergus was an unfortunate casualty. Had ye been in my position, you'd have acted in like."

"Nay. You're wrong, cousin." Reid stood, eager to rid himself of his Eoin's presence. "I would never have named Fergus Wallace as the MacGregor heir to save my own arse."

6

●
—————

~ ARRANGEMENTS ~

"Blessed be the light of day, and the Holy Cross, we say.

Blessed be the immortal soul, and the Lord who keeps it whole."

S'help me Odin! Hold your wheesht, man! She would sew the Englishman's lips together. Was it really necessary for Henrik to announce the rise of the sun? Could one not simply open her eyes to discover on her own that it was dawn?

Robbie awoke in a foul mood, with a fool taste in her mouth, and a foul kink in her neck. Oddly enough, she was as warm as fresh bread, save for her cheek. Her wet cheek.

She opened one eye and found Oscar looming over her. The cat yawned, swiped its giant tongue over its nose and then proceeded to bathe himself. A task Robbie rather wished was in her near future, but she was awake enough to know there would be no brook to wash in, nor a place of privacy to tend her morning ablutions. Much to her chagrin, Robbie knew the moment she got to her feet she would be in need of said privacy.

She twisted beneath a weight of furs that had not been there when she'd bedded down for the eve and wanted to believe Eoin had covered her during the night, but he'd never concerned himself overmuch with her needs. Most likely, 'twas Reid's doing. Her assumption only added to her sullen mood. She didn't want him fretting over her or seeing to her comforts.

Pushing out of the masses of fur, she stood, readjusted her kirtle, and worked the kinks out of her neck. The rope bed Eoin had lounged in the better part of yesterday was empty, the same as it had been when she'd retired. Exhaustion, combined with a bitter lack of caring, had prevented her from seeking him out. The man had a nose for the drink. 'Twould be just like Eoin to make nice with the crew in exchange for a dram of mead.

After neatly rolling the furs, Robbie stuffed them into a nook and plaited her hair into a loose braid as she crossed the quarterdeck.

A gromet she'd met yestereve passed with a pail and twig broom. "Good morrow, Miss Mary. Best get to the afthatch for the mornin' meal. They be handin' out biscuits and fruit."

"My thanks, Duncan." She offered the lad a smile, but food would have to wait.

After climbing the companionway, she knocked lightly on Reid's door. The little dance she did some mornings was not upon her—yet.

No answer. She tested the lever, but it was locked. Blast it! She tapped on the wood with a bit more enthusiasm.

The door jerked open. "God's legions! The damn ship had better be sinking."

Holy Loki. Robbie's entire being went limp, but her

eyes were greedy in their perusal of the fine specimen before her.

"Robbie?" Reid stood beneath the archway holding a red silk sheet low around his hip bones. Muscles rippled across his abdomen and his thick chest, and the only spot of hair to be found drew a thin line from his navel to his...

Robbie swallowed.

"Have ye need of something?"

She shook her head.

Her pulse dropped from her neck to her womanhood and throbbed. 'Twas nigh impossible for her to cross her legs any tighter, but she tried.

"Then why are you pounding on my door at this ungodly hour?"

She nodded and resisted the urge to squirm. Of course the man slept naked. Now she had his image burned onto the backs of her eyelids. There would be no escaping him. Nothing left to the imagination, save for what lie beneath the red silk sheet.

As that thought flitted through her mind, the red silk sheet began to rise.

Perfect. Just perfect. The man was getting aroused.

"Robbie, I strongly suggest ye quit looking at me like that." Reid cocked his head, dragging her out of her stupor.

She straightened her spine and found his face. The shadow of a beard darkened his jaw and his swollen red eyes held the hint of mischief, but what turned the heat inside her from lust to annoyance was his smug grin.

"I am in need of the privy pot," she finally spit out.

He dipped into a pretentious bow and motioned her into the cabin. "Dinnae trouble yourself with the bed as I'm obviously still in it."

She wouldn't oblige him with a comment. Instead,

she rounded the partition and snatched up the empty privy pot. There had to be somewhere on this bluidy ship she could find a smidgeon of privacy.

"Where are you going with my...?" His word trailed off behind her as she descended the companionway of the captain's deck.

The deck was abuzz with activity so she dropped below to the gunner deck. Jax appeared between two cannons. "Good tomorrow, *C'ak'is Ak'.*"

She was in no mood for Jax. "I amnae Fire Tongue. My name is Robbie."

He laughed and mumbled words she didn't understand. If she wasn't in dire need of the privy pot, she would've launched it at him. Instead, she unhooked a lantern from the wall and dashed down two more sets of stairs before she found a narrow passageway that was blessedly vacant. She popped open the first door on her right, held the lantern high, and inhaled the stale scent of grain. Gunny sacks five deep aligned the walls and yellow dusted the floor.

'Twould have to do. The fullness weighing down her innards demanded she make haste, but the moment she paused, the pitter-patter of spiked nails marched across the floor.

Her heart did a pitter-patter of its own.

She was hardly squeamish. Grandda had taught her how to gut a fish and skin a rabbit. She'd even killed a snake or two. But rats? Blast it all!

Deciding to retreat, she descended deeper into the ship's belly where naught but silence followed her. However, the smell that greeted her in the keel was ungodly—sweet, acidic, rotten. Something had definitely died.

"Holy Loki!" She pinched the privy pot between her elbow and side and cupped her nose and mouth, but the atrocious odor seemed to stick in her nostrils like molasses. Her eyes watered, blurring her vision, but she proceeded forward, rounding the stairway.

She walked straight into a silky web.

She jumped backward as panic seized her muscles. Shivers ripped up her spine. The tiny hairs at her nape shot straight out.

She raised the lantern between two pillars and caught a glimpse of at least three black spiders wriggling across their spun home.

Her heart punched her ribs in double-time.

Squealing, she raced back up the ladderways toward Reid's cabin as if the English regiment were at her heels. At her approach, a dozen crewmen on the main deck quickly formed two rows. She shot between them and found herself right back where she'd been only minutes before. She beat on Reid's door with a trembling fist, not caring if he answered stark naked. 'Twas doubtful she would be able to see passed the spots speckling her vision.

She hated spiders. She hated them more than the Scots hated the English.

Another shiver raked over her being just as Reid opened the door. "What is it now?"

Ignoring his question and his disgruntled look, she handed him the lantern and exited the small door at the back of the cabin that led to the narrow balcony. She freed her hands of the privy pot then scrubbed her hair, her arms, her back. Why did she feel them crawling on her?

Skittish, she checked every nook overhead and every spindle of the rail before she allowed herself to breathe and tend to her personal needs.

Feeling childish about her behavior, Robbie dallied on the balcony watching the waves roll into two white lines to form their wake. She thought of Grandda and how he'd calmed her after she'd climbed into a hollow log filled with dozens of wolf spiders. If she lived to be a hundred, she would never forget that day.

A bit of sadness washed through her. Only a day had passed and already she missed him greatly. She wished Eoin had allowed Grandda to accompany them on this adventure, but mayhap, 'twas for the best. She didn't know what dangers lay ahead, and Grandda might not have been strong enough to fight the wind and cold.

If it was within her power, she would see Grandda happy in Rannoch beside a fire to ease the pain in his bones and mayhap a small alchemist's work-house for him to mix his vapors.

Someday, Grandda. Someday.

Robbie stepped back inside the cabin and returned the privy pot behind the partition. She found Reid in breeks leaning against the edge of his desk with his arms crossed over his bare chest. He glared at her.

S'help me Odin, if the man so much as speaks—

"Are ye quite done?"

She actually heard her teeth grind. As if she needed a scolding. "Nay woman should suffer such humiliation, regardless of her status."

"Status has naught to do with the fact that you went traipsing about the ship carrying a damn privy pot. If ye felt humiliated, 'twas of your own doing."

"I demand a place of privacy."

Reid's black brows rose. "Forgive me for not making such arrangements beforehand."

It didn't occur to her until that moment why he hadn't prepared her quarters. It had naught to do with privy pots, or rats, or spiders, and everything to do with Reid MacGregor, and his deluded presumptions. "S'truth. Did ye honestly think I would be so quick to jump into your bed?" Blast the man and his arrogance!

The muscles in his arms sharpened. "You'll have

private quarters by noontide."

7

~ Intrigue ~

Taming the wildest beasts of the Yucatán proved to be an easier task than wooing Robbie Wallace.

Reid rolled his gold coin over his knuckles repeatedly and studied the charting maps atop his desk. He wondered if he should invite the woman in or leave her to lurk outside his open door. She most likely spotted the unmade bed from the helm and was itching to tidy the chamber. The woman needed a task to occupy her mind before she drove his crew to madness.

Steady winds had kept the canvas full for a sennight, pushing them into the Atlantic without event, but the past two days had proven agonizing for her as they sat in a doldrum. The sails hung like draperies and the crew lounged about the deck like seals basking beneath a high sun. Robbie, however, proved incapable of doing nothing.

She followed Jax, badgering him. "How do ye say 'good morrow' in your language?"

"Ba'ax ka wa'alik?"

"...and 'farewell?'"

"Taak tu laki."

"...and 'I'm pleased to make your acquaintance?'"

"Hach ki'imak in wo'ol in kaholtikech." Jax spent hours teaching her the language, but he eventually snuck away and hid below deck, so she sought out Henrik and Jean-Pierre.

When they ran out of duties to occupy her time, she latched onto Duncan and assisted him and a few other gromets with the tedious task of buffing splinters from the teakwood planks with a holystone. Old sails had been mended, decks scrubbed, and rails painted. He'd caught her on the gunnerdeck three days past with a soiled rag and a dirty face.

"The cannonballs needn't be polished to obliterate the enemy," he'd assured her, so she cleaned the cannons instead.

Only once did she seek Eoin out, but the red-nosed sot dismissed her with the flick of his wrist. He'd turned the storage chamber into a damn tippling house and slept from dawn to dusk wherever his arse fell. Henrik, along with a half dozen topmen, joined Eoin every eve for cigars and spirits, which suited Reid fine as Robbie avoided her intended when the man was blootered.

Reid calculated the distance between ports, deciding where to lay anchor to replenish their drink. He had no intention of letting Eoin's cup run dry.

Robbie cleared her throat outside his door, dragging him out of his musings. Now that she had her own quarters belowdeck, he doubted she was in need of his privy pot.

The woman was bored.

He wasn't one for trickery, but if he possessed any wit at all, he would nab the opportunity to spend time with her.

He made a fist around the coin and pounded the

desktop. "God's legions!" he yelled and waited to see if she fell for the charade. From the corner of his eye, he saw her step into the doorway, but only part way. Pretending not to notice her, he purposely scowled and let his forehead fall against the desk.

"Is something amiss?" she asked with genuine concern.

Reid snapped upright, feigning shock, all the while hiding his smile. "'Tis naught of import."

She disappeared from the doorway.

"I dinnae possess the wit to decipher these maps," he blurted out, which drew her back into the doorframe. Her red-gold hair glittered beneath the sun, reminding him of the ancient fire-goddess for whom he'd named his ship. He wanted to know the softness of her locks and the fire in her kiss, but he could wait.

He was a patient man.

She twirled a curl and craned her slender neck. "I used to study the maps Grandda acquired from his trips to Edinburgh. Mayhap I could be of assistance."

He controlled his enthusiasm. "'Tis doubtful. The map I need assistance with is unlike any you've seen before." He wasn't surprised when she crossed the cabin and bent over his desk, accepting his challenge.

A quick glance at the scattered charts was all she needed to question his sincerity. "Ye jest." Her thin brows popped up, and she dropped the curl she'd been toying with. "I should hope the captain of such a grand ship would know a nautical chart from a map, else we're destined to die at sea."

Och. The lass was smart. Reid decided it best to drop the pretense. "I plotted these charts and can assure you we'll reach the Yucatán in less than three sennights."

"What in the name of Odin am I to do for three bluidy sennights?" The woman's exhale ruffled the pages of his journal.

"I've a task for ye." He cleared the desktop of everything save for his journal, then spread a wool atop the surface. Nerves made his hands shake as he unlocked a strongbox carved with ivy and butterflies, then retrieved a bundle wrapped in burlap. 'Twas adolescent to be so anxious, but naught could be done to prevent it. He prayed the lass he'd known in his youth would share his excitement. "You can help me with this."

As Reid peeled back the burlap, Robbie's eyes rounded with wonder the same way his had when he found the stone stele. "'Tis a map to the gold?"

If his suspicions were correct, Xitali had left behind so much more than gold. There was a wealth of knowledge awaiting him in the Yucatán and he wanted to find it with Robbie. "Of sorts."

She trailed her fingertips over the carved pictures on the stone slab. "The symbols are similar to the markings on Jax." She looked up, her green eyes reflected the intelligence he so admired in her.

He nodded. "'Tis written in a language centuries old."

Her lashes fell against her fair cheek, and her shoulders sagged. "'Twould take a scholar years to decipher. I fear I cannae help ye."

"Not years. Months. I have the translations." He flipped open his journal to the pages explaining the symbols and their meanings. "'Tis all here. I can teach you, the same as the elders of the Mopán people taught me."

Debating, she looked out the open doorway and wrapped a curl around her finger. She didn't have to voice her concerns. Eoin would disapprove.

The man didn't deserve her. He treated her like a lowly peasant, and he drank far too much for a man in need of coin. He was arrogant, self-righteous, and worst of all, he lied to her. If she knew about Fergus, she wouldn't be so quick to defend Eoin. Reid would eventually tell her, but first, he needed her trust.

Robbie turned back toward the desk and flattened her palms on either side of the stele. Her desire to learn about the treasure must have outweighed her qualms regarding Eoin. "Where do we begin?"

"We count." The tickle in his stomach reached out to every nerve in his body as he pulled the chair out for her and proceeded to explain the numbers system to her. "A dot equals one, a bar equals five, and a shell— like this," he dipped a quill in the ink pot and drew in his journal, "represents zero."

As the day progressed, Reid instructed her on the concepts of the calendar system as well as the sacred rituals performed by the priests and priestesses of the ancient Maya. Robbie listened with intensity and questioned his every instruction. They conversed like old friends, diverting from one topic to the next without pause.

When Reid began to explain their alphabet, which really wasn't an alphabet so much as picture words called glyphs, Robbie became lost in its complexity. She studied his journal, and he studied her. He memorized the shape of her slender nose and the freckles sprinkled atop her cheeks. He noted her mannerisms—the way she twisted her curls and tickled the skin beneath her nose with the ends of her hair. When she nibbled on the inside corner of her full lips, it took all his strength not to set her back and kiss her.

The brand that marked her as a MacGregor prevented her from living a free life in Scotland. But she wasn't bound to Clan MacGregor, nor was she bound to Eoin. She could make her own choices, and someday he hoped she might choose him.

He wanted to tell her how often he'd thought of her,

thought of them—together. He'd longed for a woman to call his own, for a wife to give him bairns. When he imagined fulfilling those goals, Robbie had always been that woman. The Jaguar King had offered his daughters on more than one occasion. They were beautiful, exotic women with olive colored skin and lush black hair, but they lacked Robbie's spirit.

The qualities that drew him to her were the very attributes keeping her out of his arms: pride, devotion, faithfulness. 'Twas a contradiction. If he was to have Robbie as his own, she would have to go against the very qualities that made her the woman he wanted to share his life with.

"Five is past, and six floweth," Henrik sang out the fifth half hour of the watch. "More shall flow if God willeth. Count and pass, make voyage fast."

Robbie scratched notes in his journal, paying no heed to the call to change the guard. She was completely immersed in applying what she'd learned to decipher the symbols carved into the stone slab. He supposed he could save her the trouble, but in truth, he wanted her to discover the knowledge on her own.

He stood and rolled the wick higher inside the brass lantern to provide her more light as the moon was but a sliver this night. "I have to relieve Jean-Pierre at the helm."

She waved him away and for reasons unbeknownst to him, he bent down and kissed her cheek. It felt natural. 'Twas meant to be a courtesy. An innocent gesture of farewell. Nothing more, but the quickening of her pulse in her neck told him she hadn't received it as much.

Her fingertips touched the skin he'd kissed. Her knuckles whitened as her grip intensified on the quill. Her gaze remained pinned to the desktop.

"Forgive me." He dashed out of the cabin before she

had the opportunity to scold him.

• • •

Slightly stunned, Robbie watched Reid flee the cabin. She should've scolded him for showing such affections, but if truth be told, scolding him wasn't even on the list of things she wanted to do to Reid MacGregor.

She wanted to pull him against her and feel the heat of his body crushed against hers. She wanted to taste the salt of his skin and explore the exotic scent that had tempted her beyond reason the whole of the day. But she resisted the urge to act on her desires, knowing it would be wrong, knowing the temptation would cost her and so many others their livelihood.

Eoin would punish Robbie by ousting anyone close to her or Reid from the clan, regardless of how much gold they returned with.

Robbie coiled her hair into a knot atop her head and secured it in place with a bone stylus she found in Reid's desk drawer. She fanned the back of her neck and blamed the rising temperature for the perspiration trickling down her spine. Unfortunately, that lie didn't hold true with the heady arousal pooling low in her belly.

She would give her eyetooth for a cool brook to ease the heat from her body and free her mind of her sinful thoughts. Unfortunately, the *Obsidian* lacked such grandeur, so she opened the small door to the balcony, hoping the setting sun would push a breeze between the open doorways.

It didn't. 'Twas still as death. No breeze drifted in. Just thick, heavy air.

Thump.

Oscar jumped onto the balcony and stole a beat of Robbie's heart.

"Holy Loki, Oscar! Ye nigh scared the pink out of

me."

Oscar responded by dragging his hot, heavy tongue over her forearm, which didn't help her condition. She could go to her quarters and rid herself of her heavy wool, but she wanted to continue her work deciphering the stone tablet. With Reid occupied at the helm, the basin behind the partition was a temptation she could enjoy without guilt.

"Ye keep watch for me, aye?"

Oscar yawned, showing her his threatening teeth, then plopped down at her feet to lick his paw.

"Worthless beastie." She rounded the partition, located a cake of soap amongst Reid's toiletries, and dipped a cloth into the basin. As she washed her face, the exotic scent of his soap stimulated her senses and filled her mind's eye with unwanted images—two bodies, wet with perspiration, tangled in a sensual position that was most likely physically impossible.

She cursed her traitorous imagination and pressed the cool rag against the back of her neck, but it wasn't enough to douse the fire rushing beneath her skin. She loosened the laces of her bodice and pushed the garment off her shoulders.

She shouldn't have closed her eyes, for it was there she saw Reid bathing her. Cool water ran down her back and over her breasts, then the cake of soap slipped over her sensitive nipples—nipples Reid tormented one at a time between his teeth in her wanton vision.

A caress as soft as silk drew a line across her shoulders.

Her eyes shot open. Her hands trembled.

She sucked in air and held it. The soap shot from her hand like a boulder from the catapult. She wiggled back into her sark and crossed her arms over her small breasts.

He was behind her. His exhales cooled her wet skin and curled a shiver over the knobs of her spine. Had he purposely snuck in? Or had she been so wrapped up in her thoughts, she hadn't heard his approach?

A tiny giggle lay trapped in her throat. Blast her foolishness!

She should yell at him, tell him to leave, but she was barely capable of breathing with him so close. Her heart pounded like a drum between her ears, and she prayed her knocking knees wouldn't fail her. Sensations coursed through her body and gathered between her legs to mimic the throbbing of her pulse.

The man wasn't even touching her, yet her breasts grew heavy and her nipples turned into hard aching stones. She hugged herself a little tighter, part of her hiding, part of her desperate to alleviate this undeniable arousal.

Reid leaned into her ear and swallowed. "I forgot my...I forgot something, though I cannot recall what it was."

"'Tis late. I should go." She scrambled to pull her *plaide* back over her shoulder before she turned around. "Eoin might be looking for me."

Reid nodded, but didn't remove himself from her path. Instead, he reached up to touch her face.

The rise and fall of her chest intensified. She pulled the corner of her lip between her teeth and waited for him to touch her...but he didn't.

He fisted his hand, pivoted on his heel, and exited the cabin in three strides.

Robbie pulled in air in greedy doses. She felt as if she'd climbed the tallest mountain in Scotland. Her throat burned and her skin tingled.

She didn't know how, but she had to get the man out of her mind. Without further delay, she left and rushed below deck. A lantern in the narrow passageway lighted the way to her quarters where she found Eoin leaning against the entrance holding a flask of drink.

"Where have ye been?" he asked in a tone more curious than accusing.

Guilt had her mind racing. A trickle of sweat fell over her temple. "I've been studying a stone tablet that will lead us to the gold. 'Tis fascinating really. The symbols represent different words in a language centuries old. Would ye like to see it?" *Cease!* Robbie swiped the back of her hand over her brow. 'Twas not like her to babble or sweat. Eoin would suspect something. As well he should.

"Nay. I'm more interested in seeing ye." He blinked slowly and grinned. 'Twas the first time she'd seen him smile since they boarded the *Obsidian*.

She returned his smile more as a courtesy than a form of acceptance. Eoin wasn't uncomely. His jaw was square and strong when it wasn't covered with a beard. Dark boyish locks fell over his brow and reminded her of a man less conflicted with responsibility. A time, not long ago, she might have regarded his heavy-lidded dark eyes as seductive, but now she knew 'twas the drink.

She'd once felt giddy when he looked at her. He was the Gregarach. 'Twas a privilege to have him call her his woman, so why did she cringe when he pulled her close?

He dipped his head low and nuzzled her ear with his nose. "I love ye."

Robbie scoffed internally. Of course he loved her. The man's bollocks were undoubtedly blue, and there were no other women aboard to love.

He raised her skirt and slid his hand up the back of her thigh.

She wished she desired him. She wished he made

her toes curl when he touched her.

But he didn't.

He reeked of drink and filth and when he forced his thick bitter tongue in her mouth, she felt naught but disgust. She pushed against his chest. "Do ye intend to have your way with me right here where anyone might pass?"

"Holy Christ! I swear the man set ye up in these godforsaken dwarf quarters so I couldnae bed my own woman."

S'truth, the chamber was far from spacious. She couldn't lie flat on the narrow palette else her head and feet would touch the bulkhead. The room had walls and a door, which was more than most were privy to, so she had hardly complained.

"I have needs, Robbie." He flanked her against him, squeezed her duff beneath her skirt with the hand not holding his precious drink, and kissed her throat.

She had needs, too, but Eoin rarely concerned himself with them. Just as she was about to shove him off her, he stiffened.

"I smell him on ye." He leveled his dark eyes with hers and released her. "Ye've been with him."

"Nay. 'Tis not what ye imply." She shook her head so hard her hair came undone. "We've been at his desk studying the stone tablet all day. Reid left to tend his duties at the helm, and I washed in his basin with his soap. 'Tis all."

Eoin poured rose-colored drink straight into his gullet. "Think ye I am such a fool?" He drew up a wad of mucus and spit on the floor. "You'd do weel to remember who ye belong to and what your betrayal would cost ye." He pivoted and ducked beneath an overhead beam, leaving her with his threat.

Robbie slipped inside the dark confines of her quarters and pressed her forehead against the wooden door. She felt trapped, confined to a prison with no walls. Scotland was her home, but she was not free there, nor were any of the women bearing the mark of the MacGregor. They roamed the mountains, hiding in the mist like beggar thieves.

A warm tear fell over her cheek. Her wants were not so greedy. She wanted a home, a place to raise a half dozen bairns. She wanted a place Grandda could live out his days in peace. And she wanted a man who was proud to call her wife.

She buried her face in her hands and sobbed as she admitted to herself, she no longer wanted that man to be Eoin.

8

~ BARGAINS ~

"X-I-T-A-L-I." Robbie sounded out the letters, then double-checked her notes for accuracy. She'd done it. After three days of poring herself into deciphering a single column of glyphs, she finally reaped the rewards.

"I know her name," she announced and stood, pushing the chair backward. The discovery had her trembling. "Reid, I know her name." She turned and found a sleeping giant sprawled out atop the bed in black breeks and a white *lèine* shirt with his "kitten" tucked into his side.

She could have cooed over the perfectly charming pair for hours, but her excitement couldn't be contained. She fell to her knees beside the bed and shook him. "Reid."

His response was a quiet whistle.

She grabbed hold of his muscular arm and shook him harder. "Reid!" she hollered this time.

He shot upright, plucking a pistol out from beneath the bolster. Black waves of sweat-soaked hair lay plas-

tered to his temples as his confused gaze scanned the
cabin. "What is it, love?" In a protective gesture, he
wove his fingers through her hair and held the side of
her head.

Love? The way he used the word sounded so natural. As if he'd been calling her that for years. Most
likely, he used the same endearment on all women to
coax them into his bed. A sudden bit of jealousy made
her frown, but she pushed the thought aside and redirected her energies on the reasons she'd awoken him.
"I know her name."

"'Tis hotter than the fires of the Underworld in
here."

She would have stomped her foot had she been
standing. Instead, she growled. The man really had
difficulty focusing at times. He shoved the pistol back
beneath the bolster, got to his feet, and then peeled off
his *lèine* shirt. Sweat-slicked muscles rippled beneath
a late afternoon sun shining in through the windows.

Blast it! Now she had difficulty focusing.

She pulled the corner of her lip between her teeth
and ogled her fill while he wiped his brow. Did the
man have to be so distracting?

She stood, punched the rolled sleeves of her sark
farther up her arms, and grumbled. "Think ye are hot?
I am wearing bluidy wool."

"I see no one preventing you from taking it off," he
tossed the lewd comment over his shoulder as he
walked toward the basin to wash.

She did stomp this time and mentally searched for
a barb, but none came. S'truth, she'd been cold the
whole of her life, and the heat was a welcomed change.

The stone, Robbie, she reminded herself. "I've deci-
phered some of the glyphs on the stone. The tablet is a
burial marker. It belonged to a woman named Xitali.
She died in 857 AD. I believe she was royalty of some

sort as the stele bears the marking of 'lady.' She was a wife, but left no bairns behind."

Reid poked his head out from behind the partition. His smile lit up his entire face and warmed her insides. She'd impressed him. She could tell by the way his pale eyes shimmered with hints of blue.

"Ye did well, Robbie." He retrieved a clean *lèine* shirt from a locker and met her at the desk. He smelled good. Verra good. She wished she could name the exotic scent. 'Twas like a sweet treat combined with musk and salt and man. 'Twas delicious. She swallowed the saliva thickening in her mouth.

Mayhap she needed to eat.

"Argyle would be proud of you."

She toyed with a loose curl and tamped down the emotions that accompanied thoughts of Grandda.

"Xitali was a Maya priestess and she died in 957. You counted wrong." Reid pointed at the grouping of lines and dots on the stele.

His smell forgotten, frustration pinched her entire face into a scowl. She dropped the curl and punched her fists onto her hips. "Ye knew? Why in the name of Odin would ye trouble me to decipher information ye already knew?"

"I wanted you to discover it on your own. Tell me ye dinnae find the whole process fascinating."

She couldn't. She'd been enthralled the past few days. Each glyph revealed a little more about Xitali's life, but there was a great deal Robbie still didn't know, and damn if he was going to make her figure it out on her own. "Tell me the rest."

Reid retrieved a scroll from the top drawer. "I drafted this map of the Yucatán jungle about a year ago." He weighted it down beside the stone slab. "Xitali's tomb is beneath an old temple between these two wells." He pointed at two circles, one larger than the other.

"Ye already found the tomb?"

"Where do you think I acquired my wealth?" He snapped a wink at her.

Feeling slightly deceived, Robbie harrumphed. "If ye already found the gold, then what are we searching for?"

"More." Reid grinned and brushed a curl behind her ear. "Xitali was more than a Maya priestess. She was a goddess."

"We are searching for gold that belonged to an ancient goddess?" Did he think her so gullible?

"We are searching for more than gold. I believe Xitali left behind a library."

"A library? As in books? In the first century?"

"Their books—called codices—were made from the thin inner bark from the ceiba tree. 'Twas where they recorded their religious beliefs."

Robbie cocked her head and gave him a look that called him adder-bitten. "Point one: gods and goddesses are not human and therefore cannae be buried. Point two: a library is not gold and cannae be sold to the Laird of Luss or the king."

"Nay, but knowledge can be a treasure in and of itself." Reid pointed at a grouping of picture words at the bottom of the stone tablet. "'Knowledge is truth and truth is power.' Xitali lived by these words, and I suspect 'tis what got her killed the first time."

"The first time?"

The man chuckled. "Xitali wasnae born a goddess, but she was smart, like you. I suspect the ruler of her city felt threatened by her intelligence, which is why he threw her in the Well of Sacrifice." Reid pointed at the larger of the two wells on the map.

"If she died in the well, then why was she buried in the tomb?"

"She did not die in the well, but the people of her time believed she did."

"And ye have a different theory?"

Reid nodded and checked the empty wooden bowl sitting atop the desk. "I believe she swam from the Well of Sacrifice to the water reservoir through an underground river." He pointed at the second well on the map. "When she appeared two months after her supposed drowning, the people believed her risen from the Underworld and hailed her daughter to *Chalchiuhtlicue*—the goddess of running waters."

"Sounds like one of Grandda's tales about the Norse gods." Robbie had always believed those stories, too.

Reid strode to the table beside the bed and picked up a second wooden bowl, but it, too, was empty. "Myth or no. The distance between one well and the next is over four thousand feet."

"'Tis too great. She would have drowned." She watched him open a locker and pop the lid off a ceramic container. Whatever he was looking for wasn't there.

"'Tis my thinking she spent that two months somewhere in between. In an underground cave, mayhap." He returned to her side and propped himself at the edge of the desk. "She would have drowned, lest she could breathe in the water."

Robbie studied his crooked grin. "'Tis doubtful they tossed a diving barrel in when they sacrificed her."

"'Twas no diving barrel that kept Xitali alive. 'Twas air. Good air. If my suspicions are correct, she had planned for her sacrifice." Reid dropped to one knee in front of the same strongbox where he kept the stele and retrieved a gold container in the shape of a triangle. He set it atop the desk in front of her. "Xitali was holding this in her tomb."

The gold mesmerized Robbie, but the mystery of its

contents was what had the hair on her arms standing up. Shaking, she lifted the lid, then stared unblinking at white frosted crystals of various sizes.

"The symbols engraved on the lid name the crystals *mus ik' kuxtal*—The Breath of Life."

She pressed her palm to her chest in an effort to calm her fluttering pulse. "'Tis a bit overwhelming."

"Touch them." Reid picked up one of the crystals and set it in her palm.

It was hard, but not like diamonds. It smelled like the ocean, so she tasted it—a little salty, tangy—but cool. The crystal was cool on her tongue. "'Tis not a gemstone. What do ye suppose it is?"

"Air." From a locker, Reid retrieved a round transparent sphere with four weights soldered onto the feet of the globe. Inside was a wick soaked in oil. "Jax's woman made this for me out of sand glass."

"I dinnae know Jax had a woman."

"Aye. Black Dove. You'll meet her and her many sisters soon." Reid pulled a wooden cork out of the top and transferred fire from the lantern to the wick inside. "Pay attention." He returned the cork which immediately choked the flame.

Robbie crossed her arms, unimpressed. He knew better. Reid, Fergus, and Robbie had dabbled in alchemy in Grandda's work-house in their youth. "Have ye knots for brains? Fire cannae burn without air."

"I'm merely demonstrating. Patience, love."

Her stance loosened, her arms uncoiled. Why did she melt a little when he called her that?

"Watch. I'm about to impress ye." He set a tiny crystal in a pocket inside the globe. Again, he lit the wick and returned the cork.

The flame burned bright and steady.

"What say ye to that, Mary-Robena Wallace?" Reid asked, his tone full of bluster.

Her heart thudded, waiting for the flame to go out, but it did not. Her mouth lay open in utter amazement. "Reid, this is an immense discovery."

"'Twas Xitali's discovery, not mine. She used the crystals to breathe underwater, but I do not posses the wit to figure out how."

Robbie pulled her gaze away from the flame as understanding set it. "'Tis why ye need me?"

Reid opened his mouth, but whatever he intended to say never formed into words. For long uncomfortable moments he only stared at her with those steel-gray eyes. The attraction between them was impossible to ignore. He wanted her. 'Twas not a fact he attempted to hide.

He raised his hand to her face and feathered the backs of his fingers over her scarred cheek. That simple touch made her ache for the impossible.

Desire was present in his gaze, but his demeanor shifted with a deep inhale. His crooked grin curved his sad eyes into half moons. "You are smart, Robbie. When we reach the Yucatán, we're going to dive from the Well of Sacrifice and swim to the reservoir. I need you to figure out how we're going to accomplish such a feat without drowning."

"Have ye conducted tests? What do ye know about the crystals?"

"Verra little." He pivoted on his heel and strode toward the door. "I'll tell you want I know as soon as I get more nuts."

Nuts? Holy Loki! She rushed out of the cabin and bent over the rail of the captain's deck. "I'm going to need more than bluidy nuts!"

"The crew is at your beck and call, m'lady." He dipped a bow and disappeared down the afthatch.

Robbie's mind reeled as she mentally inventoried a list of supplies she would need to begin testing; a tub of water, salt, twine—

"Bonjour, ma chaton." Jean-Pierre waved from the helm.

Having no idea what the Frenchman said, Robbie offered him a weak smile. "Jean-Pierre, are there sheep among the livestock below deck?"

"Oui. Have you a taste for mutton this eve?"

"Aye. But I want the bladder. Raw," she added quickly, then spotted Duncan and a Mopán laddie at the starboard rail. "Duncan, I've a task for ye and Cocijo."

"Name it, Miss Mary, and 'tis done." The two laddies looked as eager to help her as she was eager to help Reid.

"Think ye two can fetch me a couple rats?"

Duncan discussed the task with Cocijo in his native tongue. Both boys shrugged, then Duncan turned back to Robbie. "Would ye be wantin' those rats dead or alive?"

"Alive."

• • •

Reid wondered if the full moon caused the crew's foul mood, or if it was the fact their casks of spirits had run dry two nights past. Regardless, every man aboard itched to lay anchor, Eoin being the most eager of all.

"Draw the sails," Reid shouted to the topmen overhead and strode toward the prow where Eoin gripped the starboard rail. Warm dry air blanketed the *Obsidian* as they glided into Rum Cove. 'Twas not where Reid intended to port, but enough supplies could be gained for the sennight it would take to reach the Yucatán.

Reid struck a flint and lit a cigar for his cousin. The sweet smoke curled between them and seemed to muffle Eoin's ripe stench. The wretch's constant snarl likely had to do with his dependence on the drink, but Reid suspected Eoin was none too happy about the amount of time Robbie spent in the cabin experimenting with the crystals. She worked day and night conducting tests which had produced little results thus far, but Reid continued to encourage her and held the utmost confidence she would stumble onto something.

Eoin drew on the cigar, staring off at the firelight glowing from the island docks. "Is this the land ye abandoned the clan for?"

The man wanted to pick a fight did he? Reid retrieved his gold coin from his pocket and began the soothing rhythmic roll. With Robbie in his cabin out of earshot, Reid was more than eager to play with his cousin. In fact, he'd prepared words days ago for the occasion. "We've yet to reach the Yucatán, but I trust you'll be going ashore with the others before we resume our journey on the morrow. Fear not, cousin. I'll see to Robbie's comforts whilst you slake your needs."

Eoin drew up a wad of mucus and launched the hawker over the rail. He glared at Reid with narrowed dark eyes. "Are ye insinuating that I've been unfaithful to Robbie?"

"'Tis not of import where you dipped your wick in the past, but by all means I encourage such debauchery in your future." Reid goaded the man on purpose. "But before you embark on such an escapade, I've a matter to discuss."

Eoin splayed his arms wide, a mocking gesture to grant Reid continuance.

"I want the chieftainship back, and I want Robbie. I'm willing to barter an exorbitant amount of coin for your concession." He snatched the coin into his fist for emphasis.

"Holy Christ!" Eoin's laughter turned into a coughing fit, which was the reaction Reid expected, but the wretch wouldn't be so jovial when they finished the conversation.

"We both know I can lay claim to the chieftainship of Clan MacGregor. Da was the eldest of our sires, and I am your senior."

"By two months, cousin." Eoin leaned against the rail and sucked his cigar until the embers burned bright orange. He blew a cloud of swirling smoke between them. "You'd be hard pressed to gain the servitude of a clan ye abandoned years past."

"They are starving. You've provided them with no place to call home. I could buy their loyalty with a warm bed and a hot bit of fare. As a result of Da's good standing with the Crown, I am at liberty to petition King James and repeal the proscription against Clan MacGregor, which would free you from bartering with the Laird of Luss."

"What is to stop me from taking the gold and doing the same?"

"King James will not barter with a MacGregor, but I am known to him as Peter Wallace's son. As for the gold," Just the thought of Eoin bartering with the Jaguar King was entertaining. "It belongs to *B'alam*—the Mopán chieftain. There is a reason their clan has survived a hundred years of Spanish invasion, and I can assure you, the Jaguar King would sooner drink from your skull than give you his gold."

The latter image turned Eoin's smug expression into a scowl clearly visible beneath his heavy dark beard. "And this Mopán chieftain will give ye the gold for what reason?"

"I've lived among his people for eleven years. I speak their language and respect their choice of religion. I've hunted with them and fought alongside their warriors to protect their lands and their people. I've earned their respect the same way I'll regain the respect of Clan MacGregor."

The moonlight cast eerie shadows over Eoin's face. His jaw twitched. A vein in his temple pulsed. Reid had the man on the chopping block, and he was fully prepared to wield the ax.

"I'll not barter for the chieftainship."

"But you'll barter for Robbie." He resumed his play with the coin to tempt the man.

Eoin's silence spoke volumes. 'Twas just as Reid anticipated. The fool cared more about protecting his status than he did about hanging on to his claim to Robbie, which was the sole reason Reid had threatened to take the chieftainship. "I'll allow you to retain your position as the Gregarach. In exchange, I get Robbie for the gold."

"I have but to tell her of your offer to purchase her like a common whore to taint her opinion of ye."

"And I have but to tell her about Fergus to taint her opinion of you," Reid countered.

Eoin pushed himself off the rail and fisted the hand not holding his cigar. "She is naught more than a soiled pleb. She isnae worth so much."

Reid feigned indifference, but inside he wanted to strike the scabbit down. 'Twas wrong to want to kill one's own flesh and blood, yet the contempt curling Reid's hands into fists was none other than pure hatred. He held Eoin's glare, waiting for his concession. "Have we terms, cousin?"

Dark eyes narrowed to near closed as Eoin contemplated his answer. He drew on his cigar, once, twice, then after the third exhale, he answered, "We have terms. But know there is one thing I'll always possess."

Reid had what he came for. He cared little about possessions.

Eoin leaned into Reid's ear. "Regardless of how much gold ye offer, you'll never have enough coin to buy back Robbie's virginity."

Reid's jaw popped, his muscles flexed, wanting to break Eoin in two. Jean-Pierre's sudden appearance beside them saved Eoin from the pummeling he deserved.

"Preparations are in order, *Capitaine*. Shall I give the commands?"

"Nay. We are finished here. Ready the longboats and do be sure to take my cousin ashore. I dare say he is in need of Giselle's services." Reid stormed away shouting orders, "Clear the anchor. Batten down the canvas…"

Within a short period of time the majority of the crew had deserted the *Obsidian* in favor of a single eve of lust-filled debauchery. Waves slapped against the hull in a billowy hum but did little to sooth Reid's petulance.

"Henrik." Reid caught the Englishman with one leg over the rail ready to descend the hanging rope ladder.

"Will you be going ashore, Captain?"

"Nay. I've other matters to tend. I trust you to acquire enough provisions to get us to the Yucatán. I've another task for you as well. Barter with Madame Francisca for suitable garments for Robbie; a lightweight gown, undergarments, mayhap new footwear. The cost is of no import."

"Giselle's dressmaker?"

"Madame Francisca once assisted the personal modiste of Anne Juliana Gonzaga. I'm certain she has something suitable for a virtuous woman."

"Aye, Captain."

Reid stalked toward his cabin and paused with his hand on the lever, waiting for his ire to lessen.

She is naught more than a soiled pleb.

Eoin would never have the satisfaction of degrading Robbie again. If the man spoke a single ill word, Reid would grind the bastaird beneath his heel.

He pulled the handle down and prepared to face the woman he'd all but purchased for the price of a small kingdom. 'Twas time he and Robbie stop fighting their attraction. When he pushed the door open, he found her sleeping on the desk facing an empty sandglass. He was to blame for her exhaustion. The woman had made it her personal quest to create vital air.

He pulled back the coverlet on the bed he'd only risen from a couple hours before then approached the desk. After untying the twine, he peeled the deflated bladder off the privy pot—the contraption she'd built for her experiments. Inside was another dead rat which he quickly discarded out the back of the cabin. He didn't know if she was making progress, but the rat population in the stock hold had diminished considerably.

He slipped an arm behind her knees and cradled her back, then raised her out of the chair without effort. For a tall woman, she weighed no more than a small child. Now that he thought on it, she only ate when he shoved food in her hands, which obviously wasn't often enough.

Careful not to disturb her slumber, he set her gently atop the down stuffed mattress, removed her old brogues and stockings, then pulled a thin blanket to just above her breasts. Bent on one knee, he simply stared at her for long moments, watching the rise and fall of her chest beneath the drapes of wool. 'Twas madness, but what he felt for her hadn't faltered since the day he left Scotland.

"Sleep well, love," he whispered and untangled a curl out of her closed lashes. He laid his lips against her soft, warm cheek and worried over the battle ahead of him—the battle to possess her heart.

Her eyes slid from closed to half opened then back in her drowsy state. She said nothing but cupped his cheek with her small hand and stroked his lips with the pad of her thumb.

The tickle was maddening, and he would have given her what her touch implied she wanted if the pain in her eyes hadn't froze him. He might have mistaken drowsiness for sadness until a tear slipped over her temple.

He caressed her brow, tortured by the anguish in her emerald eyes. "What is it, love?"

"I wish you'd come back sooner." Her hand fell away and her eyes sealed shut.

For the first time since Da died, Reid experienced a pain so fierce in his chest he wanted to weep.

9

~ SEDUCTION ~

The warm silk against her legs felt positively sinful. Robbie refused to open her eyes knowing the perfectly wonderful dream surrounding her in splendor would vanish. She stretched and wiggled her toes—her bare toes. Oh, aye, she had to be dreaming. She always slept with her brogues on so she could run if the need presented itself.

Or mayhap she'd died. Suffocated like a rat in one of her experiments. The air she breathed was warm, damp, and a subtle weight lay against her face.

A frown awoke the muscles in her face just before she punched her way out of red silk sheets. Morning light blinded her, but her accommodations were unmistakable.

Holy Loki! She'd slept in Reid's cabin. No, 'twas worse. She'd slept in Reid's bed.

She jerked upright. Hair stung her face when her head whipped to the side. Part of her expected to find Reid sprawled out beside her—in the flesh—as that's all he'd been wearing in her dream.

Thank the gods, he wasn't there.

When she bolted out of the bed and scanned the cabin to find her brogues, a simple yellow gown draped over the foot of the bed caught her eye. Sprinkled with a tiny print of green ivy, the garment had short sleeves trimmed in white ruffles. Beside the gown was a sleeveless undershift made of thin linen with scalloped lace trimming the hem. An ivory corset so stiff it held its form added to the display.

Robbie looked down at her flat chest. Having the breasts of a blossoming young girl prevented her from ever needing such a contraption, but it was nonetheless an exquisite piece of craftsmanship.

On the floor sat a pair of yellow silk slippers adorned with green beads around the toes. And lastly was a gold bauble strung with turquoise and emeralds.

Seconds ticked by before she felt brave enough to touch any of it. Much to her disappointment, the bracelet was far too big for her skinny wrist, but the gown she could easily see herself in. She held it against her and looked down at its simplicity. It was perfectly beautiful.

A thick knot formed in her throat. She'd never been privy to such finery.

"Good morrow, love." A smooth husky voice she was coming to recognize sounded from the doorway. Arms crossed, Reid leaned against the frame with one booted foot crossed over the other. "The color suits you."

Her heart did a little dance, and she didn't even try to hide the smile that stretched her lips over her teeth. "Did fairies come during the night?"

"Nay. I had Henrik procure the garments from a woman who once assisted the modiste to the Archduchess of Austria. The gown is made of cotton and more suitable to a hotter climate."

Feelings of neglect made Robbie frown. "We docked?"

"Aye, but I fear you slept through it. We've been traveling at a speed of ten knots for the past few hours." He must have sensed her disappointment for he continued to console her. "Dinnae fret overmuch. Rum Cove was no place for a woman."

She resisted the urge to stomp. "The modiste was a woman. Am I to believe there were no other women at this port?"

"No women of propriety." Why the rogue continued to grin was beyond her comprehension, lest these women of ill repute were responsible for his jovial mood. Mayhap the whores relieved his tension.

Jealousy had her nails digging into her palms. "Did ye go ashore?" Why had she asked that? If the man wanted to go ashore and lay with the tarts, then so be it.

"Nay. Everything of value to me is on board the *Obsidian*." His stance softened, specs of blue twinkled in his silver eyes.

His flattery shouldn't have tamed the green beast inside her, but it did. She broke the hold between their gazes and studied the pattern of ivy on the gown. With Reid's moral conduct intact, she posed the question she should have asked foremost. "Did Eoin go ashore?"

"He was the first one in the longboats."

"Of course." That answer didn't surprise her. "I'm certain he was anxious to feel the ground beneath his feet. The man has little fondness for water since he nearly drowned. Ye remember the incident."

Reid nodded and blew a dramatic exhale. "Is it difficult for a woman of your intelligence to feign such ignorance?"

Blast him! He knew nothing of her and the difficulties she'd endured. Furious, she threw the gown atop the bed and stomped toward the exit, but Duncan and Cocijo appeared in the doorway, each carrying two pails of steaming water.

"Captain said ye might be needin' water for your experiments." Duncan entered the cabin and poured the contents of his pails into the oblong wooden tub she used to test her theories. Cocijo repeated Duncan's actions with another two pails, filling the tub three-quarters full.

She narrowed her eyes on Reid. "I already had water." She knew full well he intended to pamper her with a much needed bath. Did the man think he could woo her with fine garments and hot water?

Duncan's thin lips spread into a grin full of crooked yellow teeth. "Weel, now ye have more and 'tis hot."

"I hardly need hot water for my experiments." She crossed her arms and tapped her bare toe, determined to prove she wasn't so easily swayed.

"Mayhap you could find another purpose for it." Not even trying to feign innocence, Reid waved a third boy into the cabin. The gromet kept his eyes downcast as he set a towel and toiletries atop the bed, then quickly dismissed himself.

Robbie harrumphed. "If ye want me to bathe, all ye need do is tell me I stink."

Duncan twisted at the waist waiting to hear his captain's response, but Reid wisely held his tongue. Duncan, however, did not. "Take no offense, Miss Mary, but a woman shouldnae be smellin' as bad as the bilgemates."

Robbie gasped as blood filled her cheeks with instantaneous heat. Her hands fisted at her sides, and the sound rumbling in her throat might have been mistaken for a growl.

The laddies fled, but Reid had the gall to laugh outright.

"I'll leave you to your *work*." He reached for the lever and started to pull the door closed, but paused. "I suggest you lock the door, least I be tempted to check on your progress prematurely." He winked and left her in privacy.

The moment the door clipped shut, Robbie sniffed beneath her arms. The smell wasn't horrendous, but 'twas not a smell she wanted tainting her new gown. She locked the door, but also propped his desk chair into the crook of the door lever. The devil most likely had a key.

Content with her privacy, she disrobed, snatched up the toiletries, and stood beside the tub. Steam danced atop the surface like the loch on May Day. She couldn't recall the last time she'd bathed in anything besides a basin or a cool brook. She'd never needed more.

As she stepped into the tub and sank into its luxurious depths, she concluded there were vast differences between what she needed and what she desired.

She needed Eoin, but she desired Reid.

She rested her head against the rim, but the second her eyes fell shut, Reid was there in her mind's eye bathing her breasts and stroking her between her thighs.

Her eyes shot open. Blast him!

She sat up and scoured every inch of her body with a fury. Did men think they were the only ones with needs? A woman ached for release every bit as much as a man, but if a woman strayed into another man's bed to scratch her itch, she was labeled a whore. But, oohhh, if a man goes frolicking in and out of multiple women's bed, he is considered virile. Well, Eoin must be bluidy virile.

Robbie dipped her soiled hair beneath the water, after which she lathered every lock with suds. Her mental rant seemed to lessen with the overwhelming scent of primrose.

Standing in the tub, she twisted her hair like a rope, making a conscious effort not to let the droplets trickle to the floor, then she pulled a brush through the tangles until they hung in wet waves down her back. Since the air was warm, she toweled dry without haste and walked out onto the balcony to hang the towel over the rail. Standing in the open stark naked felt wickedly arousing, and as she was feeling slightly rebellious, she dawdled on the balcony, flaunting her nudity, pretending to dance.

A giggle bubbled out of her throat. She was going mad.

Moments later, she stood atop the fur rug fighting the laces of the corset over top the sleeveless undershift. The boned stays dug into her hip bones as she attempted to twist the contraption around her abdomen. She bent, shook, and raised her small breasts into the formed cups. Just when she was about to rip the foolish thing off, she looked down to find actual breasts—perfect, round, plump, luscious breasts.

The sight had her giddy. The corset sculpted her bosom in a way that created a shadowed crease in the middle. Of course, it was an illusion. Nonetheless, she spent long moments admiring herself from various angles before she draped the yellow gown over her head. The material was blessedly cooler than her kirtle, and as she righted the garment, she looked down again to find her breasts brimming out of a swooping neckline far more daring than any fashion she'd ever worn.

A soft knock rapped against the door. "Robbie?"

Blast it! She wasn't ready. She should send him away.

Nay. She wanted him to see her in the gown. She

stuffed her toes into the silk slippers, snatched the bauble off the bed and rushed to the door.

"If ye need more time, I—"

She jerked the chair away from the door, unlocked the lever, and ripped the door open wide. "I'm finished." Panting, she stepped back and awaited his approval. She would be lying if she said she didn't want to please him.

The smile he'd worn when she first opened the door fell, as did his eyes. His gaze locked on her breasts and stayed there. She could hardly blame him. They looked spectacular in the corset.

'Twas a naughty thing to do, but she inhaled, which seemed to make them even fuller.

"The gown suits you well." He briefly glimpsed the length of her garment, then returned his sights once again to her breasts. "Verra well."

Hot sensations washed through her like a firestorm. The tiny hairs at her nape prickled and her nipples hardened against the stiff material of the corset. If her body reacted to his gaze with such fever, she could only imagine what would happen if he ever touched her. She would likely reach climax within seconds.

The wicked thought snapped her fragile nerves. She giggled but quickly regained dignity. She fanned her face in an effort to thwart another giggle, but it sprang forth with might. Tears filled her eyes, her palm pressed against her perky new breasts. "Forgive me," she choked out. "'Tis a horrid thing I do when I'm nervous."

"I eat nuts." His odd statement caught her unguarded.

"Beg pardon."

"When I'm nervous or fretting over a'thing, I eat nuts." His attention shifted toward a wooden tray she hadn't realized he'd been holding. Atop it sat a bowl of nuts, a ceramic honey pot, layers of yellow flatbread, and a second bowl filled with a brown substance that looked like mud. The mixture of salt and sweet smells had her mouth watering.

"Are ye trying to woo me with exotic delicacies, Captain?"

He winked, then filled his mouth with a handful of nuts saving him from a response.

Oh, the man was charming. Too charming.

He set the tray atop the desk where he proceeded to sprinkle nuts atop a round of flatbread. Next came swirls of golden honey. He rolled the flatbread, dipped it into the thick, brown syrup, and then held it beneath her nose.

The smell was his. The exotic scent she couldn't name was this sweet, robust, succulent treat.

"Taste." He licked his lips and waited for her to oblige him.

She could have taken it from him, but she didn't. Mayhap because she felt betrayed by Eoin's blatant cuckoldry and mayhap, she simply wanted to explore Reid's seduction. After all, that's what this was: the garments, the bauble, the bath, the victuals. 'Twas a dangerous game that promised to be pleasurable, though no one was likely to win.

Robbie opened her mouth and took the bite.

Her taste buds exploded. Her jaw pinched. "Oh, God!" She chewed. She moaned. It was sweet and salty and sinful.

"'Tis good, aye."

She nodded and swallowed as he re-dipped the roll again. This time she held the side of his wrist as he fed her. She wanted to be the seductress in his little game, but the savory treat proved to be a distraction. He fed her bite after bite until she'd eaten the last delicious morsel. "I've never tasted anything quite so divine. What is it?"

"'Tis called chocolate—the drink of the gods. The Mopán people make it out of the cacao bean."

"I daresay they could barter with the beans themselves."

"They do. The cacao bean is considered currency between the tribes." Reid swiped his finger over the corner of her lips and waited for her to open. He played this game verra well, but she could play it better.

Her pulse flitted in her throat as she held his hand and guided his finger inside her mouth. She stared at him from beneath her pale lashes as she slid her lips over his knuckle and suckled him between her teeth like a tiny cock.

His eyes blinked to half closed, his lips parted on a groan. The muscles in his hand flexed the same time he snatched his arm back and raked his fingers through his black hair. He scooped up a handful of nuts.

Oh, she'd ruffled his feathers and felt powerful during the act. If she were bold enough to investigate, she was certain she'd find him hard as stone beneath his tight black breeks. But he needed to go before their game got out of control. "My thanks for the fare and the gown and the slippers. I should—"

"Did you not like the bauble?" He sounded more hurt than offended.

Robbie looked at her fist where she still clutched the bracelet. "'Tis exquisite, but far too big. It falls off my hand." She demonstrated.

"'Tis not for your wrist." He retrieved the bauble out of her hand. "'Tis for your ankle."

"'Tis an odd place for a trinket."

"You'll find that the Mopán people decorate themselves with jewels in much odder places." He bent to one knee in front of her which forced her back against the desk. "I found this in Xitali's tomb and want ye to have it."

Robbie curled her fingers around the desk's edge when the side of his hand brushed her ankle. The heat that had been stirring low in her belly dropped into her womanhood and turned into a pulsing inferno.

Their game just upped a notch.

Blood rushed up her chest, burned her neck, and scalded the backs of her eyeballs. Her muscles seized as naught but silence surrounded them. Then she felt his hand slide up the back of her calf in a caress that weakened her knees.

Her body hummed. Her eyes closed, waiting for him to continue the upward path. Her nether lips swelled in anticipation as moisture gathered at her core, but then he was gone, and the aching she felt was far worse than the expectancy.

"I should go." He pivoted and strode quickly for the door.

Nay! She wanted him to stay. She needed him to stay and finish their game. She reached out to him, but he'd already slammed the door.

10

===

~ TEMPTATION ~

Eight damn days he'd performed his duties with a raging erection. Robbie's antics had all but sucked, licked, and chewed on Reid's last nerve, then spit it back out and stomped on it.

His patience was at its end.

S'truth. He suspected her seduction was only a guise for her retaliation. She'd used him as a means to strike back at Eoin for going ashore, but Reid wanted her for more than one night. He wanted her for forever; in his bed, in his life, as his wife. Unfortunately, he couldn't get past the wanting her in his bed.

Thinking about her full lips sucking his finger led to him thinking about her full lips sucking his cock. And that damn corset! He was thankful she liked the garments, but was certain she'd not taken the corset off. Mayhap she couldn't. Mayhap she needed assistance.

He twitched, wiped the sweat from his brow, and readjusted himself inside his breeks. His bollocks were heavy with unspent seed, and his cock jerked every time he thought of the wee temptress and her lips...and her long legs...and her breasts and...

God's legions, it was hotter than Satan's hearth out here.

The sun beating down on him didn't help his condition, nor did the damn sandglass that never seemed to run empty. He counted the strokes on the slate as he'd done a dozen times this day, waiting for that last grain of sand to fall. Jean-Pierre would be about to man the helm and relieve Reid of duty soon.

Then what?

The provisions they'd bought in Rum Cove were gone. The nuts were gone. The cigars were gone. And the brandy was gone. Which meant Eoin was an unbearable piss-head.

Had that cross storm not blown them off course, they'd be home by now, and Reid wouldn't have to look at Eoin's snarl every second of the day. The man had emerged from the keel two days past and had paced the main deck ever since. His cousin was much more tolerable when he was an invisible drunk.

At long last, Henrik climbed the main mast and called for the change of guard. Only minutes later, Jean-Pierre appeared out of the afthatch and strolled to the helm.

"*Salut, Capitaine.*" Jean-Pierre swiped his pointed beard and offered Reid a congenial grin. "I dare say your cousin is in danger of wearing through the planks."

Reid peeled his fingers off the tiller and stepped to the side. "I would give five doubloons for a goblet of drink to get that guzzle-guts off my deck."

"Make it seven, and I'll escort the sot to the keel myself." Jean-Pierre opened one side of his surcoat and lifted a flat, silver container partway from his pocket. "But I want the flask back."

"You're a good friend, Jean-Pierre." Reid clapped

the Frenchman on the back.

"*Oui,* that I am, *Capitaine.* Now, run along and play. I fear your kitten might need assistance killing the rats. Duncan and Cocijo haven't been hunting in days."

Reid glanced at the open door of his cabin where Robbie worked. "She is making progress." His statement lacked conviction. S'truth, he didn't know if she was any closer to creating vital air than she had been a fortnight ago. Colored smoke had rolled out of the cabin three days past which instilled panic in every man aboard, including Reid. "We should consider ourselves fortunate she hasnae blown the ship up." Reid took his leave, heading toward the companionway.

"Yet," Jean-Pierre commented over his shoulder and waved Eoin toward the helm, then gave Duncan instructions to man the tiller.

Standing before a barrel of water they'd collected from the storm, Reid scooped up a chunk of lye, stripped out of his shirt, and washed from nose to navel. With a tuned ear, he listened to Jean-Pierre work his magic, then the blessed sound of the afthatch squeaked open. Reid glanced over his shoulder to find them both gone.

There was a god.

Reid climbed the steps to the captain's deck and hung his shirt over the rail. 'Twould be dry in a matter of minutes, but he was too close to Robbie and her lips and her legs and her breasts to wait for the sun to bake his garment.

He inhaled what he hoped was a breath of fortitude, then stepped into the open doorway.

His eyes nigh popped from his skull. What the devil was she doing?

Garbed only in her undershift and corset, Robbie was bent over the rim face down in the tub of water.

She shifted on her knees and wiggled her sweetly rounded arse, which was the sign his heart needed to resume beating.

Enraged that she would attempt such an experiment alone, Reid crossed the cabin in two strides and wrenched her out of the water. "Are you trying to kill yourself, you foolish woman?"

Startled, she pulled a leather mask from her nose that was connected to a leather tube to one of her contraptions on the floor. She pushed wet ropes of dark auburn hair from her face and stared at him with innocent emerald eyes. "I am testing. The rats survived this past experiment."

"So you thought to try it out on yourself? Are ye adder-bitten? Have the vapors turned your brains to pig dung?" Aghast, Reid wanted to shake her. What if she had drown? The thought made him shiver.

His scolding sent her into a pout. Her lashes and her chin fell in unison. She picked up the sandglass beside the tub and rotated it side to side. "How long has this been empty?"

"God's legions, woman! Think ye I paid any heed to the damn sandglass?" Pout or no, he was not yet finished ranting.

She stared at him, her eyes unfocused, her mind elsewhere. "It worked." She stood and checked the pulse in her neck. "I feel right. I dinnae swoon. It bluidy worked!"

"Are you saying you've been under water for more than a half hour?"

Robbie's lips split into a toothy smile. "I did it. I created air."

Her words finally registered in Reid's head. He looked at the contraption, the water, the sandglass, then her. "You did it. By God! You really did it." Stunned by her success, Reid wrapped his hands around her skull and kissed her.

'Twas by no means fevered or passionate, but the second he pulled back, he realized his error. While he searched for words to right his wrong, she tangled her fingers into the hair at his nape and pulled him back to her mouth. She kissed him hard, like she'd been starving for it for years. Jaw spread wide, her tongue ravished his mouth, twirling, licking, thrusting. Their teeth ground together as she flattened her palm on his chest and pushed him against the wall.

He stood there like an ignorant ape, eyes open, arms hanging at his sides, dumbfounded by her fierceness. His lack of participation didn't go unnoticed.

The fingernails piercing his chest retracted. Her breasts rose and fell with her ragged breaths. And when she raised her pale lashes to him, the rejection in her pained eyes tore a hole in his heart. "Was I wrong to think ye wanted me?"

Kiss her back, ye fool! The man who'd waited far too long for her kiss awoke with a vengeance. "Nay. I have wanted ye for forever." He wove his fingers through her wet hair, tilted her head, and dove back into her mouth with a furor.

This was the kiss he'd waited for. The kiss he'd dreamed about for eleven years. The kiss that filled the place in his heart he'd saved for her.

She was fire and ice, honey and salt. An aphrodisiac that heightened his senses, hardened his muscles, and sent his blood racing through his veins and straight to his cock.

The man who typically sorted through his morals was lost to a desire that numbed his toes. Reid wrapped his hands around her tiny waist and pushed her against the opposite wall without breaking the seal between their lips. When he drove his knee between her thighs, she gasped and threw her head back, slamming it against the wall with a thud.

"Och, love. Are—"

She sucked his bottom lip between her teeth, silencing him. Her hands were everywhere; caressing his bare skin, squeezing the hardened muscles of his shoulders, his chest, his arse. Her touch thrilled him, empowered him.

She hooked her fingers over his breeks at his hip and pulled. "Dinnae stop."

Stop? Not even the threat of a pistol pressed to his skull would prevent him from claiming her.

When she ground her pelvis against his thigh, a hot bolt of fire seared through his erection. His seed boiled in his bollocks. His cock jerked and a droplet of cum leaked out prematurely.

He groaned, knowing he would never make it inside her. He'd waited too long. He would likely spill his seed before he untied the laces of his breeks.

"If ye leave me wanting again, I'll kill ye," she threatened and sucked his nipple into her mouth. She drew on it, flicked it with the tip of her pink tongue, then pulled it between her teeth.

The woman was wild, untamed, and quickly becoming more than he could handle. He captured both her wrists in one hand and drew them over her head, then feasted on her damp neck, her sharp collarbone, the tops of her breasts pouring out of the corset. Shattered patience prevented him from fighting the rigid garment, so he filled his palm with her surprisingly round rump and slid her further up his thigh.

He always imagined their first time together would be gentle, loving, a slow exploration of flesh, but the woman was an aggressor and damn if he would switch to timid tactics now.

He propped his foot on the side of the berth taking

her leg with him and spreading her wide. The musky scent of her arousal wafted through the thin linen of her undershift. It might kill him, but he would see her satisfied before they finished. He slipped his hand between their bodies, lifted the hem of her skirt, then slid his finger into the thatch of curls concealing hot, swollen, wet flesh.

"Oh, God," they said in unison.

Before he could ease inside her, she thrust into his hand, impaling herself onto his middle finger. Her eyes twitched behind closed lids. Her entire body quaked. She whimpered.

He wanted to taste her, wanted to bring her to climax with his tongue, but he'd vowed long ago to reserve such an intimate act for their wedding bed. Instead, Reid added a second finger and watched as the signs of pure pleasure smoothed her beautiful face. A trickle of sweat fell from her temple down her neck where her pulse vibrated against her skin. He stroked her velvety sheath, pumping in and out of her, flicking the pearl inside her womb.

She was beyond ready, as was he.

"I want you, Robbie," he whispered against her cheek as his thumb rotated around her most sensitive flesh hidden at the apex of her slit.

She cried out. Her nails sliced into his hand. Her body shook. The muscles inside her clenched his fingers with startling suction and before he could withdraw his fingers and enter her properly, a burst of hot release trickled over his hand.

To say he was shocked wouldn't near describe his state of mind. He'd never brought a woman to climax so quickly.

"Holy Loki!" Her eyes flickered open, weighted with desire, but snapped wide when booming applause filled the cabin.

"Good show, cousin." Eoin clapped from the doorway. "Not only do ye have her dressing like a whore, now she is acting like one."

• • •

Mortification turned to shock, then escalated to fear within two heartbeats, but Eoin didn't stay in the doorway long enough to witness the cycle of emotions.

"My God, what have I done?" Robbie peeled herself out of Reid's arms and wobbled on unsteady legs to where her gown lay draped over the desk chair. The warm trickle of her climax dripped down her trembling legs as she wrenched the garment over her head. Her throat constricted, her hands shook, and the pulse still beating in her womanhood all reminded her of her infidelity.

Tears scalded her eyes as she rushed toward the cabin door, but Reid's fingers wrapped around her arm in a bruising grip that stilled her flight. "Robbie, wait."

"Nay! Release me," she yelled, panic cracking her voice. "I must go after him. I have to explain."

"Explain what? Explain that you deserve better?"

Her entire being shook. She felt ill, disgusted with her lack of self-control. "I'm not the only one who will suffer the consequences of my actions. I'm not like ye. I'll not put my own selfish wants before the livelihood of those I hold dear to my heart." She jerked free of him and raced from the cabin, away from Reid, away from the scene of her betrayal.

Tears nigh blinded her as she stumbled down the companionway and chased Eoin toward the bow of the ship. The wooden planks burned her bare feet. Heat dried her throat to ash. The crew gathered into pairs, but the heavy footfalls pounding behind her drown out their curious whispers.

A quick glance over her shoulder showed Reid fast at her heels.

Blast him! Blast him to Hell and back! She spun. "Please, leave me to right this wrong."

Jean-Pierre appeared behind Reid, panting, his yellowed shirt soaked with sweat. "Forgive me, *Capitaine*, I tried to occupy the man while—"

Reid stilled Jean-Pierre's tongue with a menacing look.

"Ye tried to occupy the man while what, Jean-Pierre?" *While your captain seduced me?*

The Frenchman held silent. The ropes and yard-arms overhead filled with topmen like crows in the trees. She felt like they all knew. Like they'd all been part of a grand conspiracy to tear her and Eoin apart.

She narrowed her eyes on Reid. "Did ye plan to seduce me? Did ye know Eoin was there...watching?"

The vein pulsing at Reid's temple made her heart hitch, but she took a bold step forward and pushed him hard against his bare chest.

He didn't budge. Instead, he grabbed her by the hair and bent to her ear. "Did I plan for you to attack me? Did I plan for you to threaten to kill me if I left you wanting? Nay. I did not."

He released her and made no attempt to follow her the rest of the way to the prow where Eoin leaned over the forward rail staring out at a dark ocean.

She inhaled, wiped her tear-streaked face, and stepped beside the man who'd provided her protection for more than a decade. "Eoin."

He turned, but left his hip leaning against the rail in a pose she thought too casual given the situation. His face lacked emotion, his demeanor seemed oddly indifferent. Now that she was afforded a moment to gather her wits, she wondered why he hadn't attacked Reid. She'd been the one pinned against the bluidy wall. Eoin had beaten men near to death during raids, but he hadn't so much as raise a hand to defend her.

She hid her fists between the folds of her skirt and opened her mouth, but words failed her.

"The deed is done, Robbie. There is naught ye can say to remedy what has happened." He raised a flask to his lips, and took a long draw from the mouth of the container.

"I lost myself. Please, dinnae be rash."

"Rash? Your acts are unforgivable."

She followed his gaze over her shoulder to find Reid several feet behind her, arms crossed, legs spread. Mayhap her guilt made her question their every look, but she couldn't help but feel like they already knew how this confrontation would end.

She forced her attention back on Eoin. "Can ye honestly say you've never strayed from our bed? Can ye look me in the eyes and tell me you've always been faithful to me?"

The bastaird grinned. 'Twas more of a snarl really. "We are not bound by law, by God, or even by hand-fasting. I am well within my morals to take my ease with a different woman every night if I so desire."

She expected anger, rage, mayhap hurt or disappointment, but nothing in Eoin's bearing reflected the loss of someone he claimed to love. "Did ye ever intend to legitimize our union and settle at Rannoch?"

"Rannoch was always your dream, not mine." He spit over the rail. "Our union would not benefit the clan. We both know I've been biding my time until I could gain a more substantial marriage. I'd always planned to keep ye as a mistress."

A mistress? Biding my time? A flurry of blinding white spots speckled her vision. If the man thought all his eggs had two yolks, he was sadly mistaken. She wanted to rip his tongue out. Nay. She wanted to castrate him. She'd been a fool to give herself to him.

She searched for words to hurt him, something that would wipe the smirk off his face. "Ye need me to get the gold."

"Nay, I need Reid to get the gold. All I need ye to do is service my cousin the way you've serviced me in the past to fulfill our bargain."

"What bargain?"

"I traded ye for the gold. Ye have to be the highest paid whore on the continent. I hope the treasure between your legs is worth the price he is willing to pay for it."

What she thought was her heart pounding in her ears was actually Reid's angry strides. He blew past her and threw an iron fist toward Eoin's face, but the man had been prepared for an assault. He ducked the blow, spun, wrapped his arms around Reid's ribs and squeezed.

"Is that not what we negotiated, cousin?" Eoin's sardonic question was full of pomp.

"You bastaird!" Reid roared, muscles flexed and hardened in his arms just before he reached over his head and laced his fingers behind Eoin's thick neck. Reid pulled him over his back and slammed Eoin onto the quarterdeck at Robbie's feet.

She jumped back, not knowing who to defend, and thinking she didn't want to defend either of them.

Without pause, Reid lunged atop Eoin and drove fists of fury into his sides, bone-crushing jabs that stunned Eoin temporarily, but the man had been in enough fisticuffs to know how to retaliate.

They rolled, spun, and flipped.

Positions reversed, Eoin now pinned Reid to the planks and drove his knuckles into Reid's face, splitting the skin. Blood and sweat splattered the front of Eoin's *lèine* shirt and seemed to unleash a savage beast lurking inside Reid.

Veins whelped in his neck and forearms. He bucked and sent Eoin scrambling.

"Shall I put an end to this buffoonery?" Jean-Pierre stepped to Robbie's side and cupped her elbow.

"Nay. Let them kill each other."

11

~ SECRETS ~

Where the hell is she? Reid stormed up the companionway after searching the gunner deck a second time. Robbie wasn't there, nor was she in the cabin or her quarters or the storage chamber. He'd combed every nook of the *Obsidian* twice, but the woman was no where to be found.

Two days should've been an ample amount of time for her temper to cool, but the lass was still full of fire. The eve before when he'd last tried to talk to her, he swore if she'd opened her mouth, flames would have shot out.

He rubbed his aching temple and winced as a sudden jolt of pain wrapped around his skull and squeezed. His eye had turned ten shades of purple in the past two days, but he didn't regret sparring with his cousin. S'truth, Eoin deserved a beating, but Reid couldn't say he'd won. The only good that had come of it all was that she hated Eoin as much as she now hated him.

Hands on his hips, he stood at the ship's center and scanned the deserted deck. The anchor had been weighed and the crew already rowed their way ashore, all save for Oscar and Henrik who waited patiently beside him. 'Twas past time the stubborn vixen came out of hiding. Reid filled his lungs with hot air and bellowed, "Robbie-e-e!"

Of course, he didn't receive a response, but he was out of options. "God's legions," he mumbled and wiped his brow on his sleeve. Mayhap she jumped ship. 'Twould be just like the bull-headed, fire-hissing wench to do something so foolish.

"Ahem. Ahem-hem." Henrik made a show of clearing his throat. He wore an odd face—crooked smile, crazed eyes, pinched lips—then he discreetly pointed up.

"What is it, man?" Reid followed Henrik's finger up the mainmast where a hundred and fifty rungs led a ladderway straight into a burning sun. "She's in the crow's nest?" He glanced back at Henrik. "Surely you jest."

"She went up before dawn," he whispered beneath his hand.

"Why the devil did you not tell me?"

Henrik cupped his groin and peered back up the mainmast. "She threatened to cut off my bollocks and eat them for the noontide meal."

"And you took her threat literal?" Reid rolled his eyes and reached for the first crosspiece.

"She looked hungry," Henrik defended. "Practice caution, Captain. She has a blade."

Reid looked down at Henrik from three rungs up. "Take Oscar to the remaining longboat and wait for us. We'll be about shortly."

"Aye, Captain. God be with ye."

Reid climbed the mainmast, thinking God Himself

couldn't tame the shrew.

Once he'd reached the final crosspiece, Reid pushed on the hatch at the base of the crow's nest, but the small door didn't budge. He tried again, gaining an inch this time, but the weight bearing down on it refused to allow him entry. "Mary-Robena Wallace, you will cease this childish behavior and get off the damn door."

She stomped on the floor—twice.

"Och!" Reid ground his teeth and pushed air through his nostrils like a ragging bull. The woman would be the death of him.

He curled his fingers around a handle at the base of the crow's nest and pulled himself up the side, then flipped his legs over the edge of the small wooden circle. He blamed the unsettling feeling in his stomach on the gentle sway of the ship, but knew the ailment had more to do with Robbie than heights.

Curled into a ball, she hugged her knees with arms pinked by the sun and refused to look at him. He sat beside her, filling the remaining space with his massive frame and waited long minutes for her to speak.

"I hate ye."

He expected as much. "I know."

"What ye did was wrong."

"I know."

"Ye are a deceitful, conniving liar."

"I know." He really hadn't lied, but he wasn't about to argue with her. 'Twas best to accept her bitter words for the nonce.

The sun had highlighted strips of her honey-red hair to pale blonde and when he moved to push a curl from her face, she jerked back. "Ye dinnae own me, and I never want ye to touch me again."

He scowled. That was not something he could do. "Why? Do you fear the passion between us?"

Her head shot up and her eyes glowed green with fury. "'Twas lust."

"'Twas more and you well know it." If the woman weren't so mulish, she might admit how good they could be together.

"Think ye are the only man who has brought me pleasure?"

Her relations with Eoin were not a topic he cared to discuss.

She turned away from him, set her chin between her knees, and mumbled, "I'd have half a dozen bairns by now, had I married Lyall."

"Lyall?" 'Twas difficult enough to imagine her with Eoin, but Lyall was ten years her senior.

"Aye. When I turned ten and eight, he offered to take me to his cousin's in the Highlands, but I refused to leave the others behind."

The clan. It always came back to the clan. She made a better chieftain than Eoin ever would. "And now you regret your mistake?"

"'Twas not a mistake. The weak will die without the strong to protect them. The winters are nigh more than Grandda and auld Angus can bear, and now we have Alana." Robbie turned back toward him. "Do ye even know who Alana is?"

"Nay." Why did he sense a scolding?

"She is your six-month old niece."

"Niece?" To his knowledge, Reid had no other siblings apart from Shane and Kelsa who were too young to have bairns. He quickly did the math. "Shane is only ten and five, and Kelsa ten and three."

"Kelsa would be ten and four this summer had she not died."

Reid barely remembered the wee bit. She'd only been two when Da took him away. "I suspect her death was difficult for Nanna."

"Difficult? Kelsa was the only lass not marked by the Colquhouns. She was the only one who stood a chance at gaining a marriage outside the clan. Nanna sent her to Glenstrae to barter for fur, but she never made it to the tanner. The Laird of Luss's youngest bastard forced himself on her in the wood." Robbie paused to wipe her unshed tears. "Alana was the product of that rape."

Reid felt ill. Bitter saliva pooled in his mouth, and he was certain he would vomit. "Kelsa died bearing a child forced on her."

"Nay." Robbie's chuckle reflected her insanity. "Neither King James nor God has ever made anything easy on a MacGregor. Kelsa delivered Alana, but hated the wean from the moment she slipped from Kelsa's womb. She refused to feed the babe or hold her. Nanna tried to help her through it but failed. Three months past, Kelsa wrapped Alana in a wool and went to the cavern where she strapped on the iron boots and jumped into the loch." Robbie pinched her eyes shut. "Knowing how Kelsa felt about the babe, I followed her that day and raced into the cavern when I heard the splash. I managed to save Alana, but I couldnae get Kelsa back to the surface."

Reid could do little more than shake his head. Nothing he could say would bring Kelsa back. His heart went out to Nanna and for the babe who would never know her mam. He wanted to blame someone for not saving them, but deep inside he knew that someone was himself. He shouldn't have waited so long to go back. He should have been there to protect them. "Where the hell was Eoin?"

"Where the hell were you?" she countered, her eyes shining with condemnation. It was in that moment he realized she would never forgive him. She blamed him for every wrong that had occurred to the clan over the past eleven years.

"When ye bartered with Eoin, ye should have thought with your head and not your bluidy cock, for your desire to have me in your bed will ultimately cost lives. He'll not protect them. He'll leave them behind when they move camp. Anyone close to you or I will have no chance of survival. Which is why I have to make things right with Eoin."

Reid growled. His hands turned to fists. He stood and stared at the white sandy beaches of the place he'd called home for more than a decade. The longboats now scattered the shore where the Mopán people had begun to gather. He'd imagined this moment, even prepared the words. *Welcome home, love.*

But Robbie would never accept this place as her home. He looked at the windmill peeking out of the treetops. He'd spent years building Rukux and preparing for her arrival. 'Twas all for naught—the home he'd built, the garden, the butterflies....

A dark, suffocating emotion weighed heavy upon his chest. 'Twas a feeling he went to bed with at night and awoke with every morn. A man should not feel so alone.

Robbie stood with her back to the beach. "After we retrieve the gold, I'm going back to Scotland with Eoin."

"To endure a life as his mistress?"

"To protect my loved ones."

He was selfish to take her away from them, selfish to want her, but God help him, he didn't want to let her go. "The man took your virtue without intentions of taking you to wife. He is responsible for the death of your brother, yet you remain loyal to him."

Robbie stared at him, attempting to contemplate his words. "What do ye mean Eoin is responsible for Fergus's death?"

"God's legions!" Reid held his forehead in his hand and rubbed his temples. "Think, Robbie. Think back to that eve in the cavern. To the night Fergus was slain. There is a reason Eoin escaped unscathed."

Unwanted memories filled her head. Three Colquhouns had burst into the cavern after Reid sank below the loch's surface. "They came for ye and Eoin."

"Aye."

The Colquhouns had paid her little heed, she recalled in a daze. "I ran for assistance." But one followed, and caught her on the hillock. He forced her onto her stomach and punched her hard in the back, but she fought with all her might.

Her eyes pinched tight. Tears flooded her cheeks. Her pulse quickened the same as it had that night. "He kicked me in the side," she murmured, not certain which memories she voiced aloud and which she held inside.

The recollection made her dizzy, made her nauseous. She could still recall the sound of her rib snapping, could still feel the heel of his boot in her back as he held her to the ground. The sequence of events overlapped in her mind's eye. "They branded me with an iron rod."

She rubbed her wet cheek, wanting to scrub the scar away like she'd done so many times in the past.

"What else, Robbie? What else did you see?" he prodded.

Why was he making her remember? Why did he insist on torturing her? She shook her head and pressed the tips of her fingers against her eyelids, not wanting to see anymore. "Ye were there. Ye watched them burn me."

Reid gripped her shoulders. "I tried to help you, love. God help me, I tried, but Da set me on his horse and took me away. You can continue to hate me, but know that the man whose bed you plan to return to named Fergus as the MacGregor heir to save himself from the Colquhouns' blade."

"Nay." Denial came easier than acceptance, but her heart squeezed with doubt. "Eoin avenged Fergus's death. He killed the Colquhoun who murdered my brother."

"'Tis a lie." Reid's fingertips dug into her arms. He shook her. "Do not let your loyalty to Eoin blind you from the truth."

But she didn't understand what the truth was or how Reid was privy to it. "Ye were beneath the surface. Ye were not there."

"My da was there, and he battled the Colquhoun while Eoin fled."

Nay! She shook her head as age-old grief overwhelmed her. Her legs trembled, wanting to flee, but there was nowhere to run. She possessed neither the strength nor the desire to resist Reid when he pulled her into his arms. Her body convulsed as she sobbed against his chest, reliving the loss of her brother.

Reid was patient. He gave her all the time she needed, stroking her back and circling the ridges of her spine for what seemed an eternity. "Next to you, Fergus was my closest friend. I wish I could change the past. I wish with every ounce of my being I could have protected Fergus as well as you."

"Why did ye keep this from me?"

Reid set her back and wiped her cheeks. "Would you have believed me?"

Nay. She shook her head, knowing she would have defended Eoin the same as she had for years. But no more. The pain inside her turned to anger. Eoin didn't deserve her loyalty, and he didn't deserve to lead the clan. Her mind filled with vengeful thoughts, ways to make Eoin pay.

She bent to raise the hatch, but Reid caught her. "Where are you going?"

"To find Eoin."

Reid spun her around. "He has already gone ashore, as have all the others."

Robbie gawked at the scene before her. "We've arrived? Is this your Yucatán?"

"Aye."

When she climbed onto the edge of the crow's nest, Reid grabbed hold of her wrist. "Och, woman! You're completely unrestrained. Think you can spend more than two seconds debating your decisions? There are big fish in these waters. Damn big fish. Henrik is waiting for us in the longboat."

Mayhap insanity controlled her actions, but she was desperate to get off the *Obsidian*, desperate for a moment to herself. Robbie looked down and waved at the Henrik, regretting the harsh words that had passed between them. "Do apologize to Henrik for me. Tell him I lied about the blade, and that I never intended to maim him or eat his bollocks. I shall see ye ashore." And with these words, she snatched her hand free and leapt into aqua-blue water.

12

~ ARRIVAL ~

'Twas like a giant tub of bath water—warm, soft, mind-numbing. Robbie didn't want to think about Eoin or Reid or the clan. She wanted to reflect on her brother's memory.

Inside her head, Fergus smiled at her with his round cheeks. *"Fret not, Robbie. You'll get your titties soon."*

Robbie laughed and cried remembering how her brother constantly obsessed over the size of women's breasts. Pain sluiced through her heart and her tears mixed with the brine of the sea. She licked the salt from her lips and dove beneath the surface, pretending Fergus was at her side racing her to shore. She would have won. She'd always been faster than him, smarter than him, but he'd had a bigger heart. He wouldn't want her grieving over him or sacrificing the clan to avenge him.

Then you shall know the truth, and the truth shall set you free. Father MacCrouther's words sprang forth in her memory. The same words he'd used to end his sermons. She'd always believed there was some con-spiracy against the MacGregor Clan and once re-vealed, they would all be free, but this day those words had an altogether different meaning, for she'd never felt more free to live her life.

My thanks to ye, Fergus.

She came up for air, but immediately went back under, pushing crystal clear water behind her in long sweeping motions. Having spent years diving, her lungs were strong which allowed her to explore when she entered shallow water. Salt burned her eyes, but she didn't dare close them. Sunlight illuminated a beautiful world of sea-life. Schools of tiny fish darted away from her and hid in lush green plants covering odd-shaped rocks. Colorful species of vibrant yellows, blues, and oranges wove through long thin leaves swaying to and fro like a dance beneath the surface.

Oh, Fergus would have enjoyed these waters. The loch in Scotland had always been dark and far too cold to enjoy, but this, this must have been one of God's most prized creations.

Again, she returned to the surface to fill her lungs, then dove deep to witness a creature gliding gracefully across the white sandy bottom—a flat, diamond-shaped fish with wings and a long pointed tail.

Reid suddenly appeared in the corner of her vision. She might have known he would follow. The man wor-ried overmuch about her, guarding her like the farmer guarded his chattel. Had she been able to voice her thoughts, she would have informed him his protection was both unwanted and unnecessary. But as she watched him, she admitted his attention was welcome, however suffocating it was.

He swam like a mer-creature with elegance and perfection. Bubbles floated through his black hair as he scissored his bare feet with slow, fluid motions toward the odd diamond-shaped fish. He motioned her toward him, then reached down and stroked the sea creature's smooth gray hide as it drifted away.

Robbie took his extended hand and allowed herself to enjoy his companionship without guilt as they kicked to the surface. She could see herself being his friend, even though deep inside, in the place where she hid her dreams, she wanted to be so much more.

He whipped his head side to side, spraying water from his hair and then smiled that smile that made her ache to be his woman. "The stingray has a tail like a bodkin and can cut you like a sword. You must practice caution when…"

Ack. Robbie settled on her back and let her ears dip beneath the water, turning his words into a drone. The man was always lecturing her about safety. For the nonce, she just wanted to be free of fear, free of caution. Could he not allow her this single moment of peace?

She floated and licked the brine from her lips. "I dare say a person could lose themselves in a place such as this."

Reid splashed her. "You were not listening."

"Ye were blathering like auld Angus." She splashed him back, but he was in no mood for foolishness.

"Come along, love. We can play in the water later. They are waiting for us."

She spun and waded, studying the people flooding the shore. The men wore the silly little breechcloth that covered their pillicocks, but Robbie admitted to being caught unguarded by the women's attire—or lack there of. Short canvas skirts covered them from navel to mid-thigh, and naught but rows of beads hanging from their necks provided cover for their breasts, which really wasn't covering at all. Oh, aye, Fergus would have enjoyed this verra much. "The women are practically naked."

"The shock wears off rather quickly. Look your fill now, so you do not offend them when we go ashore. Ready yourself for their greeting. I'll do my best to keep the men from being overzealous."

Overzealous? Robbie fretted over Reid's statement, recalling her first encounter with Jax in the cavern and how he'd fondled her breasts.

The instant Robbie's toes dug into the sand, Reid took her hand in his beneath the water. "When you meet the chieftain, he'll check you for disease and—"

"Ye mean he will grope me."

Reid chuckled and squeezed her hand. "Aye. He verra well might. You may call him *B'alam* or the Jaguar King. He is respected by his people and should not be insulted."

The impeding meeting set Robbie on the defensive. "And if he insults me?"

A tug on her hand was Reid's way of telling her to behave. "The gold that promises to set the MacGregor clan free is on his land. You'd be wise to hide your temper."

As they rose out of a white foam wake, she scanned the scope of the beach and found Eoin with Jax and Jean-Pierre amidst a group of natives already bonding in laughter. Hatred crawled beneath her skin and sent the blood pulsing through her veins. She wanted to tell Eoin that she knew. She wanted to tell him she hated him. S'truth, she wanted to physically hurt him.

She took a single step in Eoin's direction, but Reid pulled her back with a jerk. "Robbie, please. You must save that confrontation for another time. 'Tis doubtful you even have words prepared." He released her hand and set himself behind her, retaining a firm grip on her shoulders. "The Mopán people have waited a long time to meet you. I beg ye to give them your attention."

She might have argued until a dozen bairns raced toward her, dusting the beach with tiny footprints.

They were perfectly beautiful with olive-colored skin, black hair, and white pixie teeth. They spoke the language far too quickly for her to interpret, but a smile was easily translated in any language. Curiosity rounded their dark eyes, so she settled on her knees in the sand and allowed them to examine her. They touched her clothes and her hair. Not one of them paid any heed to the scar on her cheek, but her eyes seemed to captivate them.

A small girl with the longest lashes Robbie had ever seen leaned close and pointed. "Your eyes match our jungle. They are...green. Verra pretty."

"Verra good, Pea-nut." Reid moved to the side and caught the child when she jumped into his arms.

"Welcome home, White Serpent. You were missed." The girl, no more than eight winters, pressed her tiny hands against Reid's cheeks and kissed his whiskered chin.

"Am I still your favorite white man?" Reid brushed noses with the girl and smoothed her long black hair.

She nodded fiercely. "And I your favorite Pea-nut?"

"Aye."

Watching the affectionate reunion filled Robbie's insides with warmth, but there was another emotion present—longing. She'd wanted a family since before Eoin took her to his bed, but he'd been careful not to plant a bairn in her womb, and for that she was now thankful.

Reid squat down beside them and set the girl in front of Robbie. "Pea-nut, I would like you to meet my...friend, Robbie," he stumbled over the introductions. "This is Jax's daughter, Yellow Peacock."

"Hach ki'imak in wo'ol in kaholtikech." Robbie had

practiced the phrase, but she apparently didn't put the accents in the correct places for the child stared at her with a puckered brow. Robbie tried again, "I'm pleased to make your acquaintance."

Reid pulled Robbie to her feet as a woman slightly swollen with child waddled toward them and then threw her arms around Reid's neck.

Robbie tried not to ogle her, but it was nigh impossible. Tattooed bands of delicate designs embellished her ankles, arms, and neck. Her features were exotic—thick lips, smooth light-brown skin, and lush black hair. Gold piercings decorated her face and chains of turquoise and brown beads hung around her neck, but didn't hide her ample breasts with large brown nipples.

The small lines at Reid's temples deepened with his proud smile as he set the woman back for introductions. "Robbie, meet Jax's woman, *Mukuy Ik*."

Feeling inadequate, Robbie crossed her arms over her own breasts, but quickly had to unfold them to return the woman's affectionate hug.

"Och, nay! Call me Black Dove. I be Jax's wifie an' the mither o' his bairns."

Dumbfounded, Robbie gawked at her. Black Dove sounded just like auld Angus. "Ye speak my language verra well." Robbie raised a brow at Reid, hoping for an explanation.

"When I arrived, I taught Jax my language and he taught me his. Black Dove was smitten with Jax and tried to worm her way into our lessons."

"Aye, but the dunderheid paid me no heed." Black Dove cast a scowl across the beach where Jax stood with Eoin.

Reid smiled. "As a gift, Da taught the daughters of the Jaguar King our language, and I fear his heavy burr came along with it."

Instant regret made Robbie frown. She had no idea Jax's wife was the Jaguar King's daughter. She couldn't say with any certainty whether or not Jax even liked her. "Ye should have told me Jax was close kin to the chieftain. Mayhap I'd have badgered him less aboard the *Obsidian*."

Black Dove took Yellow Peacock by the hand and backed the children away from Robbie. "Fret not. Da's bark is worse than his bite." She dipped her head toward an approaching man whose attire was not half as intimidating as his menacing snarl.

"Prepare yourself, Robbie. You're about to make the acquaintance of the Jaguar King." Reid moved aside as well. "Remember what I told ye."

He is respected by his people and should not be insulted.

Robbie's backbone stiffened. Her pulse kicked up a notch. Her smile weakened with every step the Jaguar King took toward her. Though elderly, he was built like a stone drite-house.

She swallowed and forced herself to blink as the Jaguar King set himself before her. While she tried to deny her eyes, the bands around his forearms were unmistakably human teeth. Colored feathers decorated his shoulders and chiseled bone pierced his nostrils and ears. Tribal markings in a brown color slightly darker than his skin covered his bald head, his forehead, and his cheeks.

He scowled at her with angry black eyes. Mayhap he purposely set his face rigid to intimidate her. Mayhap he wanted to instill fear in her. S'truth, the man's tactics made her tremble, but she maintained an undaunted pose when he grabbed her chin and forced her mouth open. He moved her head side to side investigating her teeth, then held her arms outright and studied her from head to toe.

Robbie understood his need to keep his people free from disease, but his callous inspection stirred the temper Reid warned her to hide. He might be their king, but when he spun her around by her neck and cupped her duff in his hand, she nigh came undone.

"Bix a k'àab'a'?" The Jaguar King posed his question to Jax, who'd followed their chieftain across the beach and now stood at Black Dove's back.

Jax dipped his head once toward Robbie, as if to offer his approval of her controlled behavior, then answered their chieftain's question, "I have named White Serpent's woman, Fire Tongue."

Robbie narrowed her eyes on Jax, but she managed to trap her reply between her teeth.

The Jaguar King grunted, then twirled Robbie back toward him with unnecessary aggression. He blatantly stared at her breasts pushed high out of her bodice.

S'help me Odin, if the man so much as—

His strong muscular hand rounded her left breast and squeezed.

A sharp intake of hot air scorched her throat. Robbie's temper crawled into her arm and took over her hand. She wrapped her fingers around the Jaguar King's heavy bollocks beneath his breechcloth and squeezed back with a grip that snapped his eyes wide.

The natives gasped.

"Robbie," Reid scolded at her side.

Mayhap her actions were foolish, but she wasn't going to let him grope her like a common tart regardless of his status.

To her surprise, he released her breast and grinned, revealing yellow teeth encrusted with gemstones. *"Ma´. B'alam* name you Handful of Seed." The chieftain threw his head back and roared with laughter.

Humiliated, she snatched her hand back and scanned the hordes of guffawing natives. Blast them and their mockery!

Just as she opened her mouth to strongly protest her new name, the Jaguar King splayed his arms wide and boasted, "Welcome to Ballace."

He curled his hand around her shoulder and forced her steps to align with his as he led her into his jungle. The man's skin was oily or mayhap sweaty, but he smelled like sweet butter.

Reid jogged to her side. "Is that what you call hiding your temper?"

"Think ye I need a bluidy lecture now?" When Reid fell back, she craned her head over her shoulder. "Did he call this place Wallace?"

"*B'alam* is determined to name this land after my da. The two of them were verra close."

"But your da's name was Calum MacGregor."

"When King James enacted the proscription against Clan MacGregor Da assumed the alias Peter Wallace, which is also the name Da used when he first arrived. As the Mopán people have difficulty making the 'W' sound, I have heard this land called everything from Ballace to Billis."

Robbie stepped over a tree root belonging to a monstrous tree and briefly pondered Reid's words. "Peter Wallace was my da."

"And my da's closest friend."

Robbie was humbled. War stole the privilege of knowing her da, nonetheless, she'd been proud of his dedication to Clan MacGregor. She smiled inside, thinking of how pleased Grandda would be to learn a land as wondrous as this bore the name Wallace, regardless of the form in which it was pronounced.

She studied her surroundings, hoping to memorize the flora and fauna so she could describe it with accuracy upon her return to Scotland. A variety of large, vibrant-colored birds with enormous beaks flew overhead beneath a canopy of lush green foliage. Black-furred beasties bounced with gusto through the tallest trees she'd ever seen. Gazing down from the treetops, one of the creatures pitched a partially eaten piece of fruit at them, then opened its mouth and screamed in high-pitched tones.

She jumped, and the Jaguar King tightened his hold. "Be not afraid. The howler monkeys will not harm Handful of Seed."

Her scowl caused the chieftain to release her and take the lead on his own. Regardless of how brief her stay might be here, she refused to be regarded as Handful of Seed. She glared at Reid. "I want a new name."

He offered her a crooked grin, shrugged his broad shoulders, then took her hand when she side-stepped around a darting lizard. "Consider yourself fortunate to have been gifted with two names. I was called White Man for more than three years. Ye cannae demand a new name. Ye must earn it."

Robbie harrumphed. "How did ye earn your name?" Most likely Reid had bravely killed a giant snake. Or mayhap he'd slithered across the jungle floor while sneaking up on an enemy. She awaited the tale, but Reid held silent and drew tiny circles round and round the skin between her thumb and forefinger. "Tell me why they call ye White Serpent."

His bronze skin tinted red. He turned away from her and stared off into the jungle.

The man had another secret, did he? "Mayhap the Jaguar King will tell me how ye got your name."

When she skipped forward, Reid jerked her back with a grunt. "You are insufferable. I'll tell ye another time."

"Nay. I want to know now."

He growled. His jaw pinched. He checked over his

shoulder to make sure no one followed too closely. "When Jax accepted Black Dove as his woman, a celebration took place in the village. I had a wee bit more spirits than I intended and awoke the following morn sprawled out naked on the ground beneath the watchful eyes of a half dozen bairns." He pushed the crown of her head down to avoid a drooping vine. "Think ye can watch where you're going?"

"Nay." She watched him, somehow knowing he would protect her. "Go on."

Reid's color turned impossibly redder. The rims of his ears shone crimson when he wove his fingers through his disheveled hair. "The sun has not baked all of my skin a golden brown. S'truth, there are parts of me that are as pale as the full moon. And that particular morn a part of me awoke before the rest. One of the bairns pointed at...it...and yelled 'white serpent.'"

Laughter bubbled in her gut. 'Twas a welcome feeling, given the emotions she'd suffered thus far this day. The quips piled up so quickly in her head, she couldn't decide which one to use. She chewed on the inside of her lip, but her giggle burst forth with an intensity that brought tears to her eyes. "Ye are named after your cock?"

The Jaguar King glanced over his shoulder and chortled.

Reid curled his hand around her waist and pulled her into his side. "Laugh all ye like, but keep in mind," his hot breath tickled her ear, "I could have been named White Stub, but White Serpent was far more fitting for a man of my size."

Her laughter ceased. The merriment tickling her insides shifted to brazen curiosity. She tried to control the direction of her eyes, but the task proved impossible. Her gaze slid down his meaty chest to the bulge filling the front of his breeks.

She slammed into the Jaguar King's back unaware that he'd stopped in front of her.

He grunted and mumbled a few syllables she didn't understand.

"We've arrived," Reid announced when they stepped into a clearing in the jungle speckled with thatch-roof huts. Their dwellings were not so different than the cot-houses in Scotland, but the way the bare-breasted Mopán women labored over their duties was an altogether different story. Again, she was forced to control her wandering eyes. 'Twas not as if she was partial to women. S'truth, it was more about comparison. Unfortunately, the only women with breasts the same size as hers belonged to adolescent girls no more than ten and six.

She was never taking the corset off. Ever.

"'Tis like a bawdy house gone awry." Eoin's lewd comment wasn't welcome nor was his presence at her side. The man made no attempt to hide the direction of his eyes when four beautiful women positioned themselves in pairs beside the Jaguar King.

They all wore braids decorated with bright yellow feathers, but one of them stood out above all the rest. Her beads clung tight to her elongated neck in layers and didn't cover her favors at all. She was the embodiment of sensuality with circular nipples protruding from perfect round breasts. If that wasn't enough to hold a man's attention, her tiny waist, decorated with a motif of black swirls and gold chains was. She looked at Reid from beneath thick black lashes and smiled with full lips.

Robbie had never felt more invisible.

"My daughters; Gentle Fawn, Stream Dancer, Songbird, and Wild Tigress." The Jaguar King named them from left to right, ending on the beauty eying

Reid.

Black Dove stepped up beside Robbie and leaned into her side. "Da calls her Wild Tigress, but the rest o' the kin call my sister On All Fours as that's how the harlot spends most o' her time."

"Come." Jax shuffled Eoin toward a group of men dispersing weaponry. He didn't refuse, but he didn't take his gaze from Wild Tigress and her favors either.

The exchange only emphasized how ignorant Robbie had been. Not only had she been faithful to a lecher, she'd been loyal to a murderer.

She hadn't realized how tightly she'd been holding Reid's hand until the Jaguar King grabbed her by the bodice and jerked her toward him.

"Stay," he demanded, then turned to Reid. "We hunt."

A wash of unexplained panic took hold. She'd grown accustomed to his constant presence on the voyage. 'Twas ridiculous, but she didn't want to be separated from him. She looked at him with pleading eyes. "I want to stay with ye."

His shoulders fell. His forehead wrinkled, and his hand rubbed his chest over his heart. "Ye cannae possibly know how desperately I wish that were true."

13

~ THE HUNT ~

If Reid had to spend another second in his cousin's presence, he was liable to spear Eoin instead of the mountain cow shaking the bushes.

Hunkered in the thicket, Eoin wiped the sweat from his face on a drape of wool hanging from his *plaide*. The sun had baked his skin a crimson red, but the fool hadn't the sense to pull his *lèine* shirt back on to protect himself from further damage. He would pay for his ignorance on the morrow, but this night Eoin would reap the rewards of the kill, if only Reid could encourage him to hunt.

"You'd do well to try to impress *B'alam*," Reid whispered to Eoin.

"I care not about your chieftain."

"You care about his gold. I strongly suggest ye flaunt your skill as a hunter."

Eoin's eyes narrowed on the Jaguar King, but *B'alam* paid him little heed. Instead, the chieftain dipped his head toward Jax, issuing the silent order to draw the beast out of the bushes.

Reid's pulse fluttered as he curled his fingers around his spear and readied himself for the run. He missed the hunt. He missed the thrill of the chase. 'Twas a shame he couldn't make the kill this time.

"Try to keep up," he challenged the competitor inside his cousin just before Jax bellowed in warbling tones.

The mountain cow shot out of the bushes into a fevered run.

Reid took the lead, with Eoin fast at his heels. Jax could've easily outrun them, but the hunt was so much more than just spearing food. 'Twas a way for a man to prove his worth.

Lungs burning, heart pounding painfully in his chest, Reid raced through the jungle's vine-thick maze until they cornered the beast in a clearing shadowed by foliage. Trapped within a wall of trees, the mountain cow grunted, snorted, and squealed in protest.

Jax raised his spear, but Reid stilled him with the shake of his head. He wanted Eoin to make the kill, and he did so with the skills ingrained in a Scotsman. Eoin's spear whistled through the air and stuck in the beast's neck, marking the end of the hunt.

"You did well." Barely winded, Jax clapped a wheezing Eoin on the back as the rest of the hunters broke into the clearing. The Jaguar King stepped before the dead mountain cow to study the kill, then turned toward Eoin and offered him a congratulatory grin. "A good kill, white man."

Panting, Reid bent over his knees and sucked in air in starving gulps. He couldn't say with any certainty whether or not Robbie had believed his words. She'd been upset, and her tears made him regret telling her the truth about Fergus, but what concerned him more was that she would hide this truth alongside Eoin's other transgressions. 'Twas past time she saw Eoin for the man he was.

● ● ●

"Psst."

Robbie stilled her hands in the dough and let the thin *tortilla* wrap over her knuckles.

"Robbie," someone whispered from behind.

She glanced over her shoulder to find Black Dove and three of her sisters peeking around Jax's dwelling. They waved her toward them.

From the secrecy of their actions, Robbie assumed they were up to mischief and was flattered to be included. As often as Reid had warned her to practice caution, he'd also warned her not to insult the Mopán people. Befriending the Jaguar King's daughters could only benefit her cause. Not to mention she'd flattened nigh a hundred of the round *tortillas* for the white-haired woman hunched over the hot bricks beside her. Robbie didn't know the woman's name, but had decided Sour Face suited her disposition.

'Twas doubtful Sour Face would even notice her absence, so Robbie got to her feet, brushed her hands free of crushed maize, then walked with haste to the back of Jax's humble abode.

Gentle Fawn, Stream Dancer, and Songbird accompanied Black Dove. Robbie gave silent thanks to discover Wild Tigress wasn't among their group. "What's amiss?"

"We're goin' to prepare for the merrymaking." Black Dove held out a basket filled with toiletries; soaps, creams, oils, as well as buffing stones, sharp black rocks and three artist brushes.

"Come." Songbird tugged on Robbie's arm, giving her little say in the matter, and the five women ran in a single line through the jungle.

Not far from the village, they burst into a clearing

and the beauty of the landscape stole the breath from Robbie's lungs. A waterfall cascaded over the edge of a cliff into a pool of blue water so clear she could see the bottom. Lush green grasses and purple flowers the size of her hand bloomed in abundance around the perimeter, filling the air with their sweet hearty scent.

'Twas perfectly beautiful. A paradise. One might wonder if this was the Garden of Eden.

A splash brought her out of her reverie as Stream Dancer dove from a flat rock into the lagoon. Her sisters followed suit and within seconds they were frolicking naked in the water.

Unable to help herself, Robbie watched Stream Dancer in awe, now understanding how the woman had acquired her name. She swam with grace, gliding across the surface in smooth even strokes. When she rolled to her back, her round breasts floated atop the water and caused Robbie to flush with heat. She turned away from the scene.

"You are shy?" Songbird posed the question, which was odd, given she was by far the most timid of the four sisters.

"Where I come from, the people are more modest about their nudity."

Without inhibitions, Black Dove rose out of the lagoon. Shimmering water rolled over her rounded belly into her nether regions where Robbie was shocked to find her completely free of hair.

"Weel, ye arenae in your Scotland now, are ye?" She giggled and gathered soaps and creams from the basket, then returned to the water.

Contemplating Black Dove's words, Robbie curled her hair round and round her finger. Why should she be embarrassed? They certainly weren't. They were a people unrestrained by social oppression. S'truth, she envied their freedom.

Without further thought, she pulled her gown over head, then fought the laces of her corset behind her back. The battle lasted longer than she would have liked, but she eventually managed to remove the rigid garment.

The women chattered in their native tongue and lathered creams in their black hair, paying her no heed, but a brief moment of indecision stole her courage to strip completely naked. Instead, she dove into the water in her sleeveless undershift and stayed beneath the surface for long minutes before finally joining the women in their circle.

Songbird tossed Robbie a cake of soap. "Make quick. We've many work to prepare ourselves for presentation."

Robbie hardly called bathing work. 'Twas more of a luxury, but as the women stepped from the lagoon and retrieved the sharp black stones from the basket, she soon understood otherwise. They applied creams to their olive skin, then shaved their legs, their underarms, and their mons with the rocks.

There was so much to be learned from these people, but when Black Dove held out the sharp stone, Robbie shook her head. "I dinnae do that."

They looked at her as if she'd sprouted horns.

"Ye should." Black Dove shrugged and tossed the stone back into the basket.

Mayhap she should.

Robbie shook off the idea before it had a chance to linger. She focused on bathing, knowing if she let her mind wander, Reid would find his way into her thoughts.

Content with her cleanliness, she climbed atop the flat rock and basked in the heat while the women braided each other's hair. Defeated by the day, she allowed herself a moment to rest.

The floral scent surrounding her was intoxicating. Her eyes slid shut.

Mayhap the serenity of this exotic place soothed her, or mayhap 'twas simple exhaustion. Regardless of the why or the how, Reid slipped into her head, and she no longer felt guilty about allowing him entrance.

Flashes of passionate kisses and gentle caresses flitted through her mind, but she'd never been one for love-play. Her fantasy advanced at an accelerated speed to the part where Reid stroked her to climax with his tongue, and because of her new-found knowledge of the Mopán women's bathing practices, she now envisioned her nether lips as silky smooth petals of flesh.

She squirmed, and the thick ache pooling in her womb only intensified every time she replayed the scene in her head.

Oh, she wanted him. She wanted to do things with him she'd never done with Eoin. S'truth, part of her wanted to flaunt her desire for Reid in front of Eoin. Her thoughts felt sinful, but only because she'd been foolishly loyal to the wrong man for too many years. She wanted to hurt Eoin. She wanted him to pay for his transgressions with something he treasured. Mostly because of what he'd done to Fergus, but also because he'd lied to her and traded her like a piece of horseflesh to Reid in their "bargain."

Well, mayhap she should negotiate a bargain of her own. One that would avenge Fergus's death and protect her loved ones. Eoin cared about no one more than himself, but there was something he valued more than any amount of gold—the chieftainship.

She lingered on that thought. Would Reid give up his life here and take the chieftainship from Eoin if she asked him to?

She had no idea how long she'd laid there debating,

but when her eyes fluttered open, she found Black Dove and her sisters looming over her with paintbrushes in hand. They were once again clothed in their short skirts and beads, but new embellishments decorated their bodies.

Robbie sat up, combing her dry hair with her fingers, and studied the artistry painting the women's skin. Reddish-brown markings that resembled fine laced gloves covered their hands. Swirls of ivy and tiny flowers coiled around their feet and ankles. Songbird sported a painted necklace that dipped low between her breasts and Black Dove's navel was adorned with an intricate sun.

"I feel like a bat among butterflies," she jested and felt even more inferior when they nodded in agreement.

"White Serpent says ye are kin to the warrior fire-goddess," Black Dove explained. "*Itzpapalotl* appears in the form of a clawed butterfly in some men's dreams. She has wings edged with obsidian spikes and—"

"Obsidian spikes?" Robbie interrupted. "A clawed butterfly, as in a bat?" She realized at that moment, Reid had named his ship for her, but instead of feeling flattered, she felt uncomely. No woman wanted to be compared to a bat. "I dinnae wish to remind White Serpent of a bat."

"We can make you pleasing." Songbird donned an innocent smile and held up a small gold pot of paint.

They offered her a gift, and the temptation to accept was far too great to deny. Robbie had never pampered her skin with creams and oils. She rarely decorated her hair in ribbons, and she didn't possess the means to dress fashionably, but for the first time in her life, she wanted to be beautiful. "Think ye I could seduce the man with paintings of butterflies?"

The excitement alighting Black Dove's face made Robbie more than a wee bit nervous. "If ye are thinkin' to seduce the mon, we must first start with the stone."

14

~ THE VICTOR ~

Well, this was an altogether new feeling.

Robbie's legs felt icy. Her freshly shaven womanhood tingled beneath her garments as she followed the others through a jungle filled with a cacophony of sounds. Twilight guided them back to the village as did the smell of cooked meat, and every step she took filled her with apprehension.

The women had spent hours painting her skin with intricate designs that mimicked the ivy print in her yellow gown. The most seductive was a vine that trailed around her neck and fell between her breasts. Songbird had fashioned Robbie's hair in a loose pile of curls and tiny braids which gave a glimpse of the designs they'd painted on her back. 'Twas meant as a temptation. A provocative lure to attract one's eyes and tease them with the mysteries of what lie beneath her gown and corset.

She didn't know if she possessed the patience to seduce Reid, but she admitted to being excited about the endeavor.

The beat of a drum sounded ahead of them and quickly escalated into a feverish tune.

"The celebration has begun," Black Dove informed Robbie over her shoulder. "We must make haste."

Robbie held the sides of her skirt high, running behind the women until they entered the village and presented themselves in a single line before the Jaguar King. He wore a headdress decorated with colored feathers and sat on an elaborate throne draped in eels of red silk. Though she didn't know all of the Mopán peoples' customs, she was familiar with the rules of respect.

The drums ceased, but Robbie's heart continued to pound between her ears. She resisted the urge to turn around and seek out Reid for comfort, knowing she must first pay homage to the chieftain.

He glanced over his daughters with indifference, but his black eyes lingered on Robbie for long moments before he finally dipped his head, granting them freedom to join the festivities.

The drums resumed, and Robbie blew out the breath she'd been holding.

"When Da awards the victor o' the hunt, follow Songbird's lead through the ritual." Black Dove gave Robbie's hand a supportive squeeze, then followed Stream Dancer and Gentle Fawn around an enormous fire shooting flames into a starlit sky.

Robbie scanned the hordes of people. Sour Face looked at Robbie with a...sour face. Duncan and Cocijo smiled and waved. Jean-Pierre grinned and winked. Then she found Eoin, and the look of disgust curling his lip was unmistakably directed at her. A month ago, she might have been shamed by his obvious disapproval of her appearance, but this eve she felt naught but great satisfaction.

Robbie pulled her gaze away from him and searched

for Reid, but before she could locate him among the abundance of natives now dancing around the fire, Songbird gripped her by the hand and guided her toward an elevated dais to the right of the Jaguar King's throne.

Wild Tigress lounged on her belly in a pile of red silk bolsters and made no attempt to make room for them until the Jaguar King spoke commanding words in their native tongue.

Robbie knew not what she'd done to garner such dislike from the woman but had no desire to spend the eve in her company.

"Sit," the Jaguar King ordered and before she could scowl at him, Songbird yanked Robbie onto her duff atop a fluffy bolster.

"We must sit here," Songbird informed her in hushed tones. "The uncoupled daughters of the Jaguar King sit to his right until a man proves worthy of our company."

"But I'm not one of his daughters," Robbie protested.

"You are his honored guest." Songbird's gaze diverted, then she sat up high on her knees and fidgeted with her necklaces. "Do I look pleasing?"

Wild Tigress rolled her dark eyes and snorted. The woman was easy to hate.

"Ye look beautiful."

Songbird flipped her long black hair over her shoulder and tucked the sides behind her ears. Why Songbird was suddenly overcome with nerves, Robbie didn't know until she followed the woman's gaze. Reid walked toward the Jaguar King with Oscar and Henrik at his heels carrying a wooden tray filled with fare. Both barefooted men wore tan breeks and turquoise necklaces over their bare chests, and while Reid looked perfectly handsome, Henrik's smile more than made up for his poor physique. In fact, Henrik's smile never faltered as Reid conversed with the Jaguar King.

"*Ah ma´na´at k´ek´en,*" Wild Tigress murmured words in her native tongue, the tone sardonic.

Songbird glared at her sister, but the silent rebuke ended abruptly as the youngest daughter of the Jaguar King returned her bashful gaze toward Reid and Henrik. It was in that moment Robbie realized Henrik's smile wasn't meant for her, but for Songbird. The timid woman lowered inky black lashes only to peek at Henrik from beneath them.

"Ye have eyes for Henrik?" Robbie's question came out with more pitch than she'd intended.

Songbird frowned. "He is not good?"

"He is bluidy English."

"Is bluidy English not good?"

Robbie gawked at her. These people had no knowledge of continental warfare. No prejudices against the English or other countries. Regardless of how odd the pairing might be, who was she to stand in the way of two peoples' attraction? "Nay. Henrik is good."

Songbird's face lit up for mere seconds before she started fidgeting again. After gaining the Jaguar King's consent, Reid and Henrik approached. Wild Tigress sat up taller which thrust her large breasts forward, but neither Reid nor Henrik paid her any heed. Oscar plopped atop a round bolster and proceeded to bathe as Henrik fell into conversation with Songbird. Reid positioned himself beside Robbie with his back to Wild Tigress, blocking her completely out of their circle. Mayhap it was wrong, but Robbie bubbled with confidence.

"You made friends?" Reid's gaze followed the design around her neck, then slid lower to her breasts sitting high out of her corset.

Shivers of delight tapped the knobs of her spine. "Black Dove and her sisters took me to a lagoon to bathe and prepare—"

Reid's pained expression cut her words short. She touched his forearm. His muscles twitched beneath her fingers. A giddy sense of accomplishment made her giggle as she realized the picture she'd painted of her naked at the lagoon may have caused his distress.

A bit of wickedness empowered her. She hadn't spent the day mentally preparing for a seduction only to sit before the man and shyly bat her lashes. She leaned close and inhaled his clean, exotic scent. "Ye smell good."

"As do you," he breathed through parted lips.

"I suspect 'tis the soap Black Dove brought to the lagoon," she whispered into his ear but was not yet done torturing him, "or mayhap ye smell the cream I used to soothe my skin after I used the stone."

Reid sucked in an audible breath. "You used the stone?" His voice cracked.

"Aye." She blew in his ear, then glanced into the gathering where Eoin stood with his arms crossed, glaring at them. His stance only encouraged her behavior. She caressed the rim of Reid's ear with the tip of her nose. "Ye should have told me about the bathing practices of the Mopán women in one of your lectures. Have ye any idea how delicious it feels to be shaven completely bare on your—?"

"Damn the Devil, Robbie!" He snatched a bowl of nuts from the tray Henrik had set beside her and shoved it into Robbie's hand. "Nuts?" He threw a handful into his mouth and chewed viciously.

She found the man's nervousness charming. "Have ye any chocolate?" She purposely licked her top lip.

His jaw twitched. "Nay."

Oh, she was going to enjoy this seduction. She would have the man agreeing to lead the clan by the small hours. Again, she caught Eoin's eyes. *And ye will have nothing.*

"But he vowed it," Songbird whined beside them.

Henrik shushed her, but she turned harsh black eyes on Reid. "You said Henrik was next. You vowed it."

Understanding smoothed Reid's expression. "Forgive me, Songbird. 'Twas months past. I had forgotten my vow."

"There'll be another hunt," Henrik assured her, but his disappointment was as evident as Songbird's.

"You are selfish," Songbird flung the insult at Reid, then propped her chin up with her fists and pouted.

Before Robbie could console her or inquire about what had transpired, the Jaguar King rose from his throne.

The drums ceased. The natives hushed.

With his arms raised toward the heavens, the chieftain gave thanks to the gods for their blessings. He then studied his people. "Victor of the hunt, rise and step forward."

Wild Tigress stood as did Songbird. Robbie imitated their actions, trusting Black Dove's instructions to follow Songbird's lead through the ritual.

Reid's eyes rounded on Robbie. "Sit down," he demanded between clenched teeth just as Eoin set himself before the chieftain.

The Jaguar King splayed his hand toward his daughters and Robbie. "Choose."

"Choose?" Robbie echoed the Jaguar King's word in the form of a question and looked to Songbird for explanation.

"The victor of the hunt is rewarded with a companion for the eve." She glanced at Reid, her slashed thin brows reflected her confusion. "The victor of the hunt is always White Serpent, but he promised Henrik would be next."

Robbie swallowed as Eoin's lips twisted into an ugly grin.

"I'm curious, cousin." Eoin crossed his arms over his bare chest and turned toward Reid. "When ye encouraged me to impress the chieftain by making the kill, was it part of your plan to have Robbie among my choices?"

"You can decline his offer," Reid rushed out.

"And insult the Jaguar King? I think not." Eoin stepped closer and ogled Wild Tigress, then he turned his attention to Robbie. He slid a finger down her throat and over her collarbone. "What say ye, Robbie? 'Tis been far too long."

She backed away from his repulsive touch. A bout of nausea gurgled in her gut. "I would sooner claw my eyes out than serve as the companion to the man responsible for my brother's death."

Eoin snorted, the dark orbs of his eyes slipped into the corners and locked on Reid for a brief moment before returning back to Robbie. "I protected the clan as is my duty."

"Ye protected yourself, and I hate ye."

"We have a bargain." Reid stepped closer, his nostrils flared, his chest rose and fell rapidly.

"That we do, cousin," Eoin agreed. "And I'll trust ye to uphold your end." He took Wild Tigress by the hand and followed her through the throngs of natives.

Robbie exhaled as the drums resumed once again. When Songbird left Robbie's side to join her kin, Reid stepped into her place and opened his mouth, but Robbie snapped her hand upright. "Why would ye set Eoin up to make the kill, knowing what the Jaguar King would offer?"

Reid matched her intense stare with one of his own, but held his tongue.

"Answer me and dinnae lie." She crossed her arms and tapped her toe, tired of being demeaned by their bartering.

"I dinnae expect you to be among his choices. Ye are determined to sacrifice yourself to save the clan. I thought it best you knew what to expect upon your return to Scotland."

"Think ye I would remain loyal to the man after what he did to Fergus?"

"I dinnae know if you believed me."

Was she a fool to trust him? "Did ye lie?"

"Nay."

"Then your efforts to taint Eoin's character were unnecessary. I knew he was a bluidy lecher. Ye accomplished naught with your scheming, save for demeaning me in front of your clan and breaking a promise ye made to Songbird."

"Forgive me." He stared at his toes. "'Twas not my intention." He sulked his way before the Jaguar King and bowed. "Much thanks for your generosity, *B'alam.*"

The Jaguar King flattened his hand atop Reid's head. "Sleep well, my son."

Reid called for Oscar to follow, retrieved the meat-stripped hind quarter leg from the discarded mountain cow, then disappeared into a blackened path leading into the jungle.

Robbie wished he'd made the kill and chose her as his companion for the eve. She wished he thought enough of her intelligence to barter with her instead of Eoin, but neither had been the case. She plopped back down atop a bolster and reached for a curl to twist, but none were there.

The Jaguar King left his throne, sat beside her, and

pushed the tray of food in front of her. "Eat."

She glared at him but stuffed a piece of pink fruit in her mouth and chewed. For long moments he said naught, but she sensed his words coming before he spoke.

"White Serpent needs a woman."

Robbie laughed outright, appalled by his blatancy. "Ye seem to have plenty to spare. Mayhap ye should give him one?"

"White Serpent declined my daughters. It would please *B'alam* if Handful of Seed were White Serpent's woman."

Blast this man and his names! "My. Name. Is. Robbie. And I belong to no man," she spit out between clenched teeth.

The Jaguar King's laugh reminded her of Grandda; an exuberant open mouth chortle. "You are much like Black Raven."

'Twas difficult to be angry in the face of laughter. "Was she one of your women?"

"She was my only woman. What you call my queen." He removed his headdress and helped himself to a chunk of juicy meat. "The Kekchí took her."

Robbie angled her head, curious. "Why do ye not fight to get her back?"

"We did, but the Kekchí are greater in number than the Mopán. They captured my woman as well as Black Dove to draw me out." His voice lowered and the stone face he wore fell with unguarded emotions. "White Serpent saved Black Dove, but lost his da in the battle. And I lost Black Raven."

Robbie's heart softened. The Jaguar King held the same look of sadness Grandda wore for years after the fever took Gramum. "Ye have my sympathies for your loss."

He blinked his eyes slowly and dipped his head in

thanks. "The gods gift us with few days. Waste them not. Your spirit will be forever lonely in the life after, if your only companion is bitterness."

Had the Jaguar King not rose and departed, she might have told him she needed no companion, but it would have been a lie. She hugged her knees and watched the natives meander into their cot-houses in pairs. A familiar longing made her think of Rannoch.

Temper replaced the longing in an instant. She'd wasted her dreams on Eoin and his lies. S'truth, she was tired of spending every moment being bitter and angry, tired of hiding her desire for Reid behind morals that had gained her naught but frustration. Why should she suffer? Why should she be alone? Eoin certainly wasn't.

She got to her feet and walked toward the path, but paused when she heard footsteps following. Jax stood behind her, torch in one hand, a machete in the other.

He offered her a small smile. "Jax will show you the way." He guided her in silence back to the shore where they followed Reid and Oscar's footsteps along a stretch of beach. The ocean hummed to her left and the night creatures screamed to her right.

She did a little skip and hooked her hand into the crook of Jax's elbow.

"Jax will keep you safe," he assured her and then reentered the jungle. He lead her through vine-choked foliage until golden flickers of torchlight revealed a wooden structure twenty times the size of the ones in the village. Mayhap 'twas a gathering place.

'Twas odd really. Seven round buildings of ascending heights formed a circle around an enormous windmill rising out of the center. Red silk sails spun round and round, illuminated by a swell of firelight from below.

"Is this your kirk? Your place of worship?" Her

question came out breathy, mesmerized as she was by the grandeur before her.

Jax shook his head, seemingly perplexed by her question. "This is *Rukux*—White Serpent's home. He built this for you."

"He built this for me?" Robbie asked long moments later in denial, but Jax had already disappeared back into the jungle.

Eager to explore, she followed a winding stone walkway though a garden of small fruit trees. Great purple bunches of orchids pooled beneath each tree and filled her inhales with an alluring sweetness.

He built this for me. She smiled inside and out, flattered by the exquisite beauty of this paradise, yet part of her wilted, wondering if Reid would give it all up to return with her to Scotland. She padded her way toward the smallest of the seven circular towers. No doors prevented her entry and a single torch illuminated walls filled with an assortment of armory; spears and machetes, basket swords and dirks, and several pistols.

Torchlight guided her through a second open doorway into a round chamber much larger than the last. A fire burned in a hearth, lighting the area for her inspection. A device the likes of which she'd never seen spun in the high ceiling. Revolving vanes of woven palm attached to a rotating hub spun round and round, pushing air throughout the interior. In the center of the chamber sat two facing oversized armchairs, one deep purple, one red, both fat with stuffing.

'Twas like a Great Hall built for two.

Reid sat in the red chair with his back to her. His hands propped on the armrests; one holding a smoking stick, the other twirling a coin back and forth across his knuckles. He stared at the empty chair across from him and raised the smoking stick toward his face.

Robbie knew with absolute certainty that the purple chair belonged to her. Beside each chair sat a small table; hers empty, his filled with nonessentials. A wooden bowl made her lips rise at the corners. The man was addicted to nuts.

She supposed she should announce herself but didn't want to break the silence or wake the enormous multi-colored bird perched beside another open doorway.

When she passed by his peripheral, Reid jumped, startled by her presence. The muscles in his bare chest flexed as he jerked his head over his shoulder. "Tell me you did not come here on your own."

She smiled, knowing his harshness stemmed from his constant worry over her well-being. "Jax brought me." Gesturing toward the empty chair, she asked, "May I?"

He nodded but said naught more, which was unusual given the man's propensity for chatter.

Their knees knocked in her efforts to settle into the seat, but a person didn't just sit in a chair such as this one. She curled into the massive space, pulling her legs close to her chest. 'Twas soft and smelled of flowers.

Reid stared at her, doing little more than breathing and flipping the coin back and forth across his knuckles. She might have been intimidated by his intense silver gaze a month past, but not this night. This night she wanted his eyes on her. She wanted to feel the rush of giddiness that accompanied his attention.

He set the smoking stick between his lips and sucked on it until the tip turned bright orange. He blinked, but his gaze never left her. He exhaled ribbons of smoke and licked his sensual lips.

Aroused by his actions, she swallowed and

squirmed. Her nipples tightened, as if in preparation. Robbie resisted the urge to lunge atop him and har-rumphed mentally, hugging her knees tighter. She made a poor seductress. She didn't know if she should ask him to lead the clan before or *after*...and there would definitely be an after. The thought had her brimming with delirious excitement. But she had no patience for love-play. A flaw, no doubt ingrained in her as a result of Eoin's hasty couplings.

Reid's tightened scowl seemed to lessen with each draw he took on his smoking stick.

"May I try that?"

His dark brows slashed, but he passed it to her without debate.

After studying it, she tasted the end wet with his saliva. 'Twas a contradictory flavor—bitter and sweet. Mimicking his actions, she drew on it, pulling searing heat into her mouth. Heavy smoke set her into a coughing fit.

"'Tis a man's sport." He sat forward, reaching out, but she stilled him, determined to try again. This time the smoke curled over her tongue like an invisible liq-uid. 'Twas bold, stimulating, yet somehow soothing. She blew out and repeated the process three, mayhap four more times.

His chuckle seemed misplaced, much like her girl-ish giggles.

"Am I doing it wrong?"

He shook his head, his charming crooked grin re-mained in place. "I've sat here many a nights pictur-ing you in that chair. I imagined you brushing your hair, studying a book, eating fruit, but never did I pic-ture you smoking a cigar."

"Then I disappoint ye?" Her lips pursed into a pout.

"Nay," he breathed, his tone husky, silk-en...controlled. He eased back and set the coin atop the side table. He checked the empty bowl, frowned, then looked to the rafters before tossing her a side-long glance. "Think ye I can have my cigar back?"

The man's steel constraint irritated her. She wanted him to lose control the way he had on the ship. Thinking of his fingers stroking her sex to climax caused moisture to gather between her legs. Her bare mons tingled in anticipation, an icy hot sensation that made her shiver.

He held out his hand, waiting, but instead of simply handing him the cigar, she crawled out of her chair and stepped before him. "We can share." She leaned forward, steadying herself with a hand on his shoulder, and then she straddled one thigh. Her knees sank into the cushion of his chair and her aching womanhood settled atop his hard muscles. Brazenly, she ground her pelvis against him, silently telling him his control was unwanted.

He inhaled a sharp breath. His muscles flexed. His fingertips gripped the arms of the chair, denting the cushion. She didn't have to seduce him. She could tell by his pained expression he wanted her, but did he want her bad enough to give up this life in paradise?

She drew on the cigar, pulling smoke into the hollow of her mouth, then she parted her lips and gently blew the silky smoke into his mouth. Their lips brushed. She held his gaze, waiting for him to kiss her, but he did not.

His slate-gray eyes turned fierce.

He snatched the cigar from her hand and snuffed it out on a glass tray atop the side table. His fingers tangled into her bound hair and yanked her head back. "Your moods are maddening."

Oh, aye, she agreed silently. When she was with him, her emotions normally battled, but not this night. "I left my temper back at the village. You'd do well to take advantage of my high spirits." She rocked atop him, knowing what she wanted, what they both wanted. Fire rippled through her core and burned too close to her greedy womanhood. Perspiration broke out between her breasts, and her nipples painfully poked against the rigid corset.

Seduction be damned. She needed release. She pulled against the hold he held on her hair, enjoying the pain a little more than she would ever admit. His grip lessened, giving her the freedom she needed to kiss his neck. While dining on his salty skin, her fingers snuck down his sculpted abdomen, pausing briefly to notice the skin beneath his navel was as smooth as his shaven jaw. "Do the Mopán men shave themselves the same as the women?"

He only nodded, his breathing loud, gravelly. His stomach quivered as she untied the laces of his breeks. Then without dalliance, she slipped her hand inside and stroked his rigid erection—his long, thick, hard erection. Remembering what he'd said about his Mopán name, she sat back and wrapped her hand around his girth—her fingertips didn't come close to touching. Roughly, she pulled him further out of his breeks, eager to see him fully. "Holy Loki! Ye are hung like a bluidy stallion." *Ack! Did she say that aloud?*

He moaned and shook. The knot in his throat bobbed up and down. Sweat now poured down his neck and trickled between the muscular grooves of his chest, but he didn't respond to her compliment. S'truth, he hadn't said anything for quite some time. Mayhap he couldn't.

"Reid," she half-spoke, half-whispered his name to gain his attention. His eyes blinked open, near black with desire. She donned a seductive smile meant to break the last of his resistance. "Do ye tend yourself the same as the Mopán men?" she asked innocently, but gave him no time to respond before she curled her hand deeper into his breeks. No nest of wiry hair hindered her perusal. When she palmed his heavy sac, she found it as silky smooth as his cock. She rolled his bollocks, enjoying the power she exuded over him.

He cried out, the sound harsh, pained, loud.

The bird she'd forgotten about in the corner squawked, then flew out an open window.

"Robbie," his voice cracked. "I've not been with a woman in a verra long time." His confession pleased her, though it obviously caused him a great deal of agony. Thick veins whelped out of his neck and arms, and she was certain he would tear the material from the cushioned chair.

Oh, he was close. She leaned in to his ear and nibbled on the lobe. If she whispered the words she wanted to say, mayhap they wouldn't sound so audacious. "Yet ye make no advances to take your ease." She rubbed her mons against his thigh and stroked his cock. "I'm wet." She stroked him, again. "I'm willing." The pads of two fingers rubbed the bulbous head of his cock, smearing his seed around the silky smooth skin. "And I want ye buried inside me."

"God's legions, woman. Why did you come here?" He grabbed her wrist and squeezed until she released him.

His question baffled her. The man couldn't possibly be that daft. She stood, pulled her gown over her head and discarded it to the floor. Fighting the corset was a moot point as she had every intention of hiding her small breasts for as long as there was breath in her lungs. She crawled into the chair with him and positioned a knee on either side of his hips. "I should think it is obvious." Holding the hem of her skirt, she slid her aching mons over the side of his manhood.

Oh, it felt good. The veins in his cock were just rigid

enough to tickle her sensitive nub.

He squeezed her duff hard enough to still her movements. "Think ye I traveled all the way to Scotland because I wanted you to ease my needs? I want to make love to you. I want our every kiss to mean something. I want you for forever, Robbie. Not just this night."

She tried to absorb his words, but the burning in her mons begged to be doused. Clinging to his shoulders, she wiggled in his grasp enough to inch herself over his arousal, then the head of his cock slipped between her throbbing nether lips. The muscles inside her flexed and squeezed, but he hadn't given her nearly enough.

"I want you to be my woman, my wife." He loosened his hold enough for her to bounce—once, twice, three times...oh, God it was perfection, but he stopped her before she could take even half of him into her tight canal. "I intend to spill my seed in your belly again and again until I plant a child in your womb."

Anger snuck passed her lust. "I'll not barter with the life of my unborn child." She started to pull off, but he held her in place.

"But you're willing to barter. You know what I want. Tell me what you want."

"I want ye to lead the clan."

His face fell, his mouth opened, but before words spewed forth, a thunderous rumble sounded to the right of them.

Reid's eyes widened. "Dinnae move." His grip intensified, bruising her soft flesh.

The fear painting his face scared her, but not half as much as the menacing growl escalating just feet away.

From the corner of her eye she saw gold fur and black rosettes. "'Tis just Oscar," she said without conviction.

His head barely shook. "Loosen your hold. She thinks you're hurting me," he ordered, his words hushed, but she felt him tremble beneath her.

Robbie retracted her fingernails from his shoulders, leaving behind eight half moons that quickly filled with crimson red. She had to look. She had to see what was there. With the slow turn of her head, she found a monstrous beast four times the size of Oscar. 'Twas more muscular, more fierce, much more threatening. It stared straight at Robbie, then it stretched its jaws wide and screamed.

Terrified, Robbie shook. "Another of your friends?" she asked hopeful.

"Not yet."

The beast slunk toward them, head dipped low, eyeing her as it approached, then it popped its forward paws onto the arm rest and growled inches from her face.

Robbie jerked. A flash of white light stole her vision for a fraction of a second. She stopped breathing. Reid's heart hammered against her palm. She was going to die with his cock still inside her.

"She's mine." Reid reached up and protectively caressed Robbie's cheek. He whispered words in the Mopán language in a voice meant to sooth, a voice meant for cooing babes back to sleep.

The beast leaned closer. Its long whiskers twitched. Its tail whipped furiously side to side. Then it pushed off the chair as if deciding Robbie was worthy and slunk back toward an open doorway. It hovered over the bone Reid had collected from the mountain cow, but seemed reluctant to take the offering and leave. The final glance it gave Robbie over its shoulder was no doubt a warning, but it snatched the bone up between its powerful jaws and departed back into the jungle.

"Holy Loki!" Robbie exclaimed. Strength depleted, she sank against Reid's chest, which pushed his still hard cock deeper inside her.

She felt him jerk, then his hot seed burst against the wall of her womb.

Nay! Panic returned in a flash. She always pulled off Eoin and stroked him to completion. She didn't want to risk a child, but 'twas too late.

16

~ RUKUX ~

"Forgive me. Oh, God, forgive me." Reid wrapped his arms around her slender frame and begged forgiveness for inviting a lethal predator into their home. "I've been trying to tame her, but she's never stepped over the threshold. What if you'd been alone? Kantico would have killed you." He shuddered and squeezed Robbie tighter.

"Reid."

"I'll build traps." He shook, the fear still so raw. "I'll set nets. I'll do whatever it takes to keep you safe."

"Reid," Robbie shouted and pushed against his chest.

"I'll kill her if I must." He held her face between his hands, forcing her attention on him. "Kantico is only one of many lethal beasts in the Yucatán. Now you know why you must practice caution. You cannae go into the jungle at night. I'll not allow it."

"Hold your wheesht!" Robbie broke out of his hold, and the sudden movement caused his softening member to fall against his thigh. Robbie raced toward the door, which was the opposite reaction he expected.

Stuffing his cock back into his breeks, he chased her into the armory where he caught her around the waist. "I'll tie you down before I let you go out there."

"Blast ye!" She hit him in the chest with a furious fist. "Blast ye to Hell and back! Ye are so selfish."

"Robbie." He caught her by the wrist when she attempted to strike him again.

Her eyes were erratic as were her quick breaths. "I dinnae care about the bluidy beast. Ye preach on practicing caution, yet ye spill your seed inside me. I told ye I wouldnae barter with a child in my belly. I told ye!"

"God's legions!" The woman was completely adder-bitten. Kantico could be hauling her bloody corpse into the jungle and the bull-headed woman is spouting heated words about bargains. 'Twas always about the godforsaken clan.

Furious, he grabbed the front of her corset, dragged her back into the sitting room, and shoved her into the purple chair. "Sit and hold *your* wheesht! You're going to listen to me. You're not going to seduce me or barter with my affections for you."

She didn't move. She didn't speak. She crossed her arms, which squeezed her breasts further out of her damn corset, and obeyed.

Her unexpected submission left his mind spinning. He bore his glare into her violent green eyes and searched for a means to explain his fury. Only three simple words came to mind. They repeated over and over in his head. The only three words he wanted to say, but couldn't.

I love you.

Pushing away from the chair, he damned this obsession. He needed to think, needed time to consider what she'd asked of him before Kantico interrupted them. He paced the open floor, scrubbing his eyes, battling his emotions. Of course, he was going to help the clan. He would do everything in his power to repeal the proscription, but leading the clan meant leaving the Yucatán and the people who'd become his family.

Damn her! He hated how selfish she made him feel. He hated that he felt a stronger sense of loyalty to the Mopán people than the clan.

"I'm waiting," she interrupted his contemplation and snagged his pacing.

"And you'll continue to wait, you impatient, stubborn woman!" He swiped her garment off the floor and forcefully threw it into her lap. "Put your gown back on. Your breasts are damn distracting."

Defeated, he gripped fistfuls of his hair and growled deep in his throat. She stole his control and rendered him incapable of rational thoughts. "Naught is the way I'd planned," he confessed. "I pictured your arrival being so verra different. I wanted to bring you here and watch your face as ye walked past the flowers I planted for you. I wanted our first coupling to be gentle and full of passion, not some hasty transgression based on barters. I wanted to make love to you in the chamber I built for us." His shoulders slumped a little lower. "I dinnae even kiss you." He felt as if he'd been beaten down and then kicked again for good measure.

"Reid," she whispered his name, her tone soft, sympathetic.

He couldn't look at her. 'Twas too hard. Instead, he stared at the fire and blathered on foolishly. "I cannae remember your day of birth or your mam's first name. I dinnae know your preferred color, or your preferred food." He squeezed his eyes tight, thinking he sounded much like the laddie who'd been miserably infatuated with Robbie years past.

"Reid." She stood behind him, her cool fingertips touched his back which worsened the pain in his chest.

She stepped to his front and met his gaze. Her emerald eyes had softened, her delicate brows no longer pinched with bitterness. "Forgive my impatience. Mayhap we can start anew." She gently stroked his hair with her small hand. "I was born on the ninth day of the month of August, and Mam's name was Mary, the same as mine. I like all the colors, but I'm growing fonder of red these days. And before ye came back, any food at all was preferred. Now, I'm partial to chocolate." She cupped his jaw and caressed his cheek with the pad of her thumb. "We've much to discuss, but first, I'd like to see the rest of Rukux. There are five more towers. I'm sure to be impressed." Her smile was a welcomed truce. "Pretend I just arrived. Pretend I am the woman ye expected me to be."

He kissed her palm and blew a breath of angst, once again baffled by her moods. "Though you challenge me at every turn, you're so much more than I ever dreamed you'd be."

His praise glossed her eyes with wetness, but her lashes fell to conceal her emotions.

Mayhap it was best to take advantage of her meekness. "Come. I've much to show you." Taking her hand, he led her through the armory and into the garden.

"One moment." She tugged at his arm. "If there are other *pets* lurking about, I would like to prepare myself in advance for introductions."

He chuckled. "There are fish in the pond out back and you saw Khan, the bill bird." He looked overhead, searching the vine-covered walls of the center tower. "Myah should be about shortly."

"Who, or rather what, is a Myah?"

"She's a spider monkey with a talent for sneaking

about unnoticed. If she startles you, dinnae speak too harsh to her. She's a wee bit sensitive."

"I hope Myah is more monkey than spider."

Reid gave her a feigned look of horror. "There are no spiders in the Yucatán."

Robbie rolled her eyes and donned a smirk, obviously disbelieving his lie, then her expression shifted again.

He followed her perplexed gaze to a firebox mounted at the top of the tallest tower. "Are there others here? Manservants? Maids?"

"Nay."

"Then who just lit that torch?"

Reid pointed at a yellow flame bobbing up the vines. The beastie holding the taper was nigh invisible against the black starlit sky. "*That* is Myah. 'Tis her duty to alight the garden at night."

"Ye've a monkey who goes about lighting torches? Surely ye jest."

"Myah is well compensated. I daresay she likes nuts more than I." Reid pulled Robbie's arm through his and escorted her toward the larder, eager to show her how the water wheel pumped fresh water into the kitchens and the bath chamber.

"Why do ye keep company with so many animals?"

"Their diet keeps the place free of insects, snakes, and small vermin. They also ease the silence." He wouldn't dampen their conversation with words of loneliness. "'Tis why there are no doors. Oscar drove me half mad wanting in and out so I removed them."

"It feels free." Robbie exhaled and hooked her arm through his.

"Aye." Reid smoothed his fingers over hers, enjoying her companionship, and explained how the windmill connected to a series of wheels that turned the fans in the ceilings of every chamber. He prattled on about the number of heartwood trees he'd felled to build Rukux and how the women spent many a summer's eve dying eels of silk to decorate the interior.

"This heartwood tree produces the dye? 'Tis why everything is red?" she asked.

"Everything, apart from your chamber." He kissed her hand and then set her before the open doorway. "I wanted it to be special for you."

Reid held his breath as Robbie walked to the center of the chamber he'd decorated in light pink silks and spun a full circle atop the fur rug. She paid no heed to the pink chair with matching footstool or the two armoires filled with baubles and lightweight gowns. Not even the cradle he'd built for their first born caught her eye.

She looked up, and a heartbeat later, her hands flew to her mouth. Though restrained, she sobbed with emotions.

His efforts had not gone in vain. Her awe-filled expression was his reward.

"Are you impressed?"

Her nod was slow in coming, but her beautiful green eyes brimmed with tears of wonder.

His insides warmed, and his heart clenched with undeniable yearning. He wanted her more than anything else, but he selfishly realized he wanted her here at Rukux.

"'Tis perfectly magnificent," Robbie whispered and swiped at the tears rolling over her cheeks. 'Twas impossible not to be touched by such a display.

Living stars twinkled through a circular glass dome in the ceiling like the reflection atop the loch. A wide ledge rounded the circumference of the chamber and overflowed with long, slender, green reeds. 'Twas like an upside down garden alight by a dozen evenly distributed candle lamps mounted to the walls beneath the ledge.

But what burned her chest with emotions were the butterflies. Hundreds of them clustered together amidst the thick lush plants. Most of them were orange, but others were vibrant blues, yellows, and turquoise.

"They winter here and are attracted by the flame." Reid's silken voice drew her back to reality.

"Why?" she breathed, bewildered. No one had ever given her such a gift.

"When the weather turns cold in other parts of the world, they flock—"

Robbie shook her head, stilling his tongue. She didn't want another of his lectures. "Why do ye attract them here? In this chamber?"

Reid strode toward her, took her hand, and flattened his palm to hers. "Do you not remember the butterflies I gave you when you were a young lass?"

"They were dead moths. And I never knew why ye gave them to me."

His dove-colored eyes held her gaze for long moments before he raised her hand to his lips and kissed the inside of her wrist. "When you were a wean and I just six, mayhap seven, winters, I went with Da to the cot-house in Glenstrae where you lived before you moved into the stronghold. 'Twas summer and Fergus wanted to race frogs, but I wanted to watch your mam rock you beneath the shade of a willow tree. Every time she attempted to set you aside, you awoke and cried."

"Grandda always said I was born with temper."

Reid's agreement came in the form of a hoot and a wee bit too quickly.

"Go on." She enjoyed his story as much as the way he tickled the inside of her wrist with the side of his thumb. "Your mam asked if I would hold you so she could tend to her duties. You were so small and delicate and precious. Your lips were rose red and heart-shaped the same as they are today." Reid brushed her cheek with the backs of his fingers, causing her throat to clench.

"And your lashes glittered like gold in the sunlight, but it was the butterfly that landed on your cheek that kept the memory alive in my mind for years to come. It sat there long moments, slowly flapping its wings and kissing your cheek." Reid paused to chuckle. "I remember being jealous of the creature." He curled a loose lock behind her ear, but his crooked grin fell away and his eyelids slid to half closed.

"Months after Da took me from you, I had a reoccurring dream. I was that same orange butterfly, but I only had one wing. I spun circles in the dirt, helpless. I couldnae fly, and just when I stopped spinning, I would awaken terrified."

She probably should be more sympathetic, but the image of Reid MacGregor being terrorized by a dream involving a butterfly struck her as humorous. "Ye poor lamb," she cooed in a teasing tone, then giggled.

Red tinted his bronze skin instantly. "The ancient Mayas believed butterflies were the spirits of dead warriors descending to earth in disguise," he defended his masculinity with a lecture. "Butterflies are a symbol of fertility, rebirth, and happiness."

"Forgive me." She patted his hand, finding his sensitivity charming, but the smile threatening her lips couldn't be contained.

The lines between his brows deepened. "If you choose to mock me, I'll not finish."

She bit the corner of her lip and pasted on a serious face. "Go on."

He blew a breath that warmed her cheek and eventually continued. "After Da died, the dream returned.

Jax insisted I pay visit to their shaman—a priest of sorts—who interpreted the dream for me. The Mopán people believe there exists two worlds: the dream world and the waking world. A being cannae find oneness until both his worlds are satisfied. The shaman said my inner being was lost and in order for my two worlds to exist in harmony, I needed to find my butterfly's other wing. My twin he'd called it."

"Your twin?" Robbie repeated, incredulous, hoping the man would soon make his point.

"The wings of a butterfly are said to be twins, one being identical of the other. The butterfly cannae function properly without both, but there is a third part that must exist to keep the butterfly alive—the core of the butterfly—the heart. This is known as the Rukux. The shaman explained that in my dream, I was the half of the butterfly that represented my waking world, and the part that was missing—my twin, my other half—was my dreams." He held her chin up with the tip of his index finger. "Robbie, you're the half of the butterfly that fulfills my dream world."

She stared at him when he finished. His words were poetic and wildly romantic, but impossibly unbelievable. No longer did she have the urge to laugh. S'truth, his words frightened her. "We are far from twins. Ye are a dreamer who thinks entirely too much, and I am a realist. Ye are patient to a fault. I act without thought. Ye are dark, where I am fair. Ye are warm and sensitive, and I am cold and bitter." As she pointed out their opposing qualities, she felt herself stepping further away from him. She lived each day with one simple goal—survival.

"Our differences can be our strengths. Without you, the Rukux has no reason to beat." He clasped his own heart.

What he was saying was madness. He placed too

much faith in the lass he'd left behind. That girl of ten and three no longer existed and the woman she'd become could never live up to his expectations. "Ye are foolish to believe that I am your other half simply because a butterfly landed on my cheek when I was but a wean."

Her words seemed to suck his soul straight out of his body. His chin fell to his chest. His arms went slack as did his body. "'Twas just a dream."

"A dream ye based your entire existence on. A dream that impacted ye in such a way that ye returned to Scotland for me. Ye named your ship for me," she added in a rush and looked up at the heavenly creation above her. "Ye built this place for me because ye believe I am capable of making ye whole. What if I'm not the other half?"

Reid's head snapped up. "What if you are, but are too afraid to accept it?"

Robbie turned away from him, unable to bear the weight of his penetrating silver eyes, but he spun her back around and forced her to look at him. His fingertips dug into her shoulders. "Unlike you, I wear my dreams on my sleeve."

"I have dreams," she spat back, insulted. "I want to free the clan from persecution. I want Grandda to awaken without pain. I want baby Alana and all the women of Clan MacGregor to have a chance at happiness."

"Those are goals, and they shadow your own dreams."

"This is foolishness." She tried to pull away from him, uncomfortable with the subject, but he pinned her in place.

"Is it? Have ye no dreams left from your childhood? Or did the clan steal those from you as well?"

She pursed her lips, her chin jutted out. She had

dreams, none of which Reid MacGregor could ever fulfill. "I wanted to marry a king and live in a castle," she blurted out. "I wanted to sleep in a bed draped in eels of colorful silks." She poked him in the chest. "Ye are no king." She poked him again. "And this is no castle."

Reid's smug smile ignited her temper. Why had she let him goad her?

"I could be your king and Rukux your castle." He released her and gestured toward the only door she'd seen thus far. "As for the bed draped in silk, mayhap you should have a look-see into *our* chamber."

Only because she was eager to free herself from the subject at hand did she barrel into the next chamber. She expected lavishness and was not disappointed. The walls were draped in red silk that formed into a cushioned bench seat circling half the chamber. The exotic scent tickling her nose told her there were flowers, but she didn't look for them as her gaze was fixed on the only piece of furniture in the chamber—a bed. But this was no ordinary bed. It was round, covered in layers of red silk, and brimming with red and gold bolsters. A masterpiece of etched gold hung from the ceiling to create a canopy over the bed. Inside was a chandelier of flickering candles that brought the chamber to a pulsing glow.

A chill rushed over her skin, and Robbie told herself it came from the rotating blades spinning overhead, but that was a lie.

I could be your king and Rukux your castle. She hugged herself, fearing the temptation. Reid offered her the Garden of Eden, and she didn't know if she possessed the strength to resist the apple.

Reid's hot breath warmed her neck before his words fell into her ear. "This time, I intend to kiss you."

17

~ SURRENDER ~

He was the devil incarnate—a serpent inviting her to the tree of life. She should run away screaming. Robbie felt vulnerable, trapped, and terrified by the kiss he placed at the nape of her neck. While desire overwhelmed her physically, this was no longer about slaking their lusts. Reid wanted more than her body. He wanted her wholly and completely.

An inner voice warned her to proceed with caution. She knew this voice well. 'Twas the same voice that stripped her of confidence. The same voice that ridiculed her for not retaining Eoin's interests, now told her she wasn't the person Reid created in his fantasies. She didn't possess his passion, but as he eased her head back with the tips of his fingers and brushed tiny delicate kisses along her jaw, she no longer cared what that annoying voice had to say.

Her lids slid shut. She nibbled on the inside corner of her lip to stifle her quickening breaths. Gooseflesh broke out over her chest and a shiver scraped up her spine.

"You are a riddle, Mary-Robena Wallace." He pressed his mouth to the skin beneath her lobe, making her pulse slip out of cadence. "Do you want to know why?"

Nay. Her lips parted, but no words came out. She didn't want to hear the man's theories or his lectures or his chatter. She wanted him to hold his wheesht and kiss her.

"An hour past, ye were mounting me like an animal in heat." Again, he kissed the nape of her neck. "And now, you are trembling like a virgin on her wedding night."

"We both know I'm no virgin," she shot back and tried to turn around, but he held her in place with one hand wrapped around her throat.

"Mayhap in body, but what of your spirit?" His fingers slid across her shoulders to the fastenings at the back of her gown. He released the top button.

She chuckled. "Think ye I'm interested in hearing more of your chatter about reincarnated butterfly warriors?"

"What *are* ye interested in?" Reid slowly pushed the buttons of her gown through their counter holes and kissed the knobs of her spine as he exposed them.

She was interested in having the man inside her— fast and hard, but his actions told her he had no intention of advancing quickly. Her skin tingled beneath his lips, and her breasts grew heavy. In fact, everything inside her thickened and pulled toward her core. His attention was intoxicating and nigh melted the bones in her legs. Her fingers flexed inside her fists wanting to assist him, wanting to expedite his task. "'Tis not necessary for ye to do that. I can simply pull the gown over my head."

"But your haste would cost ye the pleasure of anticipation."

A lump of dry air strangled her. Pleasure she wanted. It was the emotional bond he sought that frightened her. He wanted her soul.

Oh, aye, the man was the devil.

When the buttons ran out, he pushed the material over her hips to form a buttery yellow puddle at her feet. Then, at last, he stepped in front of her. His face stole her breath and his silver-blue eyes made her want to weep, so great was his beauty. She pressed her hands against his marble-cut chest, wanting the heat of his skin flush against hers.

"When I was a lad, I dreamed about kissing you." He cradled the back of her head in his palm, then dipped his face toward hers. His eyes remained open as he suckled her bottom lip, nibbling lightly. "I knew not how to kiss a lass, but I wanted to learn on your soft lips." He skimmed her top lip with the tip of his tongue.

She closed her eyes and opened her mouth to invite him in.

"Keep your eyes open when you kiss me."

When she did as he asked, he finally kissed her. His warm tongue swept through her mouth like liquid silk. He flicked the tip of her tongue, playing with her, drawing her deeper into a world of excruciating rapture. Her body hummed with desire. Her heartbeat echoed in her ears and pulsed between her thighs. 'Twas maddening, but what made her knees weak was the hold between their gazes—a connection that cut straight to her heart and threatened to consume her.

Unable to bear it, she slammed her eyes shut, wove her fingers through his hair and pulled him hard against her mouth. When he gave in to her aggression, she tugged at the waistband of his breeks.

"Nay." He wrapped his fingers around her wrist and

brought her hand back to his smooth chest. "I've waited far too long for this, and you're going to control yourself."

Her lips pursed into a pout. "But I'm not as patient as ye."

"Then I fear the coming hours might be torturous for you." He descended on her mouth once again.

Hours? She was fortunate if Eoin lasted minutes before rolling over to seek his slumber. Oh, she couldn't wait hours. Her body was as taut as a fresh strung bow. His exotic scent and his delicious warm taste made her toes curl and pop. Her nipples sharpened into painful peaks and fiery liquid saturated her smooth nether lips. Lost in euphoria, she didn't know how long he kissed her, nor did she realized he'd pulled all the laces from the back of her corset until the rigid garment fell away from her body.

She stiffened and jerked out of his embrace. Instantly, she crossed her arms over the thin material of her undershift to hide her small breasts. An altogether different heat burned her skin. Self-awareness mixed with apprehension shook her limbs. 'Twas ridiculous, but tears welled in her eyes. She pinned her chin to her chest, hiding her embarrassment. She didn't want him to see her. He'd preconceived everything about her and what he would find beneath her bodice was sure to disappoint him.

"What is it, love? What have I done?" Worry touched his raspy words.

"I dinnae want this."

"That is a lie." He raised her chin with the tip of his finger and the gentleness in his eyes pushed tears over her lids.

"I want the corset back on."

Deep creases formed between his brows. "Why?"

She plucked the bone-stiff garment off the floor and

shook her head, not knowing how to explain. "Please," she pleaded, holding the corset against her. "I'm much more appealing with the garment on."

The look of sheer bewilderment smoothed the lines in his forehead. "There's nothing about you I dinnae find exquisite." He tickled the full length of her collarbone twice, then pushed the thin straps of her undershift over her shoulders. He leaned forward and kissed her breastbone, persuading her to release her hold.

An icy tingle wrapped around her nipples. Mayhap it was best he know she wasn't the deity of perfection he'd created in his mind. "Ye will be disappointed."

"Never." He lowered her arms and pushed her garment to her waist, then stared at her breasts. Licking his bottom lip, he held silent, which only heightened her humiliation.

Mayhap she should make light of her less than adequate qualities. "Fergus always teased me about getting my titties. I s'pose I'm still waiting."

His response to her quip was a heavy exhale that sounded akin to a growl. He brushed her erect nipple lightly with the palm of his hand, running from heel to fingertip and back. "They are perfect." He cupped her right breast and rolled the hard nub of flesh between his thumb and index finger. His breathing escalated. "Like ripe peaches with pink berries atop."

The comparison made her giggle, but when he leaned down to taste the treat he'd described, she quit breathing. Reid pulled her nipple into the heat of his mouth and dined on it with expertise. Demonstrating constant gentleness, his tongue feathered over the tip and circled the areola. He sucked, licked, and flicked her nipple until the sensitive flesh stood out like the tip of her finger, then to her delighted shock, he bit her.

She gasped, pulling in much needed air. That delicious little nibble aroused her in a way foreign to her.

She wanted him to do it again.

Fisting her fingers into his hair, she set him on her other breast. "Now this one."

As Reid feasted on her favors like a starving man, she felt the flutter of an orgasm churn low in her belly. Eoin had never paid her breasts any attention, and not until this moment did she realize how deprived she'd been.

Reid pushed her undershift over her wide hips and caught her around the waist when her legs failed to hold her weight. With one muscular arm wrapped around her middle and the other supporting her duff, he carried her to the bed's center. Not once did he take his exquisite mouth from her breast as he settled her amidst cool bolsters smelling of exotic flowers. The silken coverlet eased the heat from her back, but did little to prevent the perspiration already rolling down her neck.

Straddling her thighs, he held her arms to the bed and spent long agonizing moments tasting her skin. The man was passionate, loving, and he made her feel desirable. A master of restraint, his rhythm beat in time with the ticking cadence of the spinning fan, then something inside him seemed to snap. His hold on her arms tightened, and his gentle kisses intensified, turning hard—urgent. "Your taste weakens me."

She squirmed beneath him and arched her back, thrusting her breasts toward his magnificent mouth. The ache in her womb had spread to every pulse point in her body. Everything seemed to swell—her throat, her breasts, her mons. "What do I taste like?" She regretted asking the question the moment his fiery mouth left her skin.

"Finer that the sweetest fruit in the Yucatán," he began and kissed her ribs one at a time as he spoke.

"The Mopán people ferment a drink made from the bark of the sacred balche tree." His tongue swirled then plunged into her naval, sending her stomach to convulse inward, then he nipped at each of her protruding hipbones. "Balche is addictive." He kissed the butterfly Songbird had painted just above her womanhood. "But never have I craved its taste the way I crave ye."

He drew his nose repeatedly over the soft petals of her woman's flesh—her bare woman's flesh, which was surprisingly more sensitive. She felt her impending climax squeeze and billow. The circle of candlelight spun in streaks of gold above her. She felt imprisoned by the need clawing at her insides. She wanted to spread her thighs and invite him to drink from her, but his weight pinned her legs in place and thwarted her efforts.

Reid inhaled her essence. His fingertips dug into the supple flesh of her generous hips, but he never slipped his tongue inside the place she desperately wanted his attention. Instead, he lurched back and jumped off the bed.

"By God's legions, I cannae control myself with you." He ripped his fingers through his mussed hair.

"I dinnae want your control." She reached out, grabbed him by the waistband of his breeks, and pulled him back onto the bed with shocking strength.

His eyes snapped wide.

She disregarded his reaction, straddled his waist, and held his wrists against the bed. "If ye wanted a meek, timid virgin, ye have the wrong woman." She bent to kiss him, rubbing her mound against the rock hard bulge in his breeks, but she didn't dawdle on his lips. She moved quickly to his chest, licking his salty skin, tasting his masculinity, biting his flesh.

"Ye are the only woman I have ever wanted," he

deemed in a deep husky tone, his breathing raspy.

"Then take me." She reached for the laces of his breeks, but before she could free his cock, he flipped back overtop her and trapped both her wrists above her head in one of his hands.

"Ye are wanton." He tweaked her nipple.

She winced. "I am in pain and cannae bear this torment." Frustrated, she squirmed beneath the vise-like hold on her wrists and bucked beneath him.

To her surprise, he stepped off the bed and removed his breeks. "I pamper you with gentle kisses, and ye call my love-making torture."

Her breath of relief stuck in her throat when he turned back toward her and glared at her with darkening eyes. He didn't give her enough time to gauge his mood before he wrapped his hands around her ankles and pulled her to the bed's edge.

"Ye accuse me of wanting a meek, timid virgin in my bed, but I can assure you, the woman in my dreams is by no means meek or timid." He stuffed a hard, round bolster beneath her duff, raising her mons to him. "However, she does possess far more endurance than you."

As she looked up the length of her glistening body where his cock stood proud and tall at her entrance, she didn't care that he'd insulted her. Her persuasion was about to gain her what she most desired, yet part of her was mildly curious about the woman he spoke of. "What did ye do to this woman in your fantasies?"

He crooked a devil's grin and swiped his tongue along the crevice of her womanhood. "I fear she was too impatient to find out." He held her quivering thighs wide and slid the side of his cock over her spread lips.

She raised her pelvis to him, but he held her belly down with four fingers and stroked her pulsing clitoris with the tip of his thumb.

A haze filled her head. A hum droned between her ears. She grabbed fistfuls of bedding as the rise of her climax followed the stimulating swirl of his thumb. She slammed her eyes shut.

He stopped.

Blast him!

"Dinnae hide from me. Open your eyes. I want you to know who you are talking to."

Her heavy lids opened but narrowed. "I dinnae want to talk," she ground out between clenched teeth.

He resumed his teasing tactics on the spot that would send her into bliss-filled oblivion. "'Tis only a few words. Try to manage." He slowly fed her hungry sex the thick bulbous head of his cock.

She wanted more. She needed more, but he did not oblige her.

"Vow you will be my woman."

She nodded, her eyes flickered beneath her lids. Her heart slammed against her breast.

"Say the words."

"I vow to be your woman," she spouted quickly.

"Vow to be faithful to me and call me husband."

"Aye. Aye!" she hollered, crazed.

He pulled out and pinched her suffering flesh between his thumb and two fingers. "Say it!" he demanded, his tone unyielding.

"I vow to be faithful and call ye husband."

"For forever." He stroked the full length of her slit gently.

"For forever," she echoed in a whisper, binding herself to him like she'd never done with Eoin.

"Have you anything to add?"

"Nay. Nay!"

In one powerful thrust, Reid drove himself inside her.

She screamed.

He howled, then withdrew all the way and set the rhythm. Inch by wondrous inch he pushed deeper into her canal. Her muscles clenched around his girth, squeezing, gripping, until she came with a resounding cry. Her orgasm pulsed through her body wave after wave and pushed the scorching fire from her body.

Relief. Perfectly wonderful relief.

"Thank ye," she mumbled and giggled at the foolishness of her words as her sated body grew limp.

"'Tis my pleasure."

"Nay. 'Twas mine." Again, she laughed and waited for him to find his ease, but to her surprise he kept a steady pace.

Long minutes passed in splendor, then he picked her up and held her exhausted body to his chest. "Wrap yourself around me, love."

She coiled her arms around his damp neck and hooked her ankles behind his sinewy duff. His strength was astounding, as was his stamina.

While holding her hips, he kissed her hard and slammed her repeatedly onto his thick rod. Stroke after glorious stroke, he thrust in and out of her for an inconceivable period of time. To her astonishment, another climax gripped her, followed by a series of quivering spasms.

She whimpered, and let the sensations wash over her. Multiple orgasms were certainly new to her. Never could she have imagined such passion, such delicious pleasure.

She liked it. She liked it a lot.

"You are magnificent," he spoke into her ear, then added, "wife."

She opened her eyes and found him smiling at her, then all at once, he pushed her onto the full length of him until the head of his erection touched the plain of her womb. He embraced her with trembling arms in a crushing hug and planted his seed inside her.

Not until that moment did she realize what her self-indulgent desires had cost her. She'd pledged herself to him. She was now his wife. He held power over her. What was worse, she hadn't gained his promise to lead the clan.

18

~ INDULGENCE ~

Robbie felt Reid's eyes on her before she awoke. He wasn't touching her, but she sensed he'd been staring at her for quite some time. She held still, purposely feigning sleep while she collected her thoughts. Her mind's eye filled with flashes of Reid's lovemaking, but she forced the images out of her head in order to prepare words regarding Clan MacGregor. Leading the clan was his birthright. It was the honorable thing to do. She would ask him to protect those she held dear and make him see the right in it.

It was that simple. She inhaled and slowly blinked her eyes open, but Reid was not there. Across the expanse of red silk sat a small black monkey staring at her with huge round eyes.

Robbie quickly scanned the chamber filled with a new day's light only to find it empty. She sat up and pulled a bolster into her lap to hide her nudity from the beastie's innocent inspection. "Good morrow. Ye must be Myah."

Of course, the monkey didn't comment. Instead, she carried a half-piece of green and pink fruit across the bed and held it to Robbie's lips. Myah waited for Robbie to finish the fare, then seemingly satisfied with her task, she leapt off the bed and climbed the silk drapes up the wall where she disappeared though an open window.

"My thanks," Robbie offered futilely and rose from the bed.

A dull pain stretched through her core. She cupped herself, surprised by the soreness throbbing between her legs. One would think she'd been a virgin. "Mayhap 'twas my *spirit's* maidenhead." She laughed foolishly as she made up the bed and fluffed the hordes of bolsters.

When she entered the butterfly chamber—her chamber—she was prepared for its grandeur. The butterflies' antics turned the ceiling into a moving masterpiece while Oscar bathed himself atop a pink footstool in the chamber's center.

"Ye are obsessed with bathing, Oscar." She rubbed his ears. "I dare say ye could teach Shane and Bryson a thing or two." A bout of homesickness welled within her.

The beastie paused long enough to wink at her with both eyes, then continued to swipe his paw over his long whiskers again and again.

"I like ye, Oscar," Robbie decided aloud, then stepped before an empty cradle. Her heart grew heavy with longing. She flattened her hand beneath her navel and imagined what it would be like to have Reid's child, but the babe she saw in the cradle was Alana—a precious, blue-eyed babe who didn't stand a chance at survival without someone to fight for her.

More determined than ever to gain Reid's promise to lead the clan, Robbie stepped before one of the two

armoires in search of a garment. After opening the
doors, she was met with layers upon layers of thin
drawers. Inside, she found baubles aplenty encrusted
with diamonds, rubies, pearls.... S'truth, every gemstone was accounted for. She estimated their value
based on how much food could be bought for the clan,
then a butterfly pendant caught her eye. Four emeralds made up the wings and a pink diamond represented the body—the heart of the butterfly.

"Rukux," she whispered as emotions sent her pulse
into a frenzy.

Without you, the Rukux has no reason to beat. The
man said such foolishly romantic things. She draped
the gold chain over her head and positioned the butterfly between her breasts. Mayhap, she would keep
just this one.

The bottom drawer was three times as deep as the
others and contained the oddest assortment of trinkets: colored feathers of various lengths, red silk
scarves, a strand of olive-shaped beads. She pushed
the contents from side to side and found a heavy gold
bracelet too small even for her thin wrist. A butterfly
adorned the center with protruding antennas. Though
puzzled by the bauble, she returned it to the drawer
and looked upon another odd bit of frivolity. 'Twas the
oddest trinket thus far. It sat in a velvet box embossed
with leafy vines that formed smooth ridges over the
surface. She picked it up, surprised by its dense
weight, and studied it. 'Twas raven black in color and
had a soft squishy texture consistent with day old sap.
Upon closer inspection, she realized it was a sheath of
sorts that stretched over small gold balls.

"I see you have been exploring." Reid's words startled her, but not half as much as the slide of his fingers down the curve of her waist.

She shivered and caught his roaming hand at her

navel. "What are these?"

"Trinkets. Toys. Nothing of import. They are not for you." Reid pulled her hair aside and kissed the pulse point beneath her ear. The hand she'd caught sliding down her abdomen changed course and fondled her soft breast still tender from his overzealous attentions the eve before. He was certainly feeling randy.

"They are in my chamber. If they are not for me, then who are they for?"

He kissed the back of her shoulder. "They are for another woman."

Rage gripped her like a bolt of lightning. "What other woman?" Jealousy and insecurity sharpened her muscles. She squeezed the object in her hand and felt the slight shift of the gold balls inside. "I am your wife. Ye vowed to be faithful to me."

"Actually, *you* vowed to be faithful to *me*. I made no such promises." He chuckled.

The pompous scut bluidy chuckled.

"S'help me Odin." She searched inside the drawer for a weapon and decided the club in her hand would serve her purpose. She spun around and whacked him on the side of the head.

"Och, woman! Are ye adder-bitten?" He caught her wrist with one hand and wrapped his other around her throat to hold her at bay.

"I'll not be married to a lecher." If he thought he could stray from her bed like Eoin had, then he was sadly mistaken. "I want the words."

"What words?"

"I want your vow to be faithful."

"I vow to be faithful," he obliged without thought. "Hold your temper, love. I was merely jesting with you." He tried to kiss her, but she lurched back.

"Jesting?" She trembled. "I find no humor in your words. Say what ye imply or say naught at all." His attempt to be amusing didn't soothe the doubt still on the surface.

"Forgive me." He caressed the column of her neck. "I had expected to find you in better spirits. I only intended to tease you."

He'd never teased her before. She didn't like it.

She stared at him, trying to decide whether or not to continue her tirade. "Then what other woman were ye referring to?"

"The woman in my fantasies?" he reminded her in a questioning tone. "The other woman is inside you, Robbie. I meant to imply that you are currently far too impatient for such trinkets." He tickled her arm from shoulder to elbow repeatedly.

"Oh." Not only did she feel slightly dim of wit, she now questioned whether or not she'd pleased him. Mayhap she was a poor lover. Mayhap that had been the reason Eoin strayed from their bed. She exhaled. "My impatience is a flaw I intend to overcome."

Reid offered her a roguish grin and pulled her close. "I will assist ye in your task and when we reach our goal, we can play with the trinkets as reward. Aye?" He kissed her forehead lovingly.

She peeked back into the drawer and damned her curiosity. She should let the subject rest. She didn't. "Play with them how?"

He gave her a sidelong look and seemed to ponder longer than normal before educating her on a given subject. He retrieved a yellow feather and drew it down the front of her torso. Her nipples crinkled into pointed buds, but she didn't hide them from him. 'Twas odd, but she felt comfortable standing naked before him.

"They are for…stimulation." He grinned and cocked a brow. "Or for pleasure. An indulgence."

"They are for love-play?" 'Twas no wonder she knew

nothing of such toys.

"Aye." He tickled her throat and then her lips, which caused gooseflesh to spread over her scalp.

The feather she understood. Even the red scarves conjured up interesting images in her head. "But what is this?" She held the phallic shaped object between them.

He stared at her and blinked.

"Reid?" she prodded and blinked back, mocking him.

"'Tis an *olisbos*." He emphasized the second O in the foreign word with a peculiar high-pitch note as if that would somehow convey his meaning.

She drew her brows tight and continued to wait for further explanation, now feeling even more inexperienced.

"Mayhap you have heard it called a *diletto*."

"A *diletto*?"

"*Godemiches*. A red belt. A scarlet baubon. A false pillicock. A dil—"

"Ack! Hold your wheesht." She held her hand up to stop him. A false pillicock was self-explanatory. She studied it further then scowled at him. "Ye are certainly well-educated on the subject."

The fool flashed sparkling white teeth. "I read a lot."

Her snort came automatically. She narrowed her gaze on him, debating whether or not she really wanted to know the details of his past transgressions.

"I've spent time in France as well as London. On business," he added.

"Business, aye?"

He blew a quick breath out his nose. "I'm no saint, Robbie, but I intend to be a faithful husband. You must trust in that."

'Twas easy to tell someone to trust, but it was an altogether other matter to earn said trust. "If ye intend to be faithful and not stray from my bed, then why would I need a false pillicock?"

His bronze skin reddened. 'Twas difficult to be angry with the man when he blushed.

"Put it away." He reached for it, but she held it behind her back.

"Tell me, and I'll not speak another word on the subject. I swear."

"You are insufferable." His jaw clenched as he pulled her tight to his body. He leaned into her ear as if his words were too wicked to speak aloud. "Unlike a man," the palm of his hand slid down the base of her spine, "a woman is particularly sensitive to stimulation in more than one orifice." His middle finger slipped into the crevice of her backside.

Robbie's eyes flew wide. She pushed him off her and dropped the false pillicock back into its velvet box, then slammed the drawer. "If ye dare try to stick anything false or otherwise in my arse, I will take a blade to your bollocks."

He laughed outright and unexpectedly scooped her off her feet. "How dare ye threaten to maim your new husband?" He carried her through the bathing chamber and out a back entrance.

"Put me down! I'm naked." She kicked her feet uselessly.

"I rather like ye that way."

"Blast ye, Reid McGregor! This is not amusing." Blinded by a high sun, she cupped her hand over her eyes to find herself surrounded by a landscape of broad-leaf bushes speckled with flaming red blossoms. Seconds later, he tossed her into a pool of warm water.

She hit the sandy bottom on her backside with a muffled grunt. The shallow water was crystal clear, and if fish resided in the pool, her entrance scared them away. She emerged in waist deep water, pushing hair from her face, and pivoted in the sand a full circle before she located Reid. "Think ye I deserved that?"

"Aye. I do." He stripped off his breeks. "You were spewing fire and needed to be doused." He swaggered into the water with confidence, flaunting his physique as well as his erection. "I would think a woman who'd been so eloquently ravished on her wedding night would have awoken in a better mood."

His mouth claimed her tender breast before she could grasp his words.

She winced and grabbed a fistful of his hair to pull him off, but her attempt was further thwarted when he unexpectedly slipped a finger inside her.

"Ow!" She tensed and pinched her eyes shut. She felt bruised inside and out and wasn't nearly prepared for his assault.

He quickly retracted, his forehead creased with worry lines. "You are sore?"

"Aye." She lowered her lashes. "It seems ye are deserving of your name. 'Twill take time for me to adjust." Given his current behavior, she expected him to boast over his size. Mayhap even toss out a comparison regarding Eoin, but he simply caressed her hip beneath the water and kissed her shoulder.

"Forgive me. I should have been gentler."

She cupped his jaw as pressure squeezed her chest. "No man is gentler than ye, Reid MacGregor. None more loving." He hid his sensitivity beneath muscles and brawn, but she saw the man inside and he was beautiful.

"Dinnae be blathering my secrets. I've a reputation to uphold." He kissed the inside of her wrist, then pulled her toward a rock ledge. "Come. We need to prepare for the expedition." The glass globe and a sandglass sat atop a flat rock as well as towels and various articles she'd used during her experiments aboard the *Obsidian.*

"Are we testing?"

"Aye. I need to know exactly how long each of us can be under water before we dive into the Well of Sacrifice."

She nodded, rejuvenated by the task. "I was under for more than a half hour. Think we need more time than that?" She dried her hands on the towel and set to work preparing the crystals.

"If there are no air pockets between the Well of Sacrifice and the water reservoir, then we verra well might. I'm going to take a group of men into the jungle at dawn to make preparations for the dive."

"How long will that take?"

"Six, mayhap seven days."

"Seven days?" she whined. She didn't want to be separated from him for one day, let alone a sennight.

"The current of the underground river will have changed based on rainfall. I'm taking the diving barrel into the larger well where Xitali was sacrificed. Once I locate the entrance to the underground river, I intend to release a weighted log between the wells to measure the time and distance. Once my calculations are complete and preparations made, I'll come back for you."

He had everything figured out, did he? "I'm going with ye."

"Nay. Ye are not. 'Tis not necessary, nor is it safe. Jax and his family are coming to stay with you at Rukux. I forbid you to go into the jungle until Kantico is taken care of."

Taken care of? Had he decided to kill the jaguar? She was more than a little disturbed by this thought. Reid wouldn't have given the animal a name if he didn't feel some attachment to her. "Kantico did not hurt me."

"She is a hunter. Her instincts to protect me are lethal. She could have killed you."

"Oscar could have done the same," she pointed out, frustrated by his lack of leniency on the subject. "I dinnae want ye to kill her."

"My decision is made. You are too important to me." He diverted his gaze away from her. "Jax, Moon Hawk, and Bow Hunter are already building the traps. They will protect you while I'm away."

"Am I allowed to make any decisions? Or shall I tarry about in my chamber playing dress up like some witless princess? I have a mind. When allowed to use it, I can be quite intelligent. If ye think being my husband—"

He kissed her with his eyes open.

She pulled back. "—gives ye the privilege to act as some tyrant over me, then ye are—"

He splayed his fingers around her skull and stilled her tongue with his own. Spreading his jaw wide, he covered her mouth and chased her tongue round and round until the remainder of her words fell away from her mind.

She held on to his wrists but quickly succumbed to the perfection that was his mouth. His kiss was gentle, yet hard. Loving, yet demanding. Her toes curled in the sand, her knees grew weak, and whatever they'd been arguing about no longer seemed important. He lingered full seconds on her lips before he slowly pulled away.

Her heavy eyelids blinked open to meet his silver-blue gaze only inches from her face. "Why did ye do that?"

"I was testing a theory." He kissed the corner of her lips. "I wanted to see if my kiss could tame your temper." He nipped her top lip. "While my findings are inconclusive and require further exploration, I dare say I'm onto something." He pulled her bottom lip between the seam of his smile a final time before adding, "Now, may I continue?"

Nodding, she stared at him with parted lips, trying to recall what they'd been discussing.

"I've duties for you while I'm away. Songbird already offered to help stitch a leather suit large enough for me. I'll need you to direct her on the tailoring. You will also need to build a second breathing apparatus for me and devise a means of attaching the globes to our bodies. Black Dove will assist you. There is a firing pit and tools in the alchemist's work-house." He gestured over his shoulder at a grouping of outbuildings. "But I want you back at Rukux before the sun goes down."

Robbie stood on the tips of her toes to gain a better look at the structure. "Ye have an alchemist's work-house?"

Reid gave her a sad smile. "Your grandda always enjoyed mixing the vapors. I had hoped to give Argyle a place to spend his days doing something he loved."

Tears filled the bottoms of her eyes. If Reid gave her a thousand baubles, none would ever compare to this gift. She'd called him selfish on more than one occasion. She couldn't have been more wrong.

He turned and pointed. "The smallest of the three buildings is a dwelling which is attached to the workhouse. The largest structure is a barn filled to its rafters with heartwood logs. I had intended to take the timber to London in the spring once it dried, but I will entrust Jean-Pierre to take over the venture. He has a knack for bartering."

"What are ye saying?" She wouldn't allow herself to hope until he spoke the words.

He brushed her hair back and drew a repetitious

semi-circle over the rim of her ear. "My obligations have changed as a result of my recent vows. I am a husband now, and if luck continues to follow me, I will soon sire the next Gregarach."

"Ye are going to lead the clan?" she questioned while everything inside her sank with relief.

"Is that not what you asked of me?"

She nodded fiercely and swallowed. Her mind raced. Flashes of her kinsfolk burst forth: Grandda and auld Angus, Nanna and Shane, each girl bearing the mark of the MacGregor, and baby Alana. None of them would be left behind.

Robbie's eyes refocused on an enormous deep red flower, reminding her where she was. The man had made the decision to leave the Garden of Eden, and she prayed she was worth it. "What about Rukux?"

"I care not where I sleep at night so long as it is beside you." He kissed the thin, blue vein on her wrist. "Rukux will make Jax and his family a fine home."

"Leading the clan is the honorable thing to do," she tossed out, feeling the need to convince him he'd made the right decision.

"I'm going to save Clan MacGregor for many reasons. Honor and duty are two, but mostly my decision is selfish. A man is really no man at all without the respect of his woman."

She hugged him. Everything inside her danced with victory, but the celebration ran short when Eoin slipped into her head. "Eoin will fight ye. There is naught he loves more than his status."

"Aye. 'Tis true, which is why you are going to stay away from him. If he looks at ye, turn away. If he speaks to ye, hold your tongue. For the nonce, I'll take him with me into the jungle."

19

~ REGRET ~

Reid should let the scabbit die. "I told ye to walk behind me," he reminded his cousin for the hundredth time as he searched the vine-thick jungle for a means to pull Eoin out of the sinking sand.

"Get me out!" Eoin shouted at the half dozen Mopán men circled around him. He twisted and turned frantically at the waist, for that was the only part of his body not submerged beneath the quagmire.

After wiping the rain from his eyes, Reid jerked on an old vine hanging overhead until it broke free and fell in front of Eoin's flailing arms. "Stop struggling and grab hold."

For once, Eoin did what Reid told him and slowly pulled himself back onto solid ground. He scrambled to his feet, kicking mire from his boots and swiping it off his *plaide* as if the sludge might still be a threat to his person. "Ye hesitated. For a moment ye considered letting me sink."

Reid rolled his eyes, picked up the heavy pack he'd

carried for two days in the rain, and gave a nod to Kante to resume their trek. But before the behemoth Mopán warrior could swing his machete, Eoin started ranting again.

"Admit it," Eoin yelled behind Reid. "If I never returned to Scotland, ye would have Robbie as well as the chieftainship."

Vexed beyond his normal limits, Reid spun a full circle and clenched his fists. "I have Robbie." He closed the space between them. "And if I wanted you dead, I would have let the snake you stepped on yestereve sink its fangs into your prick. *And* you apparently need reminded of this morn's incident. Had I not prevented you from wiping your arse with the *ten ts´ak* plant, ye would've choked on your own tongue by noontide. *And*," he leaned so close he could see the red veins forking through the whites of Eoin's eyes, "now I have saved ye from the sinking sand. Unless ye wish to offer your gratitude, I strongly suggest you hold your tongue else I may feel less generous should ye find yourself faced with death again."

"Your suggestion is noted." Eoin pushed a straggly chunk of wet hair out of his eyes and donned a grin that looked less than appreciative. "I will offer my thanks for one thing, cousin."

Reid exhaled and waited suspiciously.

"The savage ye call Wild Tigress was an unexpected treat. The woman certainly knows how to use the tongue God gave her. Of course ye likely already know this." Eoin winked at the Mopán men behind them as if they were all old friends. "'Twas a welcome change to fuck a woman who knows how to hold silent."

Eoin's lewd comment was laughable. No doubt the fool attempted to insult Robbie and demean Wild Tigress at the same time, but his comment only opened the field for Reid to knock him down a peg.

"'Tis odd." Reid feigned confusion. "Mayhap my memory fails me, but the time or two I had the pleasure of Wild Tigress's company I recall her screaming like a banshee." Reid turned toward his Mopán kinsmen. "What say ye, brothers? Did Wild Tigress ever hold silent in any of your beds?"

The Mopán men shook their heads in unison.

Reid actually heard Eoin's teeth grind. His nostrils flared but no retort came.

The two men inside Reid's conscience battled. The one with morals told him to defend Wild Tigress, while the other—the wicked troll who was enjoying their banter immensely—encouraged Reid to goad Eoin just a wee bit more.

The wicked troll won.

"Allow me to enlighten you, cousin." Reid scratched his unshaven jaw. "A silent woman in bed is not a sign of submission so much as a sign of dissatisfaction. Or," he slapped Eoin on the back, "mayhap the brevity of your performance stunned Wild Tigress into silence."

"Or mayhap it was the size of my cock," Eoin retorted, his bluster renewed.

After coupling with Robbie, Reid knew otherwise. The wicked troll begged him to unlace his breeks and prove Eoin wrong, but Reid found his morals. Regardless of her licentiousness, Wild Tigress was the Jaguar King's daughter and deserved respect. The woman only behaved like a tart because she thought her talents would one day gain her a husband.

"Mayhap you are right, cousin," Reid conceded and once again gave a silent order to Kante to continue clearing a path through the dense jungle with his machete. The six Mopán men that made up the tail end of their party raised the bamboo conveyance holding the diving barrel onto their shoulders and followed. The footfalls of his Mopán brothers echoed his own as they walked through the thicket. A steady warm rain kept his *lèine* shirt and breeks plastered to his skin, but the elements were a paltry irritation compared to his cousin's constant blathering. The man groused about the weather. He talked of politics, war, and religion. When those topics didn't provoke Reid, Eoin went on about the clan.

Robbie is worth it, he told himself and drew forth an image of his beautiful wife—fierce green eyes, unruly honey-red hair, velvety skin. Thinking of her elicited calm in him. Oddly enough the first memory that slipped into his head was an image of Robbie holding the Jaguar King's bollocks.

Reid laughed a little on the inside. The woman was bold, defiant, wild, and loyal to a fault. She would give her life to save the clan, and Reid hoped one day she might care as deeply for him as she did for her kin.

He loved her, but knew in his heart she didn't return his affections. 'Twould take time. Fortunately, he was a patient man.

The rain eased as the hours passed but was replaced by a scorching sun that seemed to grow more unbearable as the day progressed. He didn't recall the insects being such a nuisance the last time he'd made this trek. Nor had he been this exhausted, this drained of physical energy.

Reid suspected the elements were not to blame for the turmoil wracking his body. It was Eoin, and his constant chucking of hawkers, his wretched smell, and above all else, his incessant chatter.

"I suspect you'll be returning to Scotland for Argyle?" Eoin's question held a little more edge than simple curiosity. The man was baiting him.

"I will be returning to Scotland indefinitely," Reid answered, not yet prepared to expound on the fact that he intended to reclaim his position as the Gregarach.

"Mayhap I'll assign ye to your own battalion in the coming battle."

"What battle?" Reid tossed over his shoulder, his steps slowed.

Eoin strode forward. "Against the Colquhouns. Ye are witless if ye think the Laird of Luss will just relinquish Kilchurn Castle because the proscription against our name is lifted?"

The man lacked an ounce of wit. "The clan no longer possesses the manpower to storm the stronghold."

"Oh, but ye are wrong, *cousin*." A cocky grin angled his mouth. "I can assure ye the MacGregors of Glenstrae *will* reclaim the clan seat. Before we left Scotland I ordered Lyall to send word of our uprising into the Highlands. I issued an offering of a hundred pounds to any MacGregor who wished to return and fight the bastairds who had us exiled. I suspect an army of four, mayhap five hundred men will be awaiting my orders to retaliate."

Gawking at Eoin in disbelief, Reid stumbled over a vine. "You endanger their lives by bringing them back prematurely. Where in God's name do you plan to hide five hundred men?"

"Finglas Gorge," Eoin answered with confidence. "The MacThomases are no doubt losing cattle in droves as we speak."

Reid's shock left him nearly speechless. He calculated the enormous sum Eoin promised this army as compensation. "Fifty-thousand pounds would better serve the clan if used to purchase Rannoch or Auchingaich." That was Reid's plan.

"I want Kilchurn Castle. Use whatever coin ye must to barter with King James to repeal the proscription, but withhold enough funds to pay those who once pledged fealty to your da before he abandoned them.

We are going to war."

"God's legions, man! How many have to die to put you back on your throne?"

"As many as it takes." Eoin fell back and held silent for the first time that day.

Reid stared ahead wide-eyed and was quickly hypnotized by the to and fro thrashing of Kante's machete, but thoughts coiled through his head at an alarming speed. Fergus had only been the first of those Eoin would sacrifice to rise to power. The people Reid intended to save just multiplied by five.

A bout of dizziness threw him off-balance. He wiped the sweat from his brow and fretted over this new development. He might have been capable of acting as laird over a hundred kinsfolk. He would have built them homes and kept them safe through political relations with the Laird of Luss, but the men that awaited them in Finglas Gorge had been abandoned by Da. They wouldn't follow Reid into battle.

Unless they had no one else to follow.

Reid mulled that thought around in his head until they at last arrived at the Well of Sacrifice. While Kante and the others cleared the perimeter, Reid peered over the edge of the well. The distance to the water's surface was three, possibly four hundred feet down.

A rock bounced of the stone wall and disappeared before the plop could be heard.

"Holy Christ!" Unbalanced, Eoin faltered backward.

Mayhap the next time Eoin found himself in peril, Reid wouldn't save him.

● ● ●

Preparing for the expedition, Robbie pulled strips of dried meat from the grate and listened to Black Dove argue with Yellow Peacock. One didn't have to speak

the language fluently to know Black Dove was win-
ning. The hopeful faces of the other children peeking
in the open doorway slowly fell as the conversation
progressed.

Their appointed leader must be failing her task.

Robbie cocked her head over her shoulder and
caught Yellow Peacock pointing at her. Robbie's gut
sank. The last thing she wanted was to be the cause of
their argument.

Black Dove scowled at her daughter and stabbed a
finger toward the garden. "Go! Help yer aunties collect
fruit for the morrow. All o' ye!" she yelled in a tempt-
me-not tone. "White Serpent will be home soon
enough."

Defeated, Yellow Peacock moped out the door. The
other Mopán children followed, each of their shoulders
fell as they dragged their bare feet through the garden
path.

Black Dove sighed and wrapped several strips of
dried meat in a wide green leaf. "Pray forgive them.
The older they get, the faster they grow weary."

"Of course." Robbie offered forgiveness with complete understanding. Auld Angus's granddaughters
were restless from dawn to dusk. "But how will White
Serpent's return affect their current state of bore-
dom?"

"He taught the bairns new games e'ery Sabbath
afore he sailed for your Scotland. I fear he spoiled
them."

This explanation brought a smile to Robbie's lips.
Reid enjoyed sharing his knowledge. Picturing him at
play with the children made her long for the babe she
was not yet carrying. He would be disappointed that
her monthly flow had come, but in Robbie's way of
thinking 'twas for the best until they were settled in
Scotland.

Someday she would have her family. Someday.

For the nonce, mayhap she could teach the Mopán children a game. "I could show them one of the games my grandda taught me."

Black Dove's smile split over white teeth. "Och! They would like that."

"What kind of games did White Serpent teach them?"

"Draughts, fivestones, barley-break, glic—"

"Glic? Is that not a game of wagers?"

"Aye. The bairns play with cacao beans." She tapped her finger against her thick lips. "Come to think on it, Henrik taught them glic while White Serpent was away on business." Black Dove filled another leaf with meat strips. "Did he tell ye about his ventures?"

Robbie simply nodded and listened to Black Dove prattle on about the value of their heartwood trees. Every time she spoke of the future, Robbie felt as if she were betraying a friend. And if truth be told, she was.

"Will ye be accompanying White Serpent in the spring to barter the timber?"

A bout of nausea curled through Robbie's gut. She could answer Black Dove's question with a simple no. It would not be a lie, but nor would it be the full truth. And the truth was, Reid wouldn't barter timber in the spring, nor would he teach the Mopán bairns any more games.

"Walk with me." Robbie hooked her arm through Black Dove's and led the way into the garden. "After the expedition, White Serpent and I are returning to Scotland to help my people."

Black Dove nodded with indifference, as if she'd expected as much.

"We are not coming back," Robbie added and was

not quite prepared for the sorrow that accompanied her words. It felt like a twisting dagger in her heart.

Black Dove cocked her head, her black brows rose. "Ever?"

Robbie shook her head, confused by the emotions thickening in her throat. Why was this so difficult? She hardly knew these people.

"Ye dinnae like it here?" Black Dove splayed her arms to encompass Rukux as a whole. Gentle Fawn's basket overflowed with fruit, and the children were now fast at play chasing Wild Tigress around the base of the windmill.

"I like it here verra much." Guilt accompanied her statement. Rukux was everything she'd dreamed about for so long, but it was in the wrong country and with the wrong people. "Please try to understand. I have loved ones in Scotland who are not privy to such comforts. They have no home and need a leader like White Serpent to save them. It pains me to take him from ye, but I fear I've no choice."

Black Dove stared blankly into the garden for long moments with her lips parted slightly. "White Serpent has been a part of our family for half my life. Da will be much saddened, as will my husband." Her bottom lip quivered, her dark eyes glossed with tears. "But none will miss him more than my daughter."

That statement triggered an onslaught of tears to rush over Robbie's cheeks. She swiped at her eyes as Yellow Peacock skipped toward them full of youth and innocence.

"'Tis best if Jax and I tell her." Black Dove turned away from her approaching daughter. "Mayhap, ye can teach them one o' your games whilst my sisters and I prepare for the e'en meal."

"Of course." Robbie managed to gather her wits by the time Yellow Peacock was upon her. She pasted on a smile and squat before the child. "Have ye ever played *Harry Hurcheon?*"

• • •

"What happened to Loki after he killed Balder?" Yellow Peacock prodded Robbie, her brown eyes wide with intrigue. The two were curled up in one of the cushioned chairs beside the hearth, and Yellow Peacock was the only child Robbie hadn't put to sleep with her story.

"They bound him and placed a snake above his head so its venom would drip onto him," Robbie continued, mindlessly stroking the girl's soft skin.

"And this is how he died?"

"Nay." Robbie popped Yellow Peacock's nose with the tip of her finger. "That is a story for another night."

Black Dove appeared beside them, hand extended, eyes centered on her daughter. The woman's indifferent manner should be expected, but that made it nonetheless bitter to swallow. "Come, Yellow Peacock. 'Tis past your slumber time."

"You tell good stories." Yellow Peacock wrapped her small arms around Robbie's neck and then kissed her chin. "I'm happy White Serpent made you his woman."

And with these parting words, Robbie was left alone in the massive chair with naught but her thoughts and the lingering aroma of cacao butter—the Mopán people's scent. Reid's scent.

He was so much a part of these people's lives. The way they lived wasn't so different from the way the clan used to live years ago. The evening meal, the games, the storytelling...It all reminded her of the happier times she'd spent at Kilchurn Castle when Calum MacGregor was laird.

Myah set a bowl of nuts on the table beside the

chair across from Robbie. The monkey crept into the corner of the chair and circled several times before she finally sat. The beastie made a whimpering noise that sounded much like a sob and stared at Robbie with huge dark eyes.

"I miss him, too." Her head fell back on the armrest. She'd never felt so sad, so alone, and the thought of retiring to their empty bed made her feel cold inside and out. Her heart beat became slow inside her chest, verra slow, as if his absence caused her life force to fade.

Without you, the Rukux has no reason to beat.

She didn't want to be apart from him, at the same time she didn't know if she could bear to watch him leave everything and everyone he loved. A tear fell over her cheek as she watched the tapers burn to stubs in the candelabra overhead. Her lids slid shut.

A jingle sounded out the open doorway—the trap Jax and Moon Hawk had set two days past.

Robbie's eyes snapped back open.

Myah squealed and disappeared into the rafters just as Kantico slunk over the threshold.

Holy Loki! Robbie's eyes rounded, her throat swelled with a fear that strangled her scream.

The beast's ears laid back, her whiskers twitched.

"Jax!" Robbie bellowed and inched onto the armrest staring into the jaguar's yellow eyes.

The single beat of her heart pounded between her ears, then a whirring noise blew past her. Jax's spear stuck in the animal's throat the same time Robbie saw a spotted cub weaving unsteadily around Kantico's massive paws.

A horrendous howl echoed throughout the ceiling.

"No!" Robbie launched out of the chair and fell to her knees beside the enormous beast. Without thought, she yanked the spear out of Kantico's neck.

The jaguar cried out then collapsed onto the floor.

Deep red blood spilled into her tawny fur and filled the spaces between Robbie's trembling fingers as she pressed her hands against the gushing wound. "Noooo!" she cried.

Chaos erupted from behind in the form of gasps and terrified screams.

Robbie jerked her head over her shoulder to find men, women, and children gathered round the far wall. "Help her!" she pleaded on a sob, but naught could be done.

She watched the life fade from Kantico's golden eyes, then the rise and fall of her ribs suddenly ceased. The jaguar had brought her cub to Rukux. She wasn't going to hurt anyone.

Robbie convulsed with emotions, feeling responsible for the death of this beautiful creature. Staring at her blood-soaked hands, her mind went numb for a bliss-filled moment, then the shock of it all filled her insides with ice. She shook with an intensity that jarred her bones. She was cold, so very cold.

"This is my fault," she whispered and watched the cub nuzzle against Kantico's belly. "I am to blame."

Kantico was only the first of many things she would take from Reid. And with each grievance, he would eventually come to regret making her his wife.

20

~ GUILT ~

Robbie waded through the cluster of children frolicking in the pond and propped her elbows onto the flat rock where Wild Tigress gazed tenderly at the jaguar cub sleeping in her lap. "And how is our wee Pepem doing?"

"She is fair." Wild Tigress set the empty milk sack aside and rubbed the cub's round belly. "And fat." She beamed a wide smile full of white teeth when the beastie yawned. "And lazy." A deep silken laugh bubbled out of her throat, but Robbie no longer looked at the exotic women with eyes full of envy. S'truth, the beastie had showed Robbie a side of Wild Tigress that was loving and nurturing and kind.

When Jax insisted Pepem be taken back into the jungle to fend for herself, Wild Tigress had defended Robbie's decision to care for Kantico's offspring. They'd spent sleepless nights teaching the hungry cub to drink from the milk sack, and within those hours Robbie managed to break down the wall Wild Tigress had built between them. Behind was a vulnerable woman who sought love, happiness, and companionship—a woman not so different from Robbie.

A splash of water arced over Robbie's head and sent Pepem into a sneezing fit.

Wild Tigress hissed words at the children in the Mopán language as she protectively pushed water droplets from Pepem's whiskers, but before she could coo the wee beastie back to sleep, Myah dropped from an overhead branch to cause a ruckus of her own. The monkey squealed and bobbed to and fro like an excited child.

A winded Black Dove entered the garden holding the sides of her belly. "They've returned."

Robbie followed the children out of the water with an urgency that knocked her heartbeat out of cadence. She'd grown accustomed to their state of undress and gave no thought to the fact that her undershift clung to her body like a second skin. She stepped into the open beside Black Dove and followed the woman's gaze to the band of men walking in arrow formation past the outbuilding.

Reid led the pack, his strides wide, his approach commanding. The instant his eyes locked with hers, his unshaven jaw angled. The look of intensity tightening his face was startling, if not somewhat frightening.

Air stuck in her throat. Her skin pebbled. "White Serpent looks a wee bit...different. Does he not?"

Black Dove's chuckle seemed misplaced. "Ye are in a heap o' trouble, lass."

"Trouble?" Robbie asked without taking her eyes from her husband. Something was definitely amiss.

"I've seen that look on Jax."

"What look?" A sense of panic twirled through Robbie's gut.

"'Tis the look a mon wears when he's been away too long and is about to have monkey sex with his woman."

Monkey sex? Robbie's chin turned toward Black Dove, but her stare remained fixed on Reid in disbelief. The man had always displayed unwavering control. He wasn't the type to—

He tore off his *lèine* shirt and threw it to the ground.

Robbie's eyes widened and dried. She swallowed.

"Ye best start runnin'."

Robbie heeded Black Dove's suggestion and shot through the towers of Rukux with a speed that might have impressed Jax. She bolted through the hall, the armory, and then into the sweet-scented garden where the windmill's blades cast moving shadows across a sea of lush green foliage. She paused to gather her breath as well as her wits.

Blast her foolishness! This was madness. Reid was the most mild-tempered man she'd ever known. He did nothing hastily. Mayhap something had happened between Reid and Eoin. Mayhap they'd discovered something unexpected at the well. She peeked over her shoulder and found his massive frame emerging through the open doorway.

His boots were gone as well as his stockings. He unlaced his breeks.

"Holy Loki," she whispered as heat churned low in her belly.

She sprinted into the jungle, weaving through vines and thick foliage. A flock of colorful birds erupted through a canopy of leaves overhead. The squealing sounds of the howler monkeys followed her progress, intensifying the chase.

He stalked her. His crushing steps escalated into a run behind her.

She rounded a monstrous tree and flattened her back against the solidity of its trunk, her bare feet positioned between the forks of its large roots. Anticipation curled her toes in the debris, her fingernails dug into the bark. She waited, breathless, chest burning, delirious with the thought of someone desiring her to the point of lunacy. She moistened her dry lips and squeezed her aching breasts, surprised by the fierceness of her own need.

He ran passed her then stopped, searching, but her audible panting easily gave her away. His head whipped to the side before the rest of his body, and it was then she saw the hunger in his darkening eyes, the savagery that made her feel like a lamb in the lion's den.

Her heart stopped for a fleeting second, then he was on her. He wrapped his hand around the front of her neck and dragged the pad of his thumb down the base of her chin. His muscles flexed. His unshaven jaw tightened. He said nothing. He didn't need to. The wild look in his eyes spoke volumes.

"Welcome—"

He slammed his mouth to hers, stealing her greeting. His fingers wove through her damp hair to hold her in place as he delved deep into the hollows of her mouth. Their teeth scraped, their tongues twirled. His kiss was harsh, demanding, but brief.

"Remove your undershift." His voice cracked with the order.

A brow slid up her forehead. "Ye've had a sennight to prepare words for your homecoming. Have ye nothing more poetic to offer your wife?" she teased dangerously and nipped at his shoulder, his chest. He tasted of salt and musk, and she wanted to sample every delicious inch of him.

"By God's legions, woman. I'm in no mood for play."

"Where is my gentle giant?" Her fingers glided over his stiff nipple and down his sweat-slick abdomen, but stopped just above his navel.

He groaned and squeezed his eyes shut. His muscles tensed beneath her fingertips.

"Where is the man who speaks romantic words about butterflies and dreams?"

"Eoin choked him to death in the jungle." Reid pulled his cock from his breeks and pumped it with his fist as he descended on her breast. His hot mouth molded over her nipple through the wet material of her undershift, sending waves of ecstasy straight into her core.

A whimper blew passed her lips. She arced her back, then pulled the corner of her lip between her teeth when her shoulders blades pressed into rough bark. When he bit her tight bud, her womanhood kicked, fluttered, and swelled.

She pushed him off her, desperate to be rid of the material keeping his mouth from her breast, but he stood upright and stared at her with eyes nigh black with carnal need. "I love you."

She tried to process those words in the half second it took him to hook her leg over his inner elbow. This was not love, this was sex. Why did men confuse the two? Why did those three words seem to slip so easily from their tongues when their bollocks were blue? And why—?

He drew the head of his cock through her wet folds then thrust inside her. A groan of hoarse male pleasure vibrated out of his throat. His fingers dug into her flesh. "Oh, God! Ye feel good."

His hips bucked, penetrating her with another inch. He was feral, the dominant species forcing her to submit to his superior strength. Her woman's sheath stretched to accommodate the girth of his shaft as he withdrew and plunged deeper again and again.

The howler monkeys screamed overhead, offering their approval of the primitive coupling.

In, out, in, out. Her body responded to the friction. Her climax rose and teetered on the edge of what promised to be pure rapture, but her heart wept inside her chest. She felt betrayed by his words. She looked at his face as he drew closer to release and was reminded of the only other man who'd claimed to love her.

The blood in Reid's veins coursed through his body like scalding lava then spiraled through his bollocks on the brink of eruption. Everything about her enticed him—the floral scent of her hair, the velvety softness of her skin, the way she squeaked every time he touched the pleasure spot deep inside her.

He felt crazed but could do naught to control his actions. The sennight he'd spent away from her only aggravated his obsession for her. He'd thought of her day and night, had gratified himself with her memory in the hopes of satisfying her when this moment arrived. But he was going to fail miserably.

His tight sac drew up against the base of his cock. The muscles in his arms and legs burned. A loud vibrating grunt hung in his throat as liquid fire streaked through his erection.

"Damn the Devil!" He withdrew on a frustrated moan and fell to his knees before her. Holding his cock in a rigid grasp, he shot his seed onto the bark of the heartwood tree between her ankles.

Mortified by his performance, he hung his head low and waited for the blinding specks of white light to fade.

"Well, that was bluidy familiar," she quipped with a sarcasm that made him feel all the more repulsed by his barbaric behavior.

He raised his chin and found her eyes—those emerald eyes that often pleaded with him, that begged him to do her bidding. The same eyes currently staring down at him in disappointment.

"I daresay ye have spent far too much time in Eoin's company."

He hugged her around the hips, pressing his forehead against the flat plain of her belly. "Forgive me. That was not me."

She stroked his hair, surprising him with her gentleness. "What happened to the man determined to plant a child in my womb?"

Eoin had gotten into Reid's head. His cousin had talked nonstop of his plans to invade Kilchurn Castle. The scabbit made war sound glorious.

A MacGregor who dies old and withered is a coward, Eoin had said, playing on Reid's guilt. Damn if the fool hadn't made sense during those speeches.

Trying to regain some semblance of dignity, Reid tucked his spent cock back into his breeks and then kissed Robbie's belly before he slowly rose upright. "As much as I desire to see ye round with our babe, I'll not saddle ye with a child if I'm to die saving the clan."

Robbie's eyes twitched, then grew wide. Her palm flattened against her chest. "Dinnae say such things. Ye...ye...cannae say such things to me in jest or otherwise."

"'Tis no jest. Eoin sent word of an uprising into the Highlands before we left Scotland. He is intent on going to war."

She pushed him away, but immediately pulled him back into her now trembling arms. "We are not going to war. Ye are not going to die."

While she hadn't returned his words of love earlier, her fierce reaction gave him hope that some tender sentiments might be cultivating in that bitter heart of hers. "Careful, love, else I might actually think you hold affections for me." He winked, feeling a little full of himself.

She whopped him upside the head. "Have ye knots for brains? We've been handfasted less than a fortnight. Think ye I am eager to become a widow?" The look puckering her face was altogether new. It was that look a woman gets just before she bursts into tears. "We are not going to war."

"Shhh, love," he cooed and kissed her knuckles. "What Eoin did was not completely asinine." While Reid didn't relish the idea of a revolt, Eoin had been wise to solicit aide in the event all didn't go as planned.

Reid held Robbie's hand and explained Eoin's intentions as he guided her through the jungle to the beach. She stared at an island sitting atop a vast plain of aqua-blue water, contemplating all that he told her.

"Let Eoin gather these men he's called down." She twirled a honey-red curl round and round her finger. "While he is playing laird, ye will meet with the Laird of Luss in a tippling house in Rosneath. Somewhere non-threatening." She walked through a white foam surf and made her own alterations to Eoin's plans. "Get the man blootered and talk of politics. Every red-blooded Scot hates the bluidy English. Ye will have that in common. Ease into talk of aligning the clans as a defense. 'Tis what men do when they barter, aye?" She glanced at him, her eyes unfocused with thought.

Reid nodded, thinking himself fortunate to have her as an advisor.

"Let the Laird of Luss know ye are against Eoin's war and that ye only seek peace for the MacGregors. Naught more."

"If I inform him of Eoin's intentions, then the Colquhoun's will be prepared when we attack."

She spun, her emerald eyes sharp and unyielding. "There will *not* be an attack as we are *not* going to war."

Reid simply nodded once. Arguing with her here and now was pointless and talk of war only caused her upset.

"I can assure ye the Laird of Luss is already aware of the uprising. 'Tis why it is important for ye to succeed in wheedling the man into your favor. Buy him drinks and see to it a loose woman or mayhap two fall into his lap. When his spirits are high, offer him coin for Rannoch."

"Rannoch is not big enough to accommodate a clan of nigh six hundred. And I fear a man of his status will require more than gold and women to relinquish Kilchurn Castle."

"Have ye a suggestion?"

Of course he did. He'd had time aplenty to contemplate a hundred different ideas, but he doubted Robbie would warm to any of them. "Mayhap a betrothal would tie the clans together."

Robbie gave him a sidelong glance. "A betrothal? The Laird of Luss has only sons. Bastaird sons at that."

"Auld Angus's granddaughters are my cousins through marriage," he suggested and peeked at her through one eye.

"Nay. They are but weans. Not a day over ten winters." Robbie's head shook venomously, her hands curled into fists. "Those bastairds branded Cait and Anice. I'll not allow ye to force a lifetime of conjugal rape on either of them simply because no one else will have them."

Reid's gaze fell upon the scar on Robbie's cheek. "Do you hold the same opinion about yourself? Did you give yourself to Eoin because you felt no one else would have you?"

She didn't cower before him. In fact, his question raised her proud chin higher and made her nostrils flare. "Eoin chose me. Women of my status have few options. And a woman bearing the mark of a Mac-Gregor have no options at all save for a marriage within the clan."

He couldn't bring himself to ask the questions now dangling on the tip of his tongue. Was she with him because she felt she had no choice? And worse, did she feel his savage performance in the jungle was naught more than conjugal rape?

Repulsed by his thoughts, Reid gathered a handful of shells and tossed each one with vicious enthusiasm into the water.

"You'll not use any of my kinswomen in your bartering, nor will ye sacrifice lives for Kilchurn Castle."

"Am I to lead the clan or you?" he snapped at her, his tone reflecting his frustration. The instant the words left his mouth, he wanted to take them back. He couldn't lead the clan without her.

Her shoulders fell a little, her fists loosened. "As your wife, I should think we would lead them together."

Reid reached out to push a wild curl behind her ear, but she flinched away as if he intended to strike her. He wrapped his hands around her shoulders instead. "There are still two tasks we must complete prior to meeting with the Laird of Luss." Sadly, discovering Xitali's library no longer seemed to be a part of their goals. That dream died in the jungle with Eoin's war. Reid hid his disappointment behind a feigned smile. "We must obtain the gold as well as acquire the edict from King James."

Robbie nodded her agreement on a sigh.

"Be patient, love." He caught her chin and was

thankful she allowed his touch. "All will be right someday."

A half-hearted chuckle warbled in her throat. "I've been chasing *someday* the whole of my life. I fear I will never catch it."

He kissed the skin beneath her lobe. "'Tis the chase that makes the reward so desirable."

Robbie's fingertips feathered over his chest and just as he might have swindled a kiss from her sweet lips a squeal sounded behind them.

"White Serpent!" Yellow Peacock barreled toward him, half-skipping, half-running across the beach. A small beastie trailed behind in her footsteps not even trying to keep up with her.

"She is verra fond of ye." Robbie stepped out of Reid's arms.

"I know. 'Twill be difficult to leave her." S'truth, it was going to be difficult to leave all of them. They were his family, his brothers and sisters, his nieces and nephews. *B'alam* had been like a father to him, but they would get along without him. He didn't belong here anymore.

At least that was what he continued to tell himself.

He pasted on a smile, caught Yellow Peacock around the waist, and propped her in the crook of his arm. Her bright eyes warmed him instantly. "How is my favorite Pea-nut?" He grabbed hold of her head and turned it this way and that, studying her with exaggerated drama. "I dare say your brain is bigger."

She giggled and kissed his chin. "I learned about Loki and Balder and Odin and—"

"The Norse gods?" Reid's brows rose.

"Aye." She flattened her palms against the sides of Reid's head and brushed noses with him. "My brain will soon be bigger than yours."

Reid laughed outright. God, he loved this child. She

had so much potential.

"Did Water Butterfly tell ye about Pepem?" she asked.

"Who is Water Butterfly? And who is Pepem?"

"Water Butterfly is your woman, ye dunderheid." The wee lass rolled her dark eyes expertly and squirmed out of his arms.

Reid turned toward Robbie. "*B'alam* gave you a new name while I was away?"

Her gaze shot out over the ocean, and her fingers quickly went to work twirling her hair. "In a matter of speaking. I decided it was inappropriate for the children to call me Handful of Seed, so I told them *B'alam* would like for them to call me Water Butterfly."

"Robbie!" Reid scolded her, but chuckled on the inside. "Ye cannae give yourself a name. Ye must—"

"Ack! I know. I know. I must earn it. But I think Water Butterfly suits me, aye?"

Reid blew a breath and nodded. What did it matter? Their time here grew shorter with every passing day. "It suits you well."

The cub licking his bare ankle drew his attention downward. He squatted beside Yellow Peacock and scrubbed the beast's ears.

"This is Pepem," Yellow Peacock informed him. "She is the jaguar's cub."

"Did Jax trap Kantico?" Reid looked to Robbie for explanation and saw the sadness welling up in her eyes. She shook her head.

"Da had to kill Pepem's mam. He said she had too much wild in her to tame."

Reid closed his eyes and pushed down the grief trying to surface. 'Twas for the best. Kantico posed a threat to Jax's family. He would have forever worried about Yellow Peacock and the babe Black Dove would deliver come spring. Rukux was safer with Kantico gone.

The cub licked his palm with a sandy tongue. "You are taking good care of Pepem, then?"

Yellow Peacock shrugged. "Wild Tigress is piggish with her, but she needs someone to care for. Mam has Da, and Gentle Fawn and Stream Dancer have Bow Hunter and Moon Hawk."

Those words reminded Reid of the task he needed to complete before leaving the Yucatán. "Come. We've a feast to prepare for."

Yellow Peacock snapped upright. "A wedding feast?"

"Aye." The instant the word left his mouth Yellow Peacock was gone. No doubt racing back to Rukux to spread the word.

He offered Robbie his hand and didn't miss the excitement lifting her countenance.

Her eyes glittered like polished emeralds. "We are celebrating our vows?"

Why did he feel like he was constantly disappointing her? "I made a promise to Songbird, and I intend to fulfill it before we leave for Scotland."

"Of course." Her chin fell, her hands clasped together in front of her. At the very least she should be wearing his ring.

"If you are wanting a wedding, I promise to seek out a priest—"

"Nay. 'Tis not necessary." When she strode passed him, he felt the cold breeze of her bitterness brush across his heart.

• • •

The drums ceased, and the natives grew silent the instant the Jaguar King rose from his throne. "Victor of the hunt rise and step forward."

Robbie wasn't the least bit surprised when Henrik

emerged from the hordes of people gathered round a crackling fire in the garden of Rukux.

"I am the victor," Henrik yelled out and hastily approached the elevated dais.

The Jaguar King's jeweled smile revealed his approval as he splayed his arms toward Wild Tigress and a highly decorated Songbird. "Choose."

Robbie leaned into Reid's side. "I wonder who he'll choose?" she asked in a hushed tone that held more than a hint of sarcasm.

He shushed her and smacked her lightly on the duff never once taking his eyes off Henrik.

Reid controlled the hunt. He was their matchmaker. He knew Henrik would choose Songbird just as everyone did, but the broad grin lifting Reid's shaven cheeks showed Robbie how much pride he took in his responsibilities.

That look added another layer of guilt to Robbie's conscience.

Henrik bowed before the Jaguar King then tripped over his own feet in his haste to position himself before Songbird. After whispering in her ear, he waited for her prompt response, which came in the form of a quick nod. He managed to place a small gold band on her finger while the crowd roared and split into two separate bodies creating a path for their escape.

"They will be happy." Reid's gaze followed the departing couple through the sea of natives and never once did his lofty smile falter.

"Ye are by far the most selfless person I have ever known, Reid MacGregor." Robbie leaned into him and kissed his neck the way he always kissed hers. Heat scalded her eyes, and she prayed he wouldn't see the upset clawing at her heart, but he did.

He raised her chin and narrowed dove-gray eyes on her.

Fortunately, the drums resumed and Yellow Peacock saved Robbie from a conversation she wasn't yet
prepared to have by pulling Reid into a circle dance.
The gaiety continued for hours—eating and drinking,
laughing and dancing. Reid interacted with his family
with the vitality of a man intoxicated on life.

Robbie sat on an over-sized pillow beside the Jaguar King's now empty throne. Wild Tigress and Eoin
had snuck away hours before, which suited her fine as
her thoughts were occupied with Reid this eve and the
words she feared she wasn't strong enough to deliver.

At his approach, Robbie readjusted her skirts and
pushed the hair from her face, but Gentle Fawn and
Bow Hunter's eldest daughter stopped him just a few
feet short of the dais.

Reid waited for her to speak, but the girl held her
tongue. "Have you need for something, *Nikkay?*"

She nodded, her dark eyes swept toward a group of
laddies and then back. "When Wild Tigress no longer
controls the dais, and *B'alam* seeks the second line to
award the victor of the hunt, I will be ready."

Reid looked down at her with one brow slanted.
"'Twill be a while yet. You are still just a wean. You've
not even earned your name."

Nikkay scowled at him and popped her fists onto
her slightly curved hips. "When my turn comes, I want
Keeper of Smiles." With her eyes, she gestured toward
an adolescent boy thriving on the laughter of several
youths. "You will save him for me, *ma'?*"

"Be patient, lass." Reid smoothed the girl's long
black hair and kissed her forehead. "I'll do what I
can."

Robbie knew why his answer was vague. He
wouldn't be here to make sure Keeper of Smiles rose
up as victor of the hunt, nor would he be here to teach
the children games. His intentions to leave Rukux and

his Mopán family behind would be a decision he would come to regret in time.

"I dare say you are not enjoying yourself." He lounged out in front of her on his back and laid his head in her lap. "Mayhap ye need more chocolate."

She inhaled his sweet exotic smell and stroked his dark hair. "If I eat more, my eyes will turn brown," she quipped and studied the beauty of his face.

The fire reflected in his pale irises as he stared blindly at the sky above. "God, 'tis beautiful here. The stars sparkle like diamonds and the perfumed fragrance of the jungle is never far from one's nose, but do you know what I'll miss most?"

Robbie shook her head and choked on the emotions rising in her throat.

"Them. The Mopán are a loving, peaceful people who share their affections without expectations."

She drew a line around his perfect lips and bent over him when his arms circled her back and pulled her to his mouth. The instant their lips touched all the remorse she'd been holding inside surged to the forefront. Her eyes pinched tight, squeezing tears out of the corners, and the sob she'd been determined to stifle burst forth between his lips.

"What is it, love?" He held the nape of her neck and looked up at her. The concern wrinkling his face made her next words all the more difficult to deliver.

"I cannae ask ye to leave. I cannae take ye from these people."

"'Tis too late. You already have. I fear the guilt I've carried for more than a decade now sits on your shoulders."

21

~ DISCOVERY ~

The diving barrel seemed much larger in his youth, and Reid was certain Loch Long had never been quite this dark.

Suspended thirty-five feet below the water's surface in the very pit of the Well of Sacrifice, Reid held tight to the crossbar over his head with one hand and supported Robbie around the waist with the other. "Is your mask secure?"

Robbie's hand slid between them to check the leather mask Reid had tarred around her nose. "Aye." Her nasal answer echoed off the sides of the drum, then her cool, wet fingers checked the seams of his mask as well. "They are both airtight."

"The water is cooler than I anticipated."

"'Tis not half as cold as the loch in Scotland," she assured him with confidence. "'Tis fortunate we are both wearing a leather suit."

He hated this niggling feeling that something wouldn't go according to plan. What if Jax and Kante didn't pull them through fast enough? Or pulled them through too fast and knocked the ropes off the pulley system? What if her glass globe hit against a rock and shattered? What if... "Check the ropes again."

She sighed. "The ropes were perfectly knotted before Jax lowered us into the well. I'm certain they are still secure."

He sensed her impatience, but damned if he was going to slip into the river current pulling at his bare feet half-cocked. "By my calculations, we should reach the water reservoir in—"

"Less than thirty minutes," she finished for him. "Ye have told me this three times already."

He was fretting. He knew it. She knew it, but naught seemed to rattle her. "Are you not afraid?" He was.

"I am, but I'm excited as well." She adjusted the straps binding the leather-bound glass globe to her side. "'Tis time, Reid. Remember to exhale through your mouth."

Every second the crystals dissipated inside the globe was one less breath they might need in the end, but he couldn't bring himself to take up the horn. He touched her lips behind the tube connected to her air source. "I should have kissed you."

"Ye can kiss me when we reach the water reservoir."

But what if they didn't make it to the reservoir? Would she know how he felt about her? "If something goes amiss, if I dinnae make it and you do, I want you to know that I love you, Robbie."

She snorted. "My garment is tarred to my body, Reid. Now is hardly the time. Mayhap after the dive I'll let ye chase me through the jungle again. Let's go." She reached over his head before he could decipher the confusion shaking his brain and blew on the horn twice—the signal for Kante and Jax to start pulling them through.

"Dinnae forget to count." She slipped out of his arms and disappeared beneath the water.

The rope around his waist tightened. He stole a final breath from the diving barrel and followed her into the cool river current.

One one thousand, two one thousand... Bewildered didn't begin to describe his state of his mind. *Four one thousand, five one thousand...*

He inhaled through his nose, exhaled out his mouth.

*Seven one thousand, eight one thousand...*He tells her he loves her, and her response is *My garment is tarred to my body?*

Ten one thousand, eleven one thousand...

Inhale, exhale.

God's legions! What the devil was wrong with her? He wanted her to know how deeply he cared for her should they die, and she accuses him of lechery. Did she think he was wooing her with sweet sentiments because his bollocks were blue? Is that what Eoin had done?

Inhale, exhale. Inhale, exhale.

He recalled the two times he'd expressed his love for her: once in the jungle just before he ravaged her, and the second had been yester eve in the small tent just before he thrust his aching cock between her thighs.

Mayhap he was a lecher!

Inhale, exhale. Inhale, exhale.

His heart beat increased.

Damn! Engulfed in wet blackness, he attempted to calm himself and regain his bearings. He held his arms outright and focused on regulating his breathing else he risked depleting his air before they reached the reservoir.

Inhale...exhale...

The rope nudged him forward, guiding him through the river passage. Periodically, the ties connecting him to Robbie tugged this way and that. Knowing she was safe beside him made the whole task a little more bearable. Since the count was already lost to him he searched the passage for any splinter of light as well as a change in the current, something that might tell him where Xitali had spent her time between the wells.

Time passed slowly in cold, wet, darkness, and his mind wandered haphazardly from one subject to the next. Regardless of what he tried to focus on, his thoughts always came full circle back to Robbie.

He was no lecher. There was no man more capable of resisting the pleasures of the flesh than he. He resolved in that moment to prove to Robbie he was a man of supreme control, but more, he wanted her to see that he was a man worthy of her love.

● ● ●

Robbie burst through the surface inside the water reservoir mere seconds before Reid did. Jax and Kante, along with a dozen or more Mopán men, whooped and cheered at ground level, celebrating the success of the dive.

They did it! They survived and so much more. Excited to the point of blathering, she sucked in gulps of air through her mouth and spun toward Reid. "Did ye feel it? The change in the water flow? At thirty-seven, ten thousand."

"Nay. I lost the count," he admitted, his bearing aloof as always, but naught could diminish her spirits.

"We must go again. This time without the ropes." She swam toward the ladder draped over the well's edge, but he caught her on the bottom rung.

"Calm down, Robbie."

Calm down? Had he lost his wits? The brink of discovery was at their fingertips and he wanted her to calm down?

"'Twill be dark soon," he explained in a somber, impatient tone.

"'Tis dark between the wells. What does it matter?"

He put his finger in his ear, and shook it. "We'll go again first thing on the morrow. There is much to prepare prior to a second dive."

Robbie climbed the rope ladder grumbling. "Why do ye get to make all the decisions?"

"Because I act without haste."

Jax assisted her over the edge wearing a gapping smile. He wrapped his long fingers around her head, then squeezed her shoulders down to her wrists as if assuring himself of her wellness. "Jax was afraid for you."

The others agreed in muffled tones making hand gestures toward the sky to offer their thanks to the gods for protecting their brother.

Reid pulled himself out of the well and onto a flat of black rock then proceeded to peel the mask from his nose. His features were smooth, void of emotion which frustrated Robbie more than an empty kettle of soup.

"We need to measure the distance on the rope and mark it so Jax and Kante know where to stop on the morrow. We are not going without the ropes." He gave her a look that warned her not to argue, then began delivering a slew of orders much like he'd done aboard the *Obsidian*.

What in the name of Odin was wrong with him? Where was the man who spoke of Xitali with such enthusiasm Robbie was nigh jealous of the woman? Where was the man who'd lost his senses when she discovered vital air? Something had happened to him between the wells. Something that stole his passion.

"Robbie, prepare the air globes as well as the fire lamps then set to work cleaning the tar from your skin."

That last order she felt certain he'd given simply to keep her occupied, but she held tight to her tongue and set to her tasks the same as everyone else.

By the time their duties were complete, the moon hovered above like a giant orb of white light. The dew shimmered silver-green on the foliage, and the sounds of the jungle amplified into a soothing musical cacophony.

Secluded from the others, Robbie lay on a bamboo mat outside her small tent waiting for Reid to join her as he had the eve before. With any luck at all his sullen mood had improved over the course of the eve, and if it hadn't—she bent her knees and slid her clean undershift down her thighs—she would rid him of whatever troubled him.

Thoughts of their coupling set her skin afire. She'd never burned for a man the way she burned for him. Her flesh tingled with thoughts of him. Mayhap 'twas the way he lost control when he was with her. He strived to be gentle, and when his desire for her refused to be caged, she felt a sense of power for releasing his inner beast.

Smack. "Why are you not sleeping in the tent?"

Startled out of her musings, Robbie looked between her bare knees just as Reid slapped the back of his neck. "Because I am not yet sleeping." She gave him a side-long glance and pursed her lips in an attempt to be provocative, but he'd clearly been bitten by a sour bug.

Smack.

"The insects will eat the flesh from your bones by morn." He sat on the mat's edge and pulled his boots off one at a time. "What is that smell?"

Robbie sat up and rummaged through her satchel until she found the container of soft balm. "'Tis a liniment Wild Tigress made for me to keep the beasties from biting me. I thought it smelled pleasant."

He peeled off his shirt. "Spread some on me."

Propped on her knees at his back, she rubbed a generous amount of the liniment into his neck and shoulders, then proceeded to work the knots out of his taut muscles as she'd done so many times before for Grandda.

Reid moaned and held still. "That feels good."

She smiled and rubbed circles up and down the sides of his spine, kneading the larger muscles between his shoulder blades and backbone until he felt loose and relaxed. Feeling rather amorous, she leaned forward just enough to brush her hard nipples across his back.

The muscles she'd just thawed tightened beneath her fingertips. His back straightened, his head snapped upright.

She grinned wickedly, reveling in the power she held over him and feathered subtle kisses across his back. She nipped at his skin as her fingers snuck around his ribs, slid down his abdomen, and then reached for the laces of his breeks.

He grabbed her hand. "'Tis doubtful I'll be needing any of the liniment down there."

Blast him! He was daft and completing behaving out of sorts. She didn't know what had happened to the man with a ravenous appetite for her, but she intended to find him. She shot to her feet and started passed him in a huff.

"Where are you going?" He caught her wrist, stretching her arm at the shoulder.

"Back into the well to find my husband." She glared

down at him, acting dramatic on purpose.

His chest shook a single time on a silent chuckle as he pulled her onto his lap and pushed the hair from her eyes.

Taking advantage of his humor, she wrapped her long legs around his waist and hooked her ankles at the base of his spine. "Ye seem different. What has happened?"

"I am weary. 'Tis all."

That was a bluidy lie. He'd behaved like a buck surrounded by a dozen does in heat since the day they'd become handfasted and now was no different. His manhood thickened beneath her with every passing second. She tickled the tops of his shoulders and gently rocked atop him. "Are ye too weary to tend your wife's needs?"

He leaned forward to kiss the skin beneath her lobe. "My wife has needs does she?"

"Ye know I do." While his lips trailed a path of fire over her neck, naught could compare to the inferno burning low in her womb. Perspiration thickened around her neck. She held his shoulders and rubbed her sex against the rigidity of his hard member. The bud hidden at the apex of her womanhood pulsed, aching for relief. She held the side of his head and guided his mouth to hers, but the ferocity she sought was not there. His lips were loose, his tongue barely responsive.

She pulled back and stilled her grinding hips. "Have ye lost your desire for me?"

That question gained her a bit of fire.

"Nay." He lifted her off him and stared up at her for long moments before he finally asked, "Where is it you need me the most, wife?"

Without the slightest hesitation, she raised the hem of her undershift to her naval. "Here." The word came out in a whisper.

His breathing deepened as he caressed the fronts of her legs, his thumbs teased the inside of her thighs, coaxing them further apart. He leaned forward and kissed her directly on her shaved womanhood. "Here?"

The contact of his lips to that most intimate place made her blood boil. "Aye. There." That was the place. She pulled her garment over her head and discarded it onto the ground, then waited for him to remove his breeks.

But he didn't move.

Instead, he propped her foot onto his shoulder and kissed the inside of her knee. Then he discovered another tender spot—the inner part of her thigh. He licked it, kissed it, made swirling designs with the tip of his tongue. He came so close to the place she wanted him most, only to float away. "Is there no other place ye ache for me?"

His words tickled her, tortured her. The heady scent of her own arousal spiked her senses. Oh, she wanted his mouth on her. She could count on one hand the number of times Eoin had pleasured her with his tongue, but that had been so long ago.

She wove her fingers into Reid's hair to steady herself. "Please," she begged. "Please kiss me there."

When he used his tongue to separate her folds, she jerked, and then trembled on a whimper. His kiss was gentle at first, slow and deliberate, sliding the tip of his tongue along the layers of her quivering flesh, up and down, up and down. Watching his mouth at play only heightened her arousal. Her insides burned, her skin tingled. She moaned and squeezed her sweat-slick breasts in unison to relieve the craving tightening her nipples. She bucked, and he responded with wicked intent.

He used the tips of his thumbs to spread her swollen lips open and then delved his tongue in and out of her repeatedly, alternating between quick and slow thrusts. 'Twas maddening and divine and delicious.... And she wanted to thank him, to tell him what he was doing to her was exquisite, but when her mouth opened, the only sounds that emanated were warbling cries of rapture.

Eoin had never taken the time to pleasure her so thoroughly. He would have sought his own release long before now. She expected Reid to do the same, to throw her down and bury himself between her legs, but he did not. Instead, he inserted one finger inside her, then two, and matched the rhythm of her gyrating hips.

When the tips of his fingers scraped the roof of her womb, all rational thought dissolved into a white haze. Her eyes flickered behind closed lids. She tore cruelly at his hair, pushing him away, then pulling him hard against her mound.

Then he found it—that secret treasure hidden where all the whorls and folds came together at the top of her mons. He licked the engorged bud gently, then hard, flicking his tongue side to side.

"Aye," she cried. "There. There!" Her muscles tightened, her toes curled around his shoulder. Every particle of her being awaited her release.

"Come for me, love." His words vibrated against her clitoris just before his lips formed into an O and drew that tiny ball of fire into his mouth.

The lower half of her body shuddered as her climax burst forth in a fiery rush. Reid held her upright when her leg faltered beneath her and continued to milk the nectar of her orgasm into his mouth.

A second ripple trilled through her and stole the remainder of her physical strength.

He caught her when she melted into his arms and

carried her inside the tent.

Sated and exhausted, Robbie lay on her belly trying to recover while Reid tickled her skin. His caresses trailed along her spine, over her duff, and down her thighs only to repeat the process over and over again. Her gentle giant had returned, but there was a part of her psyche that told her all was not right. Something still ate at his mind. "Why did ye not find your release?"

He leaned over and kissed the arc of her shoulder blade. "I burn with a desire far greater than you could possibly fathom." He kissed the base of her back and then settled in behind her.

While she attempted to decipher his words, he curled his massive arms around her and flushed her back with his chest. His knee pushed between her thighs, separating them, the same time his hot hand slid down her navel and cupped her tender mound; his other hand found its resting place over her breast. "Sleep well, love."

Sleep well? What in the name of Odin was wrong with him? His cock was as hard as stone nestled in her duff. Why wasn't he taking his ease? They were husband and wife. He had bluidy rights! Why wasn't he acting on them?

While the questions piled up at an alarming rate in her head, Reid's breathing grew steady, then turned into a whistle within a matter of minutes.

● ● ●

Thirty-five, ten thousand, thirty-six, ten thousand, thirty-seven, ten thousand. Reid stopped the count in his head the same instant the rope pulling him and Robbie through the river passage went slack. At least he'd been able to keep the count this day. S'truth, he was in complete control of his person.

While he'd awoken with the same stiff cock he'd gone to sleep with, he somehow felt powerful for having controlled his urges. Robbie on the other hand awoke with temper. He knew his behavior irked her, but he held determined to abstain from his conjugal rights until she realized she was much more to him than a soft body to spend himself inside.

Reid drew a breath from the tube connected to his air source and pivoted in the darkened water until he spotted the fire globe in Robbie's hand. That faint yellow glow illuminated a scowl that was evident even behind her mask. She wouldn't give him trouble, not here, not now. He wadded before her, waiting for her to release the globe as planned.

She didn't.

"Release the globe," he demanded, but his muffled words floated away inside hundreds of bubbles.

The stubborn wench shook her head, her brows drew tighter. She spun, and swam west, perpendicular of the main rope.

That had not been part of the plan. He told himself he needn't worry. They were both still connected to the main line by a twenty foot length of rope. Reid inhaled through his nose, exhaled through his mouth and followed the hellion. What choice did he have really? The woman had a mind of her own, and if truth be told, she could out swim him.

The water temperature turned frigid as if he'd swam into the center of an underground spring, and it was then he felt the shift in the river's current. Excitement made his pulse kick up a notch. Robbie's calculations had been spot on. The woman was brilliant! He really needed to trust her more.

She paused and swiveled. A braggart's smile was the last image the fire globe reflected before Robbie released their tiny light source into the water. The globe bobbed and swooped sideways where the river branched off the main passage, then stopped all at once only feet away. Though small, the flame cast yellow light into a small circular space surrounded by smooth rock walls.

Without hesitation, Robbie swam toward the globe and stretched both arms out to touch the sides of the narrow enclosure. She looked up, searching, studying, then her eyes reconnected with his.

He panicked. Everything about that look told him she was about to do something foolish.

Robbie untied the rope connecting her to the main line, grabbed the fire globe, and shot upward.

God's legions! The woman didn't put an ounce of thought into decision making. He wanted to strangle her wee neck. Instead, he untied the rope from his waist and scissored his feet, following her up through the narrow passageway. Only seconds passed before he heard the splash above him. He swam up the length of her body and broke through the water's surface beside her.

He sucked in musty air through his mouth and had every intention of scolding her, but the sight before him stole his anger. 'Twas like standing beneath a star-filled sky during the midnight hour. The fire globe reflected the shimmering ceiling of an enormous cavern—Xitali's cavern.

"My God in Heaven." Astounded by the discovery, Reid's entire being trembled with excitement. Somehow, he managed to crawl out of the water behind Robbie who was now eagerly pulling the pack from his shoulders.

She pealed the tarred ties free and retrieved a short piece of twisted tow they'd dipped in tallow before they left Rukux. She pulled the stopper from the fire globe and ignited the oiled torch.

The cavern filled with light, revealing a treasure far grander than any king's purse. It was the treasure of the gods.

"Holy Loki!" Robbie's words were breathy, her eyes fixed on an abundance of riches piled in heaps around the floor of the cavern: statues of the gods, chalices and vessels of all shapes and sizes. And all of it made of gold and jade.

"Where do ye s'pose it all came from?"

"Xitali must have collected it from the bottom of the Well of Sacrifice. When the kings of the ancient Maya weren't sacrificing virgins, they tossed gold into the well as an offering to their gods," Reid said in monotones, but the gold no longer held him rapt. He stood in awe, staring at the treasure he'd sought since the day he found the stone stele in the jungle. He grew dizzy, and for a brief moment he thought he might actually swoon. Unable to draw enough air into his lungs, he wanted to tear the mask away from his face, but he wasn't that careless.

"What is it?" Robbie stepped up beside him and held the torch upward to illuminate the greatest discovery of all.

"Xitali's library," Reid whispered the words as he looked on in amazement at the renderings covering the walls—pictures depicting advanced theories in irrigation, alchemy, and astrology. However, the grandest rendering of all dominated the center wall. It was a celestial depiction representing the ancient Maya universe. "'Tis the Sacred Tree of Life known as *Yaxché*," he explained. "The tree's branches connect the Spiritual Realms, the planets." He made a sweeping gesture toward the top of the tree where the branches held up the eight planets of the solar system. "The base of the tree is the Earth's plane, and the tree's roots stretch into the <u>Xibalbá</u> where the nine dark deities reside."

"Hell?"

"Aye." He'd seen similar drawings akin to the one before him, but none so detailed. "This is Mars." He pointed at the fourth planet from the left. Inside the planet was a rendering of a man and a woman standing before their own tree. A serpent coiled around its trunk. "They are Adam and Eve," he mumbled in awe.

"Xitali believed the Garden of Eden resided on Mars?"

Knowledge is truth and truth is power. Reid recalled the words on Xitali's stele and snatched the torch from Robbie's hand. He walked closer to study the trunk of the Sacred Tree of Life. "Mayhap Xitali died and met the Supreme Being of the Otherworld." Reid laughed outright, not because he found it humorous in any way, but because it terrified him to comprehend its immensity. "'Twas no wonder her king sacrificed her."

"These drawings could set a course for the advancement of science. Scholars would pay a fortune to analyze them."

He tore his gaze away from the rendering and looked into her wide green eyes—eyes full of intrigue and wonder. Anxiety coiled in the pit of his stomach. Her words set him on the defense. The effects of this discovery could be life-threatening for the Jaguar King and his people. Jax, Black Dove, and Yellow Peacock were the first of those to come to the forefront of his mind.

He wouldn't endanger their lives because a woman drew a few pictures on a cave wall.

Robbie cupped her mouth behind the tube. The giddy expression on her face made him wish he'd never brought her here. He gripped her by the elbow and guided her back toward the water. "When we return to the surface, you will tell no one about this. No one," he repeated with emphasis and gestured toward the heaps of gold which no longer held the grandeur it had when they'd broke through the surface. "We came for the gold. 'Tis all. We will need to prepare nets and more rope to haul—"

"Are ye soft in the skull?" Robbie snatched her arm out of his grasp and glared at him. "Reid, we have—"

"No!" He held both her shoulders firmly, forcing her attention on him. "The Spaniards have reaped havoc across the New World for a hundred years, killing off tribes and burning their books."

Robbie's thin brows dipped low, her head shook, her lips parted ready to debate.

"Hear me, Robbie." He didn't allow her words. "I will not invite such destruction upon the Mopán people. They are my family."

The lines smoothed from her face, her entire being sank beneath his palms, and then her lashes fell against her cheeks. "I thought I was your family now."

He sighed, knowing nothing he said could change the words he'd already spoken. "Robbie—"

She raised her hand to stop him. "They are important to ye the same as the MacGregor clan is important to me. I will say naught." Her gaze never lifted off the floor. "We should go before our air is depleted. We still have to swim to the reservoir." She slipped back into the water and then disappeared beneath the surface.

Reid blew a heavy breath and rubbed his eyes, frustrated by her failure to accept her place in his heart. What did he have to do to convince the woman he loved her?

He prepared to follow, but not without a final glance at Xitali's cavern. He'd waited so long to make this discovery, and the Maya priestess had not disappointed him. Unfortunately, the work she'd left behind would forever go unstudied.

22

~ SACRIFICE ~

She should be happy. The expedition had been a
success. In a little over a fortnight, Reid and Robbie
managed to haul all the gold out of Xitali's cavern
save for a single statue of gold and jade that Reid insisted on leaving behind to pay tribute to the Maya
priestess and her efforts. More than a dozen Mopán
warriors had been called upon to transport the fortune
back to the work-house at Rukux where Black Dove
and her sisters spent three days melting the majority
of the gold into small bricks.

The treasure that would free the MacGregor clan
was now safely tucked into the keel of the *Obsidian*
anchored a short distance from the white beaches of
Reid's paradise. Provisions for the return voyage were
in order as well. Livestock, sacks of maize, and barrels
of drink laden the ship's storage chambers, and a crew
of nigh fifty men awaited launching orders from their
captain.

They were headed home, to Scotland. In less than a

month's time Robbie would once again be with her clan. She missed them—Nanna and baby Alana, auld Angus and his granddaughters, but mostly she missed Grandda. She should be eager to step into the awaiting longboat and row out to the *Obsidian*.

She was not.

S'truth, she was miserable. A warm drizzle of rain coated her face with wetness, hiding her tears, but nothing could drown the sorrow burning a hole in her heart as she watched Reid bid farewell to his friends and family. With every parting word, Reid's control seemed to slip further from his grasp. He embraced Gentle Fawn and Stream Dancer, then Songbird and Henrik, and the guilt Robbie bore was nigh unbearable.

The Jaguar King clasped Reid in a fierce hug. "May *Xau* protect you on your journey."

"I can never repay you for your generosity."

The Jaguar King set Reid back. "Be happy, my son. This is not the end. We will meet again in the Otherworld."

Reid offered him a single nod, then bent to one knee before Black Dove. He splayed his fingers around her tight abdomen. "You will take care of this boy, aye?"

"Boy? Och! 'Tis certain to be another lass." Black Dove uselessly swiped at the endless stream of tears that had fallen over her face the whole of the morning. She raised Reid up and kissed his chin. "You will have Jean-Pierre return my Jax to me safely and before spring, aye."

Reid turned his attention to Jax who casually leaned against his spear, awaiting their departure. "You should stay."

Jax cocked his head, his dark eyes narrowed. "White Serpent and Jax make the journey together."

The knot in Reid's throat bobbed, his gaze fell to

Black Dove's round belly. "Your place is here. I do not wish for ye to miss the birth of your second born because of me."

Jax stared at Reid, and the sadness in his eyes tore at Robbie's heart. She cupped her mouth to silence the sob now choking her. She hated everything about this moment.

"Jax is going." He stomped toward Black Dove and bid her farewell. "I will be back in time. It is my promise." He held her belly as he kissed her hard, then stepped into the water to steady the back of the longboat.

Reid exhaled a ragged breath, ripped his fingers through his damp hair, and watched the majority of the Mopán people slip into the thick green foliage. He scanned the barren beach, searching. "Yellow Peacock is still angry with me?" he asked Black Dove in a somber tone.

"She will come to regret not bidding ye farewell. Someday Yellow Peacock will understand why ye left." Black Dove consoled him, her gaze met Robbie's, but only for a fleeting second before she turned to leave.

Reid lingered for long moments, staring at the landscape, before he finally swiveled. "Get in the boat, Robbie." Though he kept his eyes downcast, he remained in constant control of his emotions as he assisted her into the longboat. Few words had passed between them since they'd discovered Xitali's cavern. He'd grown distant, his mind always elsewhere. He hadn't made love to her since before the first dive more than a fortnight ago. Robbie told herself their labors stole his energy, but she knew 'twas a lie. Each day that passed, he was coming to regret the bargain he'd struck with Eoin.

She had not been worth it.

Sitting on the crossbench, she lowered her lashes,

unable to look at him. "Ye dinnae have to leave." Her words were a foolish attempt to free herself from the guilt eating her insides.

"Please, Robbie. Not now. This is difficult enough." He bent to free the longboat from the shore, but before he completed the task the squall of a child sounded from behind.

"White Serpent! White Serpent!" Yellow Peacock burst through the dense leaves and raced onto the beach.

Reid whipped his head over his shoulder and quickly jerked the longboat back into the sand. He turned in time to catch Yellow Peacock when she jumped into his wide arms.

She hugged him fiercely. "I'm sorry I called you a foul-earthed frog. I take it back. I take it back." She sobbed openly. "You will always be my favorite white man."

"And you will always be my favorite Pea-nut." Reid buried his face in the small curve of Yellow Peacock's neck for long moments before he knelt in the sand and set her back on her feet. He pushed the tears from her thick lashes with the pads of his thumbs and smoothed her long black hair. "I will miss you."

Her eyes found Robbie, her dark brows puckered, and her bottom lip quivered.

Robbie almost wished the girl would curse her. 'Twas no mistaking the look of blame in her black eyes.

Reid cradled her cheeks in his palms, bringing her attention back to him. "You will behave for your mam and take care of Pepem and Myah, and Oscar and Khan."

"And you will take care of Da." Stepping into the water, she wrapped her small arms round Jax's middle and bid him farewell in her native tongue.

"Go, Yellow Peacock. I will return before the *chikoo* turns brown on the sapodilla tree." Jax kissed the crown of her head and stepped into the boat.

She nodded, pushing tears from her eyes, then set a braided length of black hair in Reid's hand. "Do not forget me."

Reid studied her gift, stroking the braid with his thumb before he clutched it in his fist and once again wrapped his thick arms around her tiny frame. "I will never forget you, Pea-nut."

Robbie held her throat and convulsed with emotions. He would always resent her for making him leave his family. As long as there was breath in her lungs, she would remember this day as the day she took a great man away from his people.

● ● ●

Reid rolled silky smooth smoke over his tongue before he blew the silver ribbons over the bow of the *Obsidian* into a night black as pitch and wished for naught more than to put this day behind him. S'truth, Jean-Pierre had relieved him at the helm over an hour before and all was quiet on deck. However, he wasn't yet prepared to face Robbie in the confines of his cabin. Part of him sought her solace, but his grievances were still too raw, and he feared what he might say should she ask the wrong questions.

Mayhap he was a coward, but he simply wanted to sulk in his misery alone. He drew on his cigar until the embers burned bright orange and fiddled with the braid Yellow Peacock had given him until the swish of skirts whispered behind him.

"Do ye intend to avoid me the entire way back to Scotland?"

Reid's eyelids slid shut. He sighed. Why did she have to sound so bitter? "I am not avoiding you, Robbie. 'Tis been a trying day. Go back to the cabin. I'll be about shortly."

No departing footsteps broke the hum of the gale filling the foremast above him. He might have known she would defy him. From the corner of his eye, he saw wild sprigs of her honey-red hair blowing this way and that in the warm breeze.

She stepped to his side, and he turned away.

"Do ye hate me for taking ye away from them?"

Appalled by her question, he swiveled and stared at her. The spark in her emerald eyes was gone, dimmed to gray-green. Though her cinnamon lashes were spiked with tears, she did not hide behind them. She pulled the corner of her lip between her teeth and awaited his answer.

A part of him wanted her to suffer the same guilt he'd lived with since the day he'd left her on the hillside, but the part of him that loved her beyond sensibility couldn't bear to see her suffer. He tossed the remainder of his cigar over the forward rail and held his hand out to her. "I could never hate ye."

She rushed into his arms with a fierceness he hadn't been near prepared for. Her arms circled his waist in an embrace he returned with equal abandon.

Lost in her comforting touch, he brushed her hair and kissed her temple. "'Twill take time for me to forget them, Robbie."

Her head snapped up, her eyes twitched. "Dinnae say such things. I never want ye to forget them. Never. They are your family. Ye promised Yellow Peacock ye would never forget her, and I want ye to keep that promise."

A sad smile lifted the corners of his lips as he looked down at the braid wrapped around his hand. Yellow Peacock's dark shining eyes came to the forefront of his mind, and he recalled the first time he met the wee bit. "I was there when she was born." The memory was not so old that he didn't remember his fear. "'Twas the eve Moon Hawk claimed Stream Dancer as his woman. Da and *B'alam* got into a debate as to whose drink was more potent—the Scots' whisky or the Mopán's balche. The entire tribe got completely blootered; men, women, and even some of the older bairns."

"All save for ye?"

"I drank my fair share." Reid chuckled and leaned against the rail, keeping Robbie tucked tightly to his side. "But I was not nearly as lost to the drink as Jax. The man stumbled off to take a piss, and I found him face down in a crop of itching weed." Reid paused, remembering how Jax's eyes had swollen nigh shut, then scratched his whiskered jaw and went on. "I managed to drag his drunk arse to his cottage and found Black Dove suffering the beginnings of her labors."

"Was she angry?"

"Seething. I dinnae recall how long it took me to get the woman to quit kicking Jax."

Robbie hid her smile behind her hand and toyed with the laces of his *lèine* shirt, awaiting the continuation of his story.

"I searched the village for someone clear-headed enough to assist her, but none could be found. By the time I returned, Black Dove was kneeling on a bamboo mat screaming as though her bones were breaking inside her." The yellow glow of the binnacle lamp blurred as Reid became lost in the memory. "She struggled for three long hours and cursed Jax with every breath until the pains became more than she could bear. Then she begged me to cut the babe out."

Robbie gasped and squeezed his hand.

"I scolded her for her cowardice. Told her she was

the least brave of all her sisters."

"Those were harsh words."

"Aye, but not nearly as harsh as the barbs she tossed back. She condemned me to the Underworld, then spit on me, but moments after that, she pushed the babe from her womb." Reid grinned, remembering the instant he caught Yellow Peacock. "She took her first breath in the palm of my hand. I was the first to hold her, even before Black Dove."

"And Jax?"

"He slept through it all." Reid welcomed the laughter warming his insides. "Jax groveled for weeks after, trying to earn Black Dove's forgiveness."

"'Tis why ye wanted him to stay. To be there for his second born."

"Aye." Reid tickled Robbie's hand from the heel of her palm to the tip of her index finger. "And I will make certain he returns before that day arrives. No man should miss the birth of his child. There is a bond that forms in that moment."

"A bond no one can ever take away from ye," Robbie said the words the same moment he thought them, then smiled that smile that melted his heart. "I helped Nanna deliver Alana."

A moment of silence passed between them in reflection, and he yearned for the day they would have a family of their own. He thought of that day he'd rocked a small delicate babe beneath the shade of a willow tree in Glenstrae and wondered if their bairns would be wild and free like Robbie or cautious and guarded like himself.

He pulled her close by her chin, and kissed the soft skin beneath her eye. "You will make a good mam. 'Tis doubtful you'll let our bairns fall off the stable roof."

"Fall?" Both her brows rose half way up her forehead. "I dinnae fall. Ye and Fergus threw me off the bluidy roof."

"Ye landed in a heap of hay. 'Twas a harmless experiment. The cats all landed on their feet." He
laughed outright and slid down the rail to a sitting position. "I'm certain it had been Fergus's idea to see if
you would land the same."

She snorted at the blatant lie. "Grandda broke
three switches tanning Fergus's duff." She joined him
on the deck, hugged her knees, and twirled a curl
round and round her finger. "Fergus ate his sup for a
sennight standing up."

"As did I." Reid let his head fall against the rail, recalling the beating Da gave him for the incident. They
reminisced for hours, sharing memories—both good
and bad. Reid told her about the mischief he and Jax
had reaped in their jungle, and for every story he told,
Robbie had one similar.

He spoke of the battles they'd fought against the
Kekchí tribe, and she recounted the grim events that
transpired the day the Colquhouns invaded Kilchurn
Castle.

"Had Lyall not warned me and Grandda about the
attack, we never would have escaped over the bailey
wall..."

Reid hadn't realized how prominent of a role Lyall
had played in Robbie's life, but as they conversed
about the raids and the havoc the MacGregors reaped
on the MacThomases, he became increasingly aware of
the reverence filling her tone when she spoke of Eoin's
seneschal.

"For every hundred head of cattle we stole from the
MacThomases, Lyall left one behind in the wood."

"And Eoin allowed this?"

Now leaning heavily into his side, Robbie fiddled
with a loose thread on the blanket Duncan had
brought earlier that night. "Nay. Lyall did it of his

own accord without Eoin's knowing. When the raids started to prove profitable, Lyall pilfered bits of the spoils to me to hide."

"You keep talking about Lyall, and I'm bound to get jealous," Reid jested, but in truth, he wanted the admiration Robbie obviously held for Lyall.

She looked up at him, and the gray light of dawn showed him the ire in her eyes. "Ye willnae deny Lyall his place in the clan because he once cared for me. He is ten times the leader that whisky-soaked drunkard wasting space in your storage chamber could ever pretend to be. Lyall will make ye a good seneschal as he is loyal."

"He is not loyal to Eoin it seems."

"He is loyal to me and to the clan."

Too tired to debate the issue with her, Reid nodded his agreement, but it seemed she was not yet finished defending the man's character.

"Lyall and I both knew how much coin Eoin wasted in the tippling houses. What little we managed to hide provided necessities for the weak of the clan."

"Then I suspect I owe Lyall my gratitude." Those words seemed to lighten Robbie's position on the subject.

Her brow smoothed, her shoulders loosened, and she once again cuddled into Reid's side. "In the vein of things, the coin we stashed over the years matters little now. 'Tis paltry pebbles compared to what lies in the keel of the *Obsidian*."

"Where did you hide it?" he asked more out of curiosity than aught else.

"In the loch." Her boastful expression told him how proud she was of herself. "Even if Eoin knew it was there, he would never go after it. The man is terrified of the water."

Clever lass. Reid returned her grin. "So you were

hiding plunder the day I returned?"

"Aye."

Their talk mentally transported him back into that cavern. His mind's eye filled with the memory of a besotted laddie who'd bartered for a kiss from a blushing lass. "Whatever became of the Spaniard's gold?"

"There was never any gold. Grandda said he tossed a few trinkets into the loch to keep us occupied while he dabbled with his experiments."

"Your grandda lied. The gold is there. I found it the eve Da took me away."

Robbie sat up, her eyes rounded with delighted surprise. "Ye jest."

Reid shook his head and could practically see the wheels turning in her head.

She tapped a finger against her lips, contemplating. "Think ye we should collect it before we pay visit to the crown?"

"If what we have in the keel is not enough to barter with King James, then another coffer of gold doubloons will not make a difference."

His fingers mindlessly settled over his pocket where he kept the gold wedding band Black Dove made for him before they left the Yucatán. At the time, he thought melting down the coin he'd found years past would be symbolic of the love he'd always held for Robbie, but he feared it would mean no more to her than all the other jewels he'd given her at Rukux—the same jewels now lying in a coffer beside the bricks of gold in the keel. She intended to use all of it to save Clan MacGregor.

He threaded his fingers through hers, deciding to wait until she professed her love for him to give her the ring, but part of him wondered if that day would ever come to pass.

"Blessed be the light of day, and the Holy Cross, we

say.

Blessed be the immortal soul, and the Lord who keeps it whole." A dozen rungs up on the mainmast, Duncan announced the dawn of day as was the lad's new duty. Only for a moment did Reid allow himself to miss Henrik. 'Twas selfish really. The Englishman was undoubtedly still enjoying the splendors of his new marriage bed.

S'truth, Reid should be doing the same. His quest to abstain from his conjugal rights became more difficult with each passing day. He wanted for naught more than to take her back to their cabin right now and feel the slide of her body against his own. He'd had the labors of their efforts to hide behind for a fortnight, but the woman was bound to get bored in the coming days, and controlling his desire for her would prove to be nigh impossible.

He pulled Robbie to her feet. "I have to relieve Jean-Pierre at the helm."

She hid a yawn behind her hand. "But ye did not sleep."

"Nay. I did something much more important." He kissed her knuckles. "I made a memory."

23

~ BATTLE OF WILLS ~

Blast the man and his bluidy restraint! 'Twas becoming utter hogwash!

Duncan announced the break of dawn an hour past. A morning sun filled the cabin with yellow light, but Reid, who lie naked in the bed snoring soundly—again—hadn't moved. Robbie knew he was weary. He'd made a show of his exhaustion every eve for nigh a sennight now when he retired from the night watch, but he always seemed to possess the energy to talk. Mostly about foolish things. She'd learned he could curl his tongue and she couldn't. But she could touch the tip of her nose with her tongue and he couldn't. He'd eaten raw monkey brains on a dare when he first arrived in the Yucatán, and she confessed she once ate a worm.

Some eves they conversed on the balcony, some eves at the desk. They debated over what little they recalled from memory regarding Xitali's theories on irrigation and alchemy, but the information she'd painted on the walls of her cavern would have taken months to analyze, much less test.

Most of their conversations took place in bed and into the small hours of night. She suspected he missed his Mopán family, and she was happy to give him the time he needed to lament over leaving those close to him. S'truth, the timing had been perfect as she'd had her menses, but now she was finished and growing frustrated.

After bathing in the basin and using the stone Black Dove insisted she take with her, Robbie coated her skin with sweet-smelling cream and then stood beside the bed.

Reid inhaled a snore and exhaled a whistle. He was oblivious to her presence.

Most days when she awoke, he was either dressed for the day or already manning the helm. However, this morn she'd made *other* arrangements for him. If he'd lost his desire for her, then she was determined he find it again. This day. Now!

But how? Her sigh was audible. She crossed her arms over her small breasts and tapped her toe, recalling the handful of times they'd been intimate. Mayhap she should dress for the occasion. Reid seemed to enjoy undressing her the night of their union.

She slipped into a sleeveless undershift, then tackled the ivory corset, repositioning herself into the stiff cups so her breasts swelled over the ribbing. Next came a pair of cream silk stockings with red bows she tied at her thighs. The garments were simply for affect. If she had her druthers, she'd mount the man where he lay.

The thought alone set her pulse to thudding between her legs, but the dull pounding paled in comparison to the painful ache in her heart. She wanted to be his lover, but more, she wanted to be his twin. She wanted to be the half of the butterfly that fulfilled his dreams.

The woman in my dreams is by no means meek or timid. However, she does possess far more endurance than you. The words he'd spoken at Rukux floated between her ears and set her back on task.

Determined to prove herself a patient lover, she curled the sides of her brushed hair behind her ears and searched the locker. Two days past, she found the love-play trinkets hidden in a leather satchel behind a container of nuts. The man packed them, so he must plan to use them someday, and she could think of no better day than this one.

Uncertain which trinket to use, she grabbed a feather, a red silk scarf, and the heavy gold bracelet. Curious, she traced the butterfly adornment with the pad of her finger and speculated over the purpose of the protruding antennas. She wished she were more experienced, but resolved to trust Reid to guide her.

Another glance inside the satchel set her cheeks afire. The velvet box embossed with leafy vines held her attention.

A woman is particularly sensitive to stimulation in more than one orifice.

The visions forming in her head made the muscles in her duff pinched tight of their own accord. Debating, she pushed air through her nostrils. Holding his interests was imperative.

"Blast it." She muttered beneath her breath and snatched up the false pillicock.

The tips of her ears burned as did the rest of her skin. With arousal or embarrassment she knew not which, but three sennights was far too long for a woman to go without being intimate with her husband. Being open-minded to experimenting was essential, even if those experiments involved her arse.

She tucked the trinkets beneath the bolster on her side of the bed in the event she didn't possess the courage to use them, then peeled back the red silk sheets. Morning's glow cast golden light over Reid's naked body. He lay on his belly, his sumptuous rump a delicious treat for her eyes. A devious grin lifted one side of her mouth.

Maybe she should use the false pillicock on him.

A giggle tickled her throat and nigh ruined her plans, so she swallowed it and crawled atop him. The feather quivered in her trembling hand as she straddled his thighs and traced the lines of his sinewy back. Her nervousness angered her, but she refused to give him just cause to stray from their marriage bed.

Inhaling a breath of courage, she drew the feather's tip through the crevice of his duff. "Are ye awake, husband?"

● ● ●

What the devil!

Reid awoke fully aroused. The tickle on his arse sharpened every muscle in his body. He shook the remnants of sleep from his head and squirmed beneath the weight atop him. A weight he quickly surmised was his wanton wife.

The vixen placed a row of hot kisses down his spine. "'Tis past time for ye to rise from your slumber."

Rise? Oh, he'd risen. His cock felt like a stone beneath him. He drew in a sharp breath filled with a scent sweeter than the ripest fruit in the Yucatán. "What are you about, wife?"

Her pause told him his question had not been well-received. This day was bound to come. S'truth, he was surprised he'd held her at bay this long. He tried to swallow, but his tongue felt like a lump of burnt biscuits.

"I asked Jean-Pierre to man the helm for another few hours." She wiggled provocatively, brushing her bare sex against his backside. "I thought we could...play."

He wasn't strong enough to deny her. He almost wanted to fail in this foolish quest, but a romp between the sheets would not gain him what he most desired. "If you'll get off me, I'd be happy to get the cards."

She huffed. "I've played enough rounds of glic to last me a lifetime." The tickle of the feather disappeared, replaced by the tempting caress of her slender fingers. "S'truth, I had something else in mind." Robbie slid down his thighs, then scraped her teeth over his arse.

His cock grew another inch.

He bucked and flipped onto his back beneath her, carefully clinging to the sheet to hide his arousal. Sunlight filtered through her brushed hair, and a glimpse at her attire thickened his bollocks—brimming breasts, smooth satiny skin, and cream-colored stockings. The beast inside him broke free of its cage. The same beast that attacked her in the jungle.

Their gazes met. Confusion puckered her brow.

"I cannae fathom why ye are hiding from me." She slinked toward him on her hands and knees like the jaguar stalked its prey.

Heart pounding, he licked his lips and inched back. "I amnae hiding."

"Nay?" Her slender brow angled, her head cocked. She tugged on the silk, but he held it tight over his groin. Her emerald eyes flashed with temper just as she jerked the sheet out of his hands to expose his erection.

"Och, woman!" When she grabbed her bolster to

cover his nakedness, his eyeballs nigh popped out of his skull. The trinkets he'd snuck on board lie on display atop the red silk sheet. Sweat instantly gathered at his temples as he watched her slip the cock ring over her fingers.

"I was thinking ye might educate me in the art of love-play." She pulled the corner of her full bottom lip between her teeth.

He gawked at her, eyes growing drier by the second. His entire body begged him to oblige her request, to introduce her to a world filled with carnal delights. He could learn the secrets of her body, discover all the places that made her whimper and moan. The temptation made his toes curl.

"I will be patient," she coerced him and gave the cock ring a spin.

Damn the Devil and his wicked ways! This wasn't what Reid wanted. "We are not yet ready for such intimacies."

He leapt from the bed and rushed behind the partition. Hands shaking, he filled his palms with cool water and splashed his face, but naught could douse the wild fire burning beneath his skin.

"I beg to differ." The hem of her undershift tickled his calves. "'Tis exactly such intimacies that will keep ye from straying from my bed."

Straying from her bed? He turned around to assure her naught was the case, but she acted before he formed words.

She pinned him in place by the hips, then bent low and took the crown of his cock into her soft mouth.

"Oh God!" He reached for the wooden crosspiece overhead to steady himself. His head fell back, his eyes rolled beneath fluttering lids. No man was strong enough to resist such pleasure.

Pull her off! He wove his fingers into her hair, intending to yank her off. Instead, he thrust further into her mouth. The swirl of her tongue was nigh unbearable, but not half as beguiling as the way she looked at him from beneath her cinnamon lashes.

Paralyzed by her deep green gaze, he could do little more than watch her full lips slide over the length of him. His knees weakened. The beam overhead popped in response to his weight.

When her teeth scraped the underside of his cock, he lost all ability to think.

A growl of lust and frustration rumbled deep in his throat. The sound only encouraged her actions. She massaged his taut sac and bobbed.

Up. Down. Up. Down.

Fire rolled through his bollocks like molten steel as her performance escalated.

Faster.

Harder.

"Nay!" He pulled her off him with a loud pop and jerked her upright by her hair. "This is not what I want."

Her eyes pinched tight, but eased back open when he released his vicious hold on her scalp. She wiped her lush lips and looked at him as if he'd just announced intentions to join a monastery. "'Tis what every man wants."

Sharp air scraped through his burning throat. Her confident words narrowed his eyes and caused a vein to pulse at his temple. "Not all men desire the same thing. Ye base your theories on the experiences you shared with one man. One self-absorbed man who used words of love to coax you into his bed."

Her brow wrinkled, and the confusion in her eyes infuriated him all the more. He rushed past her and snatched his breeks off the back of the desk chair. "I swear Eoin ruined you."

"Is that why ye suddenly willnae touch me? Because I am soiled?"

"I am not speaking of your maidenhead." He ripped on his breeks and tied the laces over his swollen cock while searching for words that might explain the complexity of his emotions. "Eoin ruined your spirit. He stole your trust." Reid stuffed his feet into his boots one at a time. "And I fear I will never dig it out of that dark abyss you call a heart."

Undoubtedly hurt by his harsh words, she stared at him, arms hanging loosely at her sides. Her mouth opened, then closed, then opened again, yet she spoke no words of love, made no professions.

"God's legions, woman! Have ye no affections for me at all?"

"Of course I do. Ye are my husband."

He stepped before her and curled his hands around her bare shoulders, wanting to shake her, wanting to drag the words out of her. "Do you ache when you're near me?" He pressed his palm over her heart. "Does it pain you here when we are apart? Would ye die for me?"

She flattened her hand over his, but her expression was an empty mask. "I dinnae know what to say."

Say you love me! He wanted to demand, but began to think Robbie had given all her love to the clan.

Defeated, he sighed heavily, lowered his gaze, and strode toward the door. "I have to relieve Jean-Pierre at the helm." He swung the door open and found Duncan standing on the other side, hand raised for knocking. Cocijo stood at the gromet's back, reminding Reid of the friendship he shared with Jax.

"Give it back." Cocijo gave the laddie a shove of encouragement.

Duncan elbowed his native companion in the ribs, then raised his chin to Reid. "Captain, might I 'ave a word or two?"

"Speak." Reid stood in the doorway, arms crossed, blocking their view of the cabin.

The gromet slipped his hand inside his soiled tunic and retrieved a brick of gold. "'Twas a temptation I couldnae resist at the time, but I've come to my senses and wish to return it."

Reid had little patience for thieves. "I've cared for you since your da died fighting brigands. Why would you steal from me?"

"I dinnae steal it." Duncan's dark eyes widened in abject denial. "That drunkard in your storage chamber gave it to me when I caught him…" The boy didn't finish his statement. He simply stared at the wooden planks of the captain's deck.

'Twas no surprise Eoin had dipped his greedy fingers into the gold. As to why he would use it to barter with Duncan remained a question. "When ye caught him doing *what*?"

"He's got Wild Tigress, Captain. And I fear he's hurting her."

Robbie gasped behind him.

"I'll kill the scabbit." Reid pushed between Duncan and Cocijo, descended the companionway, then dropped down the afthatch. He would tear the bastaird apart if he so much as plucked a hair from Wild Tigress's head.

Reid swiped a lantern from the wall peg and stalked through the narrow hallways toward the storage chamber. A vein in his temple ticked in time with his furious strides. When he kicked the door in, he found the chamber empty.

After circling back, he marched toward the small quarters he'd set Robbie up in on the initial voyage.

He heard them before he reached the door.

Moans, groans, whimpers, none of which sounded

like cries of pain. Eoin wasn't hurting the Jaguar King's daughter, he was rutting with her. This goaded Reid further. He didn't knock. Instead, he flung the door open to find Wild Tigress riding his cousin atop the small stuffed mattress.

Heedless of the interruption, Eoin groaned and continued to pump in and out of the Jaguar King's daughter, but Wild Tigress snapped her head over her shoulder and gawked at Reid with round black eyes.

Reid felt certain the vein in his temple would burst. *First* he would kill Eoin, then he would kill Wild Tigress. "What the devil were you thinking?" he shouted at both of them. "Have ye no regard for *B'alam*? Think ye your people will not miss you?"

"*Ma'!*" Wild Tigress spouted a few more heated words in her native tongue defending her actions.

"Ye ignorant, adder-bitten, foolish woman!—*Ah ma'na'at*," he added in case she didn't understand his meaning even though she spoke his language as well as any one of her sisters.

Eoin curled a thick arm around Wild Tigress's lower back and peeked at Reid beneath fluttering eyelids. "Think ye we can discuss this later, cousin? I'm about to blow."

Fury stabbed the backs of Reid's eyeballs. He took a single step into the chamber. "You, cousin, will keep your cock between your legs and out of the Jaguar King's daughter." Reid filled his fist with Wild Tigress's hair and jerked her off Eoin. "And *you* are going back to *B'alam*."

"Owww!" she squealed and grabbed hold of his wrist, but he ignored her and dragged her up the ladderways, forcing her to run to keep up with his lengthy strides. When she tripped, he hauled her back to her feet with little compassion. She made no effort to hide her nudity, but her favors no longer enticed him. S'truth, she was like a sister to him.

The crew's curious stares were expected, but the state of Wild Tigress's undress wasn't what caused their murmurs. Nay, what garnered their interest was undoubtedly the way he nigh pulled her arm out of the socket heaving her up the companionway to his cabin.

He flung her inside, then kicked the door closed behind him. "Find her something to wear," he demanded of a slack-jawed Robbie.

She obeyed without pause, retrieving garments from a locker. Robbie stepped before a scowling Wild Tigress and pulled a sark over her head. The woman looked completely out of her element, and the way she awkwardly readjusted the garment told him she felt the same.

"What were ye thinking?" Robbie asked quietly as she donned a checked kirtle overtop the sark.

"Eoin claimed me as his woman. We are what you call...husband and wife. *Ma´*?"

Reid snorted, drawing Robbie's attention. They both knew Eoin had fed Wild Tigress full of lies to ease his needs.

Reid wiped sweat from his forehead and paced the small confines of his cabin which was a frustration in itself. He was only capable of taking two thrashing strides before turning back again. "When Jean-Pierre returns to the Yucatán, you are going back with him. Until then, you will stay with Robbie in this cabin."

"*Ma´*. I stay with Eoin," she defended. "He loves me."

Robbie shook her head and cupped Wild Tigress's elbow in a consoling caress. "Men use those words to lay with a woman."

"Not all men, Robbie. There are some who actually mean it."

24

~ FOOLS ~

Not all men, Robbie. There are some who actually mean it. Those words had haunted Robbie since Reid spoke them more than a fortnight earlier.

The ink had dried on the tip of the quill she held in her hand, but she wasn't focused on studying Xitali's theories, nor was she paying attention to Wild Tigress who continued to prattle from the bed as she had the better part of the day.

Robbie twisted a curl round and round her finger and tried to understand the workings of Reid Mac-Gregor's mind.

Do ye ache when you're near me? Does it pain ye here when we are apart? Robbie curled her fist over her heart beneath the wool *arisaid* warming her shoulders. The manner in which she'd been forced to live her life had stolen her ability to *feel*, but she'd known yearning. She'd yearned for food, for warmth, for a family, but never had those wants felt like this. S'truth, the pressure behind her breast grew heavier every day. 'Twas like a disease. An unseen cancer that ate her insides.

"Robbie," Wild Tigress snapped with impatience then sighed heavily.

"Ye were speaking of the cold?" Robbie guessed as that was the topic Wild Tigress complained about most often. "I'll fetch ye another wool."

"*Ma´.*" The woman rolled onto her belly and propped her chin atop her balled fists. "I want to know why you and White Serpent fight."

"We dinnae fight," Robbie defended, wondering why Wild Tigress would make such an accusation.

"He does not come to your bed."

"'Tis because you're in it."

"Not of my choosing." Wild Tigress popped to her feet and snatched up a bit of yellow cheese from a tray Duncan had delivered to the cabin hours earlier. "You should forgive White Serpent."

"Forgive him for what?"

"For leaving you."

Wincing internally, Robbie regretted telling Wild Tigress about her and Reid's past, but they'd been more or less imprisoned in the cabin together. The woman didn't know the whole of it. S'truth, Reid hadn't left her. His da took him away, but part of her held on to those feelings of abandonment.

Wild Tigress swallowed and fidgeted with the ties of her sark. "There is much bitterness inside you."

"Ha. Ye are one to council me on bitterness." In an effort to avoid the discussion, Robbie pushed out of the desk chair and smoothed the wrinkles from the bed.

"I am not bitter." Wild Tigress turned her back to Robbie and stared out the window at a graying sky. "I am jealous," she added quietly.

"Of whom?"

"My sisters." She pivoted at the waist, but kept her

eyes downcast. "And of you."

"Me? Are ye soft in the skull? What do I or any of your sisters have that ye dinnae?"

Wild Tigress brushed her long black mane over her shoulder and traced the window pane with the tip of her finger. "My sisters have been claimed by men who worship them. They have found love."

Robbie snorted again. The woman was so naïve. "And ye think ye found that with Eoin?"

"I please him."

"Ye please his cock."

Wild Tigress glared at her and might have tossed back a retort had the *Obsidian* not pitched off kilter. They both grasped the desk for leverage.

The sound of the capstan clinked in time with approaching footfalls up the companionway just before Reid entered the cabin.

"Good eve, ladies." He paid them little heed as he whisked passed them leaving behind a fresh clean scent. His bronze skin was damp and his tight breeks were tucked into freshly polished black boots. Her perusal of his person led her gaze to his clean-shaven jaw and his hair...

"Ye cut your hair." Robbie noticed after further inspection. Short black waves flipped out at his nape.

"I left it long enough for ye to hold on to." He winked over his shoulder at her and rummaged through the lockers for a clean white *lèine* shirt.

Wild Tigress giggled, but Robbie frowned. "What are ye about?"

"I'm going ashore."

"Ashore?" Robbie poked her head out the cabin door. A crowded port bobbed ships of various sizes and among the copper keels floated men in longboats galore—men who were no doubt rowing ashore to satiate their lust. "Where are we?"

"England." A glint of blue rimmed his irises and matched an indigo surcoat that lay broad across the expanse of his shoulders. Fancy gold buttons adorned the cuffs and a basket sword now hung from his hip. He brushed a piece of lint from his shoulder then splayed his arms out for their approval. "How do I look?"

"You look pleasing. Verra pleasing," Wild Tigress cooed in a breathy voice then drew her tongue over her lips as if she'd just licked a chocolate covered cock.

Damn if he was going ashore alone dressed to the nines like the handsome rogue that he was. The whores would form two lines to ease his needs. "I'm going with ye."

"Nay, ye are not." He curled his fingers around her upper arm, stilling her beside him. "I'm merely going ashore to inquire amongst the gentry on the whereabouts of our king."

"No man dressed like that," she pointed at his attire, "intends to keep company with other men, lest that be his pleasure."

"Ye dinnae trust me."

Robbie growled between clenched teeth.

"Ye are jealous. Admit it."

"Ye are my husband. You're damn right I'm jealous."

A sparkle lit up his flirty eyes as he cupped her duff in one hand and drew her up against him. He weaved his fingers into her hair, leaned her back, and then kissed her—hard. His hot tongue filled her mouth, swirling, teasing, tasting. He hadn't kissed her with so much passion since they left the Yucatán.

Just as she entwined her arms around his neck, he pulled her off, but not before he nipped a final time at her bottom lip. "Fret not, love. I'll return shortly. And dinnae give Jean-Pierre trouble. The man has his trough full keeping Eoin occupied."

He left her on quivering legs to retrieve a pistol and a satchel of coin from the desk drawer. "Have ye any other words for me, *wife?*"

The longer the note of silence held in the air, the lower his shoulders fell. His haughty grin slid to a sad smile.

"Verra well, then." He left on a heavy sigh.

Robbie stared at the closed door for long moments and scrubbed the chill from her arms. His departure left her feeling cold to the marrow in her bones.

"You are a fool." Wild Tigress spouted the insult from the window. "White Serpent gave up everything for you. Yet you deny him what he most desires."

"And what pray tell does White Serpent most desire?"

"Your love."

• • •

Tucked behind a table in a dark corner, Reid tossed back a goblet of English ale and swiped the back of his hand across his mouth. He studied the drunkards through a haze that filled the tippling house, but could hardly complain about the cloud of smoke as he'd been the one to provide every man in attendance with a cigar.

'Twas easy to befriend the English, especially the plebs who couldn't afford to mingle with the aristocrats. All one needed was coin and coin Reid had. So long as he kept buying, the pigeons kept drinking, and the more they drank, the faster their tongues wagged.

"Ho, Wallace." Dudley, one of Reid's newfound friends, fell into the bench seat beside him. "If'n ye seek the king's whereabouts," Dudley pointed toward the entranceway with his pewter mug, "then George Villiers is the man ye need be speakin' to."

Garbed in a gaudy gold doublet topped by a wired collar with lace trim, a man glided with feminine grace toward the bar. His breeks were full and ended at the knee where began purple and ivory striped hose that tucked into heeled shoes tied with wide ribbons. Reid had thought himself fashionable based on his past business dealings, but by his accounts this Villiers gent dressed like a woman. His only masculine qualities were his pointed beard and wide mustache.

"A dandy boy, is he?" Reid eyed his bald drinking companion warily.

"Few are fancier than our Georgie. 'Tis how Queen James like his gentlemen." Dudley drew on his cigar and casually scratched the side of his enormous belly. "Georgie advanced from gentleman of the Bedchamber to master of the Horse, and then knight of the Garter, all over the course of one season. No doubt we'll be calling him Viscount Villiers by spring's end."

Reid cared little about the king's sexual preferences and wanted nothing more than to find a means to seek an audience with His Majesty as quickly as possible. If Villiers was that means, then so be it. "I fail to see why a man with such impressive titles would frequent a place as demeaning as this."

"Georgie likes to play with the plebs. His secrets are safe here." Dudley leaned closer and spoke out of the side of his mouth. "Flatter the man, and you'll have your audience with the king before the cock crows."

A shiver wracked Reid's body at the mention of flattering a man and cocks crowing in the same sentence. He would have much preferred to talk politics and tell lies about bedding women. "I dare say I'm not his preference."

Dudley raised his mug to Reid and winked both eyes in unison. "You're exactly Georgie's preference. The dandy has a taste for brutes."

The barkeep handed Villiers a mug of ale and pointed him in Reid's direction.

"Watch yourself, Wallace," Dudley warned then made as hasty of a retreat as a man of his girth could.

"I understand you seek an audience with my king." Villiers removed the hip-length cloak that had been draped artistically over his left shoulder and handed it to his manservant. After Villiers slid into the bench seat, he dismissed his man with the swoosh of two fingers.

"He is my king as well." Reid retrieved a cigar from his breast pocket and offered it to the dandy, hoping the Mopán's tobacco might douse the floral fragrance that accompanied his person. "Or must I be bedding His Majesty to call him *my* king?"

Villiers accepted the cigar, chuckled sweetly, and then raised his goblet along with his thin brows. "His Majesty is partial to those with a more delicate nature."

Reid opened the door on the candlelbox and offered the flame to Villiers. Once lit, Reid regretted giving the man a cigar for he made a show of slipping the end between his lips—repeatedly. In, then out.

Reid's arse puckered.

Villiers inched closer and Reid suddenly felt trapped. "I, however, have always professed 'the bigger the better.'" The man boldly wrapped his long fingers around Reid's thigh and squeezed.

God's legions! Reid's eyes bulged. He swiftly removed Villiers' hand from his person. "I am a married man."

"As am I." Villiers seemed completely unaffected by Reid's rebuff. The dandy actually giggled. "What did you say your name was?"

"Wallace. Peter Wallace."

"A Scot you say." Villiers ran his gaze over Reid's

physique. "A braw Scot at that. Well then, if we are to be friends, I insist you call me Georgie."

Reid would do just about anything for Robbie, but becoming "friends" with Georgie Villiers was not one of them.

"Now, what brings you to England, Peter Wallace?"

Grateful to be back on topic, Reid reached inside his surcoat, withdrew the single brick of gold he'd brought ashore, and set it atop the table beneath Villiers' nose.

The dandy crossed his legs knee over knee and gave Reid a sidelong glance. "Am I supposed to be impressed? Any thief could melt down a month's worth of stolen loot."

Reid didn't know if the man could be trusted, but relished the idea of gaining an audience with the king this night. Once the proscription against Clan Mac-Gregor was repealed, not only would he have Robbie's trust, but the trust of his clan as well. "I have in my possession a hundred more bricks."

The dandy's aloof demeanor vanished. Villiers stared at Reid, contemplating, then once again feasted his greedy eyes on the gold. "I want to see the rest."

Reid suspected as much. He tucked the gold brick back into his surcoat and rose from the bench seat. The dandy's manservant assisted Villiers to his feet and repositioned his cloak over his shoulder. With his manservant in tow, Villiers followed Reid to the exit.

"Ladies first," Reid clucked, unable to help himself, and held the door wide.

Villiers nodded his thanks with a smile and led them out of the tippling house and onto a planked walkway. The crisp night air tasted like snow, and the moon, though hidden behind a layer of thin clouds, provided light for their stroll across the pier.

Villiers actually skipped to keep up with Reid's strides. "Will you be buying yourself a fiefdom?"

"Nay."

"Then you seek rank within His Majesty's court."

"Nay." Reid withheld his intentions, knowing Villiers would care little about freeing the MacGregors. The only thing Reid needed from Villiers was his position with the king.

His position with the king, the words echoed again in Reid's mind, but this time he laughed silently at the pun.

Villiers squeezed in closer and hooked his arm through Reid's. "If you prove good on your word, I will take you to James's bedchamber this night."

Reid stumbled over a coil of rope, but caught himself before falling flat on his face. He didn't think it was possible, but his cock nearly retracted insides itself.

When they reached the end of the pier, Reid loosened the knot securing the longboat he'd rowed ashore in.

"Where is the rest of the gold?" Villiers asked.

"'Tis on my ship." Reid straightened and pointed into a vast sea of blackness, but the *Obsidian* was not at the end of his fingertip. His arm fell. "My...ship," he repeated slowly and strained his eyes, searching the dark horizon.

His heart slammed against his ribs. His entire being sank to the balls of his feet. "Damn the Devil! Where the hell is my ship?"

25

~ BETRAYAL ~

"Good morrow, ladies."

Daylight blinded Robbie the instant her eyelids slammed open. A breath later, an enormous weight landed in the bed.

"What in the name of Odin?" She twisted to find Eoin draped in his soiled *plaide* between her and Wild Tigress. "Get out of my bed!"

"I dare say ye are in *my* bed." Eoin curled an arm around Wild Tigress who looked all too happy to have her eager lover back in her embrace.

"*Your* bed?" Robbie shook the remnants of sleep from her muddled head as she leapt from the mattress, and snatched her wool *arisaid* out of the desk chair to hide her state of undress.

"Weel, s'truth, 'tis the captain's bed, but I'll promise him another brick of my gold to use his cabin for the remainder of our voyage." Eoin pulled Wild Tigress atop him and splayed his fingers around her thighs beneath her skirt.

The man was a blathering half-wit. He had to be blootered. "Reid is going to kill ye," she warned, eager to see that threat executed, and then reached for the cabin door. The simplest twist of the lever sent the door crashing open. Icy shards of snow pelted her face, stealing her breath.

"I suspect he'd try, if he wasnae still aground."

She barely heard Eoin's retort over the howling gale filling the sails. Naught but acres of water surrounded the *Obsidian*. Horror clutched her gut and panic widened her eyes.

She spun full circle. "Ye left him?"

Eoin's hands stilled on Wild Tigress's duff, a look of feigned innocence lifted his brow. "My cousin was of no further use to me as the terms of our bargain had been met. Ye for the gold," he reminded her. "And I decided *my* gold would better serve me in Scotland."

"That gold is Clan MacGregor's only salvation," Robbie hissed and glared at him. "We are taking it back to the England." She slipped on her brogues all the while trying to calculate how many hours separated her from Reid. They had to go back for him.

She slammed the door behind her and held tight to an ice-slick handrail as she cautiously descended the companionway. Bitter wind sliced into her exposed skin, but the rage boiling in her blood kept her feet moving toward the helm. The deck was nigh barren which came as no surprise. The crew would have sought refuge below deck from such frigid weather.

"Jean-Pierre, ye must turn the *Obsidian* around." She pulled the wool tighter around her shoulders. "Reid isnae aboard."

"Forgive me, *ma chaton*, but I cannot oblige you." The instant Jean-Pierre denied her order Robbie came face to face with a reality that pained her beyond words.

Jean-Pierre had betrayed Reid.

"How could ye do this to him?" Robbie shook her head in disbelief. "Reid is your friend. Your betrayal will crush him."

"Eoin's offer was far too grand to decline."

This couldn't be happening. "Reid gave ye his ship. He saved ye from your king and provided ye with a trade."

"I'll not have need to sell timber with so much gold at my fingertips." The Frenchman looked over her shoulder, bobbed his head a single time, and two crewmen seized her by the arms.

She struggled within their bruising grasp and searched for words that might convince Jean-Pierre he'd made a grave mistake. "Eoin willnae keep his promise. He will never part with the gold."

"Put her with the rest of them." Jean-Pierre tossed a key at one of her captors then pulled his wool scarf back over his face.

"Nay!" Robbie screamed as they dragged her across the main deck, but she was no match for their combined strength. One of the brutes held her while the other unlocked a latch securing an iron lattice gate to the deck.

Robbie dug her heels into the planks, but they raised her off her feet and tossed her in.

A man's knee stuck in her gut. A shoulder caught her in the chin. She grimaced from the blow, but righted herself and then stared into the dark orbs of a dozen Mopán men—Jax and Moon Hawk, as well as those who'd helped her and Reid transport Xitali's gold back to Rukux. Bits of snow clung to their faces and they'd been stripped to their breechcloths. Their sun-baked skin was nigh gray and covered in goose-flesh.

Seeing their strong able bodies reduced to such

frailty brought tears to her eyes, but the sob she so desperately wanted to expel stuck in her throat when her gaze landed on Kante. Propped against the bulkhead, the powerful warrior lie bleeding from a knife wound to his throat. Blood trickled down his meaty chest and into the only fur among them.

Holy Loki! She dropped to her knees and ripped a wide strip of linen from her skirt. "What have they done to ye?"

Kante wasn't a man of many words. S'truth, Robbie had never held a conversation with him. This fact didn't prevent her from tending his wound. She quickly tied the material around his neck and pushed the flecks of snow from his black brow.

"The drunkard wanted to give us gold," Cocijo explained between chattering teeth. "We refused him. The crew came at us with weapons. Kante tried to fight them..." the boy's voice cracked.

"All will be well come the morrow." Robbie lied and wrapped Cocijo inside her wool with her. "Where is Duncan?"

Cocijo looked up through the gate imprisoning them, his eyes glazed with unshed tears.

Robbie shook her head and scrubbed Cocijo's bare arms to warm him. Reid's Mopán kinsmen had been the only ones to remain loyal to him, and they were likely to pay for their loyalty with their lives.

She stared up at the snow spitting through the iron grate. The pain squeezing her heart was nigh unbearable. Disappointment. Regret. Worry. Her face burned with the emotions she tried to hold at bay, but her efforts failed. A single hot tear fell over her temple.

"We are going to die." Cocijo wrapped both arms around Robbie's waist and succumbed to his own despair.

"Nay, Cocijo. We are not going to die." Robbie inhaled air so cold it burned her throat. "White Serpent will save us."

He has to.

• • •

Blood or no, Reid was going to kill Eoin.

Standing on the prow of His Majesty's warship, Reid contemplated how he would do it. He could put a ball of iron in his cousin's gut. He could simply open Eoin's throat with a dagger or mayhap just feed him to the fish. Oh, but naught could be finer than the prospect of wrapping his hands around the bastaird's throat and squeezing the life from him.

Reid's fingertips dug into the forward rail, itching to do the deed. His murderous thoughts were the only thing keeping him sane. The sleet had mesmerized him for hours while the questions played havoc on his mind. Was Robbie safe? Warm? Protected?

Jean-Pierre would watch over her, as would Jax. He'd assured himself of this repeatedly, but he couldn't escape the horrific scenes unraveling inside his head. Eoin beating her...raping her...killing her.

Reid raked his fingers through his hair. "Damn you, Eoin MacGregor. Damn you to the fiery pits of the Underworld," he grumbled between grinding teeth.

That age-old feeling of helplessness resurfaced. He'd been powerless to save her from the Colquhouns all those years ago, the same as he was powerless now.

"Dudley's got biscuits an' broth below deck. Best go fill yer gut." Colonel Whitley leaned over the forward rail and stared at a darkening horizon. Reid could only gather two bits of information about Colonel Whitley's character based on his appearance: he was gray-headed from age not worry as his smooth skin was free of wrinkles. And the scar drawing a line across his chin told Reid the man wasn't afraid to fight.

But could he be trusted? S'truth, the colonel had all but stolen His Majesty's warship for his own personal gain, but few options had presented themselves yestereve when Reid had returned to the tippling house. Dudley had taken Reid aboard the *Dreadnought,* at which point Reid swiftly bartered with Colonel Whitley—passage for gold.

Reid suspected he should be grateful. Riding across England on horseback had been his ulterior option. "My thanks. I'll find Dudley when I can no longer see the horizon."

"'Tis your health." Colonel Whitley shrugged then straightened. "I've charted our speed and by my calculations, we will reach the Isle of Man by dawn. If your ship doesn't appear on the horizon with the sun, then I'll have no choice but to return the *Dreadnought* back to the Crown. His Majesty will have my ass if he discovers I've taken his ship north."

"I suspect King James will forgive you once I lay the gold at his feet."

A slow smile lifted Whitley's chapped lips. "All but three bricks, aye?"

"Catch the *Obsidian* and you'll have your three bricks as promised," Reid reminded the man of the terms of their agreement.

"How many bricks did ye say lay in your keel?"

Greedy bastaird. Reid eyed the man warily. "I dinnae say exactly."

"Might ye be saying now?"

Reid grinned. He couldn't blame the colonel for trying, still, Reid withheld the information.

"Twenty? Fifty bricks?" Colonel Whitley guessed. "Or mayhap you're harboring more than gold." When Reid continued to hold his tongue, the colonel probed further. "Are ye aiding and abetting a refugee?"

"Nay."

"'Tis my duty to protect the *Dreadnought*. Should I be forced to retaliate against a counterattack, I would know if there are nobles aboard before I blast your ship into splinters. Mayhap a prince? A duke?"

The man wasn't going to ease up on his interrogation. Reid checked his emotions and faced the colonel. "My woman is aboard that ship."

"Ahhh..." Enlightenment raised Whitley's brow. "Ye might have mentioned that bit before now. 'Twas nay wonder ye didn't take to our Georgie."

Relief forced breath from Reid's lungs. Mayhap the colonel was a wee bit romantic. He certainly seemed appeased. The waves breaking against the hull filled the long minutes of silence that passed between them.

"Ho!" The boatswain bellowed from the crow's nest.

Reid jerked his gaze back toward the horizon. He squinted. A pin light of yellow blinked where the black sea met a dark gray sky—the binnacle lamp.

'Twas the *Obsidian*. Reid knew it. He could feel it in his gut. She was miles away, but she was there just the same.

"Cor Blimey!" Colonel Whitley smacked Reid on the back. "We'll catch her, Wallace. 'Twill take a few days, but we'll catch your ship and your gold."

And my woman, Reid added mentally, never once taking his eyes off that tiny light of hope.

• • •

Robbie's eyes were open, but blackness surrounded her. Night settled over them like a cloak of foreboding. The snow ceased to fall hours before, and for that she was grateful, but the cold seeped into their prison like icy tentacles.

Her every appendage was frozen, her fingers, her toes, her nose. She hoped the reason Cocijo's teeth no longer clicked was that her wool was keeping him warm, but part of her feared the elements would take the boy's life before the sun rose. Jax and Moon Hawk had wedged her between them, but their bodies were slowly losing heat the same as hers. 'Twas too cold to move, too cold to sleep, and worrying over Reid's well-being only added to her misery.

Jax's warm breath fell over her the side of her face before his words broke through the silence. "White Serpent says the cold in Scotland will freeze a man's blood in his sleep."

"S'truth," Robbie agreed, deciding it best to hide the fact that they hadn't yet reached Scotland.

Moon Hawk voiced a retort first in his language, then he shared that opinion with Robbie. "White Serpent has monkey brains to leave the Yucatán."

Robbie opened her mouth to defend Reid's decision, but Jax's words came quicker. "White Serpent left the Yucatán for his butterfly."

The guilt accompanying Jax's statement gnawed at her gut, but Moon Hawk's snort didn't allow her time to dwell on feelings of regret. The two men bantered in their native tongue, their quarrelsome tone reminding her of Grandda and auld Angus.

"Your family should come live with the Mopán." Moon Hawk's offer was as generous as it was laughable.

The clan would accuse her of madness, the same as they had Calum MacGregor eleven years ago. "Mayhap ye should stay in Scotland and live with the Mac-Gregors."

"*Ma'!* Too cold," Jax and Moon Hawk said in unison.

An image of the beauty that was Scotland solidified behind her eyes. "'Tis not always so cold. We have seasons. Spring turns everything green and wildflowers bloom over the moorland throughout the summer months."

"Our jungle is green everyday, and the flowers bloom always in the Yucatán."

"Scotland has rivers and lochs and—"

"We have the beach." Jax's haughty tone goaded her, but what did these comparisons accomplish?

"My people were born on Scottish soil as were their forefathers before them. My kinsmen have fought and died to sow their seeds in a field of their own. Think ye I would ask them to abandon their birthplace for a land they have no claim in? They would think I'd lost my wit."

"They would think *Itzamná* had delivered them into paradise," Jax quipped, soliciting chuckles from his brothers hiding in the darkness.

"And what of my kinswomen?" Cait and Anice were the first to enter Robbie's mind, but she also thought of the older women, some already past their birthing years. "They will need husbands?"

"We have men. Strong men," another native voiced his opinion, joining in their conversation. "The Mopán are good hunters."

While their women defined beauty, Robbie didn't find the Mopán men the least bit comely, but how did she explain this without offending them. "I fear my kinswomen are a fussy lot. They wouldnae find your hunters...pleasing."

"We are not pleasing?" Jax questioned, incredulous.

"Of course ye are pleasing," she rushed out and reached for a curl to twirl. "But ye have women."

"I have no woman." 'Twas the first words she'd ever heard Kante speak.

How in the name of Odin was she supposed to respond to that? Frustration made her harrumph. They were trapped in the belly of a ship and mayhap going

to die, and they wanted to find mates among her
kinswomen. Though the topic warmed her blood, she
was not going to pay heed to such madness. Mayhap
Reid had been their matchmaker, but she most certainly was not.

She decided on a different approach. "How many of
the Mopán live in the Yucatán?"

They all chimed in, tossing around the names of
their elders, their sons and daughters, and their wom-
en. "Nineteen three times."

"Sixty. You've sixty members in your clan."

"Sixty," Jax agreed. "We had more before we battled
the Kekchí."

"I've nigh one hundred. Nineteen five times," she
clarified in case they didn't understand that Clan
MacGregor was nigh double the size of their tribe.
"And they are not all women. There are men who
would need wives as well, and bairns, and elder folk.
Are ye willing to share your women, and your land,
and your food? Think ye the Jaguar King would welcome so great a number?"

Silence was her answer. She sighed, regretting her
harsh tone. They had been loyal to Reid, and she owed
them her gratitude, not her barbed tongue. "White
Serpent would be humbled by your offer, as am I."

"White Serpent is our brother. It will be difficult to
return to the Yucatán without him." Jax's words stung
like a slap across the face. If they managed to escape
their prison, how were these men going to get home?
Jean-Pierre could no longer be trusted with the task.

Her head fell against the hard wood with a thump.

Jax wrapped his arm around her shoulders and
squeezed. "Fear not. The gods will save us."

Exhaustion stole her ability to argue further.
S'truth, she wanted to weep. Instead, she accepted
Jax's consoling embrace and rest against his chest.

The scent of cacao butter wafted beneath her nose and brought about welcome memories. The Yucatán's hot sun warmed her skin and saliva pooled in her mouth when she thought about the sweetness of the guava fruit. She no longer dreamed about Rannoch. Instead, she pictured herself at Rukux swimming in the pond with Reid. In her head, she watched him play with Oscar and Myah and the Mopán bairns. But now there were others among them. Shane and Bryson played *Harry Hurcheon* with Cocijo, and Cait and Anice giggled with Nikkay and Pepem.

Seconds turned to minutes and before she could stop herself, she began to pair her kin with the Mopán natives; the first of which was Nanna and the Jaguar King.

Her laugh turned into streaming tears of hopelessness that carried her into a restless sleep that couldn't have lasted more than a few hours before a voice called her back to reality.

"Miss Mary."

Robbie's eyes readjusted to the yellow light above her.

"Miss Mary, are ye well?" The small flame inside a candlebox alighted the gromet's face.

"Duncan?" Robbie jerked upright. She reached through the iron lattice to hold the boy's warm hand.

"Is Cocijo hurt?"

Robbie looked down at the laddie nuzzled inside her wool. His eyes opened, and then he smiled. "I am well, my friend."

Robbie blew a breath and offered a silent prayer to her maker before she returned her attention back to Duncan. "Ye must help us."

After a quick check over his shoulder, Duncan pushed a wine sack through the grate. Next came three blankets, one fur, and then a satchel full of garments. "Captain Jean-Pierre has the key."

"Where is he?" She worried over Duncan's safety, but continued to pull the items through the iron latticework and hand them to Jax for distribution.

"He is with the drunkard in the captain's quarters."

"Who is manning the helm?"

"I am." A bit of bravado lifted the boy's tone. Again, he checked over his shoulder. "What would ye have me do?"

"Kante is injured. I need a needle and whisky."

"I'll be back-a-ten." Duncan snatched up the candlebox.

"Wait. What is happening?"

"All will be right, Miss Mary. Fear not. I hung a lantern off the stern to help the captain find us."

"Which captain?"

"*My* captain. There is a ship trailing us. He's comin', Miss Mary."

Reid. Her heart skipped a beat. Her limbs instantly trembled. "Duncan, ye have to slow the ship. Whatever ye do, dinnae let the *Obsidian* lay anchor in Scotland."

26

~ CHOICES ~

Four days. Reid spent four damn days aboard the *Dreadnought* staring at the back of the *Obsidian* as they chased her through the coastal waters of Scotland. His Majesty's warship sailed like she was dragging anchor, but alas, passed the ports of Rosneath, and into the mouth of Gare Loch, he saw his ship emerge through a thick blanket of mist.

As the *Dreadnought* slowly floated alongside the anchored *Obsidian*, the sinking feeling in Reid's gut intensified. The horrifying scenarios he'd played over and over in his head couldn't have prepared him for this.

The binnacle lamp cast a yellow glow over the *Obsidian*. A thin layer of snow coated the rails. The sails were drawn, but what stole the breath from his lungs was the graveyard of bodies littering the main deck.

"God's legions," he whispered and felt certain he would choke on the foreboding strangling him.

Colonel Whitley's crew threw four-hooked grappling

irons over the rails of the *Obsidian* then wrestled the ropes until the two vessels sat abreast—bow to bow, stern to stern. The boatswain dropped a plank atop the rails, and Reid was the first to race across, sword drawn.

He spun a dizzying circle on the main deck, trying to absorb what his eyes didn't want to see. At least two dozen of his crewmen lay in pools of blood. In their hands lay the hilts of their weapons. Hysteria nearly crippled him as he searched the carnage for a mane of red-gold hair.

"Robbie!" He rushed to his cabin, flinging the door wide. Dark red stained the bedding and turned his feet into iron weights. Blood drew a line across the floor and disappeared on the opposite side of the berth. "Oh, Christ! No. No!"

Reid clenched his teeth and slowly crossed the cabin where he found Jean-Pierre lying on his back on the floor, his throat slit from ear to ear. Reid bent to one knee beside the man he'd called friend for more than five years and pushed his eyelids closed over his wide lifeless eyes.

How many have to die to put you back on your throne?

As many as it takes.

Fergus snuck into Reid's mind. Remorse burned his eyes and squeezed his heart. Eoin had already taken so much from him, and Reid knew the scabbit wouldn't stop until he sat at the high table at Kilchurn Castle. He would lead his army into a war that only promised more bloodshed. And for what? Even if they reigned victorious, how long would it be before the Colquhouns prepared a counterattack? With the MacGregor name still under proscription, the clan would never be truly free.

"Reid."

He jerked upright and strode to the open door when he heard her voice. His pulse pounded in his throat, the sound deafening. Fingers poked through the gated hatch in the main deck.

She's alive. She's alive! The words echoed over and over through his head during the time it took him to retrieve an ax from his cabin and cross the main deck. His fear still dominated his relief and wracked his limbs with tremors. Those emotions only intensified when he looked beyond the iron grid imprisoning them. She hugged Cocijo close to her side while his Mopán brothers surrounded her in a protective circle.

Whatever had transpired aboard the *Obsidian*, Reid knew they'd protected her through it all. There were no words great enough to express his gratitude.

"Free us." A cloud of breath accompanied Jax's impatient order.

Reid raised the ax high above his head, and after one swift blow the chain snapped in two. He bent to one knee and pulled Robbie out. She was cold, pale. Dark shadows sat beneath emerald eyes quickly filling with tears.

She frantically searched his person with trembling hands. "Are ye hurt?"

He stared at her, barely able to breathe. "Nay."

She wrapped both arms around his waist and burst into sobs against his chest, showing a weakness he'd never seen.

"All will be right now." His voice cracked over his words and for the briefest of moments, he reveled in her concern for him. He closed his eyes, damning his own tears, and kissed her temple. "Are ye hurt, love?"

She swiped the wetness from her cheeks and shook her head. "But Kante is."

His Mopán brothers assisted one another onto the deck. Kante was the last to rise up out of the hole. A dozen or more sutures tied a wound together along his throat.

"Fear not, White Serpent. I have much years left in me." The behemoth warrior clapped Reid on the back and donned a grin that felt ill-timed given their current predicament.

Reid looked back into their now empty prison. "Where is Wild Tigress?"

"The foolish woman no doubt followed Eoin ashore. She has it in her head that he'll be true to—" Robbie's eyes left his and then widened. "Holy Loki." She intertwined her icy fingers with Reid's and gawked unblinking at the dead layered alongside the rails. "Eoin vied the crew against one another, promising a single brick of gold for every pair of them."

And they'd paid the ultimate price for their greed. He didn't wanting to believe they'd betrayed him, but the gold may have been a temptation they'd been powerless to resist.

"Speaking of gold…" Colonel Whitley offered Reid a half-hearted smile, but the eagerness lifting his cheeks dropped when Robbie looked at him. Whitley's eyes locked on the brand marking her cheek.

She quickly turned away and pulled her hair close to her face. Not once had she hidden her scar in the Yucatán. The brand didn't mean anything there, but here it named her as a member of the most seditious clan in all of Scotland—his clan.

"Cor Blimey!" Colonel Whitney angled his head to study Robbie further. "Tell me I did not come all the way to Scotland for a bluidy MacGregor?"

Reid tucked Robbie behind him. "*I* came for her. *You* came for the gold."

Colonel Whitley's crew now filled the deck of the *Obsidian*, pistols cocked, swords drawn. They outnumbered Reid and his Mopán brothers by thirty, mayhap forty men. 'Twould be suicidal to initiate an attack.

Whitley's eyes narrowed on Reid. "Who are you?"

"I have many names."

"I should like to know them all."

"I am White Serpent, brother to the Mopán people." Reid paused long enough for his brothers to declare kinship in their native tongue. "Like my da, I took the name Peter Wallace because His Majesty's edict against the MacGregor clan forced us to do so."

"What is your real name, man?" The colonel drew his pistol, his tone agitated. Whitley had him by the bollocks, and he wasn't fool enough to offer the man another false name. S'truth, he grew weary of the pretense. He was the son of a leader who'd been fiercely protective of his people, but they'd been blind to his ambitions. Calum MacGregor was not a coward. He was a man of honor, and Reid would have made da proud if King James hadn't stolen his right to lead the clan.

"My name is Reid MacGregor. I am son to Calum MacGregor." He held tight to Robbie, raised his chin, and proclaimed, "I am the Gregarach, the rightful chieftain of Clan MacGregor of Glenstrae, and I have returned to Scotland to free my people from persecution."

Robbie squeezed his arm. 'Twas a small gesture, but it empowered him just the same. Her approval slid through his insides like warm honey.

"I should take you back to England so His Majesty can publicly execute you."

"And in doing so, you would never see a single brick of gold."

Colonel Whitley raised his arm and pointed the tip of his pistol at Reid's head. "I'll assume the gold is no longer on board. You will go ashore and get it. All of it.

I will take care of your ship as well as your woman until you return."

"Nay." Reid struggled to control the fury turning his muscles to iron while Robbie's fingertips dug into his waist. "She means naught to ye."

"'Tis true. But she means everything to ye." A single nod of Whitley's head sent his men into action. They held their weapons on the Mopán men. "Agree to my terms, or I'll give the order to have these savages plucked off one by one."

Reid lunged forward, prepared to attack, but Robbie stepped in front him. "Do as he asks. Please." She glanced over her shoulder.

Anger made him shake. He wanted to jump out of his skin.

Robbie pressed her palm against the back of his head and pulled him close. "Gather the clan, *m'laird*," she whispered in his ear. "I will meet ye ashore." She pressed her lips against the beating pulse beneath his earlobe then drew away.

What did she mean "meet him ashore?" He opened his mouth to argue the point, but she stilled his tongue with a look that demanded he trust her.

Damn her and her constant bravery! He was desperate, and she was bluidy invincible.

Whitley redirected the barrel of his pistol at a longboat. "I can assure ye, your woman will be treated with the same dignity as Queen Anne."

Reid wrapped one arm around Robbie's waist and pointed a warning finger at Whitley. "If you so much as raise your voice to her, I'll hunt you down and kill you."

• • •

'Twas doubtful Colonel Whitley would have tied his queen to the rails of a ship in weather cold enough to

mummify the two dead men lying at Robbie's feet.
Nonetheless, she gave thanks to Mother Nature, for
the sleet and snow had sent the colonel and his crew
below the decks of His Majesty's warship. All save for
half dozen crewmen huddled over a barrel of fire on
the *Dreadnought's* main deck—the same crewmen now
neglecting the colonel's order to guard Robbie and the
Mopán men.

She held her *arisaid* tight around her mouth to
block the icy wind cutting into her face and eyed the
ever-faithful gromet peeking out of the afthatch at
her. With the flick of her hand, Duncan slithered
through the snow, slowly inching his way to her skirts
and into the protective cover of her wool.

"What would ye have me do, Miss Mary?" The instant he cut the ropes around her wrists, the blood
flowed throughout her hands and burned her fingertips.

"Free the others and meet me below deck." Their
predicament didn't allow her the luxury of fretting.
She gripped the dead man to her left by the shoulders
and struggled with his rigid body until he bent at the
waist enough to take her position against the rail. The
man's name escaped her, but she recognized him as
one of Reid's topmen. As she draped her *arisaid* over
his head she wondered at one point in her life had she
become so calloused that the sight of a dead man
didn't make her tremble.

May God have mercy on your soul. She pushed his
eyelids closed.

Not a single tear warmed her eyes, and she blamed
Eoin for making her so apathetic. He stole her passion, her trust, her ability to feel, but Reid had rekin-
dled that fire. He'd taught her that she was a woman
worthy of hopes and dreams. She was a woman worthy of love.

"Miss Mary," Duncan whispered from the afthatch and waved her toward him. A dozen corpses now propped against the rail of the *Obsidian* replacing the Mopán men slithering across the deck.

Robbie shook the thoughts out of her head that would undoubtedly prevent her from tending the task ahead of her and crawled through the slush to the afthatch where she dropped below deck. Guided by Duncan's lantern, they moved quickly through the belly of the *Obsidian* to the galley where they dried themselves by the cooking fire.

Full minutes past before Robbie felt the weight of their eyes on her and realized they awaited her commands.

"What now?" Ever impatient, Jax drew on one of the two wine sacks circling round and reached for a piece of dried meat Duncan had dumped onto the hearth bricks.

Panic seized her momentarily, but she'd spent the small hours working different scenarios over in her head. Dawn would be upon them soon and burn through the mist that concealed them from their captors. They could easily row ashore in one of the longboats, but Robbie had no intention of leaving the *Obsidian* behind. She looked at Jax. "Think ye and Moon Hawk can handle the six guards?"

The same moment she asked the question, Duncan and Cocijo spilled a pile of weaponry onto a small wooden table behind them.

Jax snatched up a clawed dagger and grinned his response.

Robbie didn't relish the idea of more bloodshed, but if a single one of Colonel Whitley's men were given the opportunity to call for help, then her plan would fail. "Kante, think ye can weigh anchor alone?"

The warrior nodded once.

"You three," she selected a few others. "Hoists our sails, then get below deck to man the oars. Cocijo, I want ye to climb into their rigging and cut the ropes to their sails, then position yourself in the *Obsidian's* crow's nest. Duncan will need your eyes."

"And me, Miss Mary?" Duncan eagerly awaited his orders. "What would ye have me do?"

"Ye are going to man the helm." She cupped the boy's chin. "Go back into the firth where the sea splits into a Y. Take the route to the right. There is entry into a cavern at the end of Loch Long. 'Tis impossible to see waterside but, trust me, 'tis there."

Jax spun her around and pushed a blade into her hand. "Be safe." He kissed her forehead. "White Serpent would be angry if we failed to protect his butterfly."

They dispersed and Robbie tightened her grip around the hilt of the dagger. "Someday is upon us, my love," she whispered and let Reid's image fill her with unwavering courage.

27

~ ACCEPTANCE ~

God's legions! He shouldn't have left her. Robbie undoubtedly planned something foolish, something that would likely get her and his Mopán brothers killed. The woman never thought anything through. Reid embraced the anger warming his insides. S'truth, 'twas far more comforting than fretting over her well-being.

His chest and legs burned from the hours he'd spent jogging, but he continued to follow at least nine pairs of footprints through the snow-covered landscape of Glenstrae. Leckie's old estate lie beyond the next rise which explained the hoof prints that had crushed the frozen peat beneath his boots.

A woman's scream sliced through the frigid air from over the knoll.

His heart punched his ribs.

Robbie! He raced up the hillock. Beneath the gray light of dawn, he recognized six of the MacGregors who'd accompanied Eoin on the raid. They taunted

Wild Tigress, tossing her about in a vicious circle. Black strands tangled around her face and neck as she landed on her knees before a man unlacing his breeks.

Reid unsheathed the basket sword at his hip and started down the knoll the same instant the pounding of hoof beats shook the earth.

Lyall led two MacGregors on horseback through the cattle yard from the north, each wielded a weapon.

"Leave off her!" Lyall commanded and pointed the tip of his broadsword at the man demanding Wild Tigress to pleasure him.

The bastaird tucked his cock back into his breeks and backed away without dispute.

Their behavior sickened Reid, and for a moment he considered leaving all of them to the fate of Eoin's war. They didn't deserve Robbie's compassion, nor did they deserve his leadership.

"Wild Tigress." He extended his hand palm up.

Her face snapped toward him. Black eyes overflowed with a torrent of tears as she raced across the snow, tripping once over the unfamiliar kirtle. Arms extended, she catapulted into Reid's embrace. "I want to go back. Take me back. Please."

With a protective arm curled around her waist, Reid glared at Eoin's kinsmen. "What manner of men have ye become?"

"The Gregarach gave her to us," one of the men whined their defense.

"Eoin named me savage whore." Wild Tigress clutched his surcoat and sobbed against his chest.

Hot breath swirled out of Reid's flaring nostrils. Part of him wanted to scold Wild Tigress for her poor judgment, but now was not the time for a tongue-lashing. "This woman is no savage, nor is she a whore. She is the daughter of a king who would use his teeth to castrate ye for the manner in which you treat his kin."

The men cupped their groins and stepped backward.

"Leave your horses," Lyall commanded the two MacGregors accompanying him and dismounted. "Go back to Finglas Gorge. All of ye. Your laird awaits ye." His dark eyes narrowed on the four brutes.

"But we've no horses," again, the same man complained in a whine that grated across Reid's spine.

"Then walk," Lyall snapped. "'Twill give ye time to find your morals."

Wild Tigress eased slightly with their departure, but Scotland's frigid climate sent her relaxed limbs into shivers. Or mayhap 'twas Lyall's approach that made her tremble. S'truth, the man's size and scowl could scare the skin off a snake.

Lyall removed his fur and held it out in offering. He bent at the waist and cautiously studied her. "Did they hurt ye, lass?"

She shook her head in answer, but her grip around Reid's waist became suffocating.

Reid cooed her with soft words in her native tongue and smoothed her black hair. "Fear not. Lyall is much like me."

When Reid set her back to wrap her in the fur, she peeked over her shoulder at the man who'd once been Da's loyal seneschal. "He is good?"

"He used to be."

Lyall stood upright, tore his gaze away from Wild Tigress, and stroked his dark beard. "M'laird said ye and Robbie dinnae return."

"I suspect 'tis obvious that my cousin lied."

"Then where is Robbie?"

"She is being held captive on a warship in the Firth, along with a dozen of my native kinsmen," Reid stated evenly, although the constant fear knotting his stomach had yet to subside.

"Ye left her there!"

"The colonel of His Majesty's navy gave me little choice." Reid didn't need Lyall's accusatory tone. What he needed was his help. "Eoin and at least eight of my crew carried a hundred bricks of gold ashore. I need them back to save her."

"Your men are dead," Lyall announced.

"God's legions." Reid blew a heavy breath, hating himself. The many failures he'd endured the past several days began to weaken him.

"You are not at fault." Wild Tigress touched his forearm. "Eoin poisoned them with his promises, the same as he did me."

"Mount up and tell me exactly what the bluidy hell has happened." Lyall hooked his boot tip into the stirrup and swung a leg over the back of his steed while Reid set a skittish Wild Tigress atop a chestnut-colored roan.

"I'll guide ye," he assured her, knowing the woman had never seen a horse, much less ridden one. He mounted the third steed then followed Lyall into the wood behind the cattle yard. They reached the mouth of the cavern before Reid finished explaining the events of their journey.

"Ye took Robbie to wife then?" Lyall asked Reid, but stared at Wild Tigress.

Reid nodded and circled the wool covering the ring inside his pocket. The task had not been so simple. He'd professed words that made her his wife and claimed her as his woman, but still...he didn't possess her heart. "I love her."

"Ye always did." Lyall's mouth curved into a sad smile behind his beard. However, like Robbie, he didn't dwell on sentiments. He dismounted and then lifted Wild Tigress off her horse before Reid's feet hit the ground. "M'laird plans to invade the stronghold this eve. He's promised every man wielding a weapon monies and a place in the clan for their allegiance. Now that we have the edict from King James, we—"

"The proscription has not been lifted. Eoin stole my ship and the gold before I could gain an audience with the king."

"But m'laird said—"

"Every word Eoin speaks is a lie."

Lyall's movements stuck, his arms went slack. "Then we are not free?"

"Nay."

"Damn his black blood! That lying wretch would kill us all for Kilchurn Castle," Lyall hissed, his hands fisted. "This war is for naught. Even if we won a battle against the Colquhouns, we would still be hunted like dogs."

Wild Tigress side-stepped around him and tucked herself behind Reid's back, but Lyall's anger was exactly what Reid needed. With Lyall on his side, they had a chance at success. "I need the gold to save Robbie, and I suspect the men gathered at Finglas Gorge would return to the Highlands if they discovered there was to be no compensation for their servitude."

"And what becomes of us?"

"We offer Colonel Whitley ten bricks for Robbie's release, as well as the release of my Mopán brothers and my ship. We use the rest to barter with the Laird of Luss for Rannoch or Auchingaich."

Lyall led the way into the cavern chuckling. "And the bastairds would kill us in our sleep as would be their right according to the bluidy king."

Reid pulled in a breath tinged with smoke. "Then we lead the clan north, to the Highlands, and start anew."

"'Tis January. The weak will never survive."

"They would if we took them by ship."

Lyall mulled over that option as he struck a flint and brought a smoldering torch back to flame. A yellow glow illuminated the interior of the cavern and filled Reid's mind with ancient memories.

Bring me the gold, MacGregor, and I'll give ye your kiss. A green-eyed lass bartered with him in his mind's eye, but the mental image was quickly replaced with a picture of Fergus sprawled out on the cavern floor soaking in his own blood.

Age-old fury slithered through Reid's insides. Eoin needed to pay for all his lies.

"M'laird will never agree to such a folly." Lyall's words brought Reid out of his vengeful thoughts, but it was those same memories that reminded him of who he was.

"Eoin is nay longer your laird. I am reclaiming the chieftainship of Clan MacGregor as is my birthright."

The smile lifting Lyall's lips came instantly. "I supported your da and would be honored if ye chose me to act as your seneschal."

Reid reveled in Lyall's loyalty for the briefest of moments before giving the man his first order. "As my trusted advisor of accounts, I ask ye to answer one simple question." Reid raised his chin, commanding respect. "Where is the gold?"

Lyall pivoted and pointed at three lengths of rope disappearing into the loch water. "'Tis all there, save for the brick Eoin took with him to the gorge."

Angst fled Reid's body in the form of a heavy exhale. "My thanks to ye." He bent to one knee, eager to collect the means that would put Robbie back in his arms.

A splashing of water echoed throughout the hollows and halted his actions.

Lyall drew his sword as the tip of a longboat broke

through the blackest area of the cavern.

"Reid." Robbie clutched both sides of the small vessel as Jax rowed toward them.

"God's legions!"

Robbie's smile weakened his knees, yet somehow he managed to steady the longboat and assist her onto the rock floor. "What the devil—"

She wrapped her arms around his neck and silenced his question with a kiss. Their teeth scraped, their tongues twirled. Never had he known such heat. His face burned with emotion, his chest was afire. Her heart pounded against his, fluttering in sync—like the rapid beating of a butterfly's wings.

She pulled away, still beaming that proud grin. "Think ye we were just going to wait to be rescued?"

"How did—"

"We reclaimed the *Obsidian* then rowed up Loch Long. With any luck at all, Colonel Whitley will think we took a different inlet or fled back to sea."

"Ye are insufferable." Reid pulled her back to his mouth, this time he dominated the kiss. Her strength filled him with the vitality he needed to achieve the task ahead of them.

"Welcome home, lass." Lyall's words separated their lips and ended their brief reunion.

"'Tis good to have the earth beneath my feet, even if 'tis covered in bluidy snow." Robbie remained tentative, but Reid wasn't about to deny her the spoils of her homecoming.

A small push was all she needed to embrace Lyall. "'Tis good to find ye well, my friend."

"Ye have been missed."

Robbie eased back into Reid's side and took his hand. "How does Grandda fair? And Nanna and Alana and—"

"Those who cannae fight are at Brack Roody, preparing weaponry for the battle." Lyall stopped her before she could inquire about every member of the clan individually.

"We are *not* going to war," she bit out and narrowed her eyes on Reid as if he'd been the one to call an army down from the Highlands. She grabbed fistfuls of her skirt and ran out of the cavern.

Reid rubbed his temples and sighed.

"Ye should go with her," Lyall suggested. "I'll keep Eoin occupied at the gorge as long as I can while ye get the clan safely aboard your ship."

"Let the MacGregors of Glenstrae know they have a choice; they can follow Eoin or they can follow me."

"And what of us?" Wild Tigress posed the question beside Jax.

With Jean-Pierre and the majority of his crew dead, Reid had no choice but to see his Mopán kinsmen back to the Yucatán himself. With the wind at his back, 'twas still possible to get Jax home before spring. "I will see ye safely home. I give ye my word as your brother."

But first, he had to secure the clan in the Highlands.

● ● ●

The backs of Robbie's thighs burned as she ran up the hillock in ankle-deep snow. Icy mist carried the smell of smoke to her nose and scraped her throat raw with every draw of air. Exhaustion weakened her emotionally, but damned if she would succumb to fits before her loved ones were safe from Eoin and his treacherous war.

She forged down the knoll and into a white valley lined by a forest of barren trees. Water struggled to flow through a near-frozen brook. 'Twas bone-chilling cold, desolate, and lifeless.

Why would anyone give their life to own a sliver of this fruitless land?

She now understood the mental struggles Calum MacGregor must have endured. He'd known the beauty of a land far more bountiful than Glenstrae and the MacGregors had called him a coward when he'd tried to take them there.

A horse nickered behind her, dragging her out of contemplation.

"Your anger cannae help the clan. Ye should prepare words for them." Reid didn't look at her, nor did he debate the subject further before he dropped the reins of a second steed and then spurred his own horse ahead.

His aloof demeanor made her cringe. She wanted to drag him off his horse and rip his damnable self-control out of his chest. "Do ye ever do anything without forethought?"

"It seems every decision I've made as of late has been impulsive and based on emotions." His bleak tone reflected his obvious disapproval.

She mounted the mare and nudged the beast's sides to catch up to him. "Then ye regret your decisions?" This conversation was as much about their relationship as it was about the clan.

"I cannae determine whether or not I have regrets, as I'm still waiting to reap the rewards of my decisions." His gaze remained fixed on the terrain.

Frustrated, she spurred her horse in front of his. "I have no regrets." She finally caught his attention. "Nor will I have them in the future."

"Then you have made decisions of your own?"

She'd spent four days aboard the *Dreadnought,* pondering their options and playing over the outcomes. For once, she knew what she wanted. "I'm going to lead the clan away from here."

"'Tis exactly what Lyall and I decided as well. Now quit fighting me. I am not your enemy." He smacked the hind quarters of his mount with the reins and started out across the valley. "Heed me and prepare your words. The clan believes the proscription has been lifted, and 'twill take more than a demand to get them aboard the *Obsidian*."

Though her insides gave way to relief, she knew the task ahead of her would not be an easy one. If the clan could see Reid the way she did, they wouldn't hesitate to follow him to the ends of the earth.

They rode hard up a twisted mountain pass toward Brack Roody where the air thinned and the smoke blended with the mist to create a wall of fog. Five crofters' huts built side by side created a backdrop to the activity taking place in the yard. She thought she would be overjoyed to be reunited with her people, but what she saw sickened her. Cait and Anice tied bundles of arrows with twine and stacked them in a sled harnessed to an old ox. Beside a fire pit, Shane and a half dozen boys peeled the bark off tree limbs while another six used the strips to form rounds of debris. Brody painted the balls with tar so they would catch flame easily once placed into the catapult. Hundreds of the black shots filled a second sled.

Bent over another fire, Nanna stirred boiling black tar in a copper vat, and Robbie could only assume the bundle tucked into a sling on her back was baby Alana. Behind a group of women building ladders out of tree limbs and twine, she spotted Grandda auld Angus sitting atop a fallen log sharpening spearheads.

She wanted to scream at them, to tell them to stop, but before she could gather words, Reid was at her side assisting her off her mount.

"Control your emotions." He wiped tears from her cheeks she didn't even know were there. "They believe freedom is a battle away. 'Twill be up to ye to prove Eoin a liar."

"How am I to convince them that the man they've been loyal to for more than a decade would step over their corpses to walk through the gates of his bluidy castle?"

Reid cupped her jaw and brushed her cheek with the pad of his thumb. His touch caused a yearning inside her that demanded fulfillment. "Draw the words from your heart, Robbie. They will recognize your love for them, and in the end, ye will be their salvation."

His faith in her gave her hope. She dried her cheeks on the edge of her *arisaid*, swallowed a knot of trepidation, and then started out through the fog across the frozen peat.

"Merciful Moses," Nanna whispered and stopped stirring.

Robbie's presence caused a hush throughout the yard. But no one squealed her name or rushed into her skirts. 'Twas as if she'd returned from the dead.

"Mary-Robena?" Grandda squinted and used his crooked walking stick to push to his feet.

Tremors wracked her limbs as she jogged the final steps to get to the man who'd raised her and taught her everything he knew. She wrapped her arms around his thin frame and thought he'd lost all of the weight she'd gained. His tattered *plaide* smelled of stale smoke and a hint of fish. 'Twas atrocious, but comforting at the same time. "I have missed ye, Grandda."

"Ye foolish slip of a girl. Why did ye return?" He scolded her in a gruff tone even as he kissed the crown of her head.

"We returned to save the clan," Reid answered from behind.

Thick tears spilled over Grandda's sagging eyes as

he set her back and pointed his walking stick at Reid. "Ye should have kept her away."

"The lass is a wee bit obstinate when it comes to the clan." Reid snapped a wink at her, but his attention quickly diverted toward the large group gathering around them.

"Ye are going to save us?" Cait looked up at him through a tangle of blonde curls, and the hope shimmering in her pale blue eyes all but stopped Robbie's heart.

"I am going to try."

"Grandda, dinnae give me trouble when I ask ye to trust me." Robbie positioned herself at Reid's side, showing the clan who she supported. "Your laird has lied to ye. To all of ye. King James's edict against the MacGregor name stands."

Whispers of denial erupted, but she gathered her guts and pressed on. "The war ye prepare for holds no promise. Your laird's arrogance guides our men into battle, but I can assure ye, there will be no victory."

Shane stepped in front of Nanna. "We've an army assembled at Finglas Gorge."

"An army that will disband and return to the Highlands when Lyall informs them that the proscription is still in affect," Reid tossed out which caused upheaval among those who understood what Lyall's actions would cost him.

Grandda cursed beneath his breath and leaned heavily against his walking stick. "Lyall will be banished from the clan and the protection of our laird."

"As will I." Eoin's protection no longer imprisoned Robbie. She laced her fingers through Reid's and inhaled his strength. "I renounce Eoin MacGregor as my laird and pledge fealty to my husband and the rightful chieftain of the MacGregors of Glenstrae." She looked into the beautiful face of the man she trusted with her life and with her heart.

Tears glittered in his silver eyes, but he blinked them away and addressed his clan, "I will protect all of ye—the young and old, the weak and lame. Give me your loyalty and your trust, and I will lead ye to a place that knows no war."

"And what of our men?" A woman asked from the outer circle.

"The MacGregors of Glenstrae have been given the option to follow me or to remain loyal to my cousin and his cause. 'Tis my hope that they will follow Lyall to my ship which awaits us at the tip of Loch Long."

Silence ensued.

Robbie understood their fear, but she only needed one of them to start the chain. "Are ye with us?" She directed her question at Grandda, but Nanna was the first to speak out.

"I am with ye. I'll not make the same mistake twice in this lifetime."

"We are with ye." Cait and Anice looked at auld Angus. "We are with them, right, Grandpapa?"

Robbie's bladder nigh emptied while she waited impatiently for the elder's response.

"Where will we go?" Auld Angus asked through his wrinkled scowl.

"To the Highlands, to start anew," Reid answered.

"Aye, then. We are with ye," auld Angus agreed without pause as did Grandda, and the chain began…

"To the Highlands!" someone cheered.

"To the Highlands," the clan acclaimed their approval ten voices at a time, after which, Reid began directing the members with tasks.

"I want ye laddies to empty the sleds and layer the beds with fur. Assist the elders into the back and then fill every nook with the youngest bairns. Shane, are there more horses?"

"There are four mares harnessed to the catapult 'round back."

"Robbie, help the women gather their personal effects if they have any. And smile. Ye have everything ye wanted." Reid pressed his lips against her temple, then started out behind the crofters' huts with a lift in his step.

But Robbie didn't share his good cheer. She stared at the ground in stunned silence while everyone bustled around her.

She had no desire to go to the Highlands.

28

~ RETRIBUTION ~

The only thing that stopped Robbie from telling the clan she wanted to take them to the Yucatán was their willingness to board the *Obsidian*.

Jax, Moon Hawk, and Kante had awaited them at the cavern with three longboats. In less than an hour, they managed to safely ferry fifty-seven of their kinsfolk to the ship. Only a few women were hesitant to leave their husbands, but quickly followed suit when Lyall returned to the cavern with all the MacGregors of Glenstrae save for six men. The same six men who'd been loyal to Eoin since the day he'd taken over as chieftain. The same six men who'd accompanied Eoin on the raids. And it was undoubtedly these same six men who'd led Eoin to the cavern.

They dismounted outside the entrance and the sounds of their approaching footfalls all but stopped Robbie's heart.

"Make haste, and ready the ship," Reid ordered Moon Hawk and pushed the last of their kinsfolk away from the rock ledge.

"Holy Christ!" Eoin stormed into the cavern. He unsheathed his sword and narrowed his gaze on Lyall. "What is this?"

Never had she seen Eoin so enraged—lips tightened, nostrils flaring, muscles flexed. Torchlight cast shadows over his seething face, darkening the slits of his eyes.

"I swear on the cross, I'll gut ye down, cousin." A thick vein bulged in Eoin's forearm as he threatened Reid with the tip of his sword. "Ye cannae just take my clan."

"Get Robbie into the boat," Reid calmly ordered Lyall then unsheathed the basket sword at his hip. "They no longer wish to feed your appetite for bloodshed."

Lyall pushed Robbie into the last longboat with Jax, then climbed in behind her. She protested the separation and struggled back to the side, but Lyall wrapped both arms around her middle and pinned her in place.

"We had a deal." Eoin tried to circle Reid, but he was smart enough not to let the scut maneuver him into his cronies.

"You breached our agreement when ye stole my ship." Reid scrapped the steel of his blade against Eoin's and pushed him back two steps. His men backed up as well.

The boat rocked as Robbie fought Lyall's hold. "Get in the boat, please," she begged Reid, terrified the dreams he'd awakened inside her would all be lost at the end of Eoin's blade. "He is not worth it."

Eoin's icy glare froze her blood. "Ye have your whore. Where is my gold?"

Instead of inching his way toward the boat, Reid advanced on Eoin with a roar. Their swords clashed, once, twice, three times, ringing off the walls of the cavern. Reid's footing was sharp, but Eoin's wrath made him a deadly opponent.

Robbie's toes curled inside her brogues, and the tears filling her eyes nigh blinded her from seeing the fight. She screamed as Eoin raised his weapon high over his head and then plunged it in a downward arc.

Reid blocked the blow.

A battle of strengths ensued—blade pressed against blade, eyes locked in a war of wills. Then Reid reached between the connected steel and wrapped his fingers around Eoin's throat.

He squeezed. His arms shook.

The choking noise gurgling out of Eoin's throat had Robbie holding her breath. She gripped the edge of the boat.

Reid pushed Eoin hard enough to land the bastaird onto his duff at his men's boot tips. He sucked in large gulps, refilling his lungs with the air Reid had stolen from him.

"Ye want the gold?" Reid gripped the hilt of his sword and raised the weapon high above his head. "Then you'll have to dive for it." And with these words he slammed the sharp edge of his weapon downward, snapping the three ropes hanging over the rock ledge in a single blow.

"Nay! Nay, ye fool!" Eoin scrambled toward the edge on his hands and knees and filled his palms with the frayed twine.

Reid jumped into the longboat, pushing them away from the edge. "Row, Jax. Row!"

"Ye bluidy idiot!" In a fit of rage, Eoin retrieved his sword and threw it at them, but the weapon sank into the loch water along with his precious gold. "I'll find ye. All of ye. I'll hunt ye down in the Highlands and see ye pay for your treachery."

"I should have killed him." Reid pulled Robbie out of

Lyall's arms and crushed her against his chest.

She returned his embrace with a fierce hug, but her eyes remained fixed on Eoin. She memorized the complete look of failure twisting his face. A feeling of vindication straightened her spine. "The fate ye leave him with is worse than death. He has nothing. No chieftainship to hide behind. No clan to feed his arrogance. His fear of the water will prevent him from ever acquiring the gold to fund his war. 'Tis all the vengeance I need for what he's taken from me."

Lyall sat heavily atop a cross bench and scrubbed his beard. "Eoin MacGregor is many things, but he is far from ignorant. 'Tis true, he willnae dive, but he is more than capable of fishing those empty nets out of the loch."

"Empty?" Robbie looked at Reid for clarification.

"Jax, Moon Hawk, and the others transported the gold back aboard the *Obsidian* while we collected the clan from Brack Roody."

A tickle flittered inside her—part wickedness, part jubilation. "We have the gold." She all but giggled the words.

"We have the gold," Reid parroted, but in a somber tone that squashed her merriment. "And when Eoin discovers the nets are empty, I suspect he'll make good on his promise to hunt us down in the Highlands."

• • •

A poking finger repeatedly stabbed the back of Robbie's head. She awoke with a start and jerked upright from the desktop. Pain zinged instantly through her lower back and morning light crept beneath eyelids that refused to open.

"Are we there yet?" Cait stood beside the desk cradling a white ermine Robbie hadn't known she'd snuck aboard. The beastie's tail coiled round Cait's thin forearm and licked her fingers. "Snowball is hungry."

Anice sat up in Reid's bed, hugged her legs, and propped her chin atop her knees. "Will there be food where we are going?"

"Of course, angel." A tug instantly pulled at Robbie's heart. She knew what it was like to awaken hungry, but had learned at an early age no matter how much begging one did, if the food wasn't there, it wasn't there. She rubbed the kink from her neck and carefully stepped over four women sleeping atop furs lining the floor. She knelt beside the berth and tucked a blonde lock behind the girl's ear which uncovered the innocent's scarred cheek. "Are ye hungry?"

Anice nodded and the five other young girls sharing the bed bobbed their heads as well.

"I would sacrifice my little toe for a *chikoo*." Wild Tigress sat cross-legged on the floor in the corner where she'd held baby Alana throughout the night while Nanna snored on the settee.

"What is a *chikoo*?" Cait settled into a spot in front of Wild Tigress and mimicked her position. Anice climbed out of the bed, brogues on, and plopped down beside her sister. The other girls followed suit.

Wild Tigress smiled at her tiny audience. "A *chikoo* is a brown fruit. It grows from the sapodilla tree." Her eyelids slid shut. "It is juicy and sweet and warmed by the sun."

Cait licked her cracked lips. "I should like to try a *chikoo*."

"As would I," Lyall's aunt murmured from the floor.

"Then you should come to the Mopán. I will fill a basket for each of you. We have custard apples and guava and..." Wild Tigress held them rapt with descriptions of the Yucatán and all its decadent fruits. Not one of them paid heed to the tears falling over Robbie's cheeks, nor did they give notice to her hasty exit out of the cabin.

Exhaustion must have stolen her wits. She scrubbed her cheeks and swallowed the sob choking her. After pulling the wool of her *arisaid* tight around her, she gripped the cold rails of the captain's deck and scanned the land hugging both sides of the ship. The canvas overhead swelled, pushing them toward the outlet to the sea splayed out in front of them—the Highlands to the north, the Yucatán to the south.

I could be your king and Rukux your castle.

Was she selfish to want to go south? Would she be giving in to romantic ideals and foolishness to want to spend the remainder of her days in the Yucatán loving Reid?

"Mary-Robena," Grandda bellowed from the helm, pulling her out of her hopeless thoughts.

She gathered her senses, picked up her skirts, and descended the companionway. Draped in furs, Jax, Moon Hawk, and Lyall stood opposite Grandda and Duncan at the tiller, all five of them wore an odd smirk dripping with mischief.

"Good morrow, Miss Mary." Duncan's smirk grew into an even broader smile.

"Good morrow, Duncan," she returned congenially, but studied the odd gathering of men. Then she recognized Grandda's silver flask in Jax's hand just before he passed it to Lyall. Well, that explained their vacant expressions. She narrowed a scolding eye on Grandda. "Think ye it is a wee bit early for spirits?"

"Ack. Hold your wheesht, lassie!" Grandda's grin pushed rows of wrinkles up half his furry cheeks. "Men drink whisky when they are in deliberation."

"And what, pray tell, are ye deliberating?" Why did she feel like a lone hen in a den of foxes?

"Our course." Grandda pointed a crooked finger toward the outlet that was approaching ever quickly.

"Which way would ye go, Robbie?" Lyall asked with heavy eyes and tipped the flask to his lips.

"'Tis of no import which way I would go." A quick scan of the deck found no sign of Reid. "Your laird and captain has set the course for the Highlands. I will abide by this decision as I have vowed to honor and respect him as my lord and husband."

Jax hooted as did Moon Hawk, and Grandda tapped his walking stick atop the planks. Even Duncan gave her an incredulous look.

"And what of these men?" Lyall gestured toward the Mopán men huddled in furs along the rails. "They need to return to their homelands, to their families. We are indebted to them for their assistance."

Jax's face took on an over-dramatized expression. "Jax made a promise to Black Dove. The woman will have my head if I miss the birth."

Robbie felt her eyes widen. They weren't seriously contemplating making this decision without Reid.

"Think ye we should go south, Miss Mary?" Duncan asked her point blank from the center of their circle, his hand held the tiller steady.

Her breathing hitched, her heart beat wildly in her chest. What in the name of Odin were they thinking? "Ye all are blootered." She snatched the flask out of Lyall's hand and capped it. "Ye accused Calum Mac-Gregor of madness for wanting to take ye to the Yucatán years passed. What is different now?"

"We were protected by the stronghold then," Grandda pointed out. "Our options have changed."

"Blast it! Ye cannae make such decisions without your laird." She frantically searched the decks for her husband. "Where is he?"

"I suspect he is sleeping," Grandda answered. "The lad was up half the night rowing."

"Then wake him!" She punched her fists into her

hips.

"Miss Mary?" Duncan prodded her for a decision. The tree-covered bluffs came an end. Land had run out and the choice was upon them. "North or south?"

South. She wanted to scream, but stopped herself from making a hasty decision. "Draw the sails. I'll not—"

"Nok ol!" Cocijo bellowed from the crow's nest and pointed north. All heads turned over the starboard rail. From behind the bluff, the *Dreadnought* slid into view. The hatches in the hull flew open, and the noses of a dozen black cannons extended.

"Holy Loki," Robbie whispered just as a whirling hiss arced toward their starboard side.

An explosion shook the *Obsidian.*

"Go south, Duncan! South!" Robbie ordered and grabbed the rim of a barrel of sand to steady herself against a second blast.

• • •

"What the devil?" Reid bolted upright and gripped the edge of the wooden bench vibrating beneath him. The sound of cannon fire sent him racing up the ladderways to the main deck. Chaos engulfed the ship. Jax bellowed orders to his Mopán kinsmen swarming through the rigging while Robbie rushed the women and children out of the captain's quarters. Arms filled with bairns, the MacGregor men hastened the clan toward the bow of the ship.

The pulse of a single heartbeat was all the more time Reid had to fret over their well-being before another blast threw the *Obsidian* off kilter.

He leaned over the larboard side and caught sight of the *Dreadnought.* Wiping sea spray out of his eyes, he swiveled on his boot heel and caught Cocijo's upper arm to still his flight. "Gather three bricks of gold from the keel and a satchel. Make haste!"

The Mopán laddie dropped down the afthatch without question.

The cries of a squalling babe knifed through Reid's ears as he tipped a water barrel on its side.

"The *Dreadnought* came out of no where." Robbie dropped to her knees beside him and helped him hold the barrel while the contents drained.

"Is anyone injured?" He retrieved a blade from his boot to cut a length of rope hanging down from the yardarm.

"Nay." With damp eyes and an expression verging on a sob, she craned her head over her shoulder to check the gathering at the prow. "But they are frightened."

"I'll protect them, love," he assured her just as Cocijo returned with the gold.

"Fire!" Colonel Whitley's order commenced another blast.

"God's legions!" Reid threw himself atop Robbie and pulled Cocijo into their huddle as icy spray arced over the stern of the ship. The boy muttered an expletive, but quickly set them back on task. They tied the satchel of bricks to the barrel and then hoisted it all over the rail.

Reid climbed a dozen rungs on the main mast and watched Colonel Whitley's men haul the barrel and satchel up the side of their hull. He prayed the man would be content with the payment and turn back.

Seconds turned to minutes, and the tight anxiety eased out of his muscles when no more threatening shots were fired. Though they began to pull away from the *Dreadnought*, the warship continued to sail in the white foam of their wake. Only then did Reid study the land sitting on the larboard side of the *Obsidian*.

They were headed south.

Why the devil were they headed south?

He jumped to the deck where the clan gathered in a loose circle around him. "Who gave the order to alter our course?"

Not one person, man nor woman, answered, but they all looked at Robbie.

He didn't want to believe that she'd defied him. However, it would be consistent with her nature to do so. "Duncan, who gave the order to go south?" Reid asked the gromet, but his eyes never left his wife who was now backing up toward the starboard rail.

"Miss Mary gave the order, Captain," Duncan mumbled what Reid already knew.

The long rope of his patience had reached the frayed end. One eye twitched, while the other narrowed on her.

She shook her head vehemently and pointed at Lyall and Argyle. "'Twas their decision."

Lyall scoffed. "'Twas Jax who suggested it."

Jax denied the accusation in his native tongue then passed the blame to Moon Hawk, who swiftly returned it full-circle back to Robbie.

"God's legions! What have ye done, woman?" Reid latched onto her wrist and dragged her behind him across the deck. "How many times must I tell you not to make decisions in haste?"

"I told them to wake ye, but—"

"But nothing! Be still your tongue." He swore he pulled her arm out of the socket heaving her up the companionway. Once inside the cabin, he released her and slammed the door behind them. He needed time to think, to burn off this anger. He needed nuts. He needed to pace. Without a doubt Robbie intended to return to England to pursue the meeting with King James. The idea alone sent a vein pulsing beneath his eye. He growled his frustration.

"Reid, control your temper."

"Ye are completely adder-bitten." He ripped his fingers through his hair. "Did ye give any forethought at all to the consequences? If we return to England, ye will be delivering the MacGregors straight into the king's hands for execution."

He felt the gentle slide of her hand across his back before she spoke. "I dinnae want to go to England, nor do I wish to go to the Highlands."

He angled his chin over his shoulder. "Eoin's threats dinnae frighten me. I'm no coward."

"Reid," she stepped in front of him and cupped his unshaven jaw. Thick tears pooled in her emerald eyes. She drew a shaky breath. "I love ye, and I—"

"Nay!" He scowled at her and seized her wrist. Denial sat on his shoulder like an ugly troll. "How dare ye. How dare ye!" he yelled. "You know how long I've awaited those words. Dinnae use my affections for you to gain my approval."

Her brow stitched tight in the middle. A swift tug freed her hands from his grip. She pushed him against the bulkhead with shocking strength. "I am not Eoin. If I tell ye that I love ye, 'tis because I speak the truth."

Warm air passed through his clenched teeth. He straightened his shoulders and wound his fingers through her thick hair, forcing her to face him. "Ye are all about bargains, Robbie. Ye always have been. You bartered a kiss for gold when ye were but a lass. You gave yourself to me for my vow to lead the clan. And now ye stand before me using words of love to attain your next goal. What do ye want now, Robbie?"

Her eyes squeezed tight, and the tears flowed in earnest over her cheeks. As betrayed as he felt by her words, he couldn't bear the pain of her tears. He loosened his vicious hold on her scalp and awaited her answer.

"What I feel inside me speaks louder than any words." Robbie hooked her fingers over his inner elbows and stepped close. "I ache for a life with ye. When I dream, I dream of us in the water. When I wake, I think of a gentle man who tames wild beasts and teaches games to bairns that are not his own. I think of the man who is a matchmaker and protective brother of his people."

He stared at her, shocked by her words. The icy skepticism guarding his heart melted with every beat of his heart.

She leaned in and pressed her soft lips to the beating pulse beneath his ear. "I want to be your butterfly and call ye husband for forever."

His heart swelled, his face burned. Emotions attacked his every nerve. He wanted to rush onto the captain's deck and inform the world that his woman loved him. Instead, he reached inside his surcoat with a trembling hand and withdrew the gold ring tucked inside his pocket. "And I want to call ye wife for forever." He forced the ring onto her finger and then kissed her palm. "I have loved ye since ye were a lass. I love ye now. And on the morrow, I intend to fall in love with ye all over again." He held her face between his hands and descended on her smile with a ferocity that matched the hurricane of bliss whirling inside him.

This was the kiss he'd waited for the whole of his life, and never could he have imagined how sweet it would taste. "I am the victor this day!" he shouted and raised her off the floor.

She squealed and curled her limbs around him when he twirled her in dizzying circles. The joyous sound of her laughter added to his triumph and made him feel like a king who'd conquered a country. "How should we celebrate?"

She bathed his face with a foray of kisses. "I'm thinking a small *intimate* gathering should suffice. Attire is optional."

He squeezed her backside and was certain every drop of blood in his body surged straight to his groin. His muscles stiffened, pinning him place.

The vixen smiled against his neck and bit his earlobe. "It could be a long while before we have the cabin to ourselves again."

Without thought, he tossed her atop the berth and made quick work of removing his boots. "Then mayhap we should make love twice."

"Aye. 'Tis a good plan." Robbie removed her kirtle and sark in a single pull, then knelt in front of him—brogues still on—and fought the laces of his breeks.

Her eagerness ignited his own raw urgency—a desire heightened by her declaration of love. Wracked by blinding need, he pushed her back into the bedding, peeled off his breeks, then dove into the berth atop her.

She giggled and grabbed fistfuls of his hair when he descended on her breast and nipped the erect nipple. He intended to pleasure her from head to toe, but his lascivious wife wrestled him for the top position.

She won.

Waves of red-gold spilled over his chest, tickling him, adding to the sensations vibrating throughout his body. She held his wrists to the mattress and stared at him with shimmering eyes. "Ye make me happy."

While her words lacked eloquence, they filled him with a pride that split his lips into a wide grin. "I could make you happier if ye had time for a seduction."

She pulled her bottom lip between her teeth, rose up, and then sank atop his erection. Her eyelids fell shut. Her head tipped back.

They moaned in unison.

"Ye can seduce me when we get home." She leaned forward, covered his mouth with her own, and thrust her hips up and down like a wild animal in heat.

His need spiraled. He circled her waist with his hands, needing an anchor, but she slammed her full weight atop him. The head of his cock touched the wall of her womb.

She cried out.

Her inner walls squeezed his pulsing member. Her entire body quivered when she reached an unexpectedly quick climax. It was only after her attack on his person slid to a steady to and fro glide, did he piece together her words. "What home?"

"Rukux," she said simply and continued to ride him, slower now. "I cannae wait to see the look on Grandda's face when he sees the work-house ye built for him."

While his mind tried to comprehend her words, his cock told him to hold his wheesht and seek his release. "What do—"

She pulled his nipples hard. Sparks flickered beneath his skin. His bollocks burned. The slap-slap of flesh pulsed through his ears and nigh stole his ability to think. Desperate to control their love-making, he grabbed her hips and twisted.

They rolled off the bed and landed with a thud atop a fur.

Her husky laugh shifted to a moan beneath him as he continued to pump hard, fast, deep. She wrapped her legs around his waist. "Oh, Reid...Reid!" She pulled his hair. "Reid!"

He exploded inside her when she reached a second orgasm.

All went white. Then black veins forked together behind his eyes forming the shape of a butterfly's wing. 'Twas dreamlike. Surreal. Robbie's heart beat against his own in sync as if one in harmony.

"Rukux," he whispered and drifted away.

He couldn't say for certain how long he laid there hypnotized by the perfect rhythm, but when he managed to slip out of the dream world, he awoke with Robbie atop him again. He sat up and braced his back against the berth. She followed, limp and sated, but unwilling to separate herself from his partially depleted cock.

He pushed her hair from her face and found her smiling. "Robbie, tell me again why we are going south?"

"We are going back to the Yucatán. To return Wild Tigress and your Mopán brothers to their homelands. I dinnae act in haste. I've thought through all the options," she rushed on.

"Did ye come to this decision on your own?"

"Nay. S'truth, 'twas Jax and Moon Hawk who planted the idea in my head while we were in captivity aboard the *Dreadnought*. Then I found them deliberating over the matter with Grandda and Lyall this morn just before the attack."

"And they were in agreement?"

She nodded, her eyes flashed with the excitement of a child. "Once the MacGregors see the wonder of the Yucatán, they will never want to leave. They are hard working. They can build homes with the timber ye have dried in the barn. We can live as one clan. Together. 'Twas what your da wanted."

It seemed she'd actually thought this one through. "Ye should have discussed this with me." He stroked the curve of her waist.

"I am discussing it with ye now." She brushed his nose innocently and drew on his lips, once, twice. "I want to go home. To Rukux." She rubbed her slick breasts over his chest. "Is it not what ye want as well?"

"Ye know it is." He tried to think about the consequences, but she once again stole his ability to think when she rotated her hips.

He became fully erect inside her.

"Then there is naught more to say on the subject." She wiggled and thrust.

God's legions! She was going to kill him.

Thrust.

Oh, but he would die a verra happy man.

"Now, say something romantic, and I promise to go slow this time." Eyes closed, she rocked atop him, sliding her heated mons over his sensitive manhood.

"Ye are insufferable." The flat of his hand walloped her arse with a loud smack, but only encouraged her movements. He gave himself over to his wife's antics, but couldn't quite escape his worries.

What if the Jaguar King turned them away?

29

~ SOMEDAY ~

Trembling with anticipation, Robbie stood in front of Reid and the entire MacGregor clan under the Yucatán's blazing sun and stared at the Mopán people gathering opposite them on the beach. The wave frothing over her bare feet cooled the hot sand burning her soles, but did naught to untie the nerves knotting in her gut.

"Dinnae get your hopes up, love." Reid set the strap of her sleeveless undershift back atop her sun-baked shoulder and kissed her temple. "'Tis much ye ask of the Jaguar King."

Reid had warned her repeatedly that all might not go according to plan. They'd discussed alternate options with the MacGregor kinsfolk. They had the gold and could build a life for the clan in Cristóbal Colón's New World, but it was here where she wanted to spend her days, for it was here where Reid's heart beat the strongest.

The longboats that had ferried the MacGregors to

the beach banged against one another along the shore, but didn't drown out the excited screams gaining strength in the jungle. Stream Dancer burst through the green foliage first, followed by Black Dove and a squealing Yellow Peacock. After Moon Hawk and Jax reunited with their loved ones, Reid stepped to Robbie's side to await their greeting, but Jax snatched up Yellow Peacock when she tried to run toward him.

Robbie's heart clenched. Every worry that had plagued her on their journey surged to the forefront of her mind. What if the Mopán people didn't accept them? What if the Jaguar King sent them away? She couldn't bear to watch Reid leave his family behind a second time, nor did she possess the strength to carry the weight lowering his shoulders now. She swallowed hard and squeezed his hand. "Go to them. They are your people."

"You and the MacGregors are my people as well, and I will never abandon you or them again."

She could have easily given herself over to sobs, but a commotion drew her attention back to the Mopán people. A line of warriors carrying spears separated the natives into two groups. Robbie spotted the Jaguar King's colorful headdress before he stepped into the aisle. *B'alam's* scowl alone would send the bravest of men into the folds of their mams' skirts.

Whispers grew in volume behind Robbie. A bout of dizziness made her sway.

"Hold your wheesht and prepare yourselves!" Grandda's order ceased their comments immediately.

Reid set his hand at the base of her back. "Think ye they will remember all that we've taught them?"

She peeked over her shoulder and watched the MacGregors line up for presentation. "Aye," was all she said, but secretly prayed her kinsfolk showed *B'alam* the respect he deserved.

She squared her shoulders as the Jaguar King walked tall through his people, but Wild Tigress stepped before her da and stopped his approach. She bowed first, then launched into a diatribe of heated words in their native tongue.

"Wild Tigress is telling him all that has happened," Reid translated, but Robbie guessed there was more to their conversation besides a recitation of events when the woman turned and pointed at Lyall standing to Grandda's right.

Reid leaned into Robbie's ear. "The man is smitten with her ye know."

The smile tugging at the corners of her lips was most welcome. S'truth, Lyall had been fawning over the Jaguar King's daughter the whole of their voyage. "Lyall will make her a good match if given the chance to prove himself."

B'alam quieted Wild Tigress with a final grunt then crossed the white sand separating the clans.

The howler monkeys filled the silence with their high-pitched shrieks and made Robbie twitch with an anxiety than grew tenfold when the Jaguar King positioned himself in front of her instead of Reid.

"You have returned." *B'alam* cocked his head to study the MacGregors aligned at her back. "And you brought your family."

Robbie swallowed her pulse and bowed reverently before the man who could crush her dreams with a few simple words. "I speak on behalf of your white son when I beg ye to consider uniting our families as one clan under your rule."

The Jaguar King raised Robbie upright when he took her hand and eyed her wedding band. "You accepted White Serpent as your only husband?"

"I did. He is my twin."

The Jaguar King pressed the side of his hand

against her breastbone. "The Rukux beats strong inside you."

A cool tear fell over her cheek. "But White Serpent's heart belongs here with ye and your people."

The Jaguar King clasped Reid's hand between their chests. "You and your woman will always have a place here, my son."

Reid dipped his head in thanks. "And what of the rest of my people?"

B'alam blew a heavy breath and raised his gaze over Robbie's head. "How many?"

"Eighty-seven," Reid answered.

"Are they free of disease?"

Reid extended his hand toward the MacGregors, inviting the Jaguar King's inspection, then held tight to Robbie's wrist when she started to follow. "Patience, love."

"Cocijo, bring the basket," The Jaguar King bellowed his order when the MacGregors held out their meager offerings. The Mopán laddie collected painted rocks, woven sashes, necklaces made of fish bones, and an assortment of weaponry. On his return walk, *B'alam* checked their mouths and skin for pox, giving a more thorough inspection to the young and old. When he finished with Shane and Brody, he moved on to auld Angus, then waited for the girls hiding behind the elder's *plaide* to step out.

They didn't.

"Come," the Jaguar King demanded and pointed at the sand in front of auld Angus.

Anice immediately obeyed and opened her mouth as Robbie had instructed her to do. Once appeased, *B'alam* lifted Anice's chin and waited for Cait to do the same, but the girl remained attached to auld Angus's hip.

"Blast him!" Robbie felt her nostrils flare. "He is

scaring them."

"He is contemplating a verra big decision." Reid held tight to her shoulders.

Long seconds passed before Cait finally stepped out of her hiding place and offered *B'alam* the ermine she'd mothered all the way from Scotland.

He accepted her gift and studied the foreign beastie's furry tail.

"She is a pet. Not vittles," Cait explained and wiped her damp eyes.

"Yellow Peacock!" He shouted, sending Cait back into hiding.

"Must he be so abrasive?" Frustrated, Robbie twisted a curl so tight around her finger, the tip turned blue.

Reid rubbed the nape of her neck, gentling her. "Consider it a show of good fortune that *B'alam* didn't pop the beastie's tail off and toss it into the basket."

Robbie cringed and was thankful when Yellow Peacock rescued Snowball from such a fate. Cuddling the ermine close to her chest, Jax's daughter quickly walked back toward her family, but slipped Reid a wink en route.

"'Tis almost over," Reid assured Robbie when *B'alam* neared the beginning of the line again. He stopped in front of Nanna and snatched baby Alana out of her arms.

"Ma'!" Wild Tigress shrieked and protested her da's behavior with a heated tongue.

"Aka'an!" He silenced her then grunted at the cooing babe.

She giggled innocently, soliciting a smile the Jaguar King seemed desperate to hide. He passed her off to Lyall's aunt and returned his full attention to Nanna. "Come."

Garbed in naught but her stained sark, Nanna

stepped forward, opened her mouth, and presented her hands. *B'alam* was a bit more aggressive with his examination of Nanna. He checked her teeth, her hair, her bones. He made a full circle around her, paying her more heed than he had any of the others. Nanna's demeanor was oddly misplaced in Robbie's option. The woman grinned and thrust her sagging chest outright awaiting his inspection with a bit more enthusiasm than Robbie might have expected.

The Jaguar King lifted one of her breasts in his hand. "You are the milker?"

Nanna's grin broadened. "I was."

Robbie felt Reid's lips against the rim of her ear. "I dinnae foresee that match."

"I did." She laughed silently and waited for the Jaguar King to complete his inspection with fewer misgivings than before.

He once again stood before Reid. "Your men are good hunters?"

"'Tis only one way to find out." Reid glanced at Lyall, and Robbie knew in that instant who would be the victor should the Jaguar King call for a hunt.

The next minutes passed painfully slow while *B'alam* contemplated in silence.

Robbie took in two breaths to his every one. She tightened her jaw, forcing her teeth to keep her tongue at bay. And just as she was about to throw herself at his feet, the Jaguar King turned toward the Mac-Gregors and inhaled.

Her heart slammed against her ribs.

B'alam raised his hands high and bellowed, "Welcome to Belize."

The weight of Robbie's worries fell from her shoulders with the cheers exploding on both sides of the beach. The howler monkeys mimicked the joyous sound, adding to the excitement of the moment. The

Mopán women rushed to mingle with the MacGregors and a cacophony of chatter soon followed. Black Dove handled the introductions swiftly before the Jaguar King led them into the jungle.

Robbie's cheeks ached from smiling, her vision blurred behind her joyful tears.

"Ye are happy?" Reid pulled her through the thick foliage.

"Verra happy." She pushed a wide leaf aside, but her gaze remained fixed on the man who was the keeper of her dreams. He was her king and this was their paradise.

She tripped over a vine.

"Och, woman!" Reid caught her and swept her up in his arms. "Think ye should watch where you're going?"

"I think it best ye carry me." She wrapped her arms and legs around Reid's middle and made faces at the children over his shoulder.

They giggled at her antics, but rushed forward when Grandda squawked at them in play. She mindlessly toyed with Reid's ear and watched Grandda hack down a vine with his walking stick. "The Yucatán suits Grandda well."

"The warmer climate is easier on his old bones."

An idea surged through the multitude of plans whirling through her head. Bubbling, she leaned back and held Reid's face. "I want to take him to Xitali's cavern."

A husky chuckle warbled in Reid's chest. "And I suspect ye will be wanting to do that this day."

She smiled, knowing this day marked the beginning of the rest of their lives. 'Twas a day she would always remember. 'Twas a day she would hold forever dear in her heart. She brushed her lips over Reid's ear. "Do ye know what day it is?"

"'Tis someday," he whispered into her neck, echoing

her thoughts.

"Aye. And I never would have caught it without ye."

Author's Note

~ A MAN WHO UNITED A COUNTRY ~

On May 14, 1603, Peter Wallace left England with six ships and King James' blessing. Wallace, a Scottish buccaneer who once served as Sir Walter Raleigh's 1st Lieutenant, brought with him men from all parts of the United Kingdom. He established a settlement on the banks of the Belize River and held the position of governor of the Caribbean island of Tortuga. After being driven from office by the Spanish, Captain Wallace settled outside of what is today Belize City at Haulover Creek. This place was a hideout for the so-called Baymen, Scottish and English privateers.

Peter Wallace, whose name was also spelled Willis in some documents, is where some believe Belize derived its name.

From the Annals of Jamaica 1827:

"Willis, the notorious buccaneer, was the first Englishman who settled on the banks of the river to which he gave his name. The Spaniards called him Walis, and the corrupting influence of time softened it to Belize."

The Belize flag represents the unity of the nation's people and is the only country in the world that depicts people on its flag. On the left of the coat of arms stands a pale-skinned man holding an axe, and on the right, a dark-skinned man holds an oar. Above the coat of arms there is a mahogany tree which represents the trade that became the backbone of the colony, and below is Belize's motto written in Latin: *Sub Umbra Floreo*—Under the Shade I Flourish.

Award-winning author, **Kimberly Killion**, has been hailed by Romantic Times Magazine as an author who writes "captivating romance with characters who are honorable, intelligent and full of humanity." Her debut book, Her One Desire, was nominated for the romance-publishing industry's highest award of distinction, the RITA® Award. Her One Desire won the 2009 Booksellers Best Award for both Long Historical and Best First Book. In addition, Kimberly was recognized in the 2009 National Readers' Choice Awards, the 2009 Golden Quill Awards, and the 2009 & 2010 HOLT Medallion. Romantic Times Magazine awarded Kimberly's second Scottish-set novel, Highland Dragon, with the K.I.S.S. Award and said this is "a tale to cherish."

Aside from writing, Killion is an active member of multiple writing organizations and teaches graphic design in the Midwest.

Please visit her website at www.kimberlykillion.com

Made in the USA
Charleston, SC
19 May 2011